WANNA
PLAY
A GAME?

ALINA MAY

ISBN: 979-8-9888758-8-8
ISBN for SE: 978-1-964979-01-4
Book Cover by Tasha Richelle
Illustrations by Lulybot
Editing by Deliciously Dark Editing
Formatting by Designs by Charly

This content only suitable for 18+

To all my girlies with trauma: so you all got a mask kink too, huh?

AUTHOR'S NOTE

Hello my nasties. Please take a moment to prepare yourself that this book has very dark content (all of you screaming SOLD, you're my favorite). But seriously, this book is full of non consent and contains themes such as violence against women, primal scenes, toxic relationships, male on male sex, and much more. In an effort not to get banned on Amazon, I can't list all the content warnings here, but they are extensive. They are listed on my website at http://alina-may-books.squarespace.com/ . Alternatively, you can scan the QR below.

The only time non consent is hot is in fictional worlds!
Still wanna play? Good. It's time to be chased by some obsessive, toxic men in masks. Let's go.

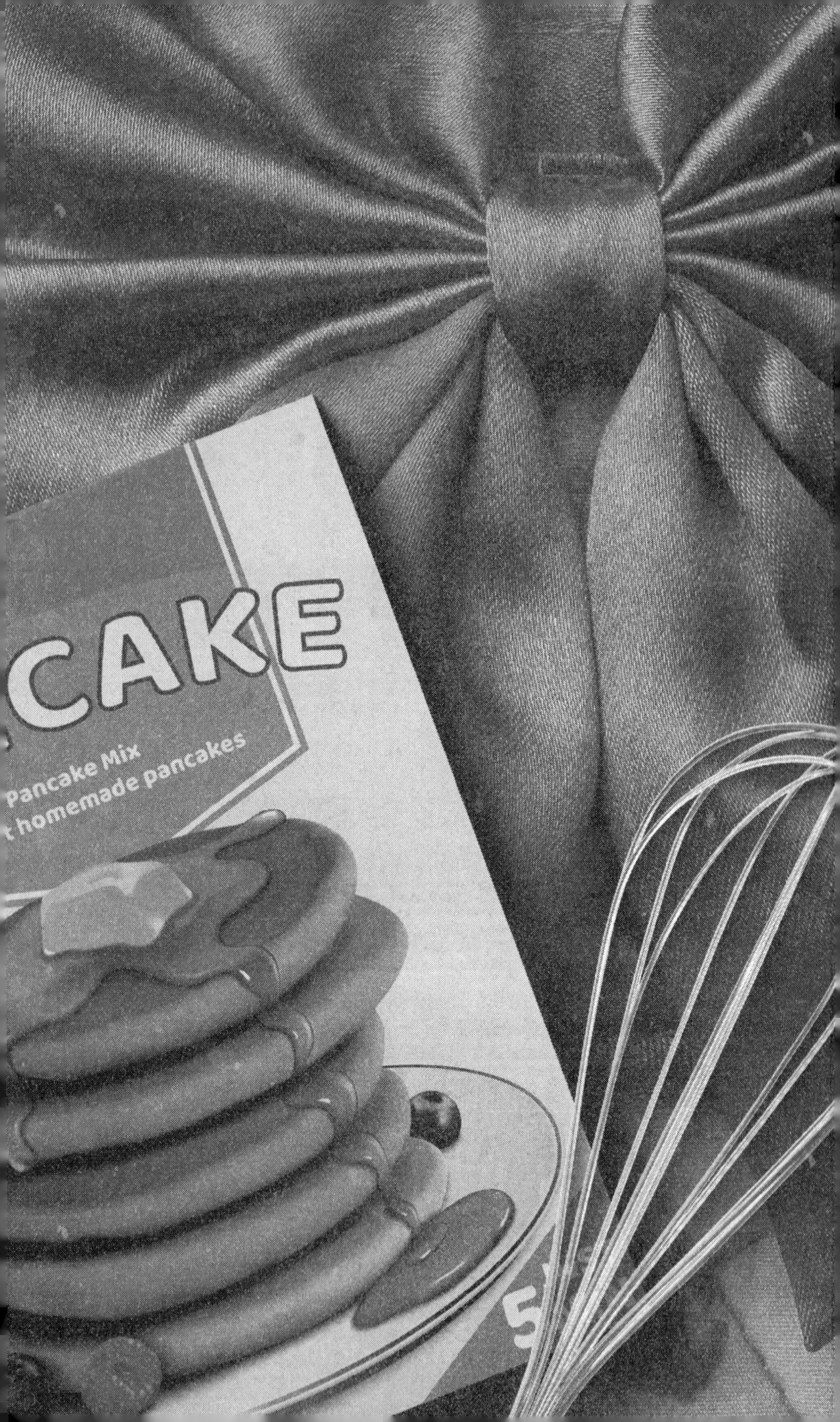
CAKE
Pancake Mix
homemade pancakes

CHAPTER 1

SAWYER

There's an itch on my goddamn arm, and I can't get it to go away. I flip my knife out and drag the canted blade down my forearm, leaving a white stripe of flaked skin. "Sawyer," Miles groans. "Keep your DNA off the pews."

I lazily move my gaze to him. He's standing with his tattooed arms crossed, watching Ryder torture the lawyer on the altar. The lawyer groans, the sound hollow in the empty church.

I flip the knife up and catch it between my fingers. "I'm not cutting, you blind asshole."

The lawyer whimpers. He's tied on his back, and Ryder leans over him, whispering something. He runs his gloved hands over the funnels he has drilled into the man's body. He's been pouring acid into them for the past few hours, 'rotting him from the inside out' or whatever.

I groan and stand up, walking between the pews.

"Want some help, Ryder? Ah shit, you got some blood on your suit." I lean over the lawyer and point at a spot on Ryder's pressed suit.

As he looks down, I flick him on the nose.

Ryder's normally blank face flickers with emotion for a second, and then it's gone. He clenches his jaw. "Stop interrupting."

I roll my eyes. Ryder goes back to his chanting – he's saying something religious. Once you've heard it for the 50th time, it gets old. Ryder's mark doesn't look like he'll last much longer. Thank god. Ryder does the same thing every time it's his turn and never lets us help for the fun parts.

"I'll wait in the car." I brush past Miles with a wink. "And watch your tone with me, pup."

Our truck is the only one in the lot. The grass is withered in the cracked asphalt and crunches as I step on it. Ryder's choice of location was in the middle of nowhere in an old asylum-turned-church.

It's two in the morning, and no one is out. I light up a cigarette and breathe in the smell of smoke and sunbaked grass. Fucking hell, these things are disgusting. But the lawyer had them on him, and I couldn't let them go to waste.

I cough around the smoke and lean against the truck. I hate the stillness here. It makes the voices in my head louder. I drag another draw of smoke in and hold it until my lungs burn.

When the boys finally join me, they smell of gasoline.

"You use the potato chips?" I snuff out my last cigarette and chuck the butt into the truck.

"No," Ryder says and gets in the back seat. Miles joins me in the front and slams the door.

"Jesus," I groan. "You know that kindling burns without a trace."

The church begins to glow in the dark night.

Ryder shrugs his jacket off, "I know how to burn a building down, cocksucker."

I swerve out of the lot, flooring it. "Okay, someone doesn't care about *art*, 'cocksucker.' And if you're hinting for me to suck your dick, you know that's more Miles' thing." I floor the gas, and we fly down the wrong side of the road.

"Sawyer," Miles grips his door handle, the tattoos on his forearm flexing. He's covered in tattoos, mostly from his military days. It's hot. I like knowing I have a badass kneeling at my feet.

I grin. No one is on the road, and for the first time tonight, I feel a flicker of life. Even helping Ryder didn't help – the lawyer's sniveling fear did little for me. I need fresh, angry, vengeful fire.

"Sawyer." Ryder gives me a warning look and pulls off his tie. He's always put together on the outside. He brushes his cuffs off. As usual, he still looks crisp and handsome with his medium-length hair styled back. It's annoying.

I just step on the gas and crank up the Bluetooth radio.

"You're stiff." I reach over and rub Miles' thigh with my right hand and brush over his crotch. "And not in a good way."

"Fuck off." He smacks my hand away.

I bring it right back and grip his groin hard. I feel him harden beneath my hand. "Good boy," I mock.

"Bitch," he snarls and yanks my hand off of him by a finger, causing a zing of pain to jolt up my arm. "Not when you're going a hundred down the wrong side of the road."

I laugh and shake my hand. "You know hurting me gets me hard, Miley."

He hates it when I call him that.

Miles doesn't take the bait. We've known each other for years and hunted together for a while. He knows I'm trying to get under his skin.

My smile fades. The last few hunts haven't been hitting the same. They're becoming predictable. Predictable is boring. Boring makes me want to slam my head into the steering wheel. It makes me want to fly down the wrong side of the road until we reach the city. Get in a chase with the cops. Kill someone. Feel their blood under my nails as they search my eyes for help.

There's a curl of interest again.

"Sawyer," Ryder barks.

I blink and look in the mirror at him.

"Get your head out of your ass."

Ryder is the most responsible of the group. He rarely drops orders, but when he does, we generally listen. If we don't, he'll make sure to take it out on our asses. Fucking sadist. Still, the thought has me hardening in my pants.

3

I grumble and slow my speed.

"Don't know what has you so fucked up." Miles leans back and closes his eyes. "It's your turn to hunt."

I tighten my hands on the wheel. That's the problem. I don't have a target. In the last three hunts, I've picked random people off the streets who have given me shit. The boys weren't happy with me — they tend to pick their hunts with more precision — but they know the rules, so they played along.

But for a while now, things have become...bleh. My last three hardly even fought back. The idea of hunting the next guy to flip me off in traffic gives me a tiny hint of life and then...nothing.

I scratch my arm again, trying to get to the itch crawling under my skin. Something's not right. I can feel it. Hunts usually make it better. So why isn't it better?

I just need to find the right person. I have a feeling the right target would change everything.

CHAPTER 2

CALI

The minute the apartment door slams open, I know Ben is in a bad mood. He appears in the doorway, wearing a cutoff tee and gym shorts. His eyes are glassy, his blond hair falling into his eyes. I catch the smell of beer as he walks past me and throws his keys down on the dining room table. He glances at the phone in my hand.

"Oh, I see. Talking to your other man while I'm gone."

"Excuse me?" I ask his back as he grabs a beer from the fridge. My fat black cat, Halloweiner, runs to the back room like he always does when Ben's around.

"You fucking heard me," he mutters, opening a can and chugging it.

I put my phone down on the couch. So it's going to be one of those nights. Last time he got like this, he threw a beer bottle at our front window, and I had to duck out of the way.

"Better keep those cans in your hand and not on the wall," I hiss.

He's downing another and completely ignores me.

"You're late," I say and move to the doorway of the kitchen. It's way past when he normally comes home from tech school. Things haven't been going well – he says he's getting bullied – and he's been drinking way more than normal. By the time I get home from work at the hair salon, he's usually drunk.

"Something you clearly took advantage of, huh bitch? Did you fuck him tonight too?" Ben locks eye contact with me. His gaze is dark, livid.

My muscles lock up. "I told you a hundred times I'm not talking to anyone else!"

The kitchen light drowns out Ben's face, making his hair look white and his eyes more red. His nostrils flare. "What the hell is wrong with you? I give you everything, and your bitch ass cheats while I'm gone?" He stalks forward, eyes locked on mine.

"I'm not *cheating* on you." I back up. "And you weren't working; it's after two in the morning!"

I've never seen him quite this bad. Alarms ring in my head. My back hits the wall, and he slams both his hands next to my head with a bang.

I flinch.

Ben sees it. He smirks and lowers his head down so he's looking into my eyes. "I work fucking hard all day, and you'd think I could get a girlfriend who cares? Even just a little bit? But fuck, clearly that's impossible! How much effort does it take to keep that slutty pussy away from other men?" His breath is sour, and he smells like sweat.

"What the hell, I—"

"Shut up!" He roars and slams his hand into the wall behind me again and again, making it shake. "Listen when I'm talking to you."

My body trembles. For a second, I see another face screaming at me. But in my memory, I'm smaller, and there's no place to run from the bruises. There never was.

Spittle hits my face, and I realize I'm back in the apartment with Ben yelling over me. Rage floods through me. This is not going to happen again.

I shove both my hands into him as hard as I can. "Get away from me!"

8

His hand comes so fast I can't stop it. It cracks into the side of my face, and my head flings to the side. Tears well in my eyes, and I feel sick for a second.

I take a minute to catch my breath, then wheeze out a laugh, "You hit like a bitch."

Suddenly, hands are at my throat, slamming me back against the fridge. I cough, the pressure crushing my windpipe. Ben is screaming something at me, but I can't tell what. I scratch and claw at his arms and face. The world feels fuzzy the longer he squeezes. I kick and claw, but my ears start ringing. They ring, and I feel warm. No, I'm hot, I'm burning up. And floating.

Suddenly, he lets go.

I slump down, and Ben follows me, holding my arms. "Oh fuck, baby. I'm sorry. I'm so sorry I didn't mean—fuck!"

I cough multiple times, blinking the kitchen back into focus.

"Baby. Baby, can you hear me?"

I glance at Ben. He has tears in his eyes. "Baby, I'm so sorry. I don't know what happened. I mixed beer and whiskey and it always does that to me. If you hadn't talked back, that wouldn't have happened. You know better than that."

My ears have stopped ringing, but the fuzziness still remains.

It happened again. I promised myself things were going to be different now. I promised.

My throat squeezes, and I swallow. I push back into the living room. Ben follows me, wailing and grabbing my hand.

I snatch it back, yanking my keys from the table.

"No, baby, where are you going?" He jumps in front of me.

"Out. I need a minute."

"No, please, I didn't mean it! Don't leave me, baby, I love you. You're my everything. Please, baby."

He snatches at my keys. Thankfully, he's too drunk to get them from me. I grab my phone from the couch.

"I'm just going for a drive." I rush out the front door, hitting the unlock button on my car over and over.

"No, wait, let's talk about this. I'll make this better, I promise." The sound of his footsteps is heavy and fast.

I sprint to my car, throwing the door open and locking it after me.

Ben slams into the window, rocking the car with the force of his chase. "Please, Cali, I'll do anything. I love you! You're my eternity. Please don't leave me."

My hands shake as I put the keys in the ignition. Stupid fucking hands. I'm not even that scared. This has happened before. Not with him, but still. It didn't even hurt that bad.

I take a deep breath before turning the key over and putting the car in gear.

Ben senses what I'm about to do and darts toward the back of the car. He stands behind it, still yelling and begging with his hands out. In the backup camera, he falls to his knees, clasping his hands together.

I throw the car in drive and jump the curb as I yank the wheel to my right. My head almost hits the steering wheel with the jostling.

Ben tries to block me again, but he doesn't quite make it. I tear out of the lot, then slam on the brakes right before the main road. My cat! I glance behind me. He always claws at Ben when he gets too close.

Ben sees me stop, starting to run toward me.

Fuck it. Halloweiner will rip his throat open if he tries anything. I step on the gas and chuckle bitterly. My cat's better than I am. At least he fights.

It takes a while before my legs stop shaking. Something is clearly fucking wrong with me because I've had less of a reaction before. I'm a moron for allowing this to happen tonight.

After my leg stops bouncing, I look around. I've left my small town, and I'm deep in the harvested fields of wheat and pastures. The only things clearly visible are the blinking red lights of the wind turbines littering the landscape. I think I took the highway out of town.

I pull over and put my forehead against the steering wheel. I still can't get my body on board. It wants to shake. My cheek burns, and my ear feels hot and tingly from where it must have gotten hit.

I swallow. I know what I need.

It's been five months. Five months since I've had a drink. It's not like I can't start over, right? It's not that hard to make up for five months. Before I can think about it too much, I pull out and head to a gas station I know is down the road.

By the time I get there, the clock says 3AM. Surprisingly, there's another car in the lot – a silver pickup truck parked right in front of the convenience store.

My cheek is still on fire, and I'm sure it's red, but I grab my wallet and head inside. The gas station is small, with only a few aisles. The normalcy of the rerun pop music, fluorescent lights, and small rack of wine makes me take a shuddering breath in. I grab the red that I already know has the highest alcohol content and head around the corner of the aisles.

I run right into a wall of muscle, slamming into the unforgiving surface.

"Oh shit, sorry –" I look up at the man and pause.

He's drop-dead gorgeous. He's tall, easily over 6 feet, with an undercut and light brown hair pulled into a bun on top of his head. A delicious cologne fills my nose. It smells clean, like cedar and sage. The man smirks, and his blue eyes are dark. It feels like he sees right into me, even though that makes no sense.

The hair prickles on the back of my neck.

"I...didn't see you there." I take a few steps back.

The man watches me retreat, his smirk growing. He tips his head so his eyes shadow further. "No worries, sugar."

He's wearing a T-shirt and blue jeans that mold nicely to his muscled thighs. Suddenly, I'm hyper-aware of my ratty shirt, leggings, and wild hair.

"Sorry," I laugh awkwardly, step around him, and flee towards the register.

I feel his gaze on me as I check out, sending a shiver up my spine.

"That all?" The employee's voice startles me.

"I'm sorry?"

"Is that all?" he asks again.

"Yeah, sorry. Yeah."

The middle-aged man looks over his glasses at me. He lifts an eyebrow and sighs, "Next."

I feel the man's overwhelming presence behind me. Vulnerability tingles between my shoulder blades. It makes me want to turn around. My instincts scream to not give him my back.

I square my shoulders and walk outside. I pull in a deep breath of hot, dry air when I burst into the night again. Almost there. I need this drink more than I need my next breath.

The silver truck is still parked right by where I stand, and as I glance up, I see two men in the front seats. In my fleeting glance, both are just as handsome as the one inside, both with darker hair. The driver is covered in tattoos up to his neck and down his hands. He glances over and catches me looking.

I hurry to my car and shut the door.

I thank the gods I kept my bottle opener on my keys and open it right in my car. My phone dings. I ignore it and put the bottle to my lips. The second the alcohol hits my tongue, I relax. This is what I needed. I'll start my sobriety again tomorrow. I just...I can't tonight.

I'm through half the bottle before I glance at my phone. It's been blowing up, and I see it's Ben.

> **Ben:** So you don't care if I kill myself, huh? Some girlfriend you are.

My cheeks heat. You know what? I don't have to take this. I swallow. I can't be like this. I can't let him beat the shit out of me like my mom's boyfriends used to do to her. That is, the few times a year that I even saw my mother. She never called the cops. She never did anything.

I take another swallow. You know what? I'm not going to be like that. I pull out my phone, hovering above the keypad. It's not that hard. Just three numbers. Something tells me not to, but the alcohol warming me says it's fine.

I dial.

"911, where's your emergency?" The woman on the other end sounds bored.

Her wording throws me off for a second. "I—it happened a while ago."

There's a pause. "Where are you, ma'am?"

I glance around and tell her the name of the gas station. "But it happened at my apartment."

"What happened?" Now she sounds annoyed and bored. I swallow. This is not going right.

"My boyfriend and I got into a fight."

"Is he still there?"

"I don't know."

"Ma'am," the woman on the other line lets out a sigh. "Where is your apartment so I can transfer you to the right person?"

I'm feeling less okay by the minute. "You know what, I'll just call when I get home."

I press the end call button and throw the phone into the backseat. My body wants to shake again, but the alcohol soothes me. Tonight doesn't feel real. It feels like I'm watching myself act from the other side of a window.

I'm still too close, though. I want it to feel like nothing. Nothing but warm and fuzzy and okay. And I'll drink until it feels that way.

The silver truck pulls out of the lot, startling me. I forgot it was even there. I watch as the taillights disappear, blurry red lights swimming into the darkness.

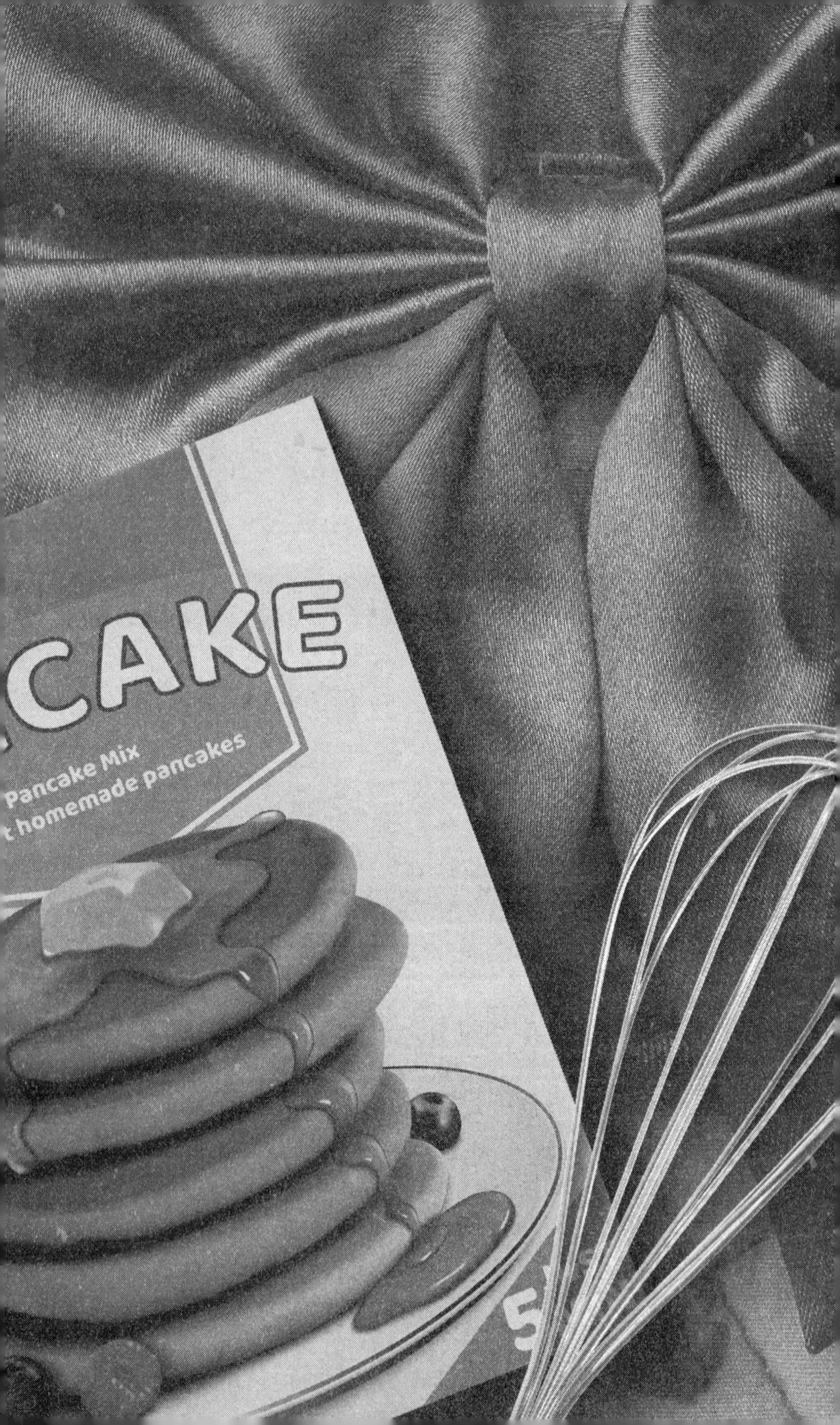
CAKE
Pancake Mix
t homemade pancakes

CHAPTER 3

SAWYER

Ryder kicked me out of the driver's seat, and now I have nothing to do. I keep thinking about the mousey girl in the gas station. The way her messy, curly blond hair begged me to grab it and force her to her knees. To give her a real reason for the fear I saw in her eyes.

I sigh and adjust myself. I had forced the boys to sit awhile longer, waiting to see if she'd run. She never did. She was like a bunny – sitting frozen in place, hoping the predator had forgotten her.

Ryder didn't let us stay longer than 10 minutes. He picked up a warrant for one of our bodies a while back, and we've had to lay low since. Ironically, it wasn't even him who killed the man – it was Miles. But somehow, they pinned it on Ryder.

When we make it back to the motel, I leap out of the car, and I'm immediately hit with the smell of tar and shit. This motel is a piece of shit. A far cry from what we can afford, but we want to stay off the radar, and we usually fuck viciously and crash right after a hunt.

Miles scans us into the room while Ryder grabs some things from the truck. I follow Miles in, smacking his ass.

A door slams, and there's a shout.

"Police!"

I stiffen. Miles beats me to the door and flings it open. Red and blue lights flood the room.

"Police! Show me your hands!"

I make it to the doorway to see Ryder illuminated in front of us, hands up. He's facing us and yells, "Stay back! Don't get involved."

Another cruiser comes tearing into the lot, and two more cops jump out. That makes four cops, all with guns pointed at Ryder.

"Don't move! Back up towards me!"

Rage burns in my throat. How dare they? I try to shove past Miles.

Miles shoves me back. "No, bro. There's too many – you'll get shot."

I shove him right back. "He's family."

"Stay back!" Ryder barks at me while he backs towards the officers.

Miles pushes in front of me again. He's slightly bigger than me from all his years in the military. He growls. "Chill, bro, we'll get him out. We can't help him if we also go to jail."

I look into Miles' green eyes, then feint off to the right. He falls for it, and I jump past him on the left.

Red and blue flashing fills my vision outside. I blame that for why I don't see the fist flying at my head. Miles hits me hard, and I pause for a fraction of a beat. It gives him time to swing again, his fist smashing into the left side of my face. Blackness softens the lights, and I feel something hit the back of my knees. I fall, trying to sort the swimming darkness.

A heavy weight falls on my back, forcing my stomach to the ground. My right arm is cranked behind me.

"Bro," Miles hisses, "I said chill. You're making things worse."

I groan as my vision clears, and I see Ryder being handcuffed.

I buck, but Miles has enough time to sink my arm into a lock. He locks up my shoulder, sending a white line of pain through it when I move.

"Pup," I growl, warning lacing my tone. "Let me go."

He doesn't.

"Let me go, or I'll fuck you up," I grunt in frustration. Ryder looks back at us. His stone-faced expression changes to worry, then anger, when he locks eyes with me. My nose is filled with the smell of tar as I watch my partner get shoved into the back seat of a cruiser.

The rage that fills me is unmatched.

Miles mutters, "Don't do anything stupid."

The pressure on my shoulder releases, and I jump to my feet. I shove Miles back hard enough that he takes a few steps back.

He raises his hands in surrender. "The cops are watching, Sawyer. Act cool."

I glance back. He's right. Now that they've nabbed their prize, they're now looking at the two of us.

After a pause, one of them walks over. "Hey, he wanted you to have his keys."

He looks like he thinks his shit doesn't stink, and I instantly don't like him. Probably beats his girlfriend at home.

Miles steps in front of me, grabbing what must have been in Ryder's pockets.

"Where's he going?" Miles asks.

"Alfalfa County jail for now." The cop looks down his nose. He and I stare at each other. I bet I could get the skin off his face in one piece. Maybe two.

"Does he have a bond?" Miles asks again.

"No." Like the pussy I know he is, the cop breaks eye contact first and turns back to the cruiser.

I watch him walk past our truck with the bed full of the instruments Ryder used to kill the lawyer. The cop glances over at it.

I stiffen.

"Hey, sir." Miles jogs to walk beside him. "I understand if you can't say – I'm prior military myself, so thank you for your service – but who called it in?"

The cop looks back at Miles and eyes his tattoos. "Not sure.

Someone at the gas station."

I clench my fists and watch helplessly as the cop climbs back in the cruiser with Ryder in it. One by one, the cops pull out of the lot.

Miles slowly turns back to me, running a hand through his hair. The crickets chirp. The angry dialogue in my head gets loud.

"Fuck!" Miles yells. It snaps me out of my thoughts. This motherfucker.

I snatch him up by the neck, shoving him back into our room. "What was that?"

I wrap my hands around his thick neck, shoving him down to his knees.

Miles gives me a look full of anger, and it makes the blood rush to my dick. I grab as much of his dark-cropped hair as I can and yank his head back. "Pup..." I growl. "What the hell was that?"

He meets my gaze and sneers. "Where's my thank you? If I hadn't done that, you'd either be shot or in cuffs on your way to jail for a felony."

I yank his hair again, causing beautiful tears to spring into his green eyes. It makes my dick harder. "Brat."

Ryder is gone. Helplessness rolls in my stomach.

Miles must see my gaze change. He reaches up and grabs my belt, starting to undo it. "We'll get him out. Not the first time he's gone to jail."

I don't stop Miles as he yanks the belt from my pants, although he can't look at what he's doing with how far I've yanked his head back. I smirk at him. "Suck it."

Miles swallows, his pupils blown. He fumbles, and his hot hand wraps around my length, squeezing hard. Pleasure shoots through me at his touch.

"Sure thing, boss," he says in a mocking tone.

He opens his mouth, swallowing me down in one motion. I groan, sinking into his hot mouth. I let go of his hair to put both hands on the back of his head to thrust deeper into him. The helplessness washes away as I take control.

Miles chokes.

"That's right. Choke on your master's dick." I snarl, pounding into his face ruthlessly. Pleasure curls up my spine, and I watch as the tears streak down his face. My mouth waters.

Miles gags heavily. I pull back enough to let him catch a breath, "If you puke, I'm going to fuck that ass until you bleed, got it?"

He groans, shifting, and I see he has his dick in his hand.

"Don't come. You don't get to come after the stunt you pulled tonight." I know it's not his fault, but he's close, and I'm pissed.

Miles groans again, right onto my dick. I throw my head back and thrust deep. His throat squeezes me, wringing pleasure from deep in my balls that sends fireworks up my spine and down my legs.

I reach down and pinch Miles' nose closed. He shifts, grabbing my thighs, but I don't let go.

I fuck Miles' face until it turns a pretty purple color. I stare into his eyes, watching him fight with himself to continue to submit. I thrust harder, raising an eyebrow. I know Miles loves absolute submission, but he fights like hell before he gives it. He makes tiny gags on my dick, his body trying to breathe mine in for air, but he doesn't pull back. Finally, as his eyes start to droop, his gaze turns blissed, and his body relaxes. I shout, pulsing my release down his throat, and yank out.

Miles swallows and tries to breathe, coughing and hacking. Finally, he catches his breath and groans, his hand twitching on his hard dick. Precum lines the top of his fist.

I tuck myself back into my pants, raising an eyebrow. "You going to obey, pup?"

"Yes." He grits his teeth and tucks himself back in his pants, standing.

"Good boy." I grip under his chin, bringing his face to mine. We look into each other's eyes for a minute. He smells like sex. "Don't ever do that again," I whisper.

"What, protect my family?" His gaze bounces between my eyes.

My voice lowers, and the back of my throat tightens. "No." I'd do anything for my chosen family, and he knows it. I run my thumb along his chin. "No," I shake my head, clearing my throat. "Never hit me on my left side again. You know that's my good side."

Miles' eyes crinkle in a smile for a second before he nods. "Sure thing, boss."

I let him go. I take a minute to collect myself and then throw myself into googling everything I can about the county jail. As I do, I think about our pretty little nark.

You fucked up, little bunny. You fucked up. I think it's time we had some fun.

CHAPTER 4

CALI

"Someone brought this for you," my coworker Rachel says. I look up from the client whose hair I've been cutting. Rachel waves a bouquet of white and pink flowers in the air.

"Jesus," I mutter. It's been a week since I kicked Ben out. He went back to his mom's house, and I didn't tell anyone what he did — I just wanted it to be over. But, of course, it can't be over. He continues to harass me.

"It doesn't have a card." Rachel looks under the flowers at the top of the glass.

My client glances at me in the mirror. "Who are those from?"

"My cunt of an ex," I say, then snap my mouth shut. Normally I have more of a filter, but I just don't give a fuck right now.

"Oh…" she drags it out.

"Sorry," I mutter.

"No, it's okay. I shouldn't have asked." She looks uncomfortable. "It's just…you don't know what those are?"

I look at them again. They look like weeds from the side of the road. He couldn't even be bothered to try. "Weeds?"

She shrugs. "Yeah, I guess. Hemlock and foxglove. They kill our cattle every year. And they'll get your kids if you aren't careful."

My stomach sinks. The fucking nerve of this fucker! This is just wrong.

I grab the flowers and dump the whole thing in the trash, the vase hitting the bottom with a loud thump.

This isn't the first thing I've noticed him do. Every day this week, I've gotten a text from a blocked number saying things like: you fucked up, and: your time is coming. I just block them and go about my day, but this? This is starting to piss me off.

It's hard to finish the rest of my shift. I feel my coworkers' eyes on me, and I'm boiling mad. This motherfucker has been pushing his luck. Of course, the first time someone ever gives me flowers, they're meant as a threat.

I desperately need a drink.

I hit up another gas station on the way home, grabbing a few bottles of wine.

Fuck sobriety. I'll start again when life isn't an absolute shit show.

I laugh at that as I walk into my apartment, gently scooting Halloweiner out of the doorway. He screams at me, rubbing against my legs like he hasn't eaten in weeks.

"You're fine," I mutter. "You're not gonna starve." He runs towards his food and looks back at me, meowing. His pink tongue is the only thing that stands out against his otherwise black self. I follow him to Ben's old gaming room and feed him. Per usual, he bumps the scoop and spills the food in his excitement. When I'm done, I feed myself. Wine, that is.

I had stopped at my PO Box on the way into the apartment and found a letter from my grandma. I glare at it across the couch and take a healthy swig from my glass. She never talks to me. Mostly because I blocked her number, but still. Part of me — the stupid part — hopes this is an apology. Maybe she wants to mend what she broke? Although let's be honest, I'm not even sure a therapist could touch that at this point.

I light my apple and cranberry candle, and only when I've gotten a good buzz do I rip the letter open. She's written my address in pencil, and my sweaty hands smear it a bit. I pull out two folded pages on lined paper.

Dear California...

I roll my eyes. My mom gave me that stupid name because she said it was her favorite place on earth. Just like she said, I became her favorite place on earth. Before she got drunk off her ass and left me to live with my grandma. Because that's what you do with your favorite things, obviously.

My eyes water, and I blink in anger.

"I wanted to say I miss you. Grandpa and I both do. We're worried about you. Living in a town with a man you're not married to is just not safe, dear. Did we not teach you better? You're straying from the righteous path into sin. Please. Your soul will be damned to hell for eternity. We love you. Stop—"

I drop the letter. That's more than I need to see.

I down the rest of my wine and snatch up the papers. I mutter, "You couldn't beat Jesus into me when I was younger, so you can't love him into me now."

I get up and stuff the letter down the garbage disposal. Turning the water on, I run it, listening to it whir.

I can see my grandma's angry face. She would get all red as she screamed at me for disrespecting her. For being a sinful child who needed cleansing. My memory is full of half glimpses of her as I turned around.

My hands shake. I should have known that letter would be more of the same. *God*, why did I want that to be a good letter, though?

I sniff away tears. Stupid alcohol. Making me soft.

I sit down and pour myself another drink. Halloweiner jumps up on the arm of the couch, purring and rubbing aggressively against my hand holding the wine glass. Cool wine sloshes onto my pants.

"Weiner!" I gasp.

He tilts his black head at me and flicks his tail, his 'tude saying he did it on purpose. I sniff back tears because, apparently, I'm being a little bitch tonight, and I head to my bedroom to change.

It's a small bedroom full of scattered things that I mean to organize, but I always get sucked into my phone before I can.

I go to grab a pair of pants and notice that one of my dresser drawers is open. I frown. I always close them. It's a pet peeve of mine. Maybe I left it open in my rush to get to work this morning?

As I pull out new pants, my phone dings. I dig it out of my pocket. It's a picture message from an unknown number.

Jesus Christ, Ben. Now's not the time.

I open the message. It's a picture of me walking out of the salon earlier today, wearing the same dark blue jeans I had just spilled wine on.

What the absolute hell? I don't remember seeing Ben today. In fact, I don't remember seeing anyone.

A text rolls in right after.

> **Unknown:** Did you like the flowers?

My nostrils flare. That's it. This needs to stop.

> **Cali:** Leave me the fuck alone.

I throw the phone on the bed and go to change my pants.
A reply comes back instantly. I snatch my phone up.

> **Unknown:** Awww, I thought they were to die for.

I grit my teeth.

> **Cali:** Stop. Following. Me. I said we were done. Leave it be.

> **Unknown:** Oh, we're far from done, Bunny.

I pause. This isn't how Ben normally talks. He must really have lost it.

I block the number and throw my phone on the bed. I flop down next to it. The room spins deliciously. Maybe I'll just move. I'd hate to lose my apartment, but this isn't worth my mental health. Plus, I've always wanted to live anywhere but here.

Halloweiner jumps up on the bed and snuggles next to me. I pass out there with my wine-soaked pants still on, bemoaning my life.

CHAPTER 5

CALI

Waking up is a struggle. My head pounds, and I'm groggy. I blink slowly, barely focusing on my room. Everything spins, and I want to throw up.

What the hell?

I try to get up, but I can't. I groan. Why won't my legs work? I lie here, staring at the ceiling. I didn't think I got *that* drunk last night. I try to get the energy to grab my phone. When I do, I see a bunch of missed messages from my coworkers.

Fuck. It's noon and way past my shift.

With supreme effort I get up, grab panties out of my drawer, and pull them halfway on before I notice they're dirty.

"Fuck." I never put dirty clothes away. Did Ben fuck with me before he moved out, and I just didn't notice? I sit panting at the edge of my bed. I feel gross, like I'm covered in a crust of nasty. I should have showered last night. That's the last time I get that drunk.

I barely make it to the kitchen before I'm puking in the trash.

My legs tremble, and I wipe the snot from my nose when I'm done. Goddamn, this is pitiful.

When I'm convinced I won't puke anymore, I grab a can of Coke from the fridge and take a sip. The bubbles irritate my stomach, but it's all I have at the moment, and I can't miss work. I am already struggling to make payments on my apartment as it is.

When I go to leave, I notice my front door isn't shut all the way. "Jesus," I mutter. I'm falling apart at the seams here.

I drag myself to work. While there, I feel like shit and puke a few more times in the bathroom. Despite that, I push through my workday. As my grogginess subsides, my pussy starts to ache, and for the life of me, I can't figure out why.

I barely make it home after work before I collapse on the couch. I lie here for a while, zoned out. I vow never to drink that brand of wine again. I feel like all my muscles got stretched out to twice their size and then folded back in my body.

My phone dings, and I groan. It's an unknown number again.

Unknown: Tired?

What the fuck? I narrow my eyes.

Another message comes through. It's a gif of Elmer Fud and says: be very, very quiet. I'm hunting wabbits.

My heart races. Something isn't right. I sit up and reply.

Cali: Who the fuck is this?

Unknown: You're pretty when you sleep. Can I call you Sleeping Beauty?

I freeze. This isn't Ben. This person doesn't talk like him at all. Plus, Ben always preferred to call. He wanted to hear the background to make sure I wasn't with anyone. It may be someone he hired to fuck with me, but I know with absolute certainty he's not the one on the other end of the phone. I glance at my front door. It's locked.

> **Unknown:** I'll take that as a yes. You know, you fucked up royally. Fitting for a princess, I suppose.

I stare at the phone.

> **Unknown:** Get it? Sleeping Beauty? Princess?

> **Cali:** Who the hell are you?

> **Unknown:** Are you so sure you don't know me?

I swallow. I think through my family and coworkers. Is this a client?

> **Cali:** What do you want?

> **Unknown:** Wanna play a game?

I swallow.

> **Unknown:** I'm going to hunt you. You're going to run. When I catch you, I'm going to make you play.

My heart starts to race. I type back *no*.

> **Unknown:** Ah, good girl. I like it when you fight.

My hands shake. I swipe to my call screen.
Ding.

> **Unknown:** I wouldn't do that, little bunny. If you call anyone, I won't give you a head start.

My hands shake so hard I drop my phone. What the hell?

I glance around my room, checking for cameras. I don't see anything. My breath is reduced to short, quick bursts.

I look closer around the room. Wait a damn minute. The dining room chair nearest to the wall looks closer to the table than normal. We never use that chair, and now the indentations on the carpet are visible. It's been moved.

I sprint to it and climb up. I glare at the ceiling. In the corner, there's a small black circle, no bigger than a pencil eraser.

Oh my god. It's a tiny device.

I grip it and yank it down. It was stuck to the wall with a tiny bit of adhesive.

My phone dings from the floor. I ignore it, searching the rest of the apartment. There's a camera in the kitchen, the office, the bathroom, and two in the bedroom. My chest is heaving by the time I'm done, and I feel sick. I drop all of them in the sink and turn the water on.

When I move to the living room, I'm almost in tears. I snatch up my phone.

> **Unknown:** I see you've found some of my toys. They're not nearly as fun as the ones I normally use.

Unknown: Ticktock, little bunny. Your time has started.

Unknown: Are you ready to run?

CHAPTER 6

CALI

Adrenaline makes my fingertips numb. Where the hell is it? I'm digging through my closet when my fingers bump into a hard plastic container, and I rip it down. My gun case.

I nearly cry in relief. Thank god — or Satan — for my conservative, terrified grandparents.

I throw it on the bed and open it. The small Glock sits there, sleek and dangerous. I last shot it six years ago. I wasn't very good, and I don't even know if I remember how. My hands shake, and I seat the magazine in it and release the slide with a loud snick.

I lay both that and the small holster on the bed while I try to throw things together. I can't stay here any longer. I don't know if this is all some fucked up joke or what, but I just can't. I throw clothes, toiletries, and my phone charger into my bag.

Halloweiner runs between my legs, meowing continuously. I grab a trash bag and throw his things in it. Fuck, I'm going to have to pack his stuff. Fuck this town, fuck this state, I'm out of here. I never wanted to live here anyway. I'll start over with the meager savings I have. All two hundred bucks of it, but that's fine. I'll make it work.

Once my car is packed with the random stuff I can find, I pick up my boy and sit him in the passenger seat. I walk around to the driver's side and slide in next to him. I need to hit the bank first.

When I turn over the key, nothing happens.

"Fuck, fuck, fuck."

I try again. Nothing. The dash doesn't even light up. I pop the hood of my trunk and gasp.

There's a note. I squint in the fading light. "I thought I said *run*."

Fuck! I open my phone. I hover over the call button, wondering if he has a way to tell what I'm doing. Did he put cameras up outside?

You know what, damn him. I open the phone app and wait for a text. Nothing.

I find Rachel's name and hit call. I figure she would get here faster than the useless cops in this town anyway.

The text comes immediately.

> **Unknown:** Ready or not, here I come.

My hands shake so badly I almost drop the phone. He must have fucked with my phone when he put the cameras up. Holy shit, does that mean he came over when I was home?

I feel sick.

Rachel picks up. "Hey babe, what's up?"

"Hey, can you come pick me up?"

"Sure. What's going on?"

Halloweiner wails from the front seat, and it makes me jump.

"I think I'm in some kind of trouble. Meet me in our spot."

"At t—"

"Shhhh," I shush her. I have no idea if he's listening, but my bet is he is. If I'm going to get out of this mess, I have to be smart. "Someone's listening. I'm in...a bit of trouble. Meet me there as soon as you can."

I hang up.

Fuck, I'm going to have to leave my cat.

My heart cramps. I glance at him through the windshield. He looks down his nose at me. The brat has been with me through everything. I can't leave him.

For a hot minute, I stand frozen, debating setting up camp here and shooting whoever this is as he walks through the door. Calling the cops and waiting.

But what if he doesn't come right away? What if he waits for days until I run out of food, and then he gets me? What if he follows me to the store, waits till I'm alone, fuck, hides in my apartment while I'm gone?

No. I need someone to help me get my car running again, then we're leaving. I'll be back in a few hours with help, and he doesn't care about my cat anyway. He wants me.

I snatch Halloweiner up and his litter and put him back inside the apartment. He stares at me through the door, and when I shut it, my heart breaks.

I'm a horrible person. But I'll make it up to him.

I grab my keys and wallet from the car and take off at a brisk walk.

I have no idea how close this fucker is. Or, if he's even serious. I keep looking back over my shoulder. Every time I face forward, my back tingles.

I've met Rachel at the local coffee shop a few times. I have no idea if the man has gone through my text history, but this was the closest place I could think of. The coffee shop is at least five blocks away.

It's fall, and with the sun down, the weather is moderate. The gun is in the waistband of my leggings, and it constantly feels like it's going to fall out. Fuck, do I even remember how to shoot it? Point and shoot, girl. Point and shoot. I kick myself for not paying attention to the lessons when I had a chance.

I make it to the main road with the coffee shop. As soon as a truck drives by, I toss my phone into the bed. If he's tracking me that way, let him try.

I speed walk to the parking lot of a strip mall. The sushi place is still open, and I pray that someone is there. I nearly cry when I see a black minivan and a mom packing her kids into it.

"Excuse me?" I walk up to her, checking over my shoulder again. "Please, my boyfriend took my phone, and now he's chasing me. Can I borrow your phone? Just for a second."

The middle-aged woman looks at her kids and then back at me. She looks skeptical.

I hold my hands up. "Please."

She shuts the car door so her kids are safely inside, and then she pulls her phone out of her pocket. "Where is he? Do you need me to call the cops?"

I swipe to the emergency call screen and realize with a sickening drop in my stomach that I don't remember anyone's numbers. They're all just entered as contacts on my phone.

Well. I remember my grandmother's.

I'm paralyzed. Do I call her? And confirm what she believes to be true? She's over an hour away. And what would she do? Pray the man away? My hands shake.

"Let me call the cops." The phone slips out of my hand as the woman takes it. She throws me a weird look and dials.

I glance over my shoulder again and catch sight of something. Adrenaline hits my bloodstream, and I look closer. There's a man standing in the shadows across the street. I can't see much of him because it's dark, but I know it's a man because he's huge.

I glance back at the woman and the car full of kids. I swallow. I already left my cat. I can't be a shitty person and let him come near them. The woman talks on the phone and tries to ask me what my boyfriend looks like.

I take off. I sprint as fast as I can. I veer to the right, where there's a neighborhood of mobile homes. I hold my gun in place in my waistband, and I throw a wild look over my shoulder.

I don't see anything. I dart down a side street, my chest heaving. I dash to the tall weeds around a dark trailer and peek around the corner.

The street is wide, with parked cars on either side.

A man stands by a sedan on the right side of the street, hood drawn over his head, but I can see he has a mask on. A Ghostface mask.

I make a strangled sound and turn and bolt in the opposite direction. I stick to the shadows, darting back and forth between homes, tripping over lawn chairs, and forcing myself to keep going.

I snatch the gun from my waistband, my hands trembling. Don't shoot on accident. Fuck, finger off the trigger.

Oh my god, he's going to try and kill me. Ben hired him to kill me. My heart races.

I spot a large patch of shadows on my right next to a white trailer. I dart to it and wait.

He doesn't have the advantage. I need to take him out before he gets one.

I gasp for breath, my heart swelling and racing.

Silence fills the park. Crickets. I desperately try to slow my breathing. It feels like my chest is squeezing together.

There's movement on my right. The man walks past the corner. He's even bigger than what I thought in a plaid jacket and a white mask.

I raise the gun up. The man turns slightly at the movement, facing me.

I pull the trigger.

Bam! The gun kicks hard, and I jump.

There's a blur of movement, and my hand is snapped to the side. I'm weightless for a second before my back slams into the side of the trailer, and a massive body crushes into me. A hand clamps over my mouth and nose, and blinding pain twists at my hand holding the gun, forcing me to drop it. I try to cry out.

The man is so tall that my face presses into his chest. He leans back slightly, his mask almost glowing.

A rich, deep voice hisses, "I kill men for less. But seeing as we haven't even started to have our fun, I'll let it slide, bunny."

I thrash in the man's hold and struggle to breathe. My heart is still pounding, my lungs screaming. He's so heavy that I barely move.

The man drags in a deep breath. "God, that's my favorite perfume. Are you afraid, Sleeping Beauty?"

I choke for air. The man doesn't let up. He rumbles in my ear,

"You'll learn soon that if you get anything, it comes from me. Food? Me. Water? Me. The air you breathe?" He rubs the plastic mask against me and whispers, "Also me."

I try to knee him in the balls, but his legs are pinning mine apart, and the lack of air is making me groggy.

"You're all mine now, bunny."

He lets his hand off, and I draw in a huge breath, then immediately start panting. He wraps his huge hand around my throat, pinning me to the trailer again. Shadowed eyes look at me from behind the mask, completely void of emotion.

Suddenly, he reaches down, and something soft is yanked through my mouth and tied behind my head. The man's massive body lets off me for a second, and I'm whirled around.

There! There's a tiny space between him and the wall. The man snatches my arms, and something cold and metal clamps down on them, tightening painfully.

There's a chuckle. "If you fight me now, it'll only turn me on. Although you'd like that, wouldn't you?"

Suddenly, I'm in the air and over his shoulder. I scream into the cloth in my mouth and kick. There's a smack and a sudden, fiery pain over my ass. He laughs. "God, hot little ass too. It's a shame I got my hands on you. We're going to have so much fun."

CHAPTER 7

MILES

I glare at Sawyer as he attempts to make pancakes. This is the third one he's bunched into a mangled mess and knocked into the burner.

I snap up from my seat at the island and stalk to him. We returned to Ryder's home after he got arrested two days ago. This home is our closest home to the jail he's being held at. The house isn't huge — just a ranch with a few bedrooms, an office, and a nice basement — but where it lacks size, it makes up in quality. The countertops and island are all marble, and the appliances are copper. Ryder put a lot of care into designing this kitchen, and he'll kill us if we burn it down.

"Not like that." I try to grab the spatula from Sawyer. "You have to be patient. It's not ready to flip yet."

Sawyer throws me a cheeky grin. He's thrown on a red and white frilly apron, probably because he knows it annoys me.

Sawyer smacks my outstretched hand with the spatula. "Back off. I know how to do it."

I cross my arms and lean against the island. Sawyer has been acting off all week. He was gone all night last night and returned at the asscrack of dawn. And now, he's damn near cheerful.

I frown. "What the hell is up with you?"

Sawyer grins, and it's the kind of smile he usually gives our marks, not us. It makes my hackles rise.

"Sawyer," I growl.

He's in my face in an instant. He presses his forehead to mine, his breath puffing against my face. "What was that tone, pet?"

I glare into his blue eyes. They're hard and calculating. He watches me for a second, his pupils dilating as I glare back at him. I hold his challenge longer than normal.

Sawyer finally pulls back with a cheeky smile and says, "I chose a mark."

My eyebrows shoot up. "Oh yeah?" Of all the things, this wasn't as bad as I was expecting. "Why didn't you say?"

Sawyer smirks. "I like the suspense."

I should have known he had something up his sleeve. "Don't you think it's a bad time for all this? Ryder can't join us."

"Sure he can. His bond hearing is at the end of the week. He'll get out. It's a weak case."

Guilt fills me. Ryder is in there because of me. I had bad luck on a hunt, and someone called the body in before it had time to decompose enough. They got a bit of Ryder's DNA off of him.

I wince. He took the fall for me, as any of us would do for each other. I still hate it. I haven't been right since, and I could use a distraction.

"So..." I pull out a stool and sit at the kitchen island. "Who is he?"

"It's the person who called Ryder in."

"Oh yeah?" I sit forward, a thrill running through me. Some good payback would be healing.

"Yep. The game's already started." Sawyer walks back to the stove. "You'll get to chase."

A grin creeps up my face. Sawyer knows I love to hunt. I throw a chase into every hunt I lead.

I lean into the counter. "Where's the map? What are the rules?"

Sawyer opens a drawer and throws down a map. "I figured you'd ask. Nerd."

I look closer. It's a topographical map of what looks like...our area?

"What the hell? We never hunt here." Misgiving creeps in.

Sawyer rolls his eyes. "Calm your tits. When's the first time a mark has gotten away from us in a game?" He gives me a challenging look.

"Never, but damn! Especially with the cops crawling up our asses?" I groan and rub a hand down my face. "Listen, is he fit? How long can he run? Does he have any survival skills? Because he could conceivably get away."

Sawyer leans over the island, looking deep into my eyes. "She's fit."

Sawyer keeps looking at me. I pause. Wait. Did he say...*she*?

He raises an eyebrow.

Oh, so this was a joke. I glare at him, huffing a fake laugh. "Stop fucking with me, dude. Not funny."

"Not a joke." Sawyer's face is serious. "Her name is California."

I laugh for real this time. "Right. Got it." I push back out of my stool and start to walk away.

Sawyer's hand clamps over my shoulder and whirls me around. "It's the woman who called Ryder in, Miles."

I glare at him. "A woman?"

"Yes." His smile is manic, and his hair is messy.

I shove him back a step.

"We don't hunt women, Sawyer."

He crosses his big arms. "You don't. Ryder doesn't." His face gets serious. "I do."

A shiver of fear runs through me. "What the hell? No, you don't!"

I've hunted with these men for years. I know their styles and kill patterns. At least, as best as I can know Sawyer and his off-the-wall decisions. He's been acting off for a few weeks, but maybe now he's truly lost it.

I lower my voice, "Are you good?"

Sawyer's face darkens, and he scratches his arm unconsciously.

"She's the one who betrayed Ryder!"

My mom's bruised face pops into my head. I shake my head to clear it. "Okay? But that's a hard limit, Sawyer. I don't hurt women. Period." He can't be for real. Sawyer knows my past.

I roughly start cleaning up the disaster in the kitchen. If I don't do something, I might have to think about the fact that this might be real. And this can't be real.

"I didn't say you had to kill her," Sawyer says.

"That's what hunt means, asshole." I turn off the burner, throwing dishes into the sink.

His voice gets low and dangerous, "Are you forgetting that you don't get to say no to me?"

I whirl on him, going nose-to-nose with him. We're almost the same height, although I'm a little heavier than him. I glare into his hard eyes. "Hard. Limit. Asshole. I said no."

He leans back with a shrug. "Well, that's too bad. Because she's in the basement right now."

CHAPTER 8

CALI

It's been hours since the man threw me in a cell and locked the door. Or at least, that's what it feels like. I've walked circles around the small room for what feels like forever, waiting for the door to open and something bad to happen.

I wonder what Rachel thinks. I hope she figured out something was wrong after I didn't show up. My stomach clenches. What if I don't show up for work tomorrow? Will I still be alive tomorrow? Dread runs through me. What will happen to Halloweiner if I die?

I sit heavily on the mattress on the floor. It has no sheet, and there is nothing else in the room. It looks like a basement with cement walls. I've circled it a hundred times. The only light comes from the crack under the door, and there's no door handle. It smells like mildew and sweat.

There's a bump from above, and I clench my fingers into fists again. My heart is racing. I don't know what the hell this man wants from me, but I'd almost rather him just come in and do it than sit in suspense.

WANNA PLAY A GAME?

I hear noises outside the door, and I jump up. Shadows fall in my line of light, and I realize that I have nothing to use as a weapon.

The door swings open, and the sudden shift from darkness to light hurts my eyes. A light flips on in the room, and I shield my eyes while angling my body to the door.

The man stands there, mask still on. He has a folding chair with him.

"Hey, bunny." He pushes the chair into the room and then grabs another from outside. I glimpse another, bigger room that looks like…a game room? What the hell?

The door is yanked shut.

The man wears jeans and a T-shirt. There are tattoos that ripple up both arms in red and black ink. It feels like he sucks the energy from the room and then shoots it back to me through the mesh-covered eye holes in his mask.

"What, no pleas for mercy?" His voice makes goosebumps run up and down my arms.

He easily handles the chair with one hand and sets it down in the middle of the room.

My chest burns with unanswered questions, but I keep my lips sealed. Whoever this is, he clearly gets off on having all the power. I refuse to play into that.

He chuckles. "Sit."

I glare at him. I can barely see the shadows of his eyes through the mask. Why does he wear that? Do I know him?

He motions at the chair again. "Sit. I won't ask again."

I lick my lips but don't move. He's going to hurt me anyway. Why obey?

He gives a light-hearted laugh and stalks around the chair. "You gotta choose your battles, pretty girl."

Adrenaline burns under my skin, and I try to run past him, but he snatches me up by my neck and plops me onto the chair. He rummages in his pocket and pulls out a zip tie. I claw at his mask, knocking it sideways enough to see a cut jawline and dark stubble. He gets one hand tied to the chair, then goes for the other.

I kick out at him. He sighs and easily does the same for my legs.

My chest heaves. Being at his mercy now makes my vision blur at the edges. And that makes me angry. How dare he?

"Fuck you, you disgusting pig."

The man adjusts his mask and pats my knee. "Pigs aren't disgusting. And relax. I'm not going to hurt you. Right now, anyway."

He pulls up the other chair and sits so close his legs wrap around the outside of mine. He's huge and warm, and fuck, there's that cologne smell again.

"Okay, let me see what I'm working with." He faces me and slowly reaches his hand out to my face.

I rear back as far as I can go. The man brushes his thumb along my jaw.

I spit at him.

The man slowly raises his hand, wipes it off the mask, and then groans. "Jesus, bunny." He adjusts his crotch.

"You're sick," I hiss.

He chuckles and pulls something out of his pocket. It's... makeup?

I stare at it.

"I have a pretty specific look I'm going for." The man grabs a bottle of something. "Sexy, hot, sleek. Primer. Close your eyes."

"Fuck you," I snarl. He can't just do whatever he wants with me.

The man shakes his head and uses one hand to cover my eyes. I jump as a cool mist settles over my skin.

"It burns the eyes," he says softly. "Pick your battles."

I stare at the man as he fishes in his lap for something else.

"Is that...a beauty blender?" It's the first question I allow to slip by, and I kick myself for it.

"Yep." He holds it up. "Don't worry, it's clean. New, actually." He grabs what appears to be foundation. "I think I got the right shade. I had to guess from the cameras in your apartment." He dabs a little on my hand and makes a satisfied grunt.

I continue to stare at him. Well, the only parts I can see. His neck is tanned, and the skin looks soft. He has a V-neck on, and I see more tattoos peeking out. He holds the beauty blender out to my face, pausing to see what I'll do. I picture grinding his face into an oven burner, but I sit still.

The man dabs the makeup gently over my face. I stiffen when he gets close to my eyes, and he slows down, carefully applying it. He's so close I can hear him breathing behind the mask. His hands smell sweet...almost like syrup.

He's a coward, hiding his identity. I glare at him. "Why don't you take that off."

"So anxious to see me?" He leans back to get something else.

"No," I huff and look away.

He works for a bit. It's the weirdest thing I've ever experienced. What are his plans for me? Get me dolled up so he can kill me while I look pretty?

Good. At least I'll look nice for my time on the news. Not that there are a lot of people who will miss me. Fuck, my cat will.

Oh my god, he's going to die locked in my apartment.

"Listen..." I pause, unsure how to say it. "I've already been gone...I don't know, a few hours. I have a cat. He's stuck at my house with no one to take care of him."

"Halloweiner," the man says.

My leg twitches. He knows my cat's name. Oh, that's right. He invaded my privacy. Sent me creepy texts and stalked me. "You have no right."

He chuckles and says in a low, gravely voice, "Bunnies run, predators hunt. That's how it works."

I shiver. He sounds so sure.

He rummages in his pile.

I clench my teeth. "The least you can do is make sure someone takes care of him."

The man looks up at me, and I catch the light of his eyes behind the screen of the mask. They're blue and ringed in dark lashes. He looks at me sincerely and says softly, "Already taken care of, bunny."

My jaw is so tight it hurts. The room grows solemn. I know this means he doesn't plan on letting me go. Against my will, tears form behind my eyes.

"Eyeshadow next," the man grabs a pallet with nude colors and leans toward me with a brush.

Of course, the fucker wants to look at my eyes right as I cry. I jerk my head back.

"Easy," he mutters. His voice is calming. "Gonna have to close those pretty eyes for me."

Flashbacks of my grandmother screaming at me to close my eyes flicker in my mind. Without thinking, I mutter, "Please, no."

I feel him staring at me, and I flush.

"You won't beg for your life, but you will beg for this?"

I press my lips together, angry that it slipped out. Angry that he's watching me with such a knowing silence. I glare at his mask. It's dirty, and there's a small crack on the right side.

The man says softly, "I said I'm not going to hurt you right now. I promise. I know you don't know me, but I'm a man of my word."

Yeah, right.

He just sits there. It's very clear he won't give me a choice. And that makes me angry. Him being so soft is almost worse than if he came in here and hurt me. What is he doing?

The man leans toward me again with the brush. I jerk my head away.

"Fight me on this, and there will be consequences. They won't hurt, but I guarantee you won't like them." His voice is still soft, but there's a hint of excitement in it.

I can't. I can't give him this. He's trying to get his foot in the door. If I submit now, it'll be easier and easier for him to tell me what to do.

He shrugs. "Okay then." He gently palms my forehead back so my head is cranked back and drags a thumb down my eye. I instinctively shut them. He pins my eye closed by my eyelashes. I try to open it, but he increases the pressure. I stop, not wanting him to poke my eye.

"Good girl."

I jump when he lets go of my eyes and gently applies the makeup. My breathing is heavy. With my other eye, I watch his other hand gripping the palette. For the first time, I notice a simple smiley face tattooed on it. His hands are big, with veins running through them.

The man continues his process for a while. Neither of us speaks. He even applies fake lashes and lipstick.

When he's done, he leans back. My cheeks flush, and I feel

ashamed, like a pig dressed up for slaughter.

"Damn," the man breathes.

Anger rolls through me.

"Now, for your punishment."

He leans in and runs both hands up my thighs. I stiffen. What the hell is he doing?

He slides his hands back down, then up again, this time tracing along the insides of my thighs, getting dangerously close to my pussy. His next swipe up, he brushes my clit.

"What are you doing?" I can't stop my voice from the shrill rise of panic.

"Punishing you." He continues and touches my pussy again.

"Stop," I whisper. The man's presence is powerful and heady, and I hate him.

He cocks the mask. "No, Cali. I am a man of my word. You break my rules, you get punished."

He kneels in front of me, and I try to close my legs, but the ties just below my knees prevent that.

The man's fingers brush over my pussy again, sending a jolt of sensation up my spine despite my leggings. I jerk.

He laughs. "So sensitive."

I grind my teeth. Fuck him. He won't get another reaction out of me. He continues massaging the inner parts of my thighs, brushing my clit every now and again. Heat runs along my thighs straight to my pussy as the large masked man kneels at my feet, teasing me. I clench my fists.

"Cali, you need to learn a few things. The first is that you can't fight me and win. I will *always* win. And the second is that this pussy is mine. All of you is mine."

He strokes my pussy directly. Immediate pleasure fills me with every touch of my clit. Good lord, has it been so long since I've been touched that I'm this desperate? I hold back a moan. None of this should turn me on.

"What a little slut." He lightly pinches, getting my clit between his fingers and pulling it.

My eyes roll back, but I keep my mouth shut.

"You're just a needy little whore aren't you?"

I grit my teeth. Fucker notices everything.

"A greedy whore. Nasty, pretty little thing." He groans and starts rubbing my clit quickly and with a steady tempo.

It feels so good, and my body wants more. I catch myself before I arch my back. Fucking hell. I think about anything other than this. I think about Ben, and that sobers me a little.

The man slaps my clit, and I cry in surprise. "When I'm playing with this pretty little body, you think about me and me only."

I hiss, "Fuck you."

He just laughs and continues his steady tempo, pressing a little harder. My hips want to press into his touch. The man moans, the sound deep and masculine.

He works me expertly, and just when I feel the pleasure building up, he stops. He reaches into my pants, stroking his fingers along my wet pussy.

The man chuckles and dips one thick finger into me.

I stiffen. It feels so foreign, but when he brushes against a spot in me, pleasure rolls through me.

The man pulls his hand out, looking into my eyes as he lifts his mask slightly, and I hear him suck on his finger.

I tense.

He pulls his finger out with a moan. "Whore."

My mouth drops open for a second before I shoot back at him. "Rapist pig."

He shrugs. "You have something against pigs?" He straightens and starts collecting his things as if nothing happened. "I have something for you to put on."

The man moves to the door. "Fight me or don't, but you'll be wearing it either way."

My cheeks are on fire. I can't believe that just happened. My body is wound tight with unreleased tension.

The man grabs something from outside and tosses it toward me. It's a grocery bag of...clothes? He removes his chair from the room and then flips open a knife.

I stiffen.

The man holds up his hands as a sign of peace. "Knives are more R—" he pauses, "Knives aren't my thing; I'm just gonna cut

WANNA PLAY A GAME?

you loose."

My heart pounds, but he does what he says, cutting my legs and arms free. He steps back. "Put those on. You have five minutes." Then he leaves, the door slamming after him.

I pull the clothes out. They're skimpy, that much I can tell. What the hell is this? I dig around more. There's pom-poms? I gasp. It's a fucking cheerleader costume, complete with a black and white scrappy top that says 'daddy' and long white stockings.

I want to scream. He can't be real. This can't be real. What the fuck did I get myself into? Clearly, he'll enjoy me fighting him on this, so I throw it on. I'd rather deal with the humiliation of the outfit than whatever other punishment he means to give me. There's tennis shoes in the bottom of the bag that fit me perfectly.

I wonder if the bag can be used to strangle him. I tuck it away in my top, just in case. He didn't give me a bra, *shocker*, so my nipples are clearly visible through the white top.

Shadows fall in front of the door right before it opens.

I jump like I've been doing something wrong.

"Ready to play, bunny?"

CHAPTER 9

MILES

I went for a run. I couldn't stand to be in that house one more minute. I run until my body feels like it's going to give out and circle back to the house.

That fucking man and his impulsive decisions. He's infuriatingly impossible. Bringing someone into our home? If the cops come here and do any snooping, we'll all get arrested. Especially now that there's a woman here. A woman Sawyer kidnapped. Jesus Christ! As much as the man acts like we're invincible, you get caught when you get sloppy.

I'm covered in sweat from the desert sun, and I wipe it off my forehead. One thing about this godforsaken Oklahoma state– it's always sunny. Our house sprawls out in front of me, the ranch looking homey against the surrounding fields and golden cow pastures.

I don't know what we're going to do with the woman in our basement.

The thought makes me want to turn around and run again. To

run and run until this irreversible problem goes away. But I can't run from this one. Ryder isn't here to take care of things, and I have to make sure Sawyer doesn't do something terribly stupid. Which he's already done.

Fuck.

Ryder is going to be so disappointed. My heart twinges thinking about him sitting in a cell, hearing about this. On top of him taking the fall for me, he tries to keep us together as Sawyer buries his problems in chaos, and I run from and beat the shit out of mine.

Sawyer appears at the front door, leaning against the doorframe. The sight of him makes me angry.

I snarl, "You better have made our little problem disappear." The second I say it, I realize he actually may have killed her. Fresh adrenaline runs through me.

Sawyer glances lazily at me. I ripped my shirt off a long time ago, and his gaze lingers on my chest. "Pup, you didn't tell me where you were going."

I shove past him. "You seemed a little preoccupied."

"So grumpy. It's just a woman." He follows me into the kitchen, where I grab a cold bottle of water from the fridge and guzzle it. He watches my throat as I take long pulls.

When I'm done, I smash the plastic bottle. "Just a woman? She's an added complication! She knows where this is now. *No one* knows where this is. Why in the hell did you bring her here, Sawyer?"

"Awww, is the good boy mad that his tactics are overwhelming his morals?" Sawyer pouts his bottom lip.

"Shut the fuck up." I move down the hallway toward the bathroom.

"Make me," Sawyer growls, his voice suddenly deep.

I whirl, and I point a finger at him. "It's always a game for you. I know you think I have too much heart, but you could benefit from having a tiny bit yourself."

Sawyer simply stares at me. "You think she's special just because she has a pussy?"

"No!" I throw my hands in the air, frustration, anger, and helplessness rolling through me.

Sawyer grins, and I kick myself for reacting. Sawyer is like a bloodhound for weakness. It's always best to pretend you don't have any around him.

I growl, "I don't kill women because I was raised right! Who the fuck raised you? Oh, that's right." I glare at him. "You wouldn't know, 'cause you had a piece of shit mom."

Anger flares in Sawyer's icy eyes. He's on me in a flash, pushing me back against the hallway wall by his forearm on my throat.

I don't fight him. I look down my nose at his seething face. "Relax Sawyer. It's just a joke."

He heaves a few breaths, then slowly smirks. He huffs out a laugh.

I glare at him.

Sawyer steps back, his eyes sparkling. "Goddamn. You've been around me too long, haven't you? Look at my pretty boy, goody-two-shoes playing my own games." He adjusts his crotch. "I'm smitten."

I cross my arms. "What the fuck, dude? You have a woman in the basement. We have to let her go, Cyrus."

He tosses me a glance at the nickname. He calls me Miley, and I call him Cyrus. Not sure why, but we always have.

"Well, I guess you're in luck." He shrugs. "Just did."

"What?" I can't help the shock from bleeding into my voice. "Did you make sure she wasn't going to say anything?"

"I don't know about all that." He starts walking towards the kitchen. "I planned on tracking her down and shooting her."

My stomach bottoms out. I can't say anything for a second. "What?"

"She's my mark. Although," he reaches the island and grabs an apple out of the fruit bowl, "I suppose...if you caught her and...I don't know, kept her away from me, I'd think about negotiating."

"What the hell?"

Sawyer takes a bite of the apple, drawing my gaze to his stubble and sharp jawline.

"If it's not worth it to you, I'll go. I'm gonna use my Glock this time. The rifle is boring." He looks at me with full seriousness in his gaze.

But he can't be serious...right?

I throw my hands in the air. "You want me to keep her away from you? How?"

"It's a game." Sawyer rolls his eyes and tosses the apple in the air. "God, you're boring." He catches it with his huge hand and eyes me. I know he's waiting for me to ask him more.

"A game?" I grit.

"You'll be her safe zone. Like tag. If she gets away from you, though, she's all mine."

I pause, trying to figure out if he's serious about this. "Where did you let her go?"

"Out the front door."

"What?" I glance out the window. I see nothing but our front yard and endless pastures. I must have just missed her on my way in.

"Jesus." Sawyer rubs an ear with the hand not holding the apple. "No need to yell. I'm right here."

I dart to grab the keys. "So she knows what the place looks like and how to get here?"

"Not important if she's dead," Sawyer mutters.

"How long has she been gone?"

"I don't know. Ten minutes?" he says around a mouthful.

"You cocksucker."

"Nope, still not me," he mutters as I rush to my bedroom to grab a shirt. As I run through the kitchen again, he throws something at me. "Oh, take this."

It's a Ghostface mask.

"What the fuck is this?"

"She doesn't know you're here. She hasn't seen my face. Thought you wanted to protect the family?" He raises an eyebrow and smirks.

I nearly crack the plastic in my grip. "You're gonna pay for this."

"Sure thing, Miley." He yawns. "Oh, and better hurry." He winks. "I told her to run as fast as she could."

CHAPTER 10

CALI

As soon as I see the open land, I bolt. I keep waiting for a bullet to hit me in the back — there's no way he's just going to let me go. I run as fast and as far as I can until my lungs burn and my spit tastes like blood. I haven't run in forever, and it's hot as ever living fuck. The sun is beating down on me. Heaving for breath, I push my legs as fast as they can go, and I feel like throwing up.

Finally, I stop, gasping, putting my hands on my knees. I look around and notice I'm in a pasture – I would guess a cow pasture – with nothing but tan and gray scrub and a tree line in the distance. I look behind me, and it's nothing but the same. I veered away from the roads, knowing that he would probably chase me down in a car first.

"Fucker," I growl. I want to keep running, but I force my racing brain to slow. I need to think. Strategize. The man didn't give me any food or water, and I'm already thirsty. I know the absolute longest I can stay out here is three days, assuming the rattlers and other creatures don't get me before thirst does. I need to find civilization.

Sweat rolls down my face and chest. I rip off the stockings, stuff my feet back in the shoes, and continue at a slower pace, trying to conserve energy while putting as much distance from me and him as possible.

Sweat creeps into the waistband of my mini skirt, itching like hell.

Is he hunting me? Why did he dress me up?

Oh my god. My grandparents are going to hear about my death on the news and see my mangled body on the desert floor in this ridiculous get-up. The thought makes me want to laugh and cry at the same time. They'll absolutely croak.

I jog for maybe another 20 minutes before I hear a motor in the distance. I cuss and sprint to the nearest tree line. It's nothing but thorns and scrub, but I duck down as best I can. I'm not sure if it is just a stranger or the man, but I can't take any chances.

I look around for a stick or rock or anything I can use as a weapon.

As the motor gets closer, my adrenaline ramps up. I see an ATV drive into my vision, and my stomach sinks. It's the man riding it with the mask still on his face. I hate not being able to see his expressions. The blank mask scares me.

The man drives up to my line of scrub and stops. The cut-off of the engine and the ensuing silence is loud.

He gets off the bike slowly.

I slide a rock into one of my stockings and wait.

The man walks toward me slowly, looking right at me. At least, I think he is. He looks menacing.

There aren't many shadows since it's midday, and I know there isn't much chance he doesn't see me.

"I see you. C'mon out now." His voice sounds different. More level.

I stay crouched. He faces the mask directly at me.

"I see you," the man repeats. "Don't make me come in there after you."

He takes one more step toward me and I dart to my feet. I take

66

off, squeezing between two bushes to get to the other pasture.

"Stop!"

Fuck, there's a wire fence. I scramble over it, hearing him chase behind me.

"Fuck," he says, and I glance back to see him get caught up in the fence.

I run harder. I have to get away. He's going to kill me when he catches me; there's no doubt about it. Probably rape me first, then kill me.

My legs are like putty from my sprint earlier. I hear the man behind me again and throw a wild look over my shoulder. He's over the fence, his huge body giving chase.

I scream and run faster, but it's not enough. I know he'll catch me.

I take the sock with the rock in it and whirl around. I swing it right for the man's face.

He ducks, and it smashes into his shoulder right before his arms wrap around me, and we hurl towards the ground. I tense, closing my eyes, but the impact doesn't come. Instead, he lands, cushioning our fall with a grunt.

Fuck! I scramble to get away.

The man flips his heavy body on top of me, pressing my stomach into the dirt.

"Easy," he growls. "Don't fight me."

"Like fuck I won't! Let me go." I struggle and kick and flail my arms. The man fights with me for a second before freezing, "What the fuck are you wearing?"

I try to push up to get away, but I can't move his heavy body. "What you asked me to, you dumb fuck."

I grab a fistful of dirt and throw it back to where I guess his face is. I hear it hit the mask, and he ducks down. "Jesus. Give me your hands, woman. I'm trying to make this easier for you."

"Sure you are, fucker." I grab more to throw at him, but he snatches my arm up, twisting it behind me.

"I'm trying," he grunts against my struggling, "to help you."

"Would you stop being a bipolar motherfucker?" I snarl. "Just kill me now. Stop playing these games."

The man's smothering weight presses the rocks and prickles into my stomach. He snatches up my other hand, pinning both against my lower back. Something hard closes around them, and I hear a zip. There's a pinch around my wrists.

No!

"Relax," the man says.

"Fuck you," I spit back. I'm still heaving for breath, and he's barely breathing.

"Did you try to smash my brains out?" he asks.

"It's a shame I failed," I growl.

"Jesus. You really are aggressive, aren't you?" Suddenly, the weight is off my body, and he heaves me over his shoulder for the second time.

I struggle anyway.

"A cheerleader," he growls. Then he says, almost too low for me to hear him, "Fucker."

He walks me back to where he found me. I try running again when he places me over the fence, but he wraps his hand in my hair, keeping me there while he hurdles the fence.

I'm flung on the ATV so I'm straddling it, and almost immediately, the man sits behind me. He wraps an arm around my waist, anchoring me tightly to him. My skirt is so low there's nothing of my legs left to the imagination.

The man grunts softly with my movements and turns on the ATV. He smells different now. More like sweat and musk and something savory.

I feel his dick pressing into my lower back. It makes me scream and thrash harder.

The ride back is short. I'm almost ashamed by how quickly we make it back. The man snatches me off the bike before he's hauling me up the front steps. I drop all my weight and go limp.

He cusses and picks me up and holds me against his chest like I weigh nothing.

I struggle again.

As we walk through the front door, I'm hit by a blessed wall of air conditioning. For a second, I gawk at the house. I didn't have time on the way up to take it all in. On our left is a small hall, a large open living room straight ahead, and on the right is a modern-looking kitchen with a long hall branching off it. Everything looks professionally decorated. This dude has serious money.

"That took a while. Get caught up in the outfit?" a male voice says.

I jump. A man emerges from behind the fridge door. He's tall as fuck, and built, with black and red tattoos on his arms and long, shaggy light hair that's tired up on top of his head. He's familiar. Alarm bells ring in my head.

He makes eye contact with me and winks, "Oh hey, bunny."

Everything slows to a stop.

Oh shit. There are two of them.

The man holding me hisses, "Not cool, dude."

I panic and struggle for real. The man's arms band tighter around me. I scream, long and bloodcurdling.

"Easy," he mutters, loosening his grip enough so I can breathe.

"Who the fuck are you?" I scream. "Fucking let me go!"

"You didn't charm her?" The man at the fridge says. "C'mon, dude. Losing your edge."

I struggle and headbutt, then dig my teeth into the man's shoulder.

"Fuck!" The man holding me drops me. I fall heavily on my ass. I scramble to get up.

"You didn't tell me she was a banshee." The man snatches my arm and drags me down the hall. "Thanks for the heads up."

"You like them that way." The other man chuckles.

"Let me go!" I kick back at the man holding me, and he flings me into his arms again. He takes us into a doorway on the right, and I notice it's a bedroom before he plops me on the bed.

"I'll kill you!" I scream.

He wrestles my leg down. "I have no doubt you would if you could." He whips out a neon blue rope from nowhere and ties my leg to the bedpost. I get a good kick in on his chest, making him cough. He just pins my other leg down and ties it too. My arms are still tied behind me.

I scream. My chest heaves for breath. And I realize, horrified, that I want to cry.

The masked man whips his mask off.

I freeze. This one has closely cropped dark hair, green eyes, and a square jaw with a dimple on his chin. He looks about the same age as the other one, in his mid-thirties. Why do they both have to be the hottest men I've ever seen?

The man above me reaches suddenly toward my head, and I flinch automatically. He freezes, staring at me. Then, slowly, he reaches behind me. "I'm not going to hurt you. What do you say you work with me, yeah?"

My adrenaline rushes, waiting for him to hit me. "I'd love to, but I don't team up with kidnapping rapists. Maybe next year," I spit.

There's a laugh from the doorway, and I glance over. The original man leans in the doorway with one hand on the frame above his head.

The man over me snaps, making me flinch again, "I thought you said you'd leave us alone if I was here, dude." He turns back to me.

"I'm gonna roll you over enough to cut your wrists loose. Don't claw my eyes out, okay?"

I just glare at him.

"I'll take that as an enthusiastic: yes, sir." He rolls me, and I stiffen at the flip of a knife. But when he cuts my hands free, I feel instant relief. As soon as I pull my hands out from under me, he snatches up the right one and straps it down. I claw at whatever I can as he does that. Quick as fuck, he leans over me to strap my left down.

Yep. Not sweet. More leather and...coconut. He smells good.

I flip him off.

The man smirks slightly, then slides off the bed. He marches to the door and shuts it, closing the other man out. I glance around the room. It's a large bedroom, clean, with no frills. Just some dressers, a chair, and a guitar. It looks like it belongs to a man.

Is this his room?

The man walks back toward me. He looks pissed. I watch as he moves past me and two large windows facing what appears to be the front yard.

The man notices me looking. "You won't be getting out through those. Trust me, you're safer with me than you are out there."

Now I can hear the difference in their voices. This man's voice is smoother and less gravely.

I see what game they're playing. A fucked up version of good cop, bad cop. "Oh, really?" I yank at my bonds. "Is that why I'm tied up looking like this, alone on the bed of the man who kidnapped me?"

"I didn't kidnap you."

I glare at him. "Sorry. I misinterpreted it when you tackled me, forced me on your bike, then tied me to your bed."

He shakes his head and moves to the bathroom. I hear the water running before he comes back with a cup.

I realize how incredibly thirsty I am. The man puts the cup to my lips, and I jerk my head away.

"There's nothing in it. Just water." His eyes scan my body, and he quickly snaps them back up to my face. "You're dehydrated. Drink it."

I turn my face away. "Just leave me alone."

"Don't be a brat. It's good for you. Drink it."

"Fuck off!" I snarl.

The man's face darkens.

I brace myself for the hit. I wait, muscles tense.

He looks at me, his body still, his face unreadable. Then he puts the water down on the nightstand and leaves the room, shutting the door behind him.

I struggle to get loose, but he's tied me too tightly. After a while, I stop fighting. My body sags in exhaustion. The fact I'm still alive rushes over me in cold relief. Tears well in my eyes as I chuckle. Jesus. What's wrong with me? I don't know that I should be celebrating the fact I'm now not only in the hands of one fucked-up asshole, but two. But I can't help but still feel relief.

Where the hell had I seen the man in the kitchen? I run through everyone I've seen at the salon recently and all of Ben's old friends. I draw up old memories until I gasp.

He was the man at the gas station. Holy shit. The one I ran into and thought was creepy.

Did he take me because I bumped into him? Did he text me all those things because he was mad at me for that? Is that what I have to pay for?

I stare at the cup of water on the nightstand. God, I'm so thirsty.

I run scenarios in my head until, eventually, despite my best efforts, my exhaustion and the soft bed lull me to sleep.

CHAPTER 11

MILES

I stare at the woman – Cali – as she sleeps. She might be one of the most gorgeous things I've ever seen. Fucking prickly but still gorgeous. Her pale skin makes her fake black eyelashes and light pink lips stand out in pretty stains of color. Her chest rises and falls with her even breaths. Her tits look amazing in the strappy top, and her torso? I shouldn't look while she's helpless, but I do. It's curvy and soft, making me want to put my hands on it and bruise it.

The skirt covers a small section of her hips, and her long, smooth legs stretch out to pretty little feet.

Goddamn. I've been hard since I first wrestled with her.

"Fucking Sawyer," I mutter. He knew exactly what he was doing. Never again will I let him look at my porn searches.

I pull up a chair at the end of the bed, but I don't sit down. I know I shouldn't. You could see right up her skirt if you did.

My mouth waters, and I clench my jaw. Goddamn. Sawyer fucked me in the living room after I locked her in here, but I'm still hard as fuck. The feel of her fighting me earlier while wearing almost nothing had me almost coming in my pants like a fucking teenager.

It's been a while since I've had a woman. After I met the guys, I didn't feel the need to. But now?

I glance at the chair again. I sit.

I know this is exactly what Sawyer wants. For her to interest me. I look everywhere in the room but at the gorgeous woman at my mercy on the bed. I stare out the windows for a long time. Every soft breath she takes makes me jerk my gaze toward the bed and then back to the windows.

I won't do it. He won't win this game.

Something thumps in the hall, and I look behind me. As I turn back, my gaze accidentally grazes across her body. I suck in a breath and stare.

She has a thong on, but it's moved to the right, probably from her struggles, and the rest of her pussy is out. It's gorgeous, with pretty pink folds surrounded by creamy white thighs.

I groan and rub my dick through my jeans. Goddamn. Raging lust burns through my skin. She's so helpless. Right there. I want to just push into her while she's tied down. I imagine doing so, the feeling of her soft body surrounding my dick, squeezing it. Her jerking awake in surprise and then in anger. The way her body would jerk my dick as she fought and screamed.

I pull my dick out of my jeans and stroke it, groaning. She'd fight me, but she wouldn't get away from me. I'd make sure of that. Her little wrists would get red from the chafing. I'd eat up every bit of pain and fear in her eyes.

I stroke myself harder, thinking about taking her soft body while she's cussing me out. Her pretty little pussy would welcome me right in, her tits would bounce in that hot little outfit, and I'd kiss all over that plump mouth while she tried to bite me. When I was ready, I'd come inside her, leaving all of me for her to feel. To remind this fiery woman who bested her.

I shouldn't want this, and that thought makes me want it more. My balls tighten, and I jolt to my feet. I come all over her legs and skirt, groaning as I do. I try to get as much on her as I can without wasting any of it.

I groan and think about if Sawyer came in here and made me lick it off her. Despite the fact I just came, my dick twitches again and swells.

The woman moans a little and moves.

Jesus fucking Christ.

I rip myself away from the bed and stuff myself back into my pants. I storm to the bathroom and crank on the shower as hot as it will go.

When I stand under the burning water, shame washes over me.

I lean my head against the shower wall. I want to treat her with complete disrespect. I slam my head against the tile, seeing my mom's purple face pop into my head. I found her beaten to death by her boyfriend right after I turned 17. I never told Sawyer that. I've never told anyone that.

Fuck.

I try to spit the sour taste in my mouth onto the shower floor. Ryder needs to come back and take control of this situation because it's getting out of hand quickly.

Goddamn Sawyer. This goddamn woman.

Saving Cali's life might be the last nice thing I'm going to do for her.

And that terrifies me.

CHAPTER 12

CALI

I wake stiff and sore. Keeping my eyes closed, I groan and roll over. The bed is so soft. So unusually soft. I blink my eyes open.

I'm not in my room.

Adrenaline burns through me, and I sit up, reality rushing back to me. I've been kidnapped. Twice.

"Ah, she awakens."

I jump. The nicer one sits in a chair across from the bed. His hands are steepled. "Sleep well?"

I rub my wrists. He's let me loose. I smell like sweat and dirt and panic.

The man watches me glance at the door. "Go ahead. But Sawyer told me if he catches you, you're all his. So, I'd suggest not."

I cross my arms and clear my throat. Sawyer must be the other man with the longer hair. The man in front of me raises a dark eyebrow but doesn't say anything. What the hell is going on?

"What do you want?"

"Truthfully?" His voice is smooth and low. He looks me up and down. "I want you gone, and I want Ryder never to have been arrested. But clearly, we all can't have what we want, can we?"

Who the hell is Ryder? I swallow. Ryder and this guy must be the other two in the car that night at the gas station. I try to look like I know what's going on.

The man lets out a sigh and eyes me from under hooded lids. "But since we can't have that, and I can't have you running off and telling people where we live, you get to stay with me. *Close* by me. Think of yourself as my little shadow from now on."

I study the tattoos on his arms. He has a few that look military-themed, including dog tags and a flag. One looks like the Air Force badge. I ask, "Who are you?"

He watches me watching him. "Miles."

Clearly, he thinks I'm not onto his game.

I cross my arms. "Sorry, I don't shadow for douches, *Miles*. Just like when you asked me earlier."

Miles stands up slowly and stalks to the edge of the bed. Good lord, he's taller than the other guy. Where do they make these men?

He leans into my space, his coconut smell drifting over me. "I'd watch your tone, little shadow. My dick has a tendency to fuck people that sass me."

I glare at his green eyes. They're light and clear, with a hint of dark menace around the edges. I growl, "Is that the only way you can get people to fuck you?"

He chuckles, and his gaze darkens. "No, but it makes it a lot more fun."

Miles pulls away. "Now, go to the bathroom. When you're done, we'll get you something to eat."

My bladder cramps from hours of not going. I watch the man for a second. Is he actually going to let me? I move off the bed, still facing him. He looks at me like a predator watching its prey — completely still. I back away into the bathroom, step inside, and shut the door. There's a lock, and I quickly twist it in place.

At the sound of the click, there's a dark chuckle from outside the door.

The bathroom is luxurious, just like the rest of the house. It's decorated in steel gray and white marble, with a large shower and a double sink.

I use the toilet and feel immediate relief. Then I drink from the sink for a long time, the water cooling and soothing me. Although, it doesn't help the hunger cramps.

I glance at the door, then quietly check under the sinks. There's nothing but extra rolls of toilet paper.

I jump at the sound of his voice on the other side of the door, "Nothing in there, shadow. Can't have you making a shank out of a toothbrush."

I glance around the sink and then check the drawers. He's right. Not a single toothbrush. Actually, there's nothing. No full-size towels, no plungers, no soap. Nothing.

I throw my hands in the air and lean against the sink. How do I play this game?

The first man, Sawyer, thinks I need to pay for something I did with Ryder. Miles wants to play good cop and get me to trust him. None of it makes any sense. What does he have to gain from being nice to me?

"Let's go." Miles' voice makes me jump. "There's food in the kitchen."

I glare at the door. I do want food. The fact that he's acting nice makes me trust him less than Sawyer.

If I play along, will I get him to relax his guard?

I take a deep breath and open the bathroom door.

Miles is standing there, and his eyebrows shoot up in surprise. "Not gonna make me kick the door down?"

"Nope." I cross my arms. "I'm hungry."

"Good." He turns on his heel. "Follow me."

I follow him out of the room. The kitchen is to the left and down the hall; to the right, it looks like more bedrooms.

Despite being dark out, the kitchen is bright, lit by lights all over the ceiling and under the cabinets. The room opens on the right to the living room, which is also lit up and full of windows. It's also extremely quiet and still.

The crack of the fridge door makes me jump.

"Take your pick," Miles says, watching me take in the house.

The room is too still. The back of my neck prickles. I glance back around the living room, checking the shadows.

Miles smirks and glances behind me again.

I check the hall behind me and jump. Sawyer leans against the wall, staring with a blank expression.

"Boo."

I grit my teeth.

Miles drones, "He thinks he's sneaky. Now, get something to eat."

I glance at the fridge. One half is full of what looks like containers of prepped meals. The other has fruits, veggies, milk, and pretty much anything I would expect in a wealthy person's fridge.

Both men watch my every move. It makes goosebumps crawl up my arms.

I grab the closest thing that doesn't appear tampered with. A pear. I turn my back to the fridge so I can face the men.

They both continue to stare. I'm painfully aware that I'm still in the dirty cheerleader outfit.

"You're gonna need more than that." Miles quirks an eyebrow.

I make a show of taking a bite.

"Awww, you already trying to take care of her?" Sawyer asks.

Miles shoots a sharp glare at the other man.

I bite into my pear again. This is weird. Very weird. Why are they fighting right now?

What in the absolute fuck did I get into?

CAKE

Pancake Mix
homemade pancakes

CHAPTER 13

SAWYER

The little bunny continues to eye us. The look on her face makes me want to wrap my hands around her throat. She thinks she can figure us out? After she already fucked us over?

"You took off part of your outfit."

My mark continues eating, glaring at me. Her missing stockings expose her long, white legs. They look so fucking smooth and biteable. What a perfect mark.

"That's against the rules," I say.

Cali continues to shoot daggers with her gaze, and when she opens her mouth, it's full of venom. "Sorry. I wasn't paying attention when you got the rule book out."

"Is trying to kill me with a rock also against the rules?" Miles leans against the sink and looks at me.

She tried to kill him? I almost laugh. That's hot. "No. That's allowed." I smirk at him.

"Don't worry, you're next," the spitfire hisses at me. I glance around at the possible weapons she might have at her disposal. "Don't make me hard, bunny. You're lucky that your attitude turns me on."

"I'm dead anyway. Why be nice about it?" She finishes her pear and holds it like she doesn't know what to do with it.

God, I love her fire. It makes me want to suffocate it. Put her out and then relight her, just for me. She's only allowed to burn for me. Fuck, I want to know everything about that fire, down to the smallest detail. I want to use it against her.

She won't let me do it willingly, and that makes me even more excited.

I point at Miles. "I won't kill you if you stay with him."

Cali glances at Miles, who looks like he wants to be anywhere but next to her. Delicious excitement curls up in me. My pup usually likes to run from the things that scare him, but I'm going to force him to interact with this one. It will provide unmatched entertainment.

"Right," Cali says, like she doesn't believe me. She throws enough sass into her tone to make it clear she doesn't understand the kind of person I am. She'll learn that there are consequences for every bit of disrespect, and I'll enjoy all of them.

I cock an eyebrow. "You'll pay for breaking the rules."

Miles looks at me with a question in his eyes.

Cali puts the core down on the island. "Clearly, I have to pay for a lot of things. Lemme just get my wallet – oh wait. I lost it when I got kidnapped."

I smile sweetly at her. I want to shove my dick so far down her throat that she passes out. Teach her that she can't fight me.

I take a step towards her. Cali flinches just slightly but stands her ground. I get close enough to her to see the fight-or-flight flair in her eyes, and then I stop.

Oh, but she's making this so entertaining. I let a slow smile stretch over my face. "Either fuck me or suck his dick." I motion at Miles.

"What?" Cali's crystal blue eyes widen, and her pupils dilate.

"Either fuck me…" I lean forward, "or wrap those pretty little lips around my friend's dick."

She sucks in a breath and holds it, eyes bouncing between me, Miles, and the rest of the room. Her lips part, still stained from the lipstick I put on her earlier.

My dick is harder than stone. I soak in her hesitation like a starving man, eating up every bit of uncertainty.

"You said I was safe with him," she whispers.

"I said I wouldn't kill you with him."

Cali's gaze bounces between my eyes. I see the second she realizes I'm serious. Her gaze darts behind me.

I laugh internally. Oh, she's going to try and fight.

Sure enough, she tries to run past me. I grab a handful of her hair and yank her harshly to her knees. Her cry makes my dick weep.

I glance down at her. Her cheeks are pink, and her tits heave. Oh, she likes this. Nasty woman.

I'm desperate to shove myself so deep in her that her eyes roll back. But that's not the game. I lean down and whisper in her ear, "What'll it be, bunny?"

She doesn't answer.

I yank her hair again, watching the pretty tears well up in her eyes. Her pupils are huge, and her breaths come fast with fear. Jesus, she really does like this. Ryder would love this.

I shift in front of her until our noses are touching. "Well?"

"Him," she hisses.

Despite the fact I knew she'd choose him, there's a slight twinge of disappointment.

I see Miles adjust himself. I know damn well this is his fantasy. I know it's hers too. I took the pleasure of going through her browsing history, and goddamn...the girl is nasty. We'll have some fun with her before I kill her.

"Take your pants off," I growl at Miles.

I turn my gaze to her. "Now you're going to be a good girl and suck him. Don't bite too hard, or I'll fuck your ass until you're screaming." I shove her head towards him.

Miles is slowly pulling his jeans down.

"Did I say take forever, pup?"

I shove Cali's face into his crotch, pressing her nose against him so she struggles to turn her head.

"Suck."

CHAPTER 14

CALI

Sawyer has a tight grip on my hair, and it causes tears to fill my eyes. The commanding grip and sharp pain send a jolt of energy down to my pussy. What the hell is wrong with me?

Sawyer yanks me back enough to let Miles' cock spring into my face. I gasp. It's long and thick.

Sawyer's deep voice rasps in my ear, "You have no choice." His tone is full of danger and promise. "Make my boy feel so good that he can't help but come down that tight little throat."

Sawyer's words and his hot breath on my neck make me shiver. A pant escapes me. My head is yanked so the tip of Miles' throbbing dick sits on my lips.

"Sawyer…" Miles grits.

Despite everything, my pussy throbs. Miles looks uncomfortable. Sawyer grabs my jaw and pinches so hard I open it. He shoves Miles' dick partially into my mouth.

Miles groans, and his dick twitches. The taste of precum fills my mouth.

"Good girl," Sawyer breathes. "More."

I bite down...hard.

Miles jerks, and a groan explodes from him. He grabs my head and shoves all the way down my throat.

Sawyer laughs. "Fucking hell, what a good girl. Yeah, bite him some more."

I gag on Miles' dick, but he doesn't let up.

Sawyer crouches beside me and runs a finger up my pussy. Electric pleasure shoots through my body.

"Ever passed out on a dick before?" Sawyer is so close to me that his lips brush the side of my forehead. He lets me back enough that I can suck in a breath. I shake my head slightly.

Sawyer shoves me back down so ruthlessly I gag again. I brace my hands against Miles' thighs, trying to push away enough to breathe. Miles stiffens and groans, his dick twitching in my throat.

"Listen to that. He loves watching you struggle."

Tears track down my cheeks. Sawyer licks them up, leaving hot tracks up my cheeks. My traitorous pussy throbs, and I shift to find some relief.

I'm shoved on Miles' dick again until I can't breathe. I sit still until my ears start ringing. Then I start struggling. Miles groans again, and Sawyer holds me still, then reaches down and pinches my nose.

"Be a good girl and fight us, Cali. Fight us until you can't anymore. And when you come back? We'll be right here to do it all again."

I dig my nails into Miles' thighs, ripping, scratching, trying to get away.

"You'll never get away from me, Cali. You're mine. You'll always be mine." My vision darkens, and sounds fade away.

Vaguely, I hear someone shout, and Miles' comes down my throat. Heat envelops my body. I become euphorically content, and then everything goes black.

CHAPTER 15

MILES

Cali slumps over. I shudder as Sawyer pulls her off my cock. I'm still twitching in ecstasy. That was the strongest orgasm I've had in...I'm not sure how long, but a very long time. I catch my breath as Sawyer lays Cali down, her head in his lap, blonde curls flung everywhere.

"Fuck, is she okay?" I kneel beside her. Sawyer has always brought me close to passing out but never pushed me over the edge. I glance at him quickly.

"She'll be fine," Sawyer says.

I wait. She doesn't wake up. I brush the hair out of her face.

"Dude..."

Sawyer snaps, "She'll be fine. Did you not enjoy it?"

I did. Immensely. I look up. Sawyer's blue eyes look haunted and angry for a second before he quickly puts on a mask of indifference. He scratches at his arms roughly. Sawyer has never really talked about his past, but I know it isn't good. Shit pops up every now and again, usually during sex, and it takes him a day or two to return to normal.

Cali twitches and moans. Sawyer gets up abruptly, and I barely catch her head before it hits the floor. Sawyer stalks out of the room.

Cali groans, and her eyes flutter open. Her gaze is cloudy for a minute, and then she focuses on me.

"Fuck," she rasps, looking around. "Why am I on the floor?"

"You passed out. How do you feel?"

She flushes and sits up. "I'm fine."

I put my hand on her shoulder to steady her.

Cali shrugs me off. "I said I'm fine." She hangs her head, muttering, "God, second time in two weeks I get choked out."

Silence fills the room, and I hone in on her. Deep anger flickers through me for some reason. "Who the hell choked you out?"

"You did, asshole! With your dick!" She motions at me. Her makeup has streaked down her face in black lines.

My voice lowers, "Besides me?" I try to ask myself why I care.

Anger flushes her cheeks. "Oh, so you're allowed to do it but not anyone else?"

Exactly.

Dread fills me. What the hell is this response?

I grunt, "Fine, don't tell me."

She sits on the floor in silence for a while, neither of us looking at each other.

God, but that attitude makes me want to wrap my fingers in her hair and fuck the sass right out of her.

Finally, she rasps, "What the hell do you want from me?"

I stare at the side of her face. She throws an attitude-filled look my way. But after seeing real anger on her face, it's clear it's just a front. This time, she's afraid. It hits me like a sucker punch in the gut.

I soften my tone, "Nothing, little shadow. Sawyer is the one who took you. I can't say what he wants."

"So you'll let me go?"

My gut twinges. "No. Sawyer won't let me let you go." That's the only reason...

Cali picks at one of her fingernails. "Does he...do this often?"

"Do what?"

"Take women."

"No." I bark out a laugh. "No, he doesn't. Actually, this is the first time for any of us."

She glances at me out of the corner of her eye. "You've never taken someone?"

I think about the many, many fuckers I've hunted over the years. She watches me. "But you said you don't take women."

"I don't."

After tense silence, she softly says, "Oh."

I run a hand through my short, cropped hair.

Cali goes to stand. I reach out to help her. She seems to have an internal battle with herself. Then, she takes my hand.

A zip of electricity shoots through me at her touch. I ignore it and help her up.

"You should eat more."

"Got any alcohol?" She laughs awkwardly.

"No alcohol." Sawyer's voice makes both of us jump. He's standing in the hall again. He still looks a little haunted.

"Fucking creeper," I mutter.

"Jesus Christ. Didn't your mom teach you that spying is rude?" There's less bite in her tone this time. "Along with kidnapping."

Sawyer shrugs. "My house. My rules."

The hatred flares in her eyes again. "That is just so beyond fucked up, you—"

I clap my hand on her shoulder and whirl her around. She winds him up like no one's business, and I think she's had enough for tonight. I shove her toward the fridge. "Eat more, then you're going to bed."

She tosses a look my way that's meant to be nasty, but just comes across sexy. Jesus, I think I've lost my mind. I only just met her, and I both can't get enough of her and can't get rid of her fast enough.

She opens the fridge. "Is any of this drugged?"

I look at what we have. Ryder prepped most of it. My gut pangs. I miss him. "Nope."

She eyes me. "You had to check?"

Sawyer laughs, sitting down on one of the bar stools. "I've been known to spike a thing or two. Sue me."

"I'll do more than sue you if you drug me," Cali says.

Sawyer groans and grabs his dick. "Like attack me? Fuck me? Come for me? So suggestive, Sleeping Beauty. Maybe I'll come fuck you while you sleep tonight."

I snap my glare at Sawyer. He ignores me completely.

I turn back to Cali, and her cheeks are flushed a pretty pink. She sees me watching, then makes a show of picking some food. She makes me take a bite before she eats it herself, but when she does eat, she shovels it down like she's starving.

I feel a pang of guilt. We've been treating her like an animal. Worse than an animal.

I shoot another glare at Sawyer. He grins at me and winks.

Jesus. Despite the haunted look, Sawyer hasn't looked this alive in months.

Cali eats until she's full, and I sit there and watch her. She demands I taste each piece of food, and I do. This woman is clearly terrified, but full of fire. Where did she get that from? Why does she throw up walls left and right? Does she have anyone at home? A boyfriend?

I glance at Sawyer. He's fully caught up in watching her, sitting still as stone.

I swallow. Sawyer is fully obsessed. Not that I blame him. Both of us love brats. We love the fight. The adrenaline. The power play. We've played with a few together before, years ago. Both men and women, but every other time, they've left at the end of the night.

And Cali doesn't get to leave at the end of tonight. In fact, she has a body bag with her name on it.

I hate that he's drug us both into this. I know why he's fucking with me. He found a weakness of mine that he's exploiting. Seeing how far he can go with it. The question is, why is Sawyer doing this? Just revenge? I look at him again. He's still staring at her with blown pupils.

Oh, this means trouble.

CHAPTER 16

CALI

Miles takes me back to his room after I've eaten. I feel so much relief with food in my stomach, and new energy runs through me.

Miles locks the door behind us. I rub my hands up and down my arms, the air conditioning chilling me in my skimpy outfit.

Not five seconds later, there's a sharp rap at the door.

"Let me in, my pretties."

Miles mutters something, then cracks the door open. "She's with me, leave us alone, asshole."

"Don't get your panties in a wad, Miley. It's just a game." Sawyer shoulders his way into the room. He beams at me. "Hand me your clothes, sugar."

I suck in a breath and take a step back.

Sawyer cocks his head like a predator, but he stays grinning. "What, you don't want to play?" His tone is playful, but his posture is threatening.

"No. I don't." I clench my jaw. It's still sore from what happened in the kitchen.

His eyes light up. "Goddamn. I've never seen a greener flag in my entire life. Take them off."

"Leave her alone, dude," Miles says, crossing his arms.

Sawyer turns to him. "You gonna get in the way of my hunt, Miles?"

Miles presses his lips together but remains silent.

Sawyer turns back to me. My knees have hit the back of the bed, and his eyes glint in excitement.

"I'll give you clothes," he says.

I look at him suspiciously. He has nothing with him.

He shrugs. "Well...I left them around the house. You'll have to find them. Without your puppy here." He nods at Miles. "Of course, you'll have to keep that delicious body away from me, too. I have a hard time controlling myself when it comes to dessert."

Miles looks uncomfortable and glances at me. "You sure that's a good idea, dude?"

They'd give me access to the escape points and possible weapons? I cross my arms. Both men glance at my titties.

I drop my arms. "Fine. I'm down."

"What?" Miles asks. But I'm already stripping off my clothes. First my top, then my skirt, then my thong. I toss them on the floor in front of Sawyer. I refuse to try to cover myself.

Sawyer looks unabashed, looking me up and down. Miles is pointedly looking at the small pile of clothes and not at me.

Sawyer whistles low. "Never gets old."

What the hell? I gather myself and mutter, "Too bad I'll never be yours."

Instantly, Sawyer's face changes. Anger flickers over it, and for a brief moment, I see a killer. Then, almost as quickly, his face softens into a mask of smiles. "You're only allowed to wear the clothes I've hidden around the house. Don't break the rules, bunny. Or do." He shrugs. "Just don't get mad when the game plays you."

He leans down, grabs my thong, and takes a long sniff. "Goddamn. Imma send this to Ryder. Night, night, lovebirds."

Anger flushes in my cheeks. "That's not—"

Sawyer shuts the bedroom door before I can finish.

I seethe.

I turn to the powerful man still left in my room. He rubs the back of his neck. "You can have the bed." He's still not looking at me.

"Fine. I'm going to shower first."

"Don't lock the door."

I stalk to the bathroom and slam the door as hard as I dare. The shower is orgasmic. I scrub my skin until it's itching. Miles comes in with some coconut-scented body wash and shampoo and leaves again. I come out of the shower smelling like Miles. There are no towels, so I do my best to wring the water from my hair, peeking out the bathroom door.

Miles is sitting in the armchair with a blanket. He's scrolling on his phone. I dart to the bed and jump in, yanking the covers over myself.

Miles glances at me.

"Don't go looking tonight, shadow. Sawyer's in a weird mood. I'm not sure what he's going to do."

His discomfort makes me unsettled. "What is his deal?" My teeth chatter from the air conditioning.

Miles ignores my question. "I'm serious. You can wear one of my shirts tonight if you want. Just stay with me."

I look at him. His green eyes are steady.

What game is he playing? Are they working together, or is he going against his friend? Is it worth losing a chance to escape? I burn with new energy and the desire to run.

Miles must see that. He raises an eyebrow. "I'll tie you to the damn bed if you try to leave this room tonight, Cali. I'm being serious."

Oh, hell no. "Fine. I won't leave. Give me the shirt."

Miles lets out a breath and pulls the shirt he has on over his head. I catch rippling muscles and dark tattoos all over his chest. It makes my mouth water. He hands me the shirt and catches me staring. He smirks.

"I didn't mean the one on you," I grumble and throw the shirt over my head.

I lay down and pull the covers over myself. I hear him sit back in the chair, and the room goes silent. I lay there for a while, knowing damn well he isn't sleeping.

I wonder who's taking care of Halloweiner. My heart pangs. He's so attached to me. He probably thinks I abandoned him. I think about all the nights he's snuggled with me as I've cried, usually because of something Ben has said or done. My chest hurts.

I wonder if Ben knows I'm gone. Or if he'd really care, honestly. Tears of self-pity fill my eyes, and I shake my head. If I ever make it out of here, I'm kicking his worthless ass.

Should I leave the room or stay? I know I can't trust Sawyer. On the other hand, I definitely can't trust Miles. He hunted me down and brought me back here. And he had no problem sticking his dick down my throat.

My pussy heats. I've never been that turned on during a blowjob. They took my body and used me ruthlessly for their pleasure.

I shudder.

What if Miles really is trying to protect me from Sawyer? Or maybe it's an elaborate game to get me to trust him and break some unknown rule.

My head spins.

What I do know is that both men are on high alert tonight. Which is bad for me. And I fucking hate that. I just want to leave *now*.

The silence eats at me. Goddamn, I could use a stiff drink. Or two. Or five.

I roll over. The bed smells like Miles. It reminds me of his dick earlier, which heats the place between my thighs all over again. Fuck.

I glance over at Miles. His eyes are closed, and his head is leaned back. His breathing is steady.

I sit up.

He cracks an eye open. "Can't sleep, shadow?"

I cross my arms. "You going to stay up all night?"

He closes his eyes again. "Yep."

I swallow. There's no way I can sleep with him in here, awake.

"Or maybe I'll tie you down so I know I can fall asleep without you doing something stupid." He glances at me through half-lidded eyes.

"I won't leave."

"Then why did you check if I was awake?"

"I was going to draw a mustache on you. Why else?" I smile sarcastically at him.

He cracks a grin. "Oh. Got a thing for mustaches?" He acts so easygoing. For a second, the tension between us seems far away.

"Gross, no." I cross my arms. "Hate them."

For a second, there's an awkward silence. We both sit stiffly. I want to bury my head back under the covers.

Then Miles says, "Gross? What are you talking about? Surely not the glorious patches of manly hair." He sits up more in his seat. "A landing strip so one knows where to plant a beautiful pussy, if you will." He smirks. "Perfection."

"I think *you* have a thing for them." I arch my eyebrow.

He chuckles. "I sure do."

We sit in silence for a bit. C'mon Cali. You're supposed to be getting him to let his guard down. I glance around the room again, seeing the guitar leaning against the wall. "You play guitar?"

"Used to. Not so much anymore." He runs a hand through his hair.

"Can I hear something?"

Miles stiffens. His toned body seems to have frozen.

I swallow. "It's fine. You don't have to."

Miles stares at the guitar.

Awesome. Now I've ruined whatever temporary truce we have.

"No, it's fine. I'll play something." He says it like he's punishing himself.

"No, really, I…"

Miles picks it up and goes back to his seat. He strums around a bit, tuning it. Then he starts playing. It takes him a bit to get into it, but it sounds like Flamenco music.

I sit back and watch the man in front of me. The longer he plays, the more he gets caught up in it, melting into the sounds. He starts humming along to the songs. I don't know them, but they sound Spanish and maybe a bit French. His big hands strum over the strings, playing them quickly and expertly. His fingers are long and tan and gorgeous. I can't stop looking.

I'm not sure how long he plays. When he finally stops and looks up and sees me, a flush runs up his neck.

"Sorry," he mutters.

"That was great. What music was that?"

He names a band I've never heard of. I nod. Miles quickly puts the guitar away. He's clearly uncomfortable.

The silence eats at me. I say, "I don't know anyone who plays. But at Christmas every year, we'd play a guitar holiday track. I always loved it."

Miles walks up to the bed, and I clutch the sheets tighter around me.

"Give me your hand, Cali."

"No. I'm sorry."

In the dark, his green eyes look gray and stormy. "I want to sleep. Give me your hand."

I know he could take it if he wanted to. I'm not sure why he's even asking.

I swallow. "I don't want to be tied up."

"I know," Miles says with a hint of sadness. He climbs on the bed beside me and grabs my hand in his strong one. The bed dips with his weight. He grabs something — handcuffs — out of his back pocket and stretches my arm up. He clasps the cold metal around my wrist, and panic hits me.

I try to get away, but Miles just swings his leg over my chest so his crotch is in my face and easily grabs my other hand. Against my will, my mouth waters. He handcuffs me to the bedpost.

I test the hold of the cuffs. They're tight but not enough to hurt.

Miles climbs off me. He says softly, "My dad used to play. Guitar, that is. Before he left, he'd play for us every night. I haven't played in a long time."

I watch him for a bit. He looks...sad. "That must have been nice," I say, my tone soft.

"It was." He smiles wistfully.

My dad left too. When I was five. Then, I only saw him every few weekends. I want to say it, but the words seem frozen in my throat. I open my mouth, but nothing comes out.

Miles returns to his seat. "Now, try to get some sleep, little shadow. There will be plenty of time to fight us tomorrow."

CAKE

Pancake Mix

homemade pancakes

CHAPTER 17

SAWYER

Why the fuck don't we keep a mark or two in the basement? I'm in desperate need of a body to hurt, and so far, bunny is playing it safe.

I pace in my room, as I have been for hours. My room is similar to Miles', but mine is messy, with vintage posters of babes from the 50s on the beach. The mess annoys Ryder and Miles so much they rarely come in here.

Jesus, Ryder will lose his shit when he finds out I've taken a mark without him.

I glare at my door. My skin itches, but I refuse to scratch it. Ryder thinks it's all in my head. That I'm crazy or some shit. Well, not crazy. That I 'don't cope well with life changes,' or some bullshit like that.

I kick a pile of clothes. Cali is naked. All that glorious, soft skin on display. Not a tattoo or scar on her. How delicious it would be to change that.

Goosebumps run down my arms. I don't normally go for

women. It's not that I haven't; I've just been bored with everyone who aren't my men. I need someone who will fight me, hurt me, and make me feel alive.

Maybe Miles is marking her right now. Scratching down her back as she rides him, drawing little whimpers of pain and pleasure from her. My dick gets hard at the idea. Jealousy also rushes through me. Why did I leave her alone with him? I want to watch.

I stop myself from running in there. I know why I left him. It's fun to fuck with him. And I'm learning it's fun to fuck with her, too. She fights so deliciously.

I stare at my laptop. I cloned her phone before I took her, and I'm tempted to scroll through it again. She had lots of pictures of her cat. Some texts with her coworkers. Some nasty porn. There were a bunch of deleted screenshots of messages between her and her ex. He sounds like a piece of shit. I wonder if I can use any of that. All her communication with him suddenly stopped the day she ran into us. And, of course, there was her 911 call, betraying Ryder.

Anger fills me again. I glance at her thong. It's lying on my pillow, begging to be grabbed. I do and bring it up to my nose, inhaling.

God. It smells like sin and fear. I shudder, and my dick hardens. Why the fuck hasn't she tried to play my game? It's early morning, and she's followed the rules. I didn't peg her as someone who would do that.

Am I wrong? Did I snatch someone who curls up under pressure?

I rip my door open and march to Miles' room. It's locked, the fucker. He thinks that can keep me out? I raise my foot and boot the door in.

It opens with a crash, and I stride in. Cali is lying on the bed, startling up at the sound.

"You didn't play my game, bunny."

"Jesus, dude," Miles comes out of the bathroom, his hair wet. "I would have opened it for you." He's wrapping a towel around his waist. I tilt my head. She's lying funny on the bed. Suspicion runs through me.

"Did you guys fuck?"

"No," she growls. Her arms are stretched above her, the morning light tracing across her. I stride up to the bed, and she stiffens. The blanket is only halfway over her.

I see why she's lying. She's handcuffed. The room is silent for a second.

That kinky motherfucker.

"So you did fuck?" I crow.

"No, dude." Miles slips some pants on.

Wait a damn minute. I turn back to her and rip the covers off.

"What the hell?" she cries.

She's wearing Miles' shirt.

I let a shit-eating grin take over my face. "Well, well, well. So you did want to play a game."

Cali's chest heaves. Her nipples peek out from under the shirt my pup gave her. My dick pulses in excitement. I turn to Miles.

Miles tries to hide it, but I see his smirk. He's smug. He knows he had her all night, and now she's wearing his shirt against my rules.

He needs to be reminded of who's in charge here. He's getting too big a head, playing savior.

"Miley..." I growl. "Hands and knees. Now."

Miles rolls his eyes at me. It makes my dick fully hard. Fuck, he's playing with me right now. He knows he pissed me off.

I growl, "You're gonna show bunny here how to take it like a good pet."

Miles stands by the windows, arms crossed. He still has no shirt on, showing off all his toned muscles and dark tattoos.

He smirks at me. "Make me, big man."

I launch at him.

There's a gasp from the bed.

Miles darts toward me to close the distance, going low to get my legs. I sprawl out over his back as he tries to knock my feet out from under me. I allow it, crushing him with my weight. Miles has learned some martial arts in the military, but I took classes for years. Miles always goes full tilt at the beginning and wears himself out early.

We roll around together for a bit, him trying hard to get the upper hand. I flow with him until he's panting. Then I get Miles in a hold that forces him to roll over on his stomach. He grunts in pain.

I glance up. Cali watches with big eyes.

"Your girl is watching you submit, pup. What do you think of that?"

Miles groans, half in pain, half aroused. He grunts, "She's probably hoping you don't pull that small dick out."

A thrill runs through me, and I laugh, yanking his pants down while holding him down. I keep my hold tight. I know damn well if I let him go now, he'll try and flip me.

"Stay down, pup," I hiss. "You think I should show her how small it is?"

I get my own pants down. My dick is so hard it aches. It springs free, and Miles shudders. He knows damn well how big it is.

"Who's in charge, Miley?"

He growls at me. I reach my free hand up to grab his hair and yank. "Who?"

"Ryder," he says.

I chuckle and smack his ass hard.

Cali gasps again. Miles flinches under me.

"What's that? Can't take the punishment?" I lean over him until I'm in his ear. "Do bad boys deserve lube?"

Miles struggles. "Go to hell."

I hold him still. "Glutton for punishment, my boy."

I spit on my hand and rub it up and down my dick. Miles doesn't get on his knees, so I line it up with his puckered hole while he's pinned under me. He stills.

"Oh, now you'll behave?" I yank his head. "I want you to look at her while I fill your ass. I want you to watch her while you get absolutely railed."

I glance at Cali. Her cheeks are flushed, and her breathing is heavy. I whisper in Miles' ear, "I think she likes watching you be humiliated, boy."

Miles swallows, the sound loud from how far I've cranked his neck back.

I push into him. I'm not gentle. He thinks he can take my game and play it against me?

Miles cries out.

"Shhhh," I whisper into his ear. "Be a good boy, and I'll let you come."

"Fuck you." Miles shudders again. I piston in and out of his tight asshole. I know it hurts – his back muscles are stiff and defined. I reach around him. Miles gets on his knees enough that I can reach his dick. I grip it, and his groan fills the room.

I plow in and out of him, glancing up at the woman on his bed. Electricity shoots through my balls as she watches us. She whimpers, her cheeks flushed a pretty pink, and her eyes heavily lidded.

My balls tighten. I slow, wanting to last. I lean over Miles and glance at Cali, who keeps her eyes on us while she tries to get her hands free. "Do you think he should come, bunny?"

She licks her lips.

"Answer me, bunny."

Her eyes widen and shoot to mine. I raise an eyebrow.

Cali nods.

"You want to watch him come?" I ask.

She nods again.

"Use your words," I say sharply.

"Yes." Her voice is husky. It makes me damn near come.

Miles moans as I stroke his hard length. I grip him tighter and yank. I cuss him in my head for tying Cali's hands and keeping her from playing with herself.

I jerk Miles off harder, playing with his body the way I know he likes. I bring him right to the edge before yanking my hand away.

"Who comes first, bitch?"

"You do," Miles groans.

"That's right." I slam in and out of him, his tight asshole gripping me perfectly. Fire fills me, and I feel an orgasm coming. I smack Miles' ass. "Are you watching her?"

"Yes."

"Good. Watch our little toy as I fill your ass with cum."

I throw my head back in ecstasy and come inside him with a

roar, my dick pulsing. Miles drains my balls, his body jerking in the need to come. I love watching him fight the pleasure. Watching him submit to me and what I want. When the pulses stop, I reach around and jerk Miles roughly. He's ready almost instantly. I warn him to watch her as he comes. He sprays cum onto the floor with a grunt.

Our girl watches the whole thing, breathing heavily. I see her hips twitch.

I yank out of Miles and walk over to her. My dick is still half hard. She watches me with eyes full of fear and lust. I lean over her, cleaning my dick off on Miles' shirt. I make sure to bump her nipples, and she sucks in a breath.

Once I'm clean and her shirt is filthy, I stretch. "I'm going to shower. Unlock her, Miles. Let her play the game. No cheating this time."

I stalk out of the room.

He spent all night with *my* mark. God, why is that small fact getting under my skin?

CHAPTER 18

CALI

I never thought I'd get turned on by two men fucking, but... damn. The look in Miles' eyes as Sawyer pounded into him with lethal power... made my pussy drip.

Ben always insisted on being in charge when fucking, but it never felt like it came from inside him. He'd slap me a few times and cuss and usually finish before I could. Then he'd roll over and play on his phone.

Sawyer leaves, and Miles uncuffs me and also steps out of the room.

I still have his shirt on. I debate for a minute, then pull it off. Sawyer was still half hard, and I know he'd happily come after me. My pussy sings at the idea.

What the hell? Am I actually craving that man's dick? I laugh bitterly to myself. Seems like I have a thing for assholes. Ben really did a number on me.

The room is quiet. I wait about ten minutes. Where did Miles go?

I open the door slowly. It's quiet in the hall. I hear the faint sound of a shower down the hall to the right.

Oh my god. Are they busy?

I sneak out of the room, shivering. I swear, they turned the heat down on purpose. My bare feet make tiny sticking sounds to the wood floor, but other than that and the shower, the house is silent.

I go for the kitchen first. It's bright and cheery with the morning sun. I look frantically for a knife block. There is none. Fuck. I quickly open the slide drawers, looking for knives or weapons. I find nothing until the last drawer. It's a rolled-up piece of fabric with a sticky note on it.

I snatch it up.

We don't play with knives until Ryder gets home.

This motherfucker.

The fabric is a thin crop top. I throw it on.

I dart to the front door that I came in. There's a note on it too.

Don't leave yet, baby. We're just getting started.

I try the door. It's locked. I check up at the top. There's a padlock along the top rim.

"Fuck," I hiss into the silence. With a jolt, I realize I can no longer hear the sound of the shower. My heart hammers. How long has it been turned off?

I whirl to go down the hall I haven't investigated yet. Maybe there's a door back here? I dart into a side room – an office. There's a fancy desk, papers, a computer, and a large window. Fuck! There's no door here. I dart to the window to see if it will open. Before I can touch it, my hair is yanked back roughly, and I fly off my feet.

I scream, falling heavily to the ground. My hair is yanked right before my head hits the ground, keeping my skull from hitting the floor. Sharp, fiery pain explodes in my head.

"Sorry to catch you so soon." A huge body drops over me. It's Sawyer. He sits on my chest, pinning my arms to my sides with his legs. He's in nothing but boxers, and his eyes look crazed and unhinged. "Miles enjoys chasing more than I do. I'm too impatient to take a bite." He winks at me, and a stray piece of wet hair falls into his face. He smells like soap.

"Let me go!"

"I see you found a shirt. Such a shame. You have pretty tits."

He plants a hand around my throat and lifts me up with him. I gasp.

"Goddamn. Gonna need a collar for this pretty neck."

Sawyer walks me into the living room. I scratch and kick and fight, but he lays me down on the floor gently next to an old-fashioned metal stove. Heat rolls from it.

I twist and try to run, but he drops all his weight and sits on my hips, pinning me to the floor.

"Stay, bunny."

Sawyer reaches beside the fireplace and comes back with gloves. I shake with adrenaline. He places them within reach.

"Where's Miles?"

It was the wrong thing to ask. Sawyer's eyes flash in anger, and he leans down, his white teeth flashing. "Miles can't save you. He's not the knight in shining armor that you think he is. You do know he kills people for fun, don't you?"

I swallow.

The sunshine dances over Sawyer's ripped abs.

"I'm gonna do some things to you, bunny. You're gonna say you don't like them, but I'll make sure that you do."

"No! Get off of me."

"No means nothing to me, Cali." Sawyer grabs the waistband of his boxers and, in one swift movement, rips them down. His dick pops out, proud and bobbing. It's longer than Miles' and already has a bead of precum dripping from the tip.

Sawyer leans forward and says softly, "Are you ready, my pretty little toy?"

I search Sawyer's blue eyes. They're harsh and excited.

I swallow down my body's desire to let him do what he wants to do. And that makes me angry. How could I want this? "No."

"What did I tell you about that word? Don't cry." Sawyer wipes a thumb along the edge of my eye. "Such pretty eyes. Don't cry, bunny. This will be fun."

I heave for breath. Sawyer remains still, waiting, watching. His pupils are completely blown. He continues to stay still until I've calmed my breath enough to stave off the panic attack. Every breath brushes my nipples against him, sending tingles shooting through my body.

"Good girl," Sawyer whispers.

He scoots down, positioning himself between my legs. I scramble to get back, but he thrusts his dick inside me with one brutal push.

I scream, and my back arches against the floor. Sawyer holds me down. The pain is sharp and aching. I thrash to get away from him. Sawyer remains inside me, waiting. I claw at him, trying to ease the pressure.

"You can take it. Be my good girl and take it."

The pain starts to subside as Sawyer remains still, replaced by fullness and throbbing. Sawyer reaches a hand down to strum my clit.

My back arches again, but this time in sudden pleasure.

"Good girl. Good fucking girl." He breathes and continues to play with me. "Look at you, taking my cock so beautifully." He adds little thrusts, his huge dick rubbing along my G spot.

I crush my eyes closed. Sawyer takes his hand away. I hear metal and fling my eyes open. He's opened the door to the furnace, and heat rolls over me.

"What are you doing?" I ask, eyes darting all over the room, looking for an escape.

Sawyer grabs the gloves and puts one on. I try to scramble away, but he just lowers more of his weight to my hips, remaining seated inside me.

"We're going to play with a little pain," he says.

I gasp when Sawyer pulls pliers out from under the furnace. A million thoughts scramble through my mind. This is where I'm going to die. He's going to torture and kill me.

"Bunny." Sawyer taps my nose with a gloved finger. "Remember, I said you're going to enjoy it."

My pulse is flying. "You're sick."

"Thank you." With one hand, Sawyer reaches the pliers into the furnace and pulls out a red hot metal plate.

I try to scramble away again. Sawyer grunts and uses one hand to pin me down by my throat.

"Don't move. I don't want to burn you by accident." His dick swells inside me.

I freeze.

Sawyer puts the plate on a tray under the furnace. He takes the hand on my throat and rips the crop top off me. "I'm going to brand you, Cali. You can fight, but don't buck up into me, or I'll burn deeper than I mean to."

"What the fuck?" I stare at the fiery red metal, then into his eyes, and scramble to get away.

Sawyer groans, thrusting a little. "Have you ever come from being hurt?"

"Let me go!"

He tsks. "You've wanted to, though. I've seen your search history."

I did look into pain play for a bit, but I never told anyone. Especially not Ben.

I want to scream and run, which, inexplicably, makes my pussy wet. "Doesn't fucking matter! You're completely insane. Let me go!"

Sawyer reaches over, grabs an alcohol pad from the floor, and kisses me right below my left collarbone. He wipes the cold pad over it. "Right here, where everyone will see it. See that this beautiful little creature is mine."

"You psycho bitch, let me go!" I swipe at his eyes. Sawyer ducks his head down, letting his soft hair brush over my nose. I scratch at his head and reach my left hand towards the pliers. His hand darts out and snatches mine up. He pins it to my stomach and then does the same with the other, holding me down with one hand. His muscles flex in the light.

I heave for breath.

With his other hand, Sawyer quickly goes for the hot metal tray. He uses the pliers to grab a scrap of glowing, hot metal and raises it over me.

I scream as he lowers it.

Sawyer gives me no time to fight. He presses the hot metal into my flesh.

Searing hot pain flashes through me. That's all I can think

about. Sawyer holds it to me, then instantly releases it. My skin is on fire, bubbling with heat. I struggle to get away.

"Good girl, you did so good." Sawyer thrusts into me. "Give it a second."

I arch my back, pain coursing through me. The pain gets worse, and I scream again.

"God, you're squeezing my dick so fucking tight, little bunny." Sawyer reaches down and starts playing with my clit.

The heat flares, and then a rush of adrenaline runs through me, and the pain starts to numb.

"Atta girl. Let the dopamine do its thing." Sawyer continues to play with me, shooting sensation into my pussy. I try to ignore it, but as the tingling and numbing spread over my body, it feels like Sawyer's fingers get bigger and my clit more sensitive while my chest pounds in pain. Sawyer starts slowly pumping into me. "Give me your moans, pretty girl. I want to hear all your little sounds for me."

Pleasure fills my foggy mind. I feel myself getting wetter. What is happening?

Sawyer releases my hands to brace one thick arm above my head. He groans, thrusting into me. "Such a greedy little pussy. You like pain? You like it when I make you hurt?"

Sawyer plays my body expertly. The tension in my muscles builds and builds, and white-hot pleasure locks up my muscles.

Sawyer lowers his head to my ear. "You're mine now. Mine to fuck with. Mine to hurt. Mine to own. No one will ever take you from me. Do you hear me?" He nips my ear. "No one."

My orgasm rolls up and explodes. Sparks flash across my vision, and I groan, my muscles locked in bliss. I stay locked like that for so long before the pleasure pulses and skitters down my legs.

Sawyer cusses and stiffens inside me. His dick pulses as he comes inside me, still braced over me.

I pant, my mind fuzzy. What the hell just happened?

Sawyer pulls out of me, panting. He looks down, his eyes shining. "Jesus Christ, Cali. Your fear is so sweet." He leans in, bumps the tip of my nose with his, then gets up. Before I know it, he's scooped me up into his arms.

Fire starts to build in my chest. I blink and look down. I can just see the angry red raised lines.

Fuck. He branded me. Fuck!

There's a loud knocking at the front door. Sawyer carries me over, sets me on the ground, then uses a key to unlock the top lock.

Miles pushes the door open, then catches sight of me. His eyes instantly open wider, and he freezes.

"What did you do?"

Sawyer chuckles. "Don't be jealous, bro."

I try to look at what he branded on me. It looks like a...5? An S? It throbs with a heartbeat, and I just want to get something cool on it.

Miles stalks up. There's silence for a second.

"What did you do?" he seethes. "You told me you wouldn't do anything."

"Don't be mad because you didn't think of it first, Miley."

"Cali." Miles puts a finger under my chin and forces me to look up at him. His eyes are full of bright anger.

I swallow.

"Are you okay?"

Anger, fear, embarrassment, and sadness wash over me all at once. I glare at Miles and shove his hand away. "I'm fine. Leave me the fuck alone."

"Here, come inside." Sawyer shuts the front door and locks it again, pulling me into the kitchen. "You're staying with me tonight, bunny. I'll take care of you."

"Like fuck she is." Miles shoves Sawyer back so hard that Sawyer grunts.

I scramble away from them.

"You branded her?"

"And made her come while doing it."

Miles swings a fist so fast I hardly see it. Sawyer ducks, but not in time, and Miles' fist glances off his head. Sawyer's eyes light in triumph. "What is your problem?"

"You can't torture her!"

Sawyer laughs. "I've seen you pull out a man's guts and light them on fire for fun."

125

"That's different!" Miles squares up again.

"How, Miles?" Sawyer steps into Miles' face, all amusement gone. "How is it different?"

"It's *her*." Miles spits. "She hasn't done anything."

Sawyer's shoulders bunch, and he steps into Miles. "She damn sure fucking did! She called Ryder in! Or did you miss that tiny detail?" The vein in Sawyer's neck throbs. "And that's the game. I do whatever I want, and you play along. Or do you just not want to play our games anymore?"

"Stop trying to push me away! Of course I want to play, but not *this*. Her. Without Ryder."

I take a tiny step back. I called Ryder in? What the hell are they talking about?

Both men circle each other, looking like killers. This is different than when Sawyer fucked Miles. I realized that that was playful. This time, it's deadly.

I glance at the front door.

"Don't run, Cali," Sawyer barks.

Miles glances at me, and Sawyer uses that tiny distraction to swing for him. He lands a brutal blow to Miles' cheek, and the fight is on. They land heavy blows, the thudding sounds filling the room.

I don't wait to see who wins. I dart to the office, instantly going to the window and attempting the latches. They flip open. I yank the window open, and an alarm screams.

I jump and scream. My mind screams to run, run, run.

I punch the screen out and swing a foot outside.

CHAPTER 19

MILES

The scream of the alarm slices through my anger, and I freeze. Sawyer stiffens, and for a second, we both pause. Cali is running.

I rip my body away from Sawyer's grip and run towards the front door. Oh my god, if she runs, he'll kill her.

"Cali!" I shout, stomach dropping when she's not there. Where the hell did she go?

There, the office door is open. I sprint to it, darting in.

The window is open. I catch a flash of movement outside. I launch myself at the window and squeeze through. Cali runs across the lawn. She's fully naked, her skin pale in the blinding sun.

"Cali!" I yell again. "Stop!"

She doesn't listen. I run after her, legs pumping as fast as I can. She's not far ahead.

"Cali, please! I'm not going to hurt you."

I'm gaining on her. She throws a look back at me, her eyes rimmed in white and full of panic. I close the distance between us and clamp my hand around her wrist.

Cali screams. It's bloodcurdling and makes my stomach twist. I flip us as we fall and make sure my body is between her and the ground.

She fights me, screaming and clawing. I hold her until she melts into sobs. We lay in the dirt as she heaves.

"Cali, I'm sorry. I'm sorry, I won't hurt you." I'm trying to comfort her, but my words make her stiffen.

"Like fuck, you won't!" Her sobs are full of anger, and she hits at me as best she can. "Get the fuck away from me!"

I hold her until her blows weaken, letting her run out of energy. Feeling her writhe, trying to get away from me, makes me hard. And I hate myself for it.

Cali must feel it. "Fuck...you." She sobs.

"Cali..."

"Just kill me. Just kill me or let me go." She's turned her face into the dirt. She's not fighting anymore, and her whole body has gone limp.

I scoop her into my arms. She lays there, not moving. My gut twists more.

I stride back to the house. Sawyer is standing in the yard, arms crossed.

I sneer at him as I pass. He's fucking with us on purpose. The game has always been to play with our marks. But now, I feel like it's me he's playing with, and not in a good way. For the first time since I met him, I wonder if we're on the same team.

Sawyer doesn't say anything. He just watches me carry Cali back in.

I take us back to my bedroom and lay her on the bed. She still hasn't moved.

"Shadow." I lean down. Her face is pale, and she's staring blankly at the wall. I clench my jaw. I've seen this look before. Mostly on people who were in the military with me and on my mom. Fuck. Sawyer took it too far.

I don't try to break Cali from it. I lay a blanket over her and leave the room, but not before I cuff her ankle to the bedpost.

I storm back into the living room to grab what Sawyer originally sent me out to get. It's birth control. At first, I thought it was in her best interest. Now, I feel like a total piece of shit.

Sawyer is cleaning something at the furnace.

I cross my arms and stare at him. He doesn't look back at me.

"You said!" I yell at him.

"I said what?" He flicks a glance over his shoulder.

"That you wouldn't do anything!"

His gaze darkens. "I *said* I'd kill her now if you didn't leave. I didn't say I wouldn't mess around. This is the game, Miley. I make the rules. Everyone else plays."

Exasperation fills me. "That's not fair."

"Life isn't fair!" Sawyer snaps at me. His eyes are wild and unhinged.

I clench my jaw. Something else is going on with him. And has been going on for months. He's fucked up, and it was bound to spill over at some point.

"I gave her an S." Sawyer gives a mean smirk. "So you'd remember she's mine."

That statement sends a jolt of anger through me so strong that I clench my teeth and taste blood. The three of us have always shared everything before. Why is he making her something we can't share?

Sawyer watches me closely, a smile on his lips.

I turn on my heel and march back to my room, slamming the door behind me. I instantly regret it when I make eye contact with the woman on my bed. It's clear she's been fighting with the cuff, and she stares at me with a startled, fear-filled gaze.

It makes anger roll through me. I swore I'd never be the kind of man who made a woman afraid. The kind of men I spent my whole life around.

I hold my hands up. "Sorry, Cali. I'm sorry."

Cali says nothing; she just watches me. I move to the bathroom, wet a hand towel, and come back out. I approach the bed carefully.

She inches away from me.

"I need to wash the burn," I say. "So it doesn't get infected."

"No." She swallows.

"I'm sorry. I'll get you pain meds and breakfast." I sit on the bed.

Cali looks like she's going to jump off the bed, despite the chain not being long enough for her feet to hit the ground. Her body is dusty from her run from me, and her hair is full of stickers from the ground. I raise my hand with the towel slowly. Her beautiful eyes watch me as I dab the burn.

I know it must hurt like fuck, but she doesn't flinch or try to get away. Instead, she stares holes into me. It's silent for a bit, and then she softly asks, "Where did you go?"

My gut twists, and I get the urge to clear my throat.

"Where?" She asks again, with more power. "Did you go?"

"I had to run and get something."

Cali's chest heaves. I glance up, and there's burning anger in her gaze. She doesn't say anything for a bit. Then she says, "I see."

I feel her shut down. Whatever slight peace we had before is completely gone now.

I continue cleaning. "You're going to need a comb for the stickers."

"And a shirt. Tell Sawyer I won that shirt fair and square." Her voice is emotionless.

Once I'm done cleaning, I grab a comb and bring it back. Cali holds out her hand. "So you just take whatever you want, fuck whoever it hurts, right?"

I stand. I clench my jaw. "I'll be back later with meds."

I stalk out of the room, catching myself before I slam the door.

CHAPTER 20

RYDER

I glance out of my cell at the digital clock in holding. Why hasn't Miles called yet? I always forget just how slowly time moves here.

Finally, a CO comes and gets me for a phone call and brings me up to the booth.

"Hey, Miles," I say.

"Hey." His voice sounds tense.

I stiffen. "What's going on?"

"Nothing. Bored. Sawyer got that package."

What the hell? His voice sounds off.

"Only instead of a men's shaving kit, it was a women's. I told him not to use it, but he opened it and did anyway. Now he's throwing it all around and ruining it. But he also says I have to use it, and if I don't, he'll destroy it completely."

My stomach clenches. Something is wrong. He never talks like this.

Miles laughs like he's joking, but I hear the tension in his voice.

"Anyway, need you back here to straighten him out."

I clench my jaw. Miles is afraid. And I know what he does when he's afraid.

He runs.

I grit my teeth, "Two more days until my hearing. Lawyer is gonna get me a bond." I name the insane amount the judge will let me out on. That, plus our extra to line his pockets.

"I'll get it," he says. "Just hurry, will ya? I'm starting to see myself shaving with a pink razor for the rest of my life, and we can't have that." He laughs, and it's a bit manic.

"I'm coming. I'll get rid of it when I get home."

I hang up the phone. I'll protect my family. Always have and always will.

I go back to my cell, and once there, I wash my hands of the germs from the phone and shoot up a prayer, like I always do. There's been a nasty flu going around the cell block. After I wash, I hold my right hand under the water again because I missed a spot with the soap. Then a few more times to make sure I got it. Then I realize I missed my left ring finger. I have to start my prayer over. I wash my finger a few times just to make sure. As I do, I think about what Sawyer brought home that caused Miles to freak out.

Fuck. Now the germs from the soap dispenser are all over my hands.

I start over. I have to be healthy to take care of my men. I'm the glue that holds them together. I clean under all my nails, but I missed a corner of the nail on my thumb.

I wash them again.

A CO bangs on my cell. "Cut it out, man. You're wasting the water."

"Almost done," I mutter. Did Sawyer bring a woman home? And why the hell would he have done that?

I wash and wash and wash.

They'll never be clean.

They'll never be good enough.

I need to get out.

CAKE

Pancake Mix
homemade pancakes

CHAPTER 21

SAWYER

I hit the punching bag again and again. I can't swing hard enough. I hit the bag again. The pain in my knuckles has turned into a numbing tingle, and there's blood on the bag. Whoopsie. Ryder is going to be pissed. He hates it when we leave messes around.

I drop to my knees and smear the drips on the mat. Then I draw a penis in it.

There.

I go back to hitting the bag. Cali turned Ryder in. She deserves every bit of what she's getting and more. Why can't Miles see that?

Fuck, but I enjoy her fight. Her fear. Despite that, I'm going easy on her, and Miles knows it. Or he would know it if he wasn't so pussy whipped.

I hit the bag again. Ryder would know. I know he's suffering right now. He thinks he can hide it, but he worries about us, even while in jail, to the point it makes him sick.

I hit it again. Ryder is the glue that holds our unit together. He does everything for us.

Punch, punch, punch.

God, Cali's eyes. So beautiful and haunted and on *fire*.

Cali reminds me of myself as a kid. And I know where my fire came from. Ugly feelings start low in my belly.

Punch, punch, punch.

Don't feel.

You're so fucked up, Sawyer. You always said you wouldn't be like me, and yet here you are.

Fuck! The voices are back. I punch harder.

Do anything not to feel. I normally don't feel things on hunts. My hunts aren't normally like this.

My hand slips with the next punch. I step back, ripping the tape off my hands. It hurts so good, but not enough. My hands shake. The ugly wants to creep in again. This time of year is always bad for me. Too many memories from the past.

You were always my favorite son. A little pervert.

I need to do something. Something to stay busy.

God, why can't Ryder be here to hurt me and take it away?

My blood drips across the basement floor as I head to the bathroom. I leave it. I march upstairs, seeing Miles on his phone on the couch. He glances briefly at me and then back at his phone like he's pissed.

"I called Ryder," he says.

"Oh, good job." I roll my eyes. "Tattling to daddy."

Miles has the bag of meds next to him, and I grab it.

"You're not going in there," Miles says, but there's none of the usual bite to his tone. It makes me pause.

"Do you need to be reminded who's in charge here?" My dick is already hard at the idea. A good attitude check would dig me out of my feelings.

Miles stares at the phone in his hand, and his voice lowers, "Sawyer. I'm not trying to defy you." He clears his throat. "Please. This is tearing us apart."

I clench my jaw. The sudden emotions make me uncomfortable. The game was to make him play against me, not make him have feelings for her.

"Please what, Miles."

"I promised my mom, Sawyer." Miles finally looks at me, the strong lines of his face shadowed and hard. He glances back down. "I promised her I'd be a better man than my dad."

I swallow.

You're no better than me.

As a rule, we don't talk about our pasts. All of us come from fucked up places, and we prefer not to dig it up. Miles doesn't ask about my mom. I don't ask about his.

A tumult of emotions washes up in me so strong it takes my breath away. I snap to my feet, grabbing the bag of meds. I'll deal with this mess, but right now, I need a distraction, and I need it now. And I'm not going to get it here. I stalk toward Cali's room.

Miles' voice stops me.

"Promise me on your brother that you won't hurt her right now."

I clench my fists.

"Please."

I grit my teeth. "Promise," I growl and burst through the door.

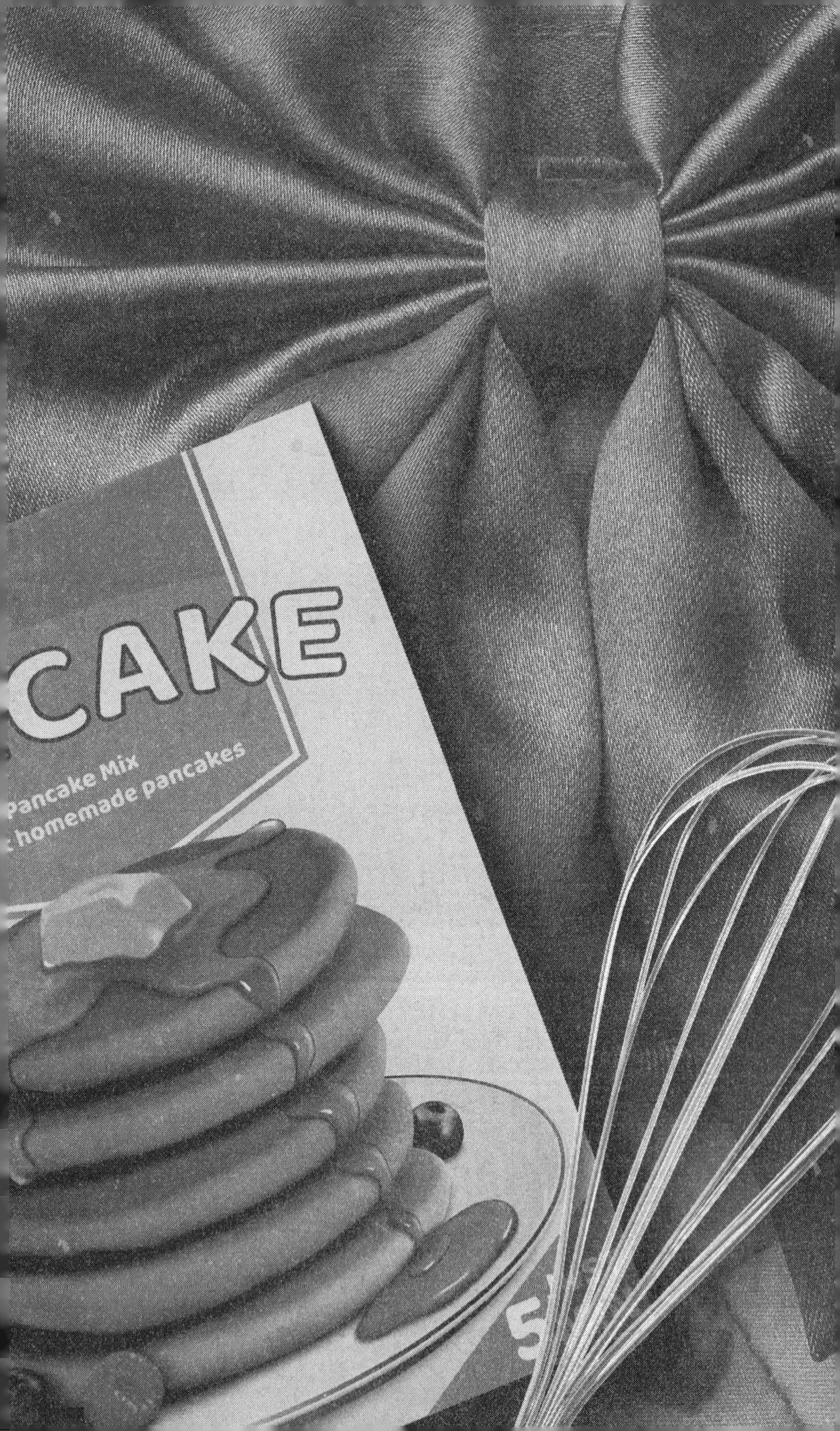
CAKE
Pancake Mix
homemade pancakes

CHAPTER 22

SAWYER

Cali scrambles up from her spot on the bed. She's still naked. Naked and rolling in a bed that's covered in Miles' scent.

I stalk to her, tossing the bag on the bed and leaning over her. I take a long sniff of her skin. Ah, she's a delicious mix of sweat, fear, and Miles. Good lord, it sends a hint of clarity through my mind.

Cali jerks back. "What are you doing?"

I straighten and rip the shirt off my head. I toss it to her. "Put that on." That'll cover her in my smell.

She clocks my bloody knuckles, but that doesn't stop the fire from flaring in her eyes.

Good. I need her to fight me right now.

Cali pulls the shirt on, covering my beautiful mark. She winces.

I smirk. "How is it?"

"It hurts, jackass."

"I meant your pussy. Are you wet still?"

Her cheeks flame red. "What? No."

Her reactions send a thrill through me. "Should I check? Are you still dripping my cum out onto the bed? Maybe I should check."

Now her whole neck is red. Oh, my little bunny loves that idea. My dick aches at the thought of her glistening pussy full of my cum.

Blessedly, the weight that was on my shoulders starts to lift.

"Here." I mess around in my bag and hold out a pill that Miles demanded I give her. "It's for the pain."

Cali turns her little nose up at me. It makes my cock jump.

"Bunny..." I warn. She's not afraid. She just likes pissing me off. I have a compulsion to own that fight. Rip it from her. Make it mine. Then give it back so she can fight me for eternity.

"You're going to take it," I tell her.

Cali's eyes widen. They're so expressive. They make me want to lean in and soak up her every expression. She's dumb for being so open with me. Maybe she isn't trying to be.

I say, "You'll like it. It's stronger than an Advil, and it'll give you a nice buzz. You like escaping in substances, don't you?"

For a second, Cali looks hurt, and then she flashes her teeth. "And you like escaping in pain, don't you?"

Oh, she's too observant for her own good. It makes the adrenaline pulse through me. I have a sudden, irrational fear that she knows that I'm running from my own mind right now. I shove it down. That's ridiculous.

"Take it," I tell her. "Or I'll make you."

Cali snatches the pill out of my hand and pops it in her mouth. I grab the water bottle I brought, and she cracks it open, taking a big swig.

"If it's in your cheek or under your tongue, I'll make you come while whipping that fine ass."

Cali's eyes glint, and she takes another gulp of water.

My dick throbs. "Good girl. It better be gone this time, or I'll whip that ass but won't let you come. Got it?"

She narrows her eyes, but she nods slightly.

"Open."

She does, and her obedience makes my dick bob. I lean over her to check. What a pretty mouth. It's so much smaller and softer than Miles'. I grip her jaw, keeping it open. I notice she's swallowed the pill. I smirk and spit into her mouth.

Cali makes a startled sound, and I let her back away. She spits on her shirt.

"You...dick!"

I snatch up the shirt and bring it to my mouth. Her pupils are blown. I make a show of licking the shirt down.

I flash my teeth at her. "You taste delicious. Now." I rummage in my bag. "Miley ran out and got you some birth control." I draw out a vial and syringe.

Cali scrambles back, her breathing becoming instantly heavy and fast. "I...I — no."

I glance at her. Instead of fire, there's a flash of raw fear in her eyes. It shoots straight to my groin. I have a sudden image of shoving into her while she fights me with that fear in her eyes. I start toward her, then freeze.

Fuck. I swore not to hurt her.

I glare at my little problem-maker. She hasn't taken her eyes off the needle. I ask, "Are you going to stay still for me?"

She swallows, trembling slightly.

That's a no. "Miles!" I bark.

Cali jumps.

There's a noise in the hallway. Out of my peripheral, I see him fill the doorway.

"Come here and hold her so I can give this to her."

Miles stalks into the room.

"Please, no," Cali says. The smell of sweat and fear has filled the room. It makes my mouth water. It's a cruel punishment that Miles made me promise not to hurt her. For me and her. I know she'll get off on it.

I give her a look. "It's either now or when you're sleeping."

"Now," she bites back quickly, then says softer, "now."

Miles sits on the bed between us. "Come here, shadow." He picks her up and puts her on his lap, caging her in with his arms.

Oh, so he's calling her nicknames now?

Cali's breathing accelerates again when he crosses his heavy arms over her.

"Miles...please." She struggles. My dick jerks. I could come from

145

just watching this.

"I won't let anything bad happen to you," Miles says. "I'll be right here." He glances at me. There's conflict in his eyes. He hates this. My gut twinges again. I don't like it when he's miserable.

Fuck. He's a fucking buzzkill. I draw up the vial into the syringe. It's a larger-than-normal gauge needle, and I throw Miles a glance. He nods slightly.

Cali trembles but has stopped speaking. I wipe down her arm and plunge the needle in.

She jolts. Miles holds her still, shushing her, whispering in her ear as I administer the contents and wipe her off. My shorts are wet. My dick is ready to go. Ready to feed off the power she's giving me. But the look on Miles' face makes my heart squeeze. I clench my jaw.

Goddamn this man and his bleeding heart. It's clear he's miserable.

I enjoy playing with Miles. I want him to be miserable, and I want him to fight me...so why does this feel wrong?

I have to do something. Something to make him feel less guilty. As I stare at them, an idea comes to me. Oh shit. This might work for both of us.

I clear my throat. "New rules."

CHAPTER 23

CALI

Sawyer crosses his arms after his declaration. He looks so menacing standing there, red and black tattoos tracing up his arms. It makes me hate him even more.

"Bunny, you are now on a point system."

Miles stiffens beneath me.

"Points will be added every time you're a good girl. Get enough points, and I'll let you go."

I suck in a breath. The world stops, and everything goes silent. Did I hear him right?

Miles' voice sounds fuzzy when he says, "What?"

"Enough points, and I'll let her go." Sawyer stares past me at Miles.

Oh my god. Oh my god, he'll let me go.

No, there has to be a catch.

"What do I have to do?" I ask.

"Plenty of things can get you points, bunny. I'm going to give you points for taking the pill like I told you to. Two points." Sawyer looks relaxed and unbothered, and he smiles.

I narrow my eyes. "How many points do I need for you to let me go?"

"I haven't decided yet." He watches the man behind me. For a second, his gaze softens. Then it snaps back to his happy mask.

"Anything we want to do to you...fuck you, mark you, hunt you, will get you points. The more fun, the more points."

I cross my arms. "So you owe me points for branding me."

"Yeah, but points also get taken away." Sawyer shrugs. "You earned one hundred points for that. But you also tried to run. Which is the biggest no-no. So two hundred points are deducted."

"Two hundred?" I sputter. This fucker! He's just playing with me again. As if my life and freedom are something he plays with like they're a game.

I throw my hands in the air. "So you can just take points away at random because you feel like it!"

"Well, I do make the rules, bunny. But no. The only hard rules are: don't run and don't try to communicate with the outside world. Those are the only two rules that you will absolutely get deducted on every time. But because I'm feeling generous, I'll let you start at zero."

Miles pushes me off his lap. "Do you swear you'll let her go?" His voice sounds disbelieving.

"If she gets enough points...I swear."

The two men share some silent communication. Sawyer's eyes are serious. Miles' shoulders relax.

I swallow. Sawyer thinks he's already won. It makes me want to punch him in the face.

I square my shoulders and turn to Miles. "I want to earn more points."

Sawyer says, "That's not how it works. We decide when you get them and what you do."

Oh, the sense of control this must give Sawyer. He knows I don't want to ask for any of this. So I look him in his triumphant blue eyes. "How much to fuck Miles?"

His eyebrows shoot up a fraction.

I cross my arms. As I do, my world spins. I blink. What meds did he give me?

Sawyer is watching me like a hawk. "You know what? I'll give you thirty points. Lay down."

I glare at him. He's testing me. Seeing if I'll obey. As much as I hate it, I have to.

I lay down on the bed so I can still see both of them. My brand burns at the movement, and the world spins again. My leg is at an awkward angle because of the cuff.

"Miles," Sawyer barks. "On your knees."

Hot hands grab my ankle and unlock me. Then they spin me around so my legs are facing them. Sawyer rips both my legs open. I fight him, but his grip is harsh and firm.

"Eat my cum out of her, pet."

Oh, fuck.

Miles' eyes flare, and he looks at my exposed pussy with pure hunger in his gaze. It makes the blood rush to my core.

I realize I've stopped struggling. I try again, weakly.

"No, no," Sawyer coos. "I know you want this nasty woman. Miles is good with his mouth. Aren't you, boy?"

Miles licks his lips and throws me an evil glance. "You want me to eat your pussy, little shadow?"

I swallow. My pussy throbs. Yes, she wants it.

Miles kneels slowly, replacing Sawyer's hands with his own.

He chuckles. "Oh yeah, you're not even fighting me anymore. What a good girl."

I briefly attempt to close my legs. My head is fully buzzing now, my skin tingling with both numbness and pleasure.

"Tsk, don't put on a show now." Miles lowers his mouth right above my pussy, his hot breath puffing on it.

My breathing comes short and fast. I can feel how wet I am as his breath puffs on it. My cheeks feel both hot and numb. How can I be this turned on by the men who've kidnapped me?

Miles watches me with those green eyes the whole time. "If you want to come, you'll keep your eyes on me, okay, pretty thing?"

Fear fills me briefly. I've always tried to avoid eye contact with Ben and the people I've fucked in the past. It feels too vulnerable.

"I..."

"You can do it, Cali." Miles licks lightly up my pussy. Electric sensation fills me as his tongue lightly swipes my clit. I jerk slightly.

Miles chuckles. "You're going to be such a delicious meal." He dives down, licking my thighs, my opening, down to my ass, and everywhere but my clit. His swipes are warm and hungry, and his pupils dilate even more. He messes with everything but where my heartbeat throbs. I squirm, and Miles holds me still.

I glance at Sawyer, who's still standing beside the bed, his face expressionless.

"Cali," Miles growls and nips my inner thigh. The bite feels both numb and sharp. Fuck. I blink to focus my eyes.

"If you want to come, you'll keep those beautiful eyes on mine. I want to see every thought that runs through that pretty little head."

Oh fuck. My clit throbs with those words. My whole body is tight with anticipation. But I can't look at him. He'll see how turned on I am. I signed up to fuck and get points, not to be vulnerable.

My gaze darts around the room, looking for an escape.

Miles growls lowly and digs his teeth into my thigh just hard enough that it hurts. I snap my gaze back to him. My chest heaves while my pussy aches.

"Be a good girl. Let me make you feel good." Miles stares at me. I tremble but don't answer. I've never come from oral. Whenever I got Ben to try it, he'd gag, and the men in my past could never get me to come.

Miles snarls and then dives into me, eating my pussy and clit with fervent energy. Pleasure fills me immediately, my throbbing clit responding so quickly it scares me. I arch my back off the bed and struggle to relieve some of the sudden sensation.

"Fighting only turns him on, bunny," Sawyer rumbles. "He's not lying. You won't come unless you obey."

Miles steadily massages my clit with the flat of his tongue. Pleasure shoots down my legs, and my skin tingles. Still, I refuse to make eye contact.

Teeth dig into my clit.

I cry out and sit up, causing the room to tumble in circles. Miles pulls back and slaps my clit with his hand. Pain explodes through me. Just as quickly, he puts his mouth back on my clit and sucks.

I moan. It feels so damn good. I want to put my fingers in his hair, yank him closer, and push him away at the same time. He sucks fervently and regularly. The pleasure overwhelms me, and I groan again.

Miles pulls away and slaps me again. "What was that, Cali? That didn't sound like my name."

I snap my gaze at him. His mouth is wet.

"I want to see the look on your face as I drink his cum out of you, shadow."

Before I can respond, Miles drops back down and focuses all his attention on my opening. He licks and sucks against it fervently, like he's trying to drink out of me. He lifts his half-lidded eyes to mine.

Fuck. He looks sinful.

Miles brings his hand up to play lightly with my clit as he puts his other finger into me.

"That's right." Sawyer's voice is raspy. "Scoop me out of her. Eat me like a good pup."

Miles dives in with more energy, groaning into me.

I throw my head back. Fuck, I want to come. I tense.

Miles' body completely leaves mine, and the pleasure fades.

I cry out and glare at him. He gives me a dark look and smacks my clit again. My back bows.

"You don't..." *smack!* "...get to come..." *smack!* "...unless you obey."

"Fuck, Miles!" I seethe and try to kick him. He just buries himself closer to me, so my kicks have little power.

"You knew the rules." He looks angry, turned on, and hungry. He dives back in, soothing the sting and immediately filling me with pleasure. He brings me to the edge again. I try to keep my body from changing so he knows, but he must feel the tension, and he stops again. He pauses just long enough that I lose the edge, then dives back in.

The pleasure is overstimulating, and I struggle to get away. Miles doesn't let me get anywhere, digging his fingers into my thighs and adding a bite of pain. Every time I glance down at him, he's looking up at me with hungry eyes.

Fuck. He leans down and eats me with more passion than

anyone ever has. I don't feel like I have to pretend I'm enjoying it.

Miles watches me. He raises his mouth just enough to rumble, "Good girl. Just like that." He goes back to licking me with the flat of his tongue, bringing his face up just enough I can see his defined cheekbones. He's so fucking hot. I feel the orgasm curling up. I reach down and grab Miles' hair, yanking his head to the tempo I need.

Miles groans, letting go of my thighs and putting both his hands under my ass, angling me more up into his mouth.

Fuck. I want to come. I need to come. I squeeze my eyes shut for a second, then yank them back open, keeping my eyes on the hooded green ones staring at me. Miles' pupils are so big there's only the tiniest ring of green. Pleasure curls up and explodes through me.

I come violently, crying out. Sparks fly all over my skin. Miles eats me through it, prolonging the pleasure. I arch into him, pulling him into me. My world is both fuzzy and buzzing at the same time. It takes me a while to come down from it.

Miles crawls up over me, kissing up my stomach as he goes. "Good girl. Good fucking girl. I knew you could do it."

As I blink back into the room, I realize the pain in my shoulder has dulled to a buzz. Miles lays next to me and pulls me into him. I feel...happy and relaxed. It's been so long since I've felt those two things.

"Shhhh. Rest now, Cali. I got you."

I glance around to see where Sawyer is. He's gone.

Miles continues muttering to me. I feel my body relax. It must be the drugs because here, right now, in this moment, I feel safe.

And that doesn't scare me nearly as much as it should.

I must zone out for a second because when I blink, Miles is combing his fingers through my hair.

"You didn't get all the stickers."

I tried. Moving my arms back pulled on my chest and hurt like a bitch. I mutter, "Sue me."

I feel Miles sit up. "Here, give me the comb."

I sit up, and the world spins. Good lord, what did they give me?

"Whoa," Miles chuckles, steadying me. He pulls me between his spread legs and leans me against his warm chest. He grabs the comb from the bedside table and grabs a section of hair. He's gentle and soothing despite all the tangles. It makes tingles roll over me.

I swallow. "You're good at that."

He hums, "I used to do it a lot."

A sharp pang of...something cuts through me. Of course, he's had a girlfriend. Do any of these men have girlfriends?

Miles must sense me stiffening, and he chuckles. "For my mom. Are you jealous, shadow?"

Oh, shit. Heat flushes along my cheeks. "No. And that's weird. Isn't your mom supposed to brush *your* hair?"

Miles grabs another chunk of hair, causing another delicious tingle to run across my scalp. My body feels slightly fuzzy. Despite that, his touch causes shivers to roll down my back.

"Well...yeah." Silence sits between us. He continues combing.

I don't know why, and maybe it's the drugs, but I feel...nostalgic. I haven't had anyone play with my hair in...well, forever.

I whisper, "I always wanted to practice hair. But I didn't have a sister to practice on. Or a mom."

Miles' fingers tickle the very back of my neck before getting another clump.

Delicious comfort and fatigue fill me. I blink slowly.

"My mom," Miles clears his throat before adding, "would come home from her shift late at night and always pass out on the couch. Her hair was always a mess." He drops some stickers into a pile he's created beside me. "Sometimes, I'd crawl up with her and comb her hair. That was the only time I got with her. After my dad left, she was always working."

I look at my hands. Miles continues to work. I want to ask what happened to his dad.

"So," Miles says. "Sawyer hasn't told me anything about you."

"Besides the fact he hates me?" I huff.

"Listen," Miles chuckles and digs his finger into my side. I struggle weakly to get away.

"You're not doing a very good job of charming your captor into letting you go."

He says it like a joke, but the air goes still, and my stomach sinks. Because that's exactly what's going on.

I clear my throat. "Yeah, can't fail at that. You might kill me."

Miles' voice lowers, "I won't kill you, Cali."

"Sure." I close my eyes again. "I didn't call in Ryder or whatever you guys think."

He traces his finger along my forehead. "Okay."

We're quiet for a bit. Then he says, "Tell me about yourself."

I frown. "I don't know what there is to say. I work as a hairstylist. I rent. I have a sassy cat who is fat and way too spoiled." A lump forms in the back of my throat. But no. I refuse to cry. I'll see him again. I'll earn enough points to get back.

Miles hums, "Boyfriend?"

I scoff. "No."

It might be just me, but it feels like he relaxes a bit.

I ask, "What about you?"

"Yeah, I have two," he chuckles.

"No, I mean a girlfriend."

"No. Those two keep my hands full."

We sit in silence for a bit. Miles continues to comb. I think he's gotten everything out, but it feels good, so I'm not complaining.

"Do you like your job?"

The question wakes me up a bit, and I shift. I realize we've gotten awfully personal. "Do I get points for this?"

Instead of answering, Miles asks another question, "Tell me why you didn't want to look me in the eye when I ate you out."

I stiffen. Because his gaze is so perceptive, I didn't want him seeing into my soul.

"I'm not answering that unless you give me points."

There's silence. Miles says, "I'll make Sawyer give you some points. Tell me."

"Are you sure? Can you do that?"

Miles' body tenses. "You know, you remind me of someone. Aggressive, pushy, and allergic to emotions. I'll get you the fucking points. Talk to me."

Fear fills me, and suddenly, I don't want to tell him. "I don't like getting close to people."

"Why?"

Because the last man I trusted let me down. Betrayed every

last sense of love and hurt me far more than hitting me. But I'll be damned if I tell him that.

"That's two questions!" I say.

"Then two points, you stubborn woman. Why don't you trust people?"

My chest tightens.

Miles traces his arms around me and hugs me. It makes me want to panic.

"Cali, you just came in my mouth. How is talking to me any different?"

"First and last time that happens," I mutter.

"Tell me." Miles' voice becomes demanding.

"Because!" Anger fills me. "Every time you get close to people, they hurt you. And I'll be damned if I fall for that again. Is that good enough for you?"

Miles says nothing.

"You happy now? Jesus, I wish you all would leave me alone. Just leave me alone and let me go!" I try to cross my arms, but they're numb. The rush of anger fills me with fatigue, and I want to close my eyes.

I feel Miles shift and get up.

I close my eyes. Maybe if I ignore him, he'll go away. Maybe all of this will go away. When I wake up, I'll be back in my own bed. With a cat that loves me. And maybe a million bucks to pack up my life and live somewhere exotic. The warmth surrounds me, making me take deep, even breaths. I'm so deliciously numb. Maybe I can get a harem of men to wait on me hand and foot. That thought makes me want to chuckle. As if.

I think I've fallen asleep when I hear a voice so soft I barely hear it say, "What are you like when you're happy, broken little thing?"

CHAPTER 24

MILES

"You have her phone," I say as I shoulder into Ryder's office. Sawyer is sitting at the desk on the computer. Sawyer grunts.

"I know you do. I want it." He's always messing with the phones of all our marks to throw the cops off our trail.

He looks up at me. "She threw it in a moving truck when I was tracking her with it. No, I don't have it."

I deflate. Fuck.

"But..." Sawyer leans back. "I did get a forensic download of it."

Hope surges in me again. Of course he did. He's good at this kind of thing. At one point, he hacked into mine and Ryder's phone to drop us dick pics all day. And they weren't of his dick, either.

Sawyer continues working. "Why do you want it?"

"Because," I say. Because she's fucked up, and I want to figure out why. Because I want to know what makes her tick. What makes her happy. What her favorite food is. What made her mom leave.

Jesus. I sound like a lovesick puppy.

Sawyer looks at me like he can see right through me. Which, he usually can. I arch an eyebrow.

"Let me see it."

"Why? You want to look at the texts between her and her ex?"

A sick feeling hits my stomach. "Who the hell is her ex?"

"Some loser. Who cares?"

Real, deep anger runs through me. I care. He fucking left her. She's angry at the world in a way I've only seen Sawyer be. And I want to know why.

Sawyer sees me get pissed, and a glint of amusement fills his eyes. He's riling me up on purpose.

"If you're a good pup, I might show you."

I arch an eyebrow. "What do you want?"

"A kiss." Sawyer grins at me. Fuck, I love that smile.

"Always bargaining," I mutter and lean to him. He licks his lips. I lower a kiss to his lips.

When I try to pull away, Sawyer grips the back of my neck and pulls me into him. He deepens the kiss, forcing my lips to part for him so he can sweep his tongue into me. My body reacts to him with sparks of electricity. I melt into Sawyer, and he groans. Fuck, why does toxicity taste so good?

Sawyer pulls away from me. "Goddamn, pup." He licks his lips and looks at me with an open mouth. "You're sinful."

I flush.

"Here." He goes back to his computer and pulls up a program. "You can see what was on her phone before I took her."

I zone in on his computer. It looks like a bunch of screens and data. "I don't know how to use this."

"Here." Sawyer grabs my hips and yanks me down into his lap. "What do you want to know about our little bunny?"

"Who the fuck is her ex?"

Sawyer chuckles and starts clicking. He brings up a text thread conversation. It takes me a bit to adjust to the formatting, but once I do, I take over the mouse and scroll. The longer I read, the more pissed I become. Who the fuck does this Ben think he is?

Ben: I'm so sorry, baby.

Ben: I didn't mean it. You know not to get me riled up.

Ben: Work has been so bad, and everything has been so hard since my grandma died. I asked you to be there for me. Where has my support been? Where? Out with your other man. What kind of girlfriend does that?

Ben: Where are you right now when I need you?

Ben: I'm just going to kill myself. I obviously have no support from the people who are supposed to be there for me. For my whole life, no one has been there for me.

Ben: So you don't care if I kill myself, huh? Some girlfriend you are.

I sit back. Sawyer is silent.

"This fucker is her ex?"

Sawyer sounds pissed. "Yeah. Been blowing up her accounts. He wants to try again."

For a second, I'm seven years old again, standing at the top of the stairs as my dad screams at my mom for being a cheating whore and telling her how much he hates her. I'd stand frozen in my dinosaur PJs, wanting to help my mom but too scared to. Then, mere hours later, she'd be believing him when he told her he loved her. She'd take him back every time, bruises and all. Until, of course, he left us.

"Pup." Sawyer grabs my wrist. "You okay?"

I clear my throat. Fuck. Why the hell does this still bother me? It was twenty-five years ago. I should be over it. "Yeah," I say. "I'm fine. Show me her camera roll."

Sawyer doesn't move for a second, then complies. Hundreds of thumbnails flash across the screen. I take over the mouse and mine through her pictures.

It's clear the woman loves her cat. She has almost no pictures of other people. Fuck. Who was there to support *her*?

Sawyer sits up straighter. "Wait."

I stop scrolling. He clicks on a picture, and an image of Cali naked, except for a man's shirt, comes across the screen. She's facing away from the camera, and she's pulled the shirt down far enough that you can see the soft and delicious curves of her body. My mouth waters. I feel Sawyer's dick twitch beneath me.

"Goddamn," I mutter. "How many points to let her go?"

"Five hundred."

I don't know where it comes from, but on impulse, I say, "Make it a thousand."

CHAPTER 25

CALI

I assume I slept all night since the sun is up again when I wake. I feel much better than before, although my brand still burns like a bitch. I've just gotten up to use the bathroom when Sawyer comes in.

"Come with me, bunny."

My gaze drops to the chains in Sawyer's hands. Why the hell does he have chains?

I take a tiny step back.

Sawyer's gaze darkens. "Don't make me chase you. You won't get anywhere, and it'll only make me want to hurt you".

"What are you going to do with me?"

"Tie you up so you can't go anywhere while Miles and I are out. Come." Sawyer turns and walks out.

They're going to leave me here? Where the hell are they going?

I follow slowly. I'm tempted to run into the kitchen, but Sawyer cocks his eyebrow at me. I glare at him. He walks further down the hallway toward a bedroom on the right that I've never been to.

I stand in the doorway. It's a large bedroom with a king-size, four-poster bed. The bed is against the wall on one side, and a huge bathroom and closet are on the other. Sawyer goes to the bathroom and motions at me.

I take one step in the room. "Where are you guys going?"

Sawyer doesn't answer. He's wearing nicer clothes than I've seen him in, with dark wash jeans and a button-down shirt.

Sawyer fastens the end of the chain to something under the sink and then looks at me. I'm still in just his T-shirt. Sawyer's gaze drifts low where the hem just covers the tops of my thighs.

"I won't ask you again. Come here and kneel."

"Why?"

Sawyer gives me a blank look. "I'm trying to be nice. If you want me to throw you in the basement again with no bathroom, I will."

Shit. Are they going to be gone awhile? I walk stiffly to him.

Sawyer arches an eyebrow when I just stand there. Then, faster than I can register, he swats my ass.

"Ow!" I hiss.

He shoots his hand up, grips my neck, and yanks me to my knees. They crack against the floor, and pain shoots up my legs. My burn also flares up with the sudden movement.

The chain clinks, and Sawyer quickly wraps the cold links around my neck. I jerk from the cold and yank back. Sawyer clicks a padlock around the chain at my neck. I catch a whiff of his cologne. He smells masculine, and I hate that I like it.

I reach up to feel. "What the hell?" It's not strangling me, but it's tight enough that there's almost no give.

"I'm sorry I don't have an appropriate collar yet, bunny." For a second, Sawyer looks remorseful. "But I don't trust you not to rip it off while we're gone."

I stand up, and Sawyer follows suit. "How long will you be gone?"

"Not sure. This is just in case," he says. "In case you get any ideas, you can't get to the windows from here, but I've given you enough slack to move around and use the bathroom. To do whatever little bunnies do when they're caged."

He's just going to leave me in a bathroom? "You can't do this!"

"Sure I can," Sawyer winks. "And you're going to be a good little girl and take it. Can't believe all it takes is a little orgasm to make you soft."

Shock rolls through me, and then rage boils under my skin. I'm embarrassed, and I'm not fucking soft.

Sawyer pulls out a phone from his pocket and, quicker than I can cover up, snaps a picture. "It's pathetic, really. Spent all night here and didn't try to escape. It'll be easy to break you now that I have you figured out."

Before I can think, I swing at Sawyer's face.

Sawyer ducks back, a shit-eating grin plastered on. "Be a good, docile little thing."

Then he's gone.

I scream. Fuck. I know better. I fucking know better! Why in the hell did I ever let my guard down?

I see my seething face in the mirror. My neck is wrapped up in a chain collar with a padlock keeping it together. I lean in, trying to figure out how to get it off. After struggling, I see that it's not going to come off without some serious tools or a key.

I want to scream again.

Anger fills my veins. Sawyer is not going to break me. He doesn't deserve to break me. I frantically search the room for anything I could use to get away. But, like Miles' bathroom, it's been stripped of anything useful.

I glance at the mirror again. Oh my god, I look terrible. Wild. Why didn't I try to escape last night? Why did I allow myself to get comfortable?

The mirror is large, covering the double sinks and almost reaching the ceiling. I could break it. But with what?

I glance down. I have about 8 feet of chain to move around with. Moving out of the bathroom, I see how far into the room I can go. There's a large walk-in closet right next to me. I make it about two feet before the chain goes tight around my neck. I cough.

Break me. He can't break me. If my childhood couldn't break me, then this motherfucker sure can't. I'll kill him for trying.

The closet is full of suits. They're lined up on either side and look pristine. All the hangers are spaced evenly apart, and everything is ironed.

I'll show them just how much they can control me.

I get to work destroying everything I can reach, ripping suits off hangers, tearing the fabric, throwing shoes around. I used the hangers to punch holes in the drywall. Then I get inspired and try to spell "fuck you" with them. But I run out before I can. I rage and smash the hangers into the bathroom mirror.

It's therapeutic. As I destroy, I think about what my life has become. Getting somehow tangled up with a man who hates me and has made it clear he intends to hurt and kill me. What the hell is wrong with me? It makes me want to cry.

I smash things into the mirror until, finally, the glass shatters. I jump back, but my leg is still cut by some of the falling pieces.

I stare at the blood, and tension boils up in me. I sit back against the wall and stare at the red streaking down my leg. Not because the cut hurts. It doesn't. But if I don't look at something, I'm going to cry. I'm alone. I'm so horribly alone. No one is coming for me. Everyone I know leaves me, so now I just try to leave them first. Fucking hell, I thought I was okay with that. Except for now. Now, I really wish I had someone.

I miss Halloweiner. My heart clenches. I miss the way he sticks his tail straight in the air when he's happy. The way he kneads the blankets when we sleep and the kisses he gives me before bed. I always told him he was a vicious little boy. I just want to tell him I love him one last time.

I let the tears roll down my face, feeling empty. The blood has dripped down my leg and onto the floor. I want to paint the walls with it, but I've used all my energy. I just want to sleep. I grab a shirt and wrap it around the edge of a piece of glass. Then I plop down outside the bathroom and wait.

Weak? I'll show them weak.

CAKE

Pancake Mix
homemade pancakes

CHAPTER 26

SAWYER

Bugs are crawling under the skin on my arms, their little legs swimming back and forth right underneath the surface.

"Dude, you good?" Miles watches me scratching.

"Fine. What the hell is taking him so long?"

Miles glances at the sheriff's office. "He said not to go in. Let's just wait a little longer."

My knee bounces.

You're such a piece of shit.

I clench my teeth.

Twisted fuck.

Jesus. Mom's voice has gotten louder and more frequent despite every attempt to run it off.

You have a pretty little sex slave at home? You're no different than my clients.

I scratch again. I left her in Ryder's room and pissed her off so he wouldn't feel so bad about playing my game.

And you did it because it turned you on. Because you'll do anything to get off.

I claw at my arm.

"There!" Miles sits up straighter. I look over.

Sure enough, Ryder walks out of the building, his stride powerful and confident. I'm struck again by his sheer size. He's taller than me by a good few inches and bulkier than me and Miles. The man is also completely covered in dark tattoos, even where his crumpled suit doesn't cover, from his feet to his neck, where they disappear into his dark hair.

My mouth waters. Ryder walks with barely concealed power over to our car.

I jump out, and Ryder grabs me up in a hug, slamming me against the side of the truck.

"Jesus," I cough, barely able to pull in a breath. But with his crushing hug, I feel the voices recede.

"Missed you," Ryder mutters into my hair.

I swallow, "You too."

"Okay, hello?" Miles pipes up. Instantly, I'm released, and the monster of a man grabs Miles' hair, yanking his head all the way back. He grins down into his mouth. "Hello."

Miles laughs. "Let go of me, you brute."

"Tsk, tsk, Miles. You know better than to make demands." Ryder descends on Miles' mouth and kisses the hell out of him. When he lets him up for air, Miles looks up at Ryder with puppy eyes.

Ryder chuckles and releases him. "Let's get out of here."

I opt to let Ryder drive, and he pulls us out of the lot.

"Goddamn, it's good to be free," Ryder rumbles.

"You want to stop for food?" Miles asks.

"Nah. Let's just go home. I desperately need a shower and a shave."

Home. With our bunny. And our game.

Ryder is staring at me in the rearview mirror. His tone changes to a demanding one. "Something you want to tell me, Sawyer?"

Like that I have a hot piece of ass captive in our home? Who fights so beautifully that it makes me want to hurt her more? Who makes Miles want to curl up under her skin and save her from everything, including us?

You love playing your sick games. You're fucked up.

I shrug.

Ryder doesn't buy it. He goes silent, then glances over at Miles. Miles' jaw is so tight I see the muscle twitch.

"No one's gonna tell me what's going on?"

"That's on Sawyer," Miles grits. "It's his mark."

The car goes deathly silent. We've never picked marks without the others involved. For years, it's been a group effort.

You're no better than me, Sawyer. You always hated me, but look at you now.

My abuser's voice is so loud I almost hear her right next to me. I squeeze my eyes shut.

Ryder jerks the car to the side of the road. A small thrill of fear runs through me.

My door is yanked open. Ryder's voice is so soft I almost miss it. "Get the fuck out."

I do. Ryder grips the back of my neck and shoves me to the other end of the car.

"Open both doors, Miles."

Ryder shoves me against the seat where Miles sits, between the doors, so no one can see.

His huge body hovers over me, his breath ghosting the back of my right ear. "Did you forget how this works, Sawyer?"

I clench my fists.

"I ask questions, you answer." I hear the whisper of his belt being taken out.

A delicious shiver runs through me. He's going to hurt me. I want it. I need it. I need it to chase away the voices.

"I don't care if the question is what you had for lunch or what your greatest fear is." In a violent move, Ryder rips my jeans down. "I ask. You answer."

I drop my head onto the leather seat and grab Miles' thigh, bracing for what I know is coming next.

The whistle comes before the hit, and when it makes contact, my entire body jerks as pain shoots through me. Holy fuck. The whistling comes again and again, and I'm laced with fiery pain.

I groan.

"Take your dick out," Ryder demands softly. "You too, Miles."

I obey.

Whistle, hit. Fuck.

I groan, completely turned on. The pain soothes me in a way nothing else can.

Sick fuck.

Whistle, hit.

I stroke myself, my dick swelling impossibly hard. My ass is on fire. Ryder is precise with his strikes, hitting the same spots every time on purpose for maximum pain.

With the next strike, I whimper in pain.

Ryder groans behind me. "You gonna cry for me, Sawyer?"

"No," I grit. He hits me again, lighting my entire body in pain, and damn me, I want to. I'm on the edge of coming.

"No welcome home tears, Sawyer? What a..." *hit* "...bad boy..." *hit.*

"Fuuuck," I groan.

I jump as Ryder traces his hand softly over my ass. The skin feels hot and welted. Ryder whispers in my ear, "Do you want to come?"

"Yes," I grit.

"Then talk to me." He steps back and hits me again. I cry out, pain and pleasure curling through my whole body.

"Come," he demands.

I do, coming into my hand and sagging against the car.

"Miles, you wait."

Miles groans.

Ryder chuckles. He pats my shoulder. "That was a fun warm-up."

I choke back a sob. Holy fuck, I'm being weak today. What the hell is happening to me?

Ryder runs his hands down my arms. "Sawyer, what did you need to tell me?"

I pull my pants up, straighten, and turn to face him. I banish every trace of emotion from my voice and stare over his shoulder into the desert behind him. "I took the girl who called you in, made her my mark, and now she's chained up in your bedroom."

CHAPTER 27

RYDER

I take in what Sawyer just said, glancing between his eyes. They're glassy with the beautiful tears I just caused. Fuck, I want to fuck the tortured look out of him. He looks worse than when I last saw him. I know he fights his demons. I know what his mom did to him haunts him. But this? This seems worse.

Sawyer hates women. It was only a matter of time before he took one as his mark. Although, I suppose I thought his mom would be the first.

I shake my head. "Get back in the car."

For once, Sawyer obeys, and it makes me even more concerned. He always fights me any chance he gets.

I follow him into the car. Sawyer brought a woman back to our home. Why in the *hell* would he bring her there?

I glance at Miles to see his reaction. He won't look at me.

My gut twists. What happened in these few short days?

"Sawyer," I say, trying to keep my emotions in check. "Why is she at our house?"

Sawyer shrugs, then sees me watching him and answers verbally, "Never done it before. Thought it would be fun."

Miles scoffs, and Sawyer shoots him a glare.

The two of them fighting settles me a little. They always fight. It's Sawyer's toxic way of showing love.

We drive the rest of the way in silence. I know both of them are waiting for me to ask more questions.

I don't. I want to go home and make them cry their answers to me while I play with their limits. Goddamn, I need a brutal fuck. Need to remind them who they belong to. To remind them that they *never* do things without me.

We pull into the driveway, and I glance at my bedroom window. What the hell is waiting for me in there?

I head straight to my room with both men following me and throw the door open.

There, on the wall by my bathroom, sits a feral little creature. She's naked from the waist down, and one leg is covered in blood. She jerks when I walk in. Our gazes meet, and I stop. Her blue eyes are arresting, and they spark with hatred. She's gorgeous. A perfect little plaything to destroy my men. Where did she come from?

"Oh, you must be Ryder." The woman sounds bored, but her entire body is tense. She's surrounded by a complete mess. I look closer. Hangers, suits, and glass. And she's...chained by her neck? My room is trashed. My sanctuary. Gone. My stomach clenches.

I turn to Sawyer, who looks smug.

"Sawyer," I growl. "Why did you leave her in my room?" I already feel the panic from the chaos creeping into my bones.

Miles' angry voice cuts through my anxiety, "What did you do to her, Sawyer?"

"Nothing." Sawyer raises his hands. "And even if I did, that's the game, Miles."

Miles looks over, and his eyes spark in real anger. It mirrors the anger I feel in my soul.

Usually, we fight over small things. Leaving food out overnight and leaving the truck empty on gas. Sawyer messes with Miles to get a reaction. I fuck the attitude out of both of them. This is more serious.

I came home to a house divided, which has never happened in the history of our relationship. And all because of this girl.

Immediately, I don't like her.

Fuck, I feel like shit. This should not be happening right now. I need to wash the germs off from our trip. I can't crumple now. Not when they both need me so badly. I need to get them both set back in our system.

I snatch both Miles and Sawyer up by their necks and shove them toward the bed.

"I'm going to punish you until you tell me what's really going on here. Neither of you will come unless I think you deserve it."

I'm going to fuck them, and then I'm going to get rid of our vicious little problem.

CHAPTER 28

MILES

The growl in Ryder's voice makes me shiver. He's fucking pissed. I'm not sure how I got wrapped up in this, but Sawyer's a big boy, and he can admit how he fucked up. I glance at Cali again. She watches us with shrewd eyes. The blood on her leg has dried, so she must not be hurt too badly. Still, the fact that she's injured makes me murderously angry.

"Miles. Help me," Ryder barks. He's spreading Sawyer on his knees on the edge of the bed, tying each hand to the opposite bedpost. The bedposts come up higher than most – a feature Ryder uses to his advantage.

I grab Sawyer's other hand, securing him so his arms are spread to either side.

He sneers at me. "Aren't you just a kiss-ass, obedient pup."

Ryder smacks Sawyer's bruised ass. Sawyer jerks, and Ryder growls, "That obedient pup is going to suck your dick until you're squirming, so shut the fuck up."

In one move, Ryder rips Sawyer's shirt off. Sawyer tests the limits of the bonds, his muscles flexing. Fuck, he looks good.

Ryder pulls off his suit jacket and shirt and stops to look at Cali. She glares at him.

Ryder turns back around and says lowly, "Sawyer. I'm disappointed in you. You know better than to bring a mark here. We don't piss where we drink."

"More fun this way," Sawyer grits.

"More dangerous this way." Ryder leans in to bite Sawyer's ear. "You've been leaning far too close to self-sabotage recently, and you're going to tell me why."

Sawyer clams up immediately.

Ryder throws me a look. I see the excitement in his eyes. "Undo his pants."

I do. I feel Sawyer is hard before I even get them down. He's still kneeling, so I can't get them all the way off, but I go as far as I can. Sawyer's dick bobs. Ryder yanks off Sawyer's shoes and socks.

"Miles, you're going to play with yourself. Let Sawyer watch what happens when you're an obedient pup."

I lie on the bed so I can see both Sawyer and Cali. Her breathing is fast. Seeing her pink cheeks and huge pupils shoots pleasure straight down my dick.

Ryder moves towards the closet, and I see Cali tense.

Wait. She has something in her hand. The fire burns in her eyes, and her body stiffens for action.

"Cali!" I bark, my tone changing immediately.

She startles and looks at me.

"Don't fucking touch him."

Ryder glances at me, a hint of curiosity in his gaze. I know he'd kill her easily. Whatever stupid idea she had to hurt him was only going to be dangerous to herself.

Ryder squats down within her reach, saying softly, "Were you gonna try and stab me, vicious thing?"

Cali is still tense, her body trembling. She wisely chooses to say nothing.

"Why is my pup defending you?" Ryder cocks his head. "Hmmm?"

Cali swallows but still doesn't say anything.

Ryder chuckles and stands. He retrieves what he wants from the closet and returns to the bed. Clothespins.

"Maybe you need a little pain to motivate you, Sawyer." Ryder leans in and runs his nose across the skin on Sawyer's ribs. I see the goosebumps prickle on Sawyer, even though his face doesn't change.

"Touch yourself, Miles," Ryder barks. "I'm not going to ask again."

I do. I'm already sensitive from playing earlier and not being allowed to get off, so I go slowly.

Ryder runs a clip up and down Sawyer's side, tickling him. He chuckles, and then pinches the skin on Sawyer's ribs, clamping the clothespin on it.

Sawyer closes his eyes and bows his head.

"You're gonna be a good boy for me and take whatever I have to give you," Ryder rumbles. He grabs another clothespin and pinches it right above the first. He works until Sawyer's whole right side is lined with them.

"Sick fuck," Ryder murmurs. "Liking the pain I give you. Loving it. Begging for more."

The clothespins shudder with every breath Sawyer takes. I slowly stroke myself to how turned on both of them are.

Ryder goes up Sawyer's other side, then clips both of Sawyer's nipples. Sawyer doesn't react, but he keeps his eyes closed. I know it hurts like a bitch. He's done it to me once or twice, and I don't like it.

"Nasty, dirty slut." Ryder continues degrading him. The more he does it, the more Sawyer's dick bobs and leaks precum. I stroke myself.

"What a good boy, closing your eyes for me." Ryder clips a clothespin to each of Sawyer's eyelids, right under his eyebrows.

That gets a reaction. Sawyer groans a little.

Ryder chuckles. He gets up and goes to his dresser, coming back with a crop.

Ryder hasn't taken off his pants, but I see he's straining against the seams. This man is huge, and I know Sawyer's ass is going to pay. Sawyer's dick bobs again, and my mouth waters.

"You ready to talk to me, Sawyer?"

Sawyer grunts. "Go fuck yourself."

A delicious grin spreads across Ryder's face, and he snaps the crop onto the underside of Sawyer's foot.

There's a gasp from across the room.

Sawyer groans deeply.

"Suck him, Miles," Ryder demands. I scramble to obey, gripping his dick and pulling it into my mouth.

Sawyer trembles.

Whack, whack, whack. With every hit, Sawyer jumps a little. I know Ryder hits hard as hell. I have no idea how Sawyer is being so quiet. I suck him with energy, pulling him into the back of my throat. His salty precum fills my mouth.

"Sawyer," Ryder singsongs. "Sawyeeeeer. Answer me." He hits him again, and the smack is loud as fuck. Sawyer bucks into my mouth.

"What," Sawyer grits.

"Who's in charge?"

He doesn't answer, and another barrage of heavy blows land.

"You," Sawyer chokes.

"That's right," Ryder purrs. He hits some of the clothespins with the crop, causing them to violently snap off and fall onto me.

"Fuuuck." Sawyer swells in my mouth.

Ryder throws me a warning look. I know he doesn't want me to let Sawyer come yet. I pull back just a little and lap at his dick.

"Fuckers," Sawyer moans.

"What do you need?" Ryder asks.

Sawyer's whole body is tense, every muscle standing out. He fights the restraints. "More," he rasps.

Ryder's eyes light up. He stalks to the other side of the room and swoops to grab one of the glass shards Cali broke. He walks back to us, gripping the glass. It cuts his hand, but he doesn't even wince. Ryder takes his bloody hand and pulls out his dick.

"I'm gonna fuck you in the ass with my blood as lube. And you're going to thank me, you disgusting whore."

Ryder closes the distance and presses his dick to Sawyer's ass.

"Fuck!" Sawyer barks. His entire body tenses. "Fuck you, fucker!"

"Oh, now you want to talk to me?" Ryder knocks off a few more clothespins and, with a violent shove, presses all the way into Sawyer's ass.

I take Sawyer into the back of my throat again. He groans and throws his head back, pistoning into me with the force of Ryder's thrusts.

"Talk to me then. Tell me how much you hate me," Ryder hisses.

I glance up at both of them. Ryder has the glass to Sawyer's neck, a trickle of blood dripping down. I don't know if it's Ryder's blood or Sawyer's. Sawyer's head is resting on Ryder's shoulder. The tortured look is gone, and now there's only bliss.

I stroke myself harder. Fuck, I want to come just looking at them.

"You don't get to come until Miles has," Ryder grunts. "You're the bottom of the pack today, Sawyer. Putting your safety at risk, our safety at risk." He pounds into Sawyer's ass.

I groan and stiffen, glancing at Ryder. He's pressing the glass even deeper into Sawyer, lapping at the blood.

Their violence makes pleasure roll through me.

I pop off Sawyer long enough to gasp, "Please."

Ryder looks down at me, his lips red. "Yes, pup."

Pleasure explodes through me, and I do. I come in long spurts, exploding all over the sheets and my hand.

Ryder follows soon after, stiffening behind Sawyer.

"Tell me why, Sawyer," Ryder grunts.

Sawyer moans, blissed out. "For fun."

"You can run from yourself, Sawyer, but you can't run from me. Now come."

Sawyer's dick stiffens and swells in my mouth. Then he's pumping cum down my throat. There's so much of it I choke, trying to swallow it all down.

Sawyer trembles. Ryder immediately pulls out and undoes Sawyer's hands.

Sawyer collapses next to me, both of us limp and sated. Before I know it, Ryder has returned with warm, wet cloths, gives one to me, and starts to clean up Sawyer.

"Talk to me, Sawyer," he demands. "What's going on?"

Sawyer throws a look at the other end of the room. Fuck, I forgot Cali was there for a second. Her cheeks are flushed.

Ryder glances back and then looks at us again. "We'll get rid of her today. Talk to me."

I stiffen, as does Sawyer. He looks at Cali for a second too long. Ryder looks back at her, then at both of us. Suddenly he grabs my chin and puts his face in mine. "Tell me," he demands. I see a flicker of fear cross his face before he shuts it down again.

I clear my throat. I don't know how Ryder is going to take this. "Sawyer took her as his mark. She's on a point system. If she gets enough points, we'll let her go."

CHAPTER 29

CALI

I watch the men with rapt attention. Ryder doesn't move after Miles' statement. I wish he was facing me so I could see his expression. I watch Miles instead. Is he mad? What the hell does he think?

Miles just looks into Ryder's face. When he glances at me, I think I see fear.

"Outside. Now." Sawyer gets up and yanks his pants up. He doesn't throw on a shirt, and I stare again at the angry, raised scars all over his back. He and Ryder are covered in them.

The other two stay locked in a stare-off for a second.

"Let's go," Sawyer demands.

"Wait," my voice comes out gravely. I clear my throat. "I'll do it! I'll earn the points."

Miles shoots me a shut-the-fuck-up look. They leave the room and shut the door.

My heart races. Fuck. Sawyer always said he'd kill me, but he hadn't seemed done fucking with me. Ryder? I think he'd have no problem putting a bullet in my brain. The hierarchy has been overthrown, and I feel frantic.

I try to get out of the chains, but I can't. For the first time since I've been here, I have a full-blown panic attack. I feel death knocking on my skull.

This is it. This is the end.

I try to draw a breath in, but I can't. Fuck. I need a drink. I really need a drink.

I spiral, sitting almost naked on the floor of the men who kidnapped me.

What would I have done differently with my life if I knew it was going to be this short? Fuck, I wish I found love.

I picture my grandma at my funeral, looking down her nose and judging. Saying I turned out just like she expected.

No. My chest heaves. They don't get to see me like this. They don't deserve to. They don't get to see me weak. I draw in my first full breath.

I've been here for myself for my whole life, and I'll continue to do it until I go. They can take my life and my peace, but they can't take my fucking dignity.

I square my shoulders.

Footsteps come down the hall, and then the door opens. Sawyer stands there, looking completely put together again.

"Hello, bunny. Wanna play a game?"

CHAPTER 30

CALI

Sawyer approaches me, stopping just short of reaching my allotted distance. "I'll unlock you, but if you try to stab me, I'll only get turned on."

I glare at him. His blue eyes look less manic. Icy and calm. He's fully clothed and put together again. It's like what I just saw didn't happen, except for the red mark on his neck.

"You deserve to get stabbed," I growl. "Let me go."

"I'm trying." Sawyer reaches under my chin, his hot fingers grazing my neck softly. It makes me shiver.

"Maybe one day I'll let you stab me. Sounds kinky. Now, you're going to get dressed, and I'll explain the game." Sawyer grabs my hand and starts walking.

"Wait," I pull against his strong grip. For all I know, he's walking me outside to get shot.

He just tightens his grip. "Don't fight me right now, bunny." His voice lowers, "I'm doing my best to keep you alive."

I stop pulling. Sawyer yanks me down the hall and into a room that's across the way from Miles'. Once we're in, he shuts the door and lets go of me.

I rub my neck. It feels so much lighter without the chain. I glance around.

"Clean up in the bathroom." Sawyer barely looks at me as he shuffles through his drawers. This room is a mirrored version of Miles' room, but it's cluttered and covered in posters of half-naked men and women. This must be Sawyer's room.

I move to the bathroom. It's fully outfitted with everything a bathroom should be. Suddenly, I want to brush my teeth so fucking bad.

I wet a towel and run it under my arms and down my bloody leg.

"If you try to hurt me with anything in there, just know it's going up that pretty pussy," I hear from the room. "So choose wisely."

I glare out the door. Sawyer shows up, his face lit up in a grin. He tosses a pair of sweatpants, boxers, socks, and my tennis shoes at me. "Get dressed."

I eye the clothes. "Is this going to cost me points?"

"Only if you don't obey."

I do. The comfort of the clothes instantly makes me feel safer. I feel slightly comfortable for the first time since I got here. I have to roll the sweatpants a few times to keep them on my hips, but otherwise, they're soft.

Sawyer watches me with a satisfied look. "You look so hot in my clothes, bunny. Now, freshen up." He motions at the sink and walks back into the room.

I look through the drawers. There's only one toothbrush. Fuck it. I lather toothpaste on it and nearly groan at how good it feels. I find deodorant and use it, too. I really smell like Sawyer now. It makes my mouth water a little, and self-disgust immediately follows.

Sawyer pops back up. "There's hair ties under the sink."

Sure enough, I find a pack. I watch Sawyer as I pull my hair back. This man is moody as fuck. I ask, "Why are you being nice to me?"

Sawyer smiles. "I wouldn't call it being nice. You stink. Plus, we're going out, so I want you to look normal."

I flush and then freeze. What? We're going out?

Sawyer leans against the doorframe, one hand gripping the top. "New game. Hide and seek. You and I hide, Ryder and Miles seek."

I swallow. Holy fuck.

Sawyer looks at his nails. "Starting ten minutes ago, we had an hour to hide. Anywhere within a twenty-mile radius."

I stop breathing. "The time has already started?"

Sawyer chuckles. "Relax."

"Relax?" Adrenaline runs through me. "What happens if we get caught?"

"We probably get fucked within an inch of our lives." He shrugs. "It gets you out of the house so Ryder doesn't decide to... you know...kill you and end the game now. He's a little pissed about his room."

My stomach bottoms out. "Well, let's fucking go." I push past Sawyer, and he laughs. I can't believe this is happening.

"Why are you hiding with me?"

Sawyer follows me to the kitchen. "So you don't run."

I make a beeline to the front door.

"Ah, wait." I hear the jangling of keys, and I whirl. Sawyer is holding a set. "We can run if you want, but driving is faster."

Oh my god, they're going to let me get in a car.

Sawyer holds out his arm like he's a gentleman escorting his date. I glare at him.

He shrugs with a mischievous look and leads us outside.

The air and sunshine hit me, and I feel a rush of gratitude. They're letting me outside. For a brief second, tears prick my eyes.

Sawyer climbs into the same pickup I saw at the gas station. Oh my god, that feels like months ago.

For a second, I hesitate. I think about taking off on foot. Then I banish that stupid thought and hop in the passenger seat.

"Strap in, bunny. I have a stop to make."

"Wait, no." Panic runs through me. "We're going as far and as fast as we can."

"Well, yes." He winks at me. "We'll run *and* make a little pit stop."

I cross my arms. This is all so weird. What is his ulterior motive? "How do I know you're not just taking me right to them?"

"I'm not. You have my word." Sawyer looks me in the eyes. He looks sincere, as far as I can tell. I'm not convinced the man is ever genuinely sincere.

We pull out of the dirt driveway and head south. I soak in the landscape, memorizing the location. We're truly out in the middle of nowhere.

"What are the rules?" I ask.

"You'll get fifty points to play the game. And another fifty if we don't get caught. You'll lose it all if you break the only two rules."

I glance at Sawyer. I thought he was huge until I saw Ryder. That man is a giant. Sawyer looks so relaxed, with one hand on the wheel and one resting loosely on the center console.

"How many points to let me go?"

"A thousand. Should Ryder decide you're allowed to stay."

My stomach twists again. "You sick fuck." I look outside again. This game would get me a tenth of the way there. If I live past it. "How do I get him to decide to keep me?"

Sawyer's voice gets serious. "I don't know, bunny."

We drive in silence for a bit. I want to cry again.

No. I'm done with this. I'll win their stupid little game. Twenty miles is a huge radius. How will they find us without Sawyer cheating?

"Where's your phone?" I ask.

"In my pocket."

"Give it to me."

"Do you think I'm stupid?" Sawyer looks at me, his eyes twinkling.

"They're probably tracking you with it. And you can tell them where we're at."

"I promise I won't. I'll get fucked just as hard as you will, and I'm sore."

I narrow my eyes at him. "I don't think you'll care that much."

Sawyer chuckles, then fishes in his pocket and takes his phone out. He powers it off in front of me. "Good?"

I cross my arms. No, not good. But better.

I watch him drive. He looks so different than when he forced me on his friend's dick, branded me, and said he was going to kill me. Right now, he looks calm. That *look* isn't in his eyes.

"You're crazy as fuck, aren't you?" I ask.

Sawyer throws his head back and laughs. Almost as quickly, he sobers and looks at me. For a moment, he looks the most normal I've ever seen him. His voice comes out soft, "Am I crazy, Cali? Or am I just playing a game?" He maintains eye contact while driving 50 down the road.

I clench my jaw. "Look where we're going."

Sawyer winks, then looks back at the road.

I clench my jaw. "Where are we stopping?"

"A buddy of mine made something for me. I need to pick it up."

I glance at the time on the clock. It's almost 5pm, which means we only have thirty-five minutes before they come looking. What the hell does he need to pick up?

I'd like to get as far away as possible before ditching the car. I know they know this car, and I don't trust Sawyer not to have a tracking device on it somewhere. I know there isn't one in my clothes. I checked.

We roll past a few homesteads out in the distance and pull into a tiny town. I sit up straighter. There are people here. People could help me.

"You'll lose all your points, Cali." Sawyer's voice is soft. "And Ryder won't look kindly on you running."

I ask emotionlessly, "Does he look kindly on anything?"

"Yes. The people he likes." Sawyer stops in front of a beat-up, single-story house. He gets out, walks around the truck, and opens my door. "Give me your hand."

"Where are we?"

"Friend's place." The place looks about 50 years old, with the paint peeling off the sides and bushes almost as tall as the roof. Sawyer grabs my hand and escorts me down. He holds my hand as we walk up to the door, and a few cats dart off the steps. Sawyer knocks. The door opens, and I shrink back. An old woman with gray hair and a nightgown stands there. She takes one look at

Sawyer, and her eyes crinkle. "Sawyer, I was just thinking about you!" She eyes me and says, "Who's this?"

"This is my date. Cali, this is Jenny." Sawyer beams down at me. His smile is megawatt, and if I didn't know better, I would have damn near swooned at him. He's startlingly handsome.

Sawyer slightly nods at me. I blink out of it. Oh my god. I'm supposed to say something.

I swallow. "Hey, Jenny."

She grins. "Oh my god! Sawyer, she's gorgeous. I knew you'd find a good woman to settle down with. Come in, come in." She bustles inside.

We step inside, and the place is as run-down as the outside. Cats scurry out of the way, and I jump. I glance at Sawyer, but he still looks pleasant. Who the hell is this woman?

She bustles around. "I'm getting it for you. You still have that cat? The orange one?"

"No, he ran from me as soon as we got home."

She chuckles. "Ornery little things they are. Orange ones especially."

She brings back something silver. It's...a necklace. It looks like a choker with a delicate silver band and two small rings on the ends. There are tiny stones set in the sides that catch the fading light. It's gorgeous.

"Thanks, Jenny." Sawyer takes it with his other hand and leans down to give her a kiss on the forehead. "You're the best."

The woman blushes. "Oh lord, have mercy, I'm not, but I do what I can." She wiggles her eyebrows at me. "You're a lucky woman."

I flush.

Sawyer laughs and scoots me back. "I'll be back, Jenny."

As we step outside, she says, "Come back when you're ready for the ring!" She wiggles her fingers at me.

I flush.

We climb back in the car.

"Who was that?" I ask.

"Someone I've known since childhood." Sawyer turns to look at me. He holds out the necklace. "I told you I'd get you a proper collar."

I swallow and look at the necklace in his hand. It's gorgeous and sparkly, with a solid band of silver on the inside. The outside looks like intertwining bands of solid and studded strands with rings on either end. What's the catch?

"Look." Sawyer turns it over. Flowers are engraved on the smooth inside. "Recognize those?"

I squint. "No?"

"Foxglove and hemlock. The first flowers I got you."

I glance up at him and swallow. No one has ever paid that much attention to me. Emotions rise in my chest. Sawyer searches my gaze, his becoming concerned. "Are you okay?"

I clear my throat. "Yeah, I'm fine. It's just a little creepy."

"These mean something. Better than roses. Come here."

I don't move. His gaze softens, "It's a gift, bunny. Let me put this on you." He holds up the necklace.

"How does it go on?" I ask.

"Goes around here." He leans over, pulling the necklace around the back of my neck, and I catch his cologne again. He smells amazing. "And I lock it in front." He fishes in his pocket.

"Wait, don't lock it." I pull back.

He doesn't let me pull away. "That's the point of a collar, pet."

I glare. "I'm not your pet."

Something flashes in Sawyer's eyes. The darkness is there, hovering on the edges. "Well, you don't belong to Ben anymore. I took you. Marked you. You sleep in our beds. You fuck us and us only. That makes you mine."

Heat flares under my skin. "That's not how relationships work!"

"No?" Sawyer leans in with a smirk. He looks devilishly handsome. "Did you want roses instead?"

"The flowers aren't the problem!" I sputter. "Ben got me without giving me flowers. You can't just say I'm yours and have it be true!"

Sawyer's eyes darken more. "Ben never gave you flowers?"

"You're missing the point!" I throw my hands up. "You can't just kidnap me and call it a relationship! I have to have a choice in the matter."

Sawyer leans close, his breath brushing over me and his voice low and dangerous, "With me, you'll never have a choice, bunny. I chose you. That means you're mine. Your life, your breath, your hopes and dreams. You will always belong to me until your dying breath. I will never let you go, Cali." He stares into my soul. "No matter what you do or how hard you fight. You're mine. Now put on the fucking collar."

I swallow.

He grabs the ends of the choker and clicks the lock down. "You're mine. Get fucking used to it."

CAKE

Pancake Mix

homemade pancakes

CHAPTER 31

SAWYER

I let her lean back away from me. Her delicate neck looks so pretty in my collar. God, it makes me hard to look at her. She says she doesn't want it, but her pupils are wide, and her breath comes in tiny pants. She's a goddamn freak, and she loves it.

"Now." I lean back. "Where to, boss?"

"I..." she blinks like she forgot we were playing a game. Then she says softly, "I don't know."

"I have a place," I say and pull out from Jenny's driveway.

"No." Cali sits up straighter. "We need to ditch the car."

I smile a little. Smart little fighter. I wasn't allowed to tell her about the tracker in the truck bed, but clearly she doesn't trust it.

"Okay." I swerve the truck to park it in town. Cali hops out, and I grab the backpack of supplies from the back. "We can walk to my spot."

"Do they know about your spot?" she asks, catching up to me as we walk.

"No," I say. "It's just an empty farmhouse. I used to hang out there all the time as a kid."

It's almost dark out now. There's silence for a long time. I usually hate the silence, but right now, Cali's presence keeps the demons at bay.

We walk for a bit, then Cali asks, "What were you like as a kid?"

The question surprises me. "A little shit," I say.

"Wow, I'm so shocked," Cali says sarcastically.

It sends a thrill through me and straight to my dick. She's such a smartass. "What were *you* like?"

Cali pauses. "I was told I was disrespectful."

Despite myself, a laugh pops out. "Not you."

She huffs. "Yeah, well, they beat it out of me, can't you tell? I'm reformed."

I recognize that deflecting humor. I do that. Someone fucked this woman up. I clench my jaw. We walk in silence again. The house is a few roads away into the sticks. I get lost in my thoughts.

"You like cats?" Cali asks. The question startles me.

"What?" I look at her.

"You know. Cats. Pussy. The animal." She rolls her eyes.

God, when she rolls her eyes, it makes the blood run straight to my dick. "Yeah, I do like pussy. And cats."

"Why?" she asks.

"What kind of question is that?" I glance at her. The sun is down completely, and her hair looks pale and ghostly in the twilight, the curls catching the faint light.

She says, "I have a cat, the one you saw. He's an ass," she scoffs. "But I love him. He's been there for me."

Love. I turn to fully look at her.

Cali pauses, looking uncomfortable. "What?"

"Nothing. Didn't think you could love anything. With your prickly attitude and all." I motion at her.

She turns away and keeps walking. "Don't project. I doubt you've loved anything ever."

I catch up with her. "That's not true."

"What have you loved?"

I swallow. My chest feels uncomfortable, and my muscles tighten.

I love the boys.

You loved me.

I clench my jaw. Even when we lost all our money to her habit, I did love my mother. Even when I went without food. Even when she was high off her ass. Even when her Johns came over.

Even when she pimped me out to them.

I was an idiot back then.

And you're a fucking idiot now.

Cali's hand brushes mine as she walks next to me, and it yanks me out of my memory with a startle. I clear my throat. She looks at me like she expects an answer.

Oh fuck, she asked a question.

I purse my lips like I'm thinking. "I had a cat as a kid. I loved it."

Cali gives a tiny smile as she looks at the ground. I don't think she even knows she's doing it. She looks so goddamn beautiful. It chases the darkness away for a brief second, and I want to see it again.

I continue, "Well, it wasn't really mine. It followed me home from school every day, so I called it mine. I named it Raisin Bran, 'cause that makes sense when you're seven."

"You walked to school at seven?"

I shrug. "I did everything at seven. Raised my brother, too."

Cali pulls in a breath and shoves her hands in her pockets. The smile is gone from her face, and I don't like that. I want it back.

"I snuck Raisin Bran inside a few times and fed him hot dogs. He loved them."

There, a bit of light comes back to her eyes. She chuckles. "I would have been whipped within an inch of my life if I tried that."

A yucky feeling moves through me. Who the hell was whipping her? She belongs to me. No one touches her, even if it was in her past.

I want to get that look off her face, so I keep talking like an idiot. "Yeah, well, one of my mom's..." I pause before adding, "clients tried to kill him one day, so I never did that again."

Her voice is soft. "Oh." But she doesn't pry further.

We keep walking in the darkness, listening to the crickets. I relax a little.

Cali asks softly, "Who is taking care of Halloweiner?"

I tense. After I took her, I couldn't just leave him at her apartment. "I took him to the shelter."

"The animal shelter?" Cali whirls on me. Even in the darkness, I see the fear in her eyes. "What if someone adopts him? He belongs to me!"

I say nothing. There is nothing to say.

She shoves her small hands into my chest. I barely move.

Cali yells, "He's mine!"

Something uncomfortable curls in my stomach. Am I feeling... guilty?

I can't see her perfectly, but I think I see tears in her eyes.

Fuck. She can't make me feel like this! I haven't felt this in a very long time. It makes me want to crumble. My voice comes out rough, "Stupid girl. You should know better than to show weakness."

Cali whirls so she's no longer facing me. "You know what? You're a horrible person, Sawyer."

The feeling curls deeper in my stomach. I grunt, "Just trying to teach you something. Someone will always take advantage of you."

"Whatever." She walks faster. Her shoulders shake, but she doesn't make a sound.

I feel sick.

I'm not wrong. The world will eat you up and spit you out. The sooner she learns that, the better off she'll be.

So why does this feel wrong?

CHAPTER 32

RYDER

I have the water on scalding hot. It feels good against my skin and kills the germs. I still feel like I'm on the edge of coming down with something.

I scrub my skin and think about the look on Sawyer's face after I said we would kill the woman. He looked...scared. Then, when they pulled me into the hallway, they both asked for the same thing.

I'm still floored. I've never heard them ask that throughout our entire relationship. And we've had plenty of marks over the years. We met at a club in the big city and then from there, were included in a private hunting club off the coast of Japan. Only, we hunted people. The men and I hunted together and instantly fell for each other. After hunting there as a team for years, we got bored with the map and branched out on our own.

I clean under my fingernails again.

We've killed many men. And never once felt regret. But for the first time in the hallway, my men asked me not to kill a mark.

Not only that, but instead of fighting, they came together on a decision.

Any other time, it would make me happy. Sawyer has been going off the deep end for months. But they're coming together over a woman who they brought into our house? A woman who has already caused havoc? She's dangerous for them. For us. She'll run the second they drop their guard.

I clean my nails again. I should have been there for them. I should never have left.

She made me leave.

I scrub the scruff on my face. I shouldn't have fucked them while I felt sick. Whatever was going around the jail was bad. It sent two to the hospital. But they needed it. Sawyer needed it. Fuck, he was falling apart.

I shoot up a prayer to keep them from getting sick, not that I believe in god anymore. I can't after the things I've seen. It's just a habit that I can't shake.

A knock on the door startles me, and I stiffen.

Miles comes in and leans against the counter. I had to shower in Sawyer's room because, for some goddamn reason, everything was gone from my bathroom.

Miles watches me through the glass shower doors, looking me up and down. "Well damn. I was going to say the hunt countdown is on, but..."

Anger makes my mouth stiff as I ask, "What, you want a little dick before you chase that pussy?"

He grimaces. "It's not like that."

"No?" I get out of the shower and towel off. "You're not hitting that?"

Miles watches me dry off. He looks good. Deliciously good. I know how that toned body feels pinned under me. I'm not used to going days without fucking, and I'm ready to go again.

Miles doesn't answer me.

"I'll take that as a yes," I grunt. I have no problem with them fucking women. Hell, we've all fucked women together. But bringing one into our home? She's going to get all of us landed in jail, and money only goes so far when a case gets publicized. I can't stand to be separated from them again. For what, a little pussy?

A pretty little pussy, but still.

Miles crosses his arms. I throw on my clean clothes. It was hard to find a suit that wasn't ruined, and that pisses me off more.

"Miles. What do you think you're doing here? She can't live. She's seen us. Knows what we do. You kidnapped her, for Christ's sake."

"I know," he rubs the back of his neck. It looks like he wants to say something but doesn't.

God, my teeth feel nasty. "Fuck dude, where's my toothbrush?"

"Probably in the basement."

The basement? Why the *fuck* would it be in the basement? Goddamnn it, fuck this.

I continue to dry off my hair and eye Miles. I hope to god he sees some sense right now. "You know she can't live, right?"

Miles looks uncomfortable. "There's a way to keep everyone safe without killing her."

My stomach sinks. "And what in the ever living fuck could that be?"

I search under Sawyer's sink for an unopened toothbrush or razor. I don't find one but I do find a pack of hair ties. I toss it back with disgust.

"We keep her with us."

I freeze. The stuff under the sink goes out of focus. Oh, this has gone way farther than I originally thought.

"Miles," I grit. "You called me and asked me to get rid of her."

"I called because Sawyer was out of control."

"And he's not now?" I slam the doors closed and straighten. "Is he or is he not running around with this liability, playing a stupid game of hide and seek? Instead of killing her?"

Miles bites his lip. "I'm just saying there are multiple solutions."

I step up into Miles' face. He doesn't back down. His green eyes stare into my own. "What? Do you think she'll fall in love with you? Be your little girlfriend and keep all our secrets?" I lean in closer.

A muscle along Miles' sharp jawline ticks.

I whisper, "You think that Stockholm won't wear off and we'll all live happily ever after? What happens when she gets pissed at you, Miles? When she remembers how she got here? All it takes is you loading the dishwasher wrong and all of us land in prison for the rest of our lives. Is that what you want?"

He winces. "No. That's not what I want."

"Good." I straighten. "I was starting to get worried that you dropped everything for this one girl."

He doesn't say anything. And I don't like that.

I growl, "Now, show me where my fucking toothbrush is. I have to go beat some sense into Sawyer."

CHAPTER 33

MILES

I shoot a text off to Sawyer.
Ryder isn't on board.
He doesn't respond.
Change of plans, you might want to call him.
Both texts come back as undeliverable.

"Fuck." I grip my phone tightly. Fucker must have turned his phone off. Ryder wants her gone.

Even the thought of that makes me sick. This isn't right. We fucked up, and now she's paying for it.

Ryder walks past me. He tucks a gun into his waistband. "Let's go."

CHAPTER 34

CALI

"Here we are," Sawyer says.

"Where?" I stop and look around. It's completely dark now, and I'm struggling to make out the shapes in the fields.

"Our five-star hotel." Sawyer motions to the right. I can barely see the shape of what looks like an old farmhouse in a clump of trees.

I follow Sawyer as he goes off-road. The ground is uneven, and with my next step, I drop down violently to the right.

"Ow!" I try to regain my balance.

"Careful," Sawyer warns.

"Thanks." I roll my eyes. Before I realize what's happening, Sawyer swoops down and picks me up, carrying me under my knees and shoulders.

I screech, struggling. "What are you doing?"

"Carrying you so your dumbass doesn't get hurt. Don't think I can handle the bitching and moaning."

"Put me down!" I fight against his strong hold.

"No," he answers, sounding bored.

Sawyer's grip is unrelenting, no matter how much I buck. Finally, I stop, panting for breath. Sawyer continues walking, unbothered. His chest is warm and hard against me.

"I don't need to be carried." I push him with the one arm that has mobility.

"Cali, for the love of god, pick your battles." Sawyer's voice rumbles against the arm pressed into his chest. He walks us up to what I can clearly see now is an abandoned, two-story farmhouse. Sawyer carries me up the backstairs and boots the door in.

The door bangs into the silence with a loud crack.

I yelp. "Jesus! Was that really necessary?"

Sawyer sets me down. "Do you ever stop complaining?"

"Only when I'm kidnapped."

He glances down at me.

I smile sarcastically.

Sawyer rolls his eyes. "Be careful in here, and stay on the first floor. I cleaned it up years ago, but it's old. I'm shocked it's still standing."

It smells musty in here. From the meager light that trickles in through the windows, it looks like we're standing in an old kitchen. The floor is discolored all over, and pieces of the ceiling have fallen in. Sawyer moves closer to the front of the house.

I follow, banging my shin on something. A zing of pain shoots up my leg, and I hiss, "It's dark in here."

"Yeah, well, it's dark outside."

I sneer. This man.

There's a bit of light coming through the front windows. I shuffle over and look out. I see nothing but empty fields separated by scrub trees.

"There used to be..." Sawyer is shuffling around. "Ah! God, I'm a genius."

The more my eyes adjust, the more I can see. Sawyer is carrying something dark and drops it on the floor. The air wafts over me, and I can almost taste the mothballs; they're so strong.

"I used to crash here. Some of my blankets are still here."

I cross my arms and glance back at the window. "Do you think they're looking for us now?"

"Yes." He gets to work spreading the blankets out.

"We're sleeping here?" I eye Sawyer.

"More chances of getting caught if we stay mobile. People are nosey in these parts, especially late at night."

I swallow. "I don't know. I feel weird hanging out waiting for them to find us."

"Ohhh, so you're the expert in hiding from my boyfriends, huh?" Sawyer smirks, flashing his white teeth at me.

I instantly feel defensive. "No! I just feel like you're setting me up."

Sawyer's voice lowers. "I gave you my word, Cali." There's a tone of warning in his voice.

I huff and glance outside again. Maybe if he goes to bed, I can leave for good. This is the only chance I'll get. I'll steal the car and leave.

"Come here." Sawyer pats the blankets.

Absolutely not. Not while people are actively hunting me. Not when this is my chance to escape. I feign disinterest. "I'm not going to bed."

"What, afraid you won't be able to resist my draw? That you'll start humping my leg in the middle of the night?" Sawyer tosses me a smirk. He looks so handsome it makes my pussy grow hot.

My cheeks flame. Thank God he can't see it. "No!"

"Don't worry, you already have my consent." He stretches out. "I love free use."

I narrow my gaze. "What the hell does that mean?"

"You know. Fuck me anytime, whether I'm awake or asleep...or drugged." He wiggles his eyebrows.

I flash back to the times I used to wake up to Ben's hand down my pants. He wouldn't take no for an answer and would pressure and whine and manhandle me until I gave up and let him get off in me. I grit, "Oh, cool. Ben loved that."

The room goes deathly still. I feel the hairs prickle on the back of my neck.

Sawyer's voice is so dark it makes me jump, "Oh yeah?"

219

I rub the back of my neck. "Jesus, you're being weird."

Sawyer growls, "Cali. What did he do to you?"

Oh shit, could he see the change in me? I don't want him prying into the things I'd rather not talk about. What right does he have? White-hot anger runs through me.

I snap, "Why do you care? You literally kidnapped me!"

Sawyer flashes a look at me. He looks more violent than I've ever seen him. "Yeah, well, you're mine. And I want to know why you suddenly got so weird."

"That's not how it works! You don't get to just kidnap me and demand to know my thoughts."

Sawyer keeps me locked in an unnaturally still stare.

Fuck. I've shown weakness. I should know better than to get defensive.

Sawyer cocks his head. Instantly, his face clears of anything that was there before, and he says, "Come here."

"No." My muscles sing with energy. I want to fight and run at the same time. "I'm not going to bed. Not tired."

The creepy grin is still on Sawyer's face. He barely moves his expression. "I want to sleep, and I'm not doing it without you, so you don't run away and do something stupid."

I take a tiny step back. "Sawyer, please."

It was the wrong move. Sawyer springs up.

I scream. I dart towards the front door. My body seems to move in slow motion. Adrenaline rushes through me, and I launch myself off my right foot, then my left. Fuck, he's right behind me.

My fingertips brush the handle before a hard body slams into me from behind.

"Gotcha."

My breath whooshes out of my body as Sawyer pins me to the door.

"Did you really think you could get away from me, Cali?"

I struggle against a hard wall of muscle. The more I fight, the more Sawyer presses in. He leans against me until I feel him everywhere.

Sawyer runs his nose down my neck to where my necklace rests against my skin and bites me. Pain shoots into me, mixing with the adrenaline.

"Let go of me!"

"I do what I want with my toys," Sawyer growls.

He's everywhere and heavy and breathing my air. The fact he referred to me as a toy pisses me off. "I'm not yours," I pant.

Suddenly, I'm ripped away from the door and shoved into the living room. Before I can catch my balance, Sawyer snatches me up again and shoves me against the window. "Do you need me to show you how much you're mine? Fuck you against the window so everyone can see? Make Miles and Ryder jealous before they come in and take you?"

The glass is cold against my hot skin.

"No." A thrill runs through me at the idea. The idea of him claiming me in front of anyone to see.

Sawyer puts his nose by my cheek and pulls in a breath. "There's that delicious word. Does this embarrass you, pet?"

I push against the glass, but he holds me there easily.

"No," I say. Despite my struggles, my pussy is hot. It pulses with its own heartbeat, and I can feel every inch of my clothes touching my skin. "No one will see it anyway."

"Oh, Cali. You think they won't find us?" Sawyer reaches a hand around me and slips it under the sweatpants.

I squirm.

"They track people for a living, bunny." He chuckles. "And I think you're hot for this." He inches his hand down my stomach and under my borrowed boxers. I realize with horror that if he goes any further, he's going to feel that I'm wet.

"I think it turns you on to think of them watching me get you off. You like the idea of them getting hard watching you scream my name."

I gasp as his fingers brush my pussy.

Sawyer chuckles again and whispers, "Goddamn, Cali." He rips his hand out, grabs my shirt, and yanks it over my head. It's way too big and comes off easily.

"Press your tits against the glass," Sawyer demands.

Fuck. My clit is desperate for friction. I shift. I hesitate a second too long, and Sawyer grabs the back of my neck. He pushes me into the window. My choker clinks against the glass, and a sharp shock runs through me as the cold glass hits my nipples.

Sawyer wastes no time pulling my pants down, and immediately, I feel his dick against my ass. "Let's show them, hmmm? Let's show them how beautiful you look when you're mine."

Sawyer shoves inside me with one brutal thrust. Immediate pain and pleasure fill me, and I gasp.

"Good girl. Show them."

I instantly shut my mouth.

Sawyer pulls out slowly and pounds into me again. He then smacks my ass so hard it echoes in the empty room.

I cry out.

"Mmmm," Sawyer moans. "What a pretty sound."

He pushes in and out of me. The heat in my pussy compared to the cold of the window and the fear of people watching mixes in a heady cocktail. It feels so fucking good.

Sawyer picks up his pace, bringing one hand around to play with my clit. The other comes up and grabs my neck just under my jaw, tilting my head back so my breasts are fully pressed into the glass.

"All of this is mine," he grunts. "Every last bit of you. From your hair to your tits, to your sweet pussy, to your toes. Mine. And Miles'. And even Ryder's."

Sawyer rubs my clit, sending a sensation ripping through me. I moan, and his thrusts come more furiously.

"You don't keep anything from me, Cali. Nothing." Pleasure fills me and starts to build in my clit. I tense. Sawyer rips his hand away and groans. He swells inside me, slams inside once more, and then stills inside me, coming.

"Fuck," he moans. "Fuck, Cali, you feel so good."

My high is starting to fade, and I put my hand down to my clit.

"No." Sawyer snatches my hand away and presses me even closer to the glass. "Bad girls don't get to come."

The high fades even more, and I moan. My clit throbs, craving the attention. I can't move to relieve it.

"Fuck you," I hiss.

Sawyer half chuckles, half moans. "A punishment is a

punishment, bunny." He pulls out of me, dropping his head to the back of my neck.

"Fuck, you feel so good."

I struggle to get away. I'm still naked from the top up.

"Jesus, dude."

Sawyer takes a step back so I can move. He looks at me approvingly.

"Do you want me to get a UTI?" I yank the rest of my clothes on.

He watches me, evaluating. "No. Go piss in the yard."

"What?" I whip my head around to stare at him.

Sawyer raises his hands in surrender. "Sorry, pretty girl. Don't have a bathroom here. Or toilet paper."

I flash my teeth in a snarl. This motherfucker. I march to the back door. As much as I hate it, I do need to go, and I do not want to deal with a UTI.

Heavy footsteps follow me out of the house.

I whirl on Sawyer. The sound of crickets fills the air. "Are you really going to watch?"

He smacks a hand over his eyes. "No. Proceed, fair lady."

I glance around. There's no privacy. Nowhere to squat. I've never done this before. Will I pull my pants down and just go right here? I glance up. It's even brighter out here now that my vision has adjusted. He's peeking through one of his fingers.

My cheeks burn. I've lost all sense of privacy in every aspect of my life.

I bark, "Do you have a piss kink, dude? Turn away."

He does as I say.

"No, but Miles might."

"Gross." I pull my pants down right where I'm at and squat. "TMI."

"How's that? You've had the man's dick down your throat and tongue in your cunt."

I glower. The more I find out about these men, the more I see them as real people. And that's unacceptable. "Just fuck off, dude."

When I'm done with my business, I use dead grass to wipe off and brush past him. I move inside. "You coming to bed, pretty boy, or what?"

"Pretty boy?" He sounds genuinely offended. "Miles is the pretty one."

I toss a glance back at the blue-eyed, dark-haired, chiseled god behind me. I arch an eyebrow. He raises an eyebrow back.

I sit on the blanket he's laid on the floor, and Sawyer lies down next to me.

"Lie down," he demands.

I grit my teeth. I need him to believe I'm complying, but it pains me to do so. I lie down stiffly. As soon as I'm down, he puts an arm around me and yanks me back toward him. He pulls me until I'm fully settled against his body. He buries his head into the back of my neck.

"Did you use Miles' shampoo?"

I frown. "Yes?"

He groans, and I feel him stiffen behind me.

"Jesus," I squirm to get away. He just pulls me in tighter.

"I won't do anything," he says. "I wouldn't trust myself not to let you come, and we can't have that."

Sawyer relaxes once I'm completely pulled against him. The house is full of silence.

I think about the other men. How close are they? Were they able to track the car? If so, how long would it take them to find us in the dark?

Sawyer rumbles behind me, "What did Ben do to you?"

I stiffen immediately. Ben would whine and complain until I finally gave in. He'd be done quickly anyway, come, then roll over and fall asleep. It's not like I didn't consent. I just feel yucky about it. And the fact that Sawyer is digging into something so personal terrifies me.

"Nothing," I say. "I'm trying to sleep."

"Bunny..." Sawyer's voice rumbles against my back. "I know you're lying."

"I'm not!" I close my eyes.

Sawyer pulls me tighter against him. "Tell me why you're panicking then. Do I need to kill him?"

Jesus! I turn my face into the blanket. "Just leave it the fuck alone, okay, Sawyer? Leave it alone. Leave *me* alone."

Sawyer growls. I lay there, stiff, waiting for him to fight more. To push me more. But he doesn't. We just lie there, him with his arm around me in the quiet building. It takes a long time for me to relax even slightly and even longer before his breaths even out.

My thoughts bounce from the boys hunting us, to escaping, to our conversation tonight. Sawyer is opening up more. He's getting more comfortable. But he also wants to dig into my own life, and that scares the absolute shit out of me. I have a feeling he'll figure out how to force the secrets out of me somehow.

I don't get close to people. I just don't.

I know I don't have much time, but I also can't try to sneak away too early.

How long can I afford to wait?

CAKE

Pancake Mix

homemade pancakes

CHAPTER 35

SAWYER

The smell of cigarette smoke – old and new – fills my nose. It's all I choose to focus on as my mom laughs in the kitchen. She must have just lit up a new one. I made a mistake, followed a routine for too long, and she got a hold of me.

I ignore everything she's saying to her client and focus on the worn-down carpet in front of me. It has something spilled on it. It's dark and sticky and covered in old dirt. Maybe it's food?

"Sawyer!"

I jump at my mom's harsh voice. Shit. I didn't realize she'd come to sit next to me on the couch. I can smell the alcohol on her now.

"Sawyer, pay attention. I said say hi to Jerald."

I don't even glance at the man on the couch. I know without looking that he's ugly and hungry, just like all of the men mom brings into the home. All of the men she makes me play games with.

"Hey," I say.

Mom rubs my back and continues talking to her John. I direct my gaze back to the carpet. Did I make that stain? Probably. Mom would say

I did. What could it be, though? I try to eat every meal away from here. I dread being caught here.

Today, I was weak. I found Raisin Bran dead on the side of the road, and I came home for the third night in a row. I wanted to see if Mom knew what happened to him. To see if she killed him because I snuck him in again.

"Sawyer," Mom snaps again.

I jump. Maybe the stain is chocolate milk. It looks kind of like it. But there's texture to it.

"Mr. Jerald has come to play the game with you."

I squeeze my eyes shut. I know Jerry. Dread rolls through me. Applesauce? Maybe it's applesauce.

I jump as a heavy hand drops on my shoulder. Instantly, my arm itches. Mom said we have bugs, and I'm pretty sure they've been biting me when I sleep here at night.

"Sawyer, Jerry said your technique sucks. I'm going to teach you how to do it right."

I scratch the bugs out of my arm. No, if it was applesauce, Raisin Bran would have tried to eat it. He was obsessed with food. Once I hear Jerry's belt unfasten, I completely zone out. Probably just old cigarette ash.

I wonder if Miss Jenny has anti-itch cream?

Maybe she could tell me what the stain is.

CHAPTER 36

RYDER

I track the truck pretty quickly. It's in one of Sawyer's old haunts. I park my own truck next to it and feel the familiar thrill I do when I hunt people. Single-minded focus burns through me, and I feel alive.

"Think he took off on foot?" Miles asks. It's the first thing he's said to me since leaving home. He's pissed, but he's going to have to deal with it. I'm protecting our family.

I take in every detail surrounding us. It's fully dark now. Sawyer left the truck on the edge of town, facing into the countryside.

I'm honestly shocked he brought her here. And a little mad. Sawyer always comes here when he's on the edge of losing it. He never tells me what he does, but he comes back a little less broken and almost always with a dirty animal of some sort that I make him keep outside.

I shrug. "I'll go ask the trailer if they saw anything." Sure enough, after speaking to the neighbors, they saw my friends, who ran out of gas, walk into the countryside about an hour ago.

Oh, he can't hide from me now. I pull the hand sanitizer out of my pocket and squirt some in my hand.

"Sawyer turned his phone off," Miles mutters.

I glance at him. He's pissed.

I ask, "What, you afraid he'll actually get away from you?"

"He broke the rules," Miles grits. "He's supposed to leave it on."

I arch an eyebrow. "He's also supposed to kill his marks, not fuck them and keep them for pets."

Miles pulls his heatseeker out of his pocket and scans the area. He's quiet. "Let's keep moving."

It'll only be a matter of time. Our world is crumbling around us, but I'll put it back together again. We'll get rid of the girl and then get rid of this court case. We have to.

I'm not losing anyone else.

CHAPTER 37

CALI

Sawyer stiffens next to me. His breathing becomes heavier. I snap my eyes open, but he doesn't say anything. Just whimpers a little.

Fuck. He's dreaming.

I try to wiggle out of his hold, but he clamps down on me harder, crushing me to his chest in his hold. I feel his hard dick pressed into my back.

"Sawyer," I pant.

He lays there, frozen. It's hard for me to breathe, and his grip hurts.

Do I wake him? I know you're not supposed to wake someone out of a dream.

He groans again and squeezes harder. Goddamn, that hurts.

"Sawyer!" I shout and scratch at his arms. His hold loosens a fraction, and I buck and scramble enough to get away. He sits up, breathing heavily.

I freeze as his gaze runs across me. He doesn't look present.

The darkness is front and center in his eyes, and he looks wild. I'm afraid to move.

A deep voice from the other side of the room barks, "Sawyer!"

I scream and whirl toward the sound of the voice. Two shadows hulk in the kitchen.

Sawyer jumps up and throws himself in front of me. "Fuck off, and maybe I won't kill you." A knife flashes in his hand. Since when did he have a knife?

"Sawyer, it's me."

Is that...Miles? Fuck. They found me.

I turn and sprint to the front door. There are scratching boots against the floor and heavy footsteps. Reaching the door, I yank on the handle, but it's stuck. I immediately change plans and dart toward the staircase. A hand reaches out to grab me. I duck, and strong fingers rip into my bun.

I cry out as pain burns through my scalp.

The hand lets me go.

"Cali, don't run." It's Miles.

I scramble up the steps. Footsteps follow me. The house groans. The top opens into a hallway, and I skitter to a halt. The floor has rotted away.

Strong arms band around my waist and yank me back. I'm shoved against the stairwell, and immediately, I smell coconut.

"Jesus, Cali! You could get yourself killed." His handsome face looks concerned.

I screech in frustration and push against him. He caught me again. Miles doesn't let me go. He just presses his hard body closer to mine.

Miles puts his lips to my ear. "God, I could fuck you right now. You fight me so deliciously."

I shudder. The way he's pressing possessively into me fills me with a shiver of pleasure. Something is very wrong with me.

Angry voices come from downstairs. Miles sighs and throws me over his shoulder.

"Put me down!" I beat on his back. The world flips again, and he puts me down in the living room, grabbing my hand tightly.

Sawyer is in Ryder's face. They're both nose to nose and heaving for breath.

"It's my game," Sawyer grits.

Ryder clocks me downstairs. He moves his hand, and time slows. Ryder raises his hand so that it's pointing at me. He's holding a gun.

In slow motion, Sawyer moves to get between us, and Miles yanks me behind him.

"Jesus!" There's the sound of heavy blows, and something metal hits the ground.

I jump, trying to yank away from Miles. A full fight or flight hits me, and all I can see is the back of Miles' shirt.

He pointed a gun at me. I need to get away. I need to.

I scramble and kick and claw, my world growing fuzzy. There's shouting, but I can't make it out. I'm fighting for my life. I feel more and more trapped.

"Cali!"

I blink.

My name is shouted again. I focus on Miles' face right in front of me.

"Cali, I won't let anything happen to you."

I blink again. I feel trapped. My chest hurts. Ryder just tried to shoot me!

I glance around. Miles has me pinned against the wall. My breathing is so heavy I feel like I can't get in a full breath. I look around again.

"Cali." Miles catches my gaze again with his green eyes. "He won't hurt you. I won't let him."

I hear the other two men still fighting. I try to jerk away, but Miles doesn't let me. "We'll go outside in a minute, Cali. I just need you to take a few breaths for me."

I don't feel like I can. He's pressed too close to me.

"Get off me," I gasp.

Ryder's deep voice growls. "You've taken the game too far. I'm stepping in."

Miles looks back over his shoulder. "Would you fucking stop? You can't kill her."

Miles shifts just enough that I can see the other two men.

Sawyer yells, "So she won't get all the points, and we'll handle it then! Nothing has gone too far."

They're both panting, hair and clothes disheveled. They look like they've rolled around with each other, and the taste of dust and mothballs fills the air.

"Cali is my mark," Sawyer is heaving for breath. "You don't get to change my rules just like I don't get to change yours when it's your turn. Just because you decide not to fuck your marks doesn't mean I can't do what I want with mine."

My gut twists. Fuck.

I try to move, but Miles leans into me again and whispers low, "Easy, Cali. He's trying to help."

"Sawyer," Ryder growls. "I have a murder case pending in court. What the hell happens if the cops find her or her DNA at our house, hmm? Did you think about that?"

Sawyer says nothing.

"Yeah, I didn't think so. You guys will go away, too. I'll go away for life, if not death, Sawyer. Is that something you want?"

"No! So we'll move."

"With a captive?" Ryder looks over Sawyer and right into my eyes. "Doesn't look like she'll go anywhere without causing a scene, Sawyer."

I stiffen.

Sawyer glances back at me. Then he turns back to Ryder. "She's mine."

The room goes deathly silent. Miles grabs me a little tighter.

"You need to get rid of this problem, and it needs to be soon." Ryder points at Sawyer. "I respect the rules of the hunt, but I need her figured out. We have too much going on right now."

Ryder turns and leaves the house.

Sawyer stands still, looking out after Ryder.

Miles steps back and holds out his hand. He says so quietly I almost don't hear it over the ringing in my ears, "Come on, little shadow. Let's get you home."

CHAPTER 38

CALI

I ride with Sawyer and Miles in the truck back to the house. The whole ride back, all I can think about is how much I need a drink. Wine, tequila, whiskey, hell, even beer. I'm feeling all kinds of things that I don't want to feel right now. Especially panic. Sawyer marked me as his but acts like he's going to kill me as soon as I bore him. Miles is continuing his nice-guy act, and Ryder clearly wants to kill me. I'm a liability to all of them.

I turn to look out the window. It's still the middle of the night, but I feel so wound up I'm not even close to being tired.

When we get back, Miles doesn't grab me. He gives me the illusion of choice as we walk back up to the house. And I walk in with no fight. What other choice do I have? Clearly, running is not going to work for me.

I need to work smarter than I have been. I need to figure out the game.

When we get inside, I roughly ask, "Where's Ryder?"

"Probably in the shower already." Miles goes to the fridge and starts pulling food out.

Holy shit, I'm starving. And shaking.

Sawyer watches me. "I'll make pancakes."

"No, dude," Miles groans. "You make a fucking disaster, and I can't handle it right now."

I take a seat at the kitchen island, and Sawyer winks at me. It makes me pause. In the light, I can see his eye is swollen and red. Ryder must have gotten him. And yet, he's acting like nothing happened.

"You're just hangry." Sawyer grabs some things. "Bunny, come help."

I stand robotically. It's better than sitting still, letting the panic crawl over my skin. Sawyer grabs a boxed mix out of the cabinet. "Bowls are under the island."

I lean down to grab them. When I come back up, Sawyer is wearing a pink frilly apron.

I blink. It's so opposite to the unpredictable killer I've come to expect that it throws me.

Sawyer looks at me. "Oh good, you found them."

"Sawyer," Miles asks, "what the hell is on her neck?"

I jump at his sudden sharp tone like I've done something wrong. Sawyer laughs. "My collar."

Miles raises an eyebrow and takes me in. I look at him with uncertainty. I expect him to yell at Sawyer, but he doesn't. He simply nods. "Looks hot."

I flush.

We set about making the food. We are all acting like their boyfriend didn't just try to kill me. Like they don't have plans to kill me later.

Miles hands me a fork to stir and gives me a little smile. A lump forms in my throat, and against all reason, I wish that the rest of my life would just slip away and this scene right here could be real.

Sawyer burns the first few pancakes. Miles yells at him, and it just encourages Sawyer more. He trashes the kitchen but feeds us pancakes as they come out. He drenches them in copious amounts of syrup before he hands them over, and they taste heavenly.

As we eat, Miles grows more quiet. I watch Sawyer keep an eye on him discreetly. I look at him, too. He looks like he's drawing back into himself.

"Got any mimosas with this?" I mumble.

"No alcohol." Sawyer goes to hand me another pancake, and I push my plate back with a groan.

"Jesus, Cali, you didn't tell me you were a quitter." Sawyer motions at me with a spatula. "Eat more, you need it."

"I can't handle another one, I'm stuffed."

Sawyer smirks.

I glare at him. "Grow up."

"Oh, you haven't felt stuffed yet." He wiggles his eyebrows, and his blue eyes sparkle. "Right, Miley?"

Miles barely even looks up.

Sawyer looks at Miles. "Speaking of stuffed, you haven't thanked me yet, Miley."

I stiffen. Something is clearly bothering Miles, and he's really going to pick another fight with him?

Miles glares at Sawyer. "For what?"

Sawyer's look turns dark. "Want to rethink your attitude there, pup?"

I expect Miles to get angry, but instead, his green eyes light up. He mutters something under his breath.

"What was that?" Sawyer leans in.

"Make. Me." Miles says, but I see a hint of life returning to his eyes.

Sawyer rounds the island and grabs Miles' neck. "How about you thank me on your knees, pretty boy?" He yanks Miles off his stool and shoves him down.

They're right in front of me. I back up on my stool just a smidge but don't bother to move.

"My dick is still covered in Cali's pussy. Clean her off of me, pup." He shoves Miles back by his neck. "Now."

Heat fills me, and my clit throbs.

Miles' eyes grow hungry. Sawyer rips his apron off and yanks his pants down, his stiff cock bobbing free. Miles immediately takes him into his mouth, hollowing his cheeks. Sawyer groans.

Miles bobs up and down, then licks Sawyer's length, moaning.

"That's a good boy. That's how to properly thank me." Sawyer runs his fingers through Miles' hair, then down his face.

Suddenly, Sawyer lifts his hand and hits Miles in the face.

I jump, panic running through me. But Miles doesn't use his big body to push Sawyer back. Instead, he moans, and his eyes flutter back.

Sawyer gives a rough chuckle. "Gonna sass me next time, boy?"

Miles nods as best he can, continuing to suck Sawyer off. Sawyer smirks. "I thought so. Now let me use that pretty mouth." He grabs ahold of Miles' head and takes over, pistoning in and out of his mouth. Miles gags, and tears trickle down his face, but he keeps his eyes on Sawyer's. It makes me hot watching them.

"Fuck, pup. You're going to make me come already." Sawyer stiffens and groans, pounding into Miles one last time and stopping.

Lust fills me as Sawyer comes down Miles' throat. They watch each other as he does, pleasure filling both their faces.

I clench my hands. Fuck. My pussy is dripping.

Sawyer yanks out, brushing his hand down Miles' face, wiping away the tears. "Good boy. That's a good boy."

They both stay where they are for a minute. Then Sawyer wraps his hand around Miles' throat, just under his jaw, and pulls him to his feet.

I shift to relieve some of the pounding in my clit. Both men glance at me like they forgot I was there.

Sawyer gives me a small smile. "Miles, why don't you show her around the place? I'm gonna shower."

Miles nods, and Sawyer leaves. I'm not sure what just went on between the two of them, but this is the first time I've ever seen them get along.

And a strange part of me likes it.

CHAPTER 39

MILES

I give Cali the grand tour of the house. She's already seen most of the upstairs, but I show her the office again, then take her downstairs. Her eyes widen when she sees the huge couch, TV, and gaming system. There's also a pool and foosball table, and, of course, our makeshift cell. We didn't intend to bring people here, but Ryder is always overly prepared. I skip over the sex room. I'm not sure that she's ready for that yet.

Cali runs her hand across the pool table. "Where the hell do you guys make your money?" She's still in the clothes Sawyer gave her, her hair messy, and her eyes are heavy with sleep. She looks beautiful.

I look for that spark of jealousy seeing her covered in Sawyer's things. It doesn't come.

"Ryder plays in the stock trade. He's actually really good at it. He's our sugar daddy, if you will."

Cali throws me a look that screams she doesn't believe me.

I chuckle. "Ryder's too smart to get mixed up in the mafia or whatever else you're thinking. Too many rules, too much risk. Come on, we'll watch a movie."

I grab her hand. It's so small and soft in mine. For once, she doesn't pull away from me, and it shoots pleasure straight through my arm and into my dick. It's probably because she's exhausted, but still.

I set her down on the couch next to me. "What movies do you like?"

She tries to hold back a yawn. "I don't know. What do you like? Slasher movies?"

I glance at her. She gives a tiny, cheeky smirk.

I shake my head. "Don't sass me unless you want to get spanked, shadow."

I pick out an action movie and play it. Cali yawns again.

"Come here." I throw a pillow on the floor in front of me. "Sit." She looks confused.

"Sit. I'm going to do your hair."

For a minute, Cali looks torn. Then, slowly, she drops down in front of me. That small sign of trust shoots another bolt of pleasure through me, this time to my chest. I don't deserve it, but she's giving it anyway. Fuck.

I clear my throat and grab the remote, putting it on the accent table right behind the couch. Putting both my feet on either side of her, I pull her hair out of her messy bun. It takes a few tries, but I do it as gently as I can.

We watch the movie for a while as I finger-comb her hair. Or, she watches. I stare at her hair and get lost in my thoughts.

I feel horrible about Ryder earlier. This is his first day back, and everything is all wrong. I know Sawyer was going to check on him. He brought a stack of pancakes to his shower.

Cali's soft voice breaks me out of my thoughts. "So...what is your guys' deal?"

"What do you mean?" I massage my fingers along her scalp. She shivers, then pretends she didn't.

"Like...is Sawyer a Dom?"

"He's a switch," I say.

She's silent for a minute. "And you're a sub?"

248

I chuckle. "I'm a switch, baby. I mostly sub to the men, though."

"Why?"

I grab a clump of her hair and braid it. Why? I don't know. I like it that way. It calms the chaos in my mind when I can't just…let go.

I clear my throat, "I've always been that way. Why do you like to submit?"

She stiffens. "I don't."

I grab another clump of hair. "Cali, I'm talking about in the bedroom, not your mind. But we can talk about that too if you want."

"I'd rather not," she says.

I play with her hair in silence. The movie plays in front of us.

"Is Ryder also a switch?" she asks.

The thought of his bossy, controlling ass submitting to one of us makes me laugh. "No, babe, he's all top."

"So if Sawyer's a switch, why didn't he…after he came…you know."

"Return the favor?"

She shifts.

I braid three pieces together, focusing on the different shades of blonde in her hair. "Sawyer doesn't give head."

"Why?"

I stiffen. "That's not my story to tell, shadow."

I expect her to keep pushing, but she just nods and keeps watching the movie. Bright colors flash, and images move across the screen, but I don't pay any attention. As I run my fingers through her hair, my body relaxes. She does too. Her head bobs forward a few times.

"Miles?" Cali asks softly.

"Yeah?"

"What's going to happen to me?"

I clench my jaw. The only scenario I can think of where she stays safe is if she's with me. Close by me, as my shadow. It's the safest thing for her at this point.

That, and I don't want to let her go. She's so feisty and strong and intriguing. Every time she's in the room, I gravitate towards her. I just want to touch her. Feel her. Make her feel good. She makes me feel happy, and I'm not sure why.

But I can't tell her that. Not now. I can't even talk to her about trying to keep her safe...it's not the right time. I know she'll just fight me on it. She's too scared to see reason.

"Miles?"

I sigh. "Let's not talk about it right now."

Her body stiffens.

"Please, Cali. We can talk later. It's late, let's get some sleep."

She continues to stare at the TV. I pull her up and lay her next to me. She's stiff for a second, then relaxes. I cuddle up next to her, and it just feels right. She smells like a mixture of Sawyer and her own natural scent.

And I feel at peace. It feels like having her here fills something that was missing.

And I don't think I ever want to let her go.

CHAPTER 40

MILES

"Mom! Where's my suit?" I sort through a stack of papers on the table. My prom date is supposed to be here any minute, but Mom hasn't paid the rent. My date's a cheerleader I've crushed on since Freshman year.

Fuck. Mom used to have the checkbook in here. Where is it? I grab another pile of papers from the table. She throws everything that doesn't have a place here...which is everything.

"What?" Mom yells from upstairs.

"My suit!" Fuck, it's not here either. A roach skitters across the pile, and rage fills me. I throw the papers to the floor. We can't be late on this. We've already been warned about eviction once. I'm not even sure what I've put in the account is enough, considering Mom lets her current boyfriend run around with her card.

Footsteps come down the steps. I whirl. Mom's smoking a cigarette, dark circles under her eyes. "Your suit was in your room last time I checked."

I pinch my eyes closed. It's not new. It's probably been owned by *three different people, but I've been saving for months. I didn't think her boyfriend would steal it. There's almost no value in it.*

I clench my jaw. I'm going to be late. And we're going to get kicked out. Again. There's almost no landlord in town who hasn't heard of or kicked us out of somewhere.

"Mom. Where's the checkbook?"

She takes another drag. "It's not on the table?"

"No, it's not on the table!" I explode. "Why the hell do you not keep it somewhere special? This house is a mess, and I'm the only one who tries to help!"

She snarls, "Vinny helps!"

Rage coats my vision. "Vinny does not help!" I get in her face, leaning down to her level and yelling, "He steals your money, Mom! Steals your money and beats your ass, and what do you do? You thank him for it!"

Mom flinches back from me, even while she yells something back at me.

I instantly step back. My stomach sinks, and the world slows. This is the exact look she gave my dad.

The exact look I always swore I'd never put on another person's face.

I back away. "Mom...I'm sorry."

She just continues to yell.

"I..." my heart is racing. "I'll find the checkbook. I'll find it, and it'll all be okay."

I bump into the table.

I'm just like him. I'll never be any different. I swore I'd never be him, but I'm just like him.

CHAPTER 41

MILES

I startle awake, breathing hard. Loud sounds fill the room. A woman - Cali - lays in front of me. I snap back to reality. Cali starts to sit up. "What's going on?"

I sit up fully. It was just a dream. Just a dream. I didn't realize that was going to be the last time I saw my mom alive. I've been having that dream more and more recently. It's time to kill again. Every time I wipe an abusive fuck from the earth, the dreams go away again.

The sound of an explosion fills the room. Fuck, the TV is still on. Where's the remote?

That's right, on the dresser.

I reach over Cali to grab it.

She flinches back violently, throwing her hands in front of her face.

I freeze.

Cali scoots back, looking at me from behind her hands.

Ice fills my stomach. She acts like she thought I was going to hit her. She thinks I'd hit her? Guilt fills me immediately, chased closely by anger.

"Cali..." I swallow, then growl. "Has someone been hitting you?"

She backs away more. "Sorry. I'm sorry! I...didn't mean to uh... sorry."

I clench my jaw as her eyes dart around the room, looking for an escape.

My voice comes out dark, "Care to tell me why this is the second time you've flinched like that?"

I can see Cali's pulse racing in her throat. She sits up straighter. She looks like she's scrambling for an excuse. "Maybe I'm just afraid of you," she says.

Those words hit me like a punch to the gut. I swallow. Anger rolls in just as quickly. No, she's just trying to cover up.

I narrow my eyes and grit, "You didn't seem too afraid sleeping right next to me."

Cali's eyes dart away again. "Yeah...well! I was tired! Doesn't take away the fact that you kidnapped me!"

I remember the first time she flinched with me. I brushed it off because I believed she might be afraid of me because of that. Not anymore.

"Cali," my voice is low and full of warning. "I think it's time for a little talk."

She clenches her jaw. "No."

Her eyes are full of fear. It makes my blood boil. I vowed I'd never get that look again.

I feel like throwing up.

"Refuse all you want," I say, louder than I intend. "You're not leaving this couch until you're honest with me."

Cali pulls her legs up and wraps her arms around them. She looks at me, her eyes wide in fear.

Goddamn it, I've done it again. I heave in a breath. My hands are shaking. I'm fucking this whole thing up. What the hell is wrong with me? I'm not my dad. I'm not him.

But you are like him. You scare people.

"Cali," I clear my throat and try again, softer. "Do you know the kind of people I hunt?"

She stares at her hands and doesn't answer.

I want to reach out and tilt her chin up to look at me, but I couldn't live with myself if she flinched again.

"Cali," I say, trying to keep my voice from shaking. Jesus, I'm being so weak right now. I don't want her to hate me because of this. I clear my throat. "My marks are wife-beaters. Pieces of shit. The kind of people who make women flinch."

I watch Cali swallow, her delicate neck bobbing. She won't look at me.

I wait, my heart racing.

She takes a breath, and her gaze darts up.

I glance away, too afraid to see fear in her eyes. I need her to fully understand. I take a deep breath. "I snatch them out of their miserable lives and give them a water bottle and a knife. I make them run, and when I catch them, I beat them just like they do to their women."

I beat them with my fists until the life drains out of them. It sends a thrill of excitement running through me just thinking about it. Which also sends self-hatred following right after.

You're just like him, but stronger. The bigger bully.

"What about the knife?" Cali whispers, drawing me out of my thoughts.

The knife? That's what she's concerned about? I blink. "Sometimes they try to cut me with it."

There's silence. It stays silent for so long that I dare a glance at Cali. She doesn't look afraid.

I can't help the massive wave of relief that flows through me. But even if she was afraid, I'd still do the next thing I'm going to do. Her not being afraid makes it easier, though.

I lean forward. "So tell me who it is, or I'm going to figure it out myself. I'll sort through everyone in your life, and there won't be anything you, or any of them, can hide from me. And I don't think you want that."

Cali looks at me with those blue eyes and asks, "What will you do to them?"

"Who, shadow?"

"The ones who didn't do anything?"

A sick sense of victory settles in my chest. I growl, "So there is someone who did something."

She clenches her jaw shut and remains quiet.

"Why aren't you talking to me?" I ask. Frustration rolls through me. I'm fucking all this up.

Cali looks at me and holds my gaze with anger in her own. "Sawyer told me it was stupid to show weakness."

I grind my teeth. Yeah, that does sound like something that dumb fuck would say.

"Sawyer is a dumbass sometimes."

"But he's not wrong, Miles," she says, exasperated. "I don't know if I'm going to survive the next week. Because of your boyfriend! Why would I talk to you?"

I lean back a little. I won't let him touch her. I told her that.

I try to keep my voice even, "Cali, I'm not going to let him kill you."

She scoffs. "Those are pretty words, aren't they? But when push comes to shove, are you really going to pick me over your boyfriend?"

I grit my teeth. "It won't come to that."

"How? What are my options, Miles?" Cali's eyes glisten. Fuck, are those tears?

My heart cracks.

"You'll come with us," I say. "He'll allow you to stay with us if you're no threat."

"What about getting enough points?" A tear traces down her face.

I swallow. "If Ryder even *thinks* you'll say anything about us, he'll hunt you down."

"I won't! I swear on everything." She reaches out to grip my thighs. "You need to believe me."

I freeze. She's touching me. I want to reach out and hold her, but I'm afraid she'll flinch. "I do."

"Do you?" she shoots back angrily. "Do you, or are you just saying that?"

Fuck. She's shaking. I slowly reach out to her.

"Don't touch me!" she cries.

260

I close the distance between her and wrap her in my arms. She fights for a second. I just hold her tighter. I wish I could get rid of all of this for her. I just don't know how.

The tension leaves Cali's body, and she breaks into sobs. "I want to go home. I want to go home, and I want my life to go back to normal. I want my cat. I want my bed and my food and my drinks. Please, Miles."

I stroke her hair down over the braid I gave her earlier. My heart breaks.

"Please." Cali continues to cry.

Part of me wants to give in to her. I hate seeing her so broken. But I know that old life can never be a reality for her anymore. She can't leave us. She can't be allowed to run around knowing who we are and what we do.

A voice in me screams that she won't say anything.

But I don't want her to go.

I won't let her go.

"Ben," she whispers.

"What?" I lean down.

She hiccups. "It was Ben who hit me."

CHAPTER 42

RYDER

I'm sitting at the dining room table with my family. Dad sits down heavily at the head of the table, making the silverware rattle. He's in a bad mood tonight.

"Ryder, say grace," he demands.

I swallow but bow my head. Maybe if I do this right, he'll be happier. There's a different prayer for every day of the week, and it's so hard to remember them. I start softly, "Dear God, forgive—"

A fork clinks and I jump. Dad is glaring at me from his bowed head. What part did I say wrong?

I start over. "Dear God, give us the forgiveness that we need and don't deserve. We are wretched sinners..." I say the prayer to the end, squeezing my eyes shut.

When I'm done, there's silence. I peek up.

Dad raises an eyebrow. I swallow.

"That's the wrong prayer, son."

Dread hits my stomach. Dad says if I don't say it right, God won't hear it, and the food won't be blessed. That we'll get sick if the food isn't blessed.

I start over.

"Ryder, you forgot 'in your mercy save my soul.'"

My stomach growls. "Can you remind me?"

Dad's voice is angry. "Do you even try? Do you want to get sick? It would be a horrible death to die at the hands of an angry god."

I say the correct prayer again.

Dad shakes his head. "Do it right the first time, next time." He grabs the mashed potatoes.

I wait for the food. I'm starving, but I don't want to set him off. Mom passes me the broccoli, coughing deeply. She's been sick for a while now.

"So, son," Dad asks. "How was school today?"

I glance at him. He doesn't look mad. He doesn't look...anything.

"Good." I pick at the skin around my nails. Please don't ask about my grades. Please. Maybe Mom didn't tell him.

"How'd your test go?"

I chew on the skin on the inside of my mouth. "Fine."

"What score did you get?"

I squeeze my eyes shut. "It was hard."

The table goes silent. "I asked what grade you got, not if you thought it was hard. Answer me."

"B," I whisper.

Dad's silverware clinks against the table, and Mom winces.

"Son, I see a major problem here. You don't try. You don't do your best. I've tried to help you over and over, and it's not working." He shakes his head. "We're going to have to go to the bathroom again."

"No." I tense. "Please, no."

"Honey, he did try—" Mom tries to help, but Dad speaks over her.

"Either you're a bad child on purpose, or you have an evil spirit in you. Your mother homeschools you to teach you the ways of God, and your heart is hardened."

My back itches. It hasn't fully scabbed over from the last time we went in there.

Dad yells, "Get your ass up!"

I flinch. I'm showering again. The house Sawyer was hiding in was filthy and covered in dust, lead paint, and asbestos.

I told the boys they needed to wash, too, but they shrugged me off to spend time with their little girlfriend.

The shower takes longer than normal. When I step out, I feel my cheek throbbing where Sawyer hit me. I can't check my reflection since his woman broke my mirror.

Feisty little thing. I'll bet she's fun in bed.

Fuck! No, I can't be thinking that. I need to be the strong one. Maybe after a few days, the men will get her out of their systems. They have to.

I won't let them go to prison for a woman. No matter how beautiful she might be.

CAKE

Pancake Mix

homemade pancakes

CHAPTER 43

SAWYER

I bring breakfast to Ryder after his shower. He grunts in appreciation. I go to leave, but he reaches out and pats the bed beside him.

"Stay," he demands.

I freeze. I'm not sure how mad he is about our fight.

Ryder softens his gaze. "I've had to sleep with one eye open for the past few days. Please. Stay."

Inwardly, I wince. I hate that he had to experience that. I slide into bed next to him, and he passes out within minutes.

I sneak out to grab one of my books and then read, snuggled up next to him.

At some point, I hear the front door slam and the truck start up. I get a text from Miles:

Cali's asleep in the basement. Going out. Be ready when I get back.

I sit up straighter. Be ready? What is he talking about?

I check on Cali, who is indeed asleep, curled up on the couch downstairs. I stand there looking at her. She looks so soft and defenseless.

I'm torn between Ryder and Cali. I can't just leave her unattended. But Ryder asked me to stay.

Reluctantly, I go back to Ryder's room, leaving the door cracked to listen for Cali.

There's no movement for a few hours. Then, I hear Miles return, and I meet him at the front door.

Only it's not just him. He has a body over his shoulder.

"Miley!"

"Hey, Cyrus." He shoulders past me and marches inside. "Do me a favor and get the basement door." I smell sweat and piss. Miles' eyes are alive with life, and he looks hot, shouldering another full-grown man with ease.

Excitement sinks into me, and I dart forward to assist. "What have you gotten yourself into, Miley?"

"It's my turn for a hunt. So I'm hunting."

Holy shit. Delicious excitement rolls through me, and I follow closely. Blood drips behind Miles on his way downstairs. The man must be passed out because he isn't struggling. He looks vaguely familiar, but I can't quite see his face.

Miles takes him to the cell, and I follow as close as I can. He heaves the man over his shoulder and onto the cement ground.

The man's head makes a hollow crack.

"Dude," I punch Miles on the shoulder. "What a waste, he's not even awake. Who is it?"

Miles motions inside with disgust.

I soak in the drama he's treating this with. Miles is pissed. How exciting.

I step over the body and crouch down.

"Well, well, well." I stand. Disgust runs through me. "If it isn't Ben."

CHAPTER 44

MILES

I peek out into the basement. Cali hasn't stirred. I shut the door to the cell. It's thick and slightly sound-resistant.

I dragged a gurney in here earlier. Sawyer helps me load Ben onto it, strapping him down. He even looks like a pussy ass bitch with his box died, blond hair and mouth in a permanent pout.

Pure hatred runs through my veins. My body hums with the idea of another hunt. I grab the smelling salts from my pocket and wave them under his nose.

Ben jerks.

I lean over the piece of shit, running my finger down his cheek. "Wakey, wakey, sleepyhead."

He groans.

I'm at my calmest when I'm killing. My most peaceful. It feels like the rest of the world falls away, and my only goal is to complete the kill in front of me.

Well, my calmest until I met Cali. She does something for me. Something that I don't know how to describe. It's like my soul is...

home around her. And that scares me.

I focus on Ben with efficient energy. He moans and looks around with watery eyes.

"Welcome back, sleepy. Did you have a nice nap?"

Ben partially focuses on me and jerks back. Well, as best as he can. His helplessness makes a thrill run through me and straight to my dick.

"You…" he sputters.

"Yes, me," I smile. "You can call me Karma. I'm going to make you pay for what you did to Cali."

"Cali?" He blinks slowly, still not focusing on anything.

"What the hell did he do to Cali?" Sawyer growls.

Rage boils in me. Ben acts like Cali is forgettable? Like what he did to her means nothing? I slam my hands on the edge of the gurney hard enough to make the whole thing shake.

Sawyer turns all his attention on me. "What. Did. He. Do?" The darkness flickers in his eyes again. He's afraid. He knows what my marks do.

I step in front of the gurney. "Sawyer, this is my fucking mark. Don't fucking touch him."

He clenches his jaw, his breathing getting heavy. "Tell me."

I swallow. He's going to kill him. I don't want to tell him.

Sawyer must see it in my eyes anyway.

Sawyer lunges at the gurney. I throw myself into his body to stop him. "Sawyer! Don't kill him. Don't kill him!" I shove him back an inch. "I can't play if he's dead."

"I don't give a fuck about playing," Sawyer growls.

"He's my mark!"

I shove Sawyer with all the strength I have. He takes a single step back.

"Fuck all the way off, Sawyer. He's mine to kill."

"Don't kill me!" Ben cries from the gurney. "Oh my fucking god, don't kill me!"

Sawyer grits his teeth, the veins in his neck bulging. "He touched Cali? I'm going to rip his head off his body. Get out of the way."

"You guys know Cali? Is she here? Cali! Cali, help me!"

Sawyer's lethal gaze moves slowly to the table.

Ben sobs, "That's my girl! Please tell me you know where she is."

I'm over Ben in an instant, my fist cracking down on his face. "She's our girl," I hiss. "She's way too good for you."

Ben yells, thrashing back and forth and crying. Sawyer is frozen at the end of the gurney, the darkness barely restrained in his eyes. "Miley," he grits. "Pick a different mark. Let me kill him."

"Oh, now you want *me* to give up *my* mark?" I growl at him. "Because you were so willing to do that with your little girlfriend?"

Ben struggles against his bonds. "Girlfriend? Cali! You fucking cheating whore!"

I see red. Did he just call my girl a whore? On top of everything else? I snap, punching into Ben's body, punch after punch, keeping just enough of my head not to hit his face so I can keep him alive. I sense Sawyer on the other side doing the same.

A commanding voice rings out. "What the hell is going on?"

My haze clears enough for me to look back. It's Ryder.

He leans against the doorway with a blank look on his face. "You playing without me again, boys?"

CHAPTER 45

RYDER

Neither man responds.

I glance over the man on the table. He mouths something unintelligible, bleeding out of his mouth.

I raise an eyebrow at my men. Miles' chest is heaving. He's out of control. He takes a few deep breaths, then straightens. "I have something else in the car. Sawyer, I'll kill you if you kill him."

Miles pushes past me and mutters, "Keep your hands off him, Ryder. He's mine."

Miles is being so possessive. I glance back at the man on the table. He's moaning about something and crying for someone to help him.

Usually, Miles lets us help him chase them down. What is different about this one?

I make eye contact with Sawyer for a second. His eyes are dark and haunted again.

Fuck. I thought I fucked that out of him. Both men are spiraling. Jesus, we need this kill, and then we need another good fuck.

Miles returns and throws a jerry-rigged cage and a bag on the ground. It's full of...rats.

I realize what he's doing, and my dick gets hard. Damn. This kind of torture isn't Miles' normal thing.

Sawyer snaps out of whatever haze he was in. He leans down over the man. "I'm going to show you just how much she belongs to us."

Tightness fills my muscles. "Belongs" to them? She's just a toy and a dangerous one, too. Not a fucking girlfriend.

Miles grabs some items from the bag and asks, "Wanna play a game, motherfucker?"

CHAPTER 46

CALI

I wake up partially when Miles and Sawyer come downstairs. I'm exhausted, and my body feels heavy with sleep. When was the last time I slept well?

I lie on the couch, lucid dreaming. Faint arguing filters into my dreams.

The angry voices trigger a flashback. It starts off like it always does. Normal.

I'm perched on the armrest of the floral print couch. I know that if I pray to Tinker Bell, she'll let me fly.

I clutch my toy. She has a sparkly green skirt with a yellow bun on her head. She's pretty, like my mom. Like my grandma.

The textured couch digs into the bottom of my five-year-old feet. Grandma tells me that if I'm a good girl and pray, then my prayers will be answered. And I've been good all week.

I close my eyes hard and pray that Tinker Bell will please, please let me fly. I trust her, and I trust my grandma, who says prayers are always heard. I take one breath, excited, my toes tingling. Then, I jump.

For a swooping second, I fly. Then I hit the shag carpet with a thud. The fluttering of my chest takes a minute to calm down, and slowly, a hint of sadness flits across.

It's okay. That was just a mistake.

I climb up on the couch again, asking Tinkerbell to please help me. I try again.

Again, nothing. I refuse to let that creeping betrayal set in and try again and again. Grandma said prayer works. Why didn't she listen?

"California!"

I jump.

Grandma storms to the room. I know she's mad by the way she grips the wooden spoon she uses for the pasta.

Grandma is mad a lot. I've come to expect it.

Her lips stretch thin over her teeth. "Did you not clear your bowl?"

My bowl? Oh! From dinner. I swallow.

Grandma looks at me like I look at my older brother when he wrecks my Lincoln Log barn. Like she hates me.

"Come here, California."

My legs stiff, I obey, tripping over Tinker Bell. She skitters under the couch.

Grandma leans down. "Turn around."

I look at the spoon, my heartbeat slamming through my chest. Is she going to hit me? Only my brothers hit me, and they get in trouble for it.

My hands start to sweat.

"Pull your pants down."

I stand there, frozen. Pull my pants down? We are always hiding underwear on our clothesline so people can't see it. It's embarrassing to show your underwear.

"No."

"I'm not going to tell you again." Grandma's voice picks up volume, and her lips curl like she smells something bad.

There is the anger again. I know this. This is comfortable. All I have to do is yell, and my heart will stop beating like a drum set inside of me.

My chest heats. "No!"

Grandma's eyes widen in a way I haven't seen before, like she's trying to see any tiny move I make. Then she wraps me up in her arms so quickly that I stand there, loose for a second. This is what it feels like to be hugged *at the end of each day. How it feels when she pulls me to her to kiss the top of my head.*

Only it lasts for a blink, and then she sits and pulls me down with her. My stomach digs into her knee. Heat runs through my veins, and my heart starts thumping fast. Something is very wrong.

I feel her hands on my pants.

I yell and push back hard, my cheeks burning.

"Don't fucking turn around, Cali."

Something is not right, and I can't see what she's doing. I scramble and turn at my waist to see. Grandma's face is red and...smiling. Only she isn't happy, like when I get good grades. And her hands aren't moving like they do when they pick out my clothes for the day.

For a moment, she looks like someone I haven't seen before.

"Turn around, or you'll get more!" She forces my chest back down.

The spoon! Where's the spoon?

Her knee digs into my stomach. Fear hits me so hard I can't breathe. I can't see. I can't see!

The comfort she held is gone, leaving a blank emptiness that I scramble to get away from.

"No!" I cry and struggle, but she doesn't let up. I hate that crack of fear in my voice, the way tears start to burn in my eyes. This is going to hurt. More than a shot at the doctor's office. More than when I fell off my bike. I know she wants it to hurt badly by how she looks at me.

I can't fight the fear. I fight and cry and scream.

Why won't she let me look?

I sit straight up, heaving for breath. Fuck. Where am I? I look around. I'm in the basement. The basement where the boys are.

Where I'm being held.

I realize tears have streaked down my face. I wipe them away. I hate that flashback. I looked for that toy when I got older. I thought that maybe the flashbacks would stop if I just found where she disappeared. I guess it's a good thing I didn't find her. I stopped believing in her that day.

I hear muffled, angry voices. For a second, they sound like my grandma, and I stiffen. I relax as soon as I hear the voices are lower and male.

I glance around. Where are they coming from?

As I do, the door to the cell they kept me in opens, and not just Sawyer and Miles but Ryder steps out as well. Miles closes the door behind them. All of them look at me, and Ryder crosses his arms.

Miles and Sawyer stare at me, but their gazes are blank. Sawyer cocks his head slowly. He looks like a predator.

My muscles tighten. Something isn't right.

"What...what are you guys doing?" I ask.

A slow smile stretches across Sawyer's face. "Hello, bunny."

What the hell? I scoot to the edge of the couch. This isn't the normal Sawyer. He's flipped whatever switch he does.

Even Miles looks different. He looks detached.

I draw in a deep breath. My eyes flit to the stairs.

Sawyer drawls, "Either she's going to fight, or she's going to run, can't decide which."

"Why would I need to do either? What are you guys doing?" My heart is hammering.

"Let's play a little game." Sawyer stalks around the side of the couch closest to the stairs.

I take a step back.

Miles' voice comes from partially behind me. "You'll get points, bunny."

I jump. Miles has rounded the couch on the other side, cutting off my escape from Sawyer. Behind me is blocked by the TV.

Sawyer smirks. "Ryder, get the cross."

My gaze snaps to Ryder.

He's standing like a silent sentinel.

He growls lowly. "I'm not your pet, Sawyer. Get it yourself."

"Fine." Sawyer shrugs. "All you, Miley."

When Sawyer turns and walks to the other side of the basement, leaving my path to the steps open.

I dart toward freedom.

CHAPTER 47

CALI

Miles moves at the same time. I reach the bottom step before his huge hand clamps over my wrist.

I scream. Miles yanks me back toward him, and I whip my hands up and claw at his eyes.

"Jesus." He snatches me up, pulling me into his chest.

"Let me go!" I scream. My arms are pinned against his chest. I kick my knee up to hit him between his legs. He drops us both down on the couch, moving so he's lying on top of me.

"Easy, Cali. I'm not going to hurt you."

"Get the fuck off me!" I claw at whatever skin I can get.

Miles buries his head in my neck. "No."

My chest heaves for breath. He has me pinned, and I can hardly move. His coconut scent fills my nose, mixed with something else.

"What the hell is wrong with you?" I ask. "What is going on?"

Miles doesn't answer me, and it makes my heart beat faster.

Sawyer comes back, and from what I can see, he's dragging a

wooden X-shaped cross. A St. Andrew's cross.

I freeze.

Sawyer drags it to right in front of the TV.

"No," I whisper.

Miles says into my ear, "A hundred points. Right here, right now."

I swallow.

Sawyer pants. "Good lord, that's heavy." He looks across the room. "Is that why you wouldn't get it?"

There's no response.

Sawyer moves over to us, an eyebrow lifted. "Run *and* fight? Did you want me to be right that bad, bunny?"

I growl at him.

Sawyer turns to Miles. "Think you can get it on her, Miley? You seem to be struggling as it is."

I jerk my head to try and see what it is he's talking about.

"I can do it."

Sawyer drops a piece of fabric. Miles pushes off me a little.

"Miles! What are you doing?" I try to turn away, and he lets me. I scramble onto my stomach before he sits heavily on me. He leans down, "Have you ever messed with sensory deprivation?"

I freeze.

"We're going to fuck that pretty pussy so hard you can't walk after."

I draw in a breath.

Miles pulls fabric over my eyes, plunging my world into darkness. Oh my god, I can't see.

Adrenaline runs through me, and I fight. "No!"

Miles ties it behind my head. He lifts off me, and instantly, I'm whisked into the air. I feel myself moving.

I can't see anything. The movement is dizzying. I move to rip the blindfold off, but hands grab mine and yank them above my head as my back is slammed into something hard.

I can't see. They're not letting me see. I can't do this. "No! No, no, no."

"Hey, Cali. Hey." Miles' voice comes right at my ear. "Easy, baby."

I heave for breath. "Take it off. Take it off, I want to see."

Cold leather buckles against my hands, pinning them in place against the cool wood.

I struggle, and my heart races. Fuck. Why the hell am I acting like this? The flashback is fresh in my mind, but I know she can't touch me anymore.

"Cali, are you okay?" It sounds like Miles asking.

My chest heaves. No. No, don't show weakness.

I nod my head once.

Suddenly, Miles' voice is loud in my ear. He growls, "Don't fucking lie to me, shadow. What's going on?"

My heart thuds, and I pray he can't hear it.

"Nothing," I whisper.

It sounds like one of them walks away. My heart hammers. There's the sound of a door and then some clattering. Then again, silence.

I test my bonds. They're tight. Is everyone still in the room? Is Ryder still here?

Hands brush my hips, and I jump.

A low voice says from across the room. "You're going to get punished for lying, pretty thing. Don't ever lie to us."

I swallow, trying to find the anger that usually gets me through. I say, "You can't tell me what to do."

Rough chuckles fill the room. It sounds like they come from all over.

I yank on my bonds again.

"I fucked her against the window," Sawyer says. He sounds close. "Our little bunny likes to be watched."

My cheeks heat, and warmth flares through me.

A low voice whispers, "Nasty thing. Do you like people watching you get off?"

Heat rushes to my pussy.

"No." I try to keep my voice level.

"No? So the idea of everyone in this room getting hard watching me play with this pretty body does nothing for you?"

My clit forms a heartbeat. What the hell is wrong with me?

There's a muffled moan, then the sound of a strike.

I jump.

A hand traces along the band of my sweatpants, and I jerk. "Pretty girl, no one is going to hit you unless you beg for it."

Whoever it is chuckles, and my pants are yanked down. Cool air rushes over my pussy, and I realize how wet I am. Horror rushes through me.

Someone's body presses into me. I feel a brief moment of panic, not being able to see them. But the pressure of his body grounds me. His fingers trace down until they brush my clit.

Another pair of hands brushes over my nipples.

"What a perfect girl, being so good for us." It sounds like Sawyer, but I can't tell which hands belong to whom.

The one right in front of me traces circles around my clit, and it sends electric pulses up my body.

"We're going to fuck you right here. You're ours. You belong to us and us only, and we'll kill anyone who touches you."

"Sawyer," I say. I know it's him who is saying that. He always tries to claim me. I struggle to focus. The hands make me feel so good. My senses are heightened with my sight gone. Goosebumps run up and down my body. They play me expertly, tweaking my nipples and giving just the right amount of pressure to make my pussy clench around nothing.

Someone shifts, there's the rustle of clothing, then I feel the hot tip of a dick pressed against my pussy. Whoever it is rubs it up and down on my clit, groaning.

"Christ, you're so wet, nasty girl." That sounds like Sawyer.

The movement feels so good. I moan and let my head fall back.

The dick presses against my entrance. My body trembles. I need that extra friction.

He shoves into me.

Pleasure immediately fills me. Sawyer groans. "Fuck, dirty girl. You feel so fucking good."

He slides in and out of me, keeping me against the cross.

"Goddamn, Cali. Miles is hard as fuck. You like watching me take our girl, Miley?"

Sawyer hits a spot inside me, and I moan, sparks tightening my muscles.

"Fuck." That was Miles. His voice is breathy and tight.

Not being able to see heightens the sensation while also filling me with fear. My skin is covered in goosebumps, and yet I feel euphoric.

"You're my woman. Our woman." Sawyer grunts as he pushes into me. "Does it get you hot to know that you have all the men in this room hard for you?"

I try to reach up to pull the blindfold off, but the ties stop my hand.

"No, no." A hand reaches out and swats my right nipple.

I yelp.

"Let them hear you, bunny. Let them hear those pretty little sounds." Sawyer slams harder into me, and it makes me groan. His breathing is heavy. He reaches down to play with my clit. "Miles is touching himself. He can't help it, watching me claim you. His dick is so hard right now it looks painful."

Sawyer presses hard into my clit, and I stiffen, throwing my head back. He pinches my clit hard and growls, "Let them hear you, Cali."

I moan. Sawyer instantly rubs the sting away. It's followed by delicious waves of pleasure.

Sawyer leans against my ear and whispers, "Ryder can hardly keep from touching himself, bunny. How does that make you feel?"

Fuck. I know I shouldn't want that, but a rush of powerful elation runs through me.

"He hates that he wants you. He can't help it. You're so fucking hot." Sawyer kisses along the side of my neck.

That's my undoing. I come, blinding pleasure washing through my body.

"Fuck, Cali," Sawyer grunts. "You're squeezing me so fucking hard."

Colors dance behind my eyes. I'm locked in the waves rolling through me.

"What's my name, Cali?"

"Sawyer," I moan.

"Good girl. Good fucking girl," he groans, then rips out of me.

I gasp, hanging my head as I come down.

"Oh, you're not done, princess." Hands are at my wrists,

unbuckling me. I stagger, and warm hands catch me. "Careful. Miles is in front of you."

I try to pull the blindfold off, and another harsh swat hits my right nipple while an arm pushes my hands down.

"Come here, shadow." Hands guide me to my knees. I feel what must be Miles lying on the ground. My hips are grabbed, and I'm pulled over Miles so I'm straddling him. "Ride me, Cali."

Miles guides himself to my entrance and slowly shoves me down over himself.

I groan as his fullness presses into me again. My pussy clenches around him, and he moans. "Fucking Christ, woman. Don't make me come so soon."

Hands run along my breasts, flicking my nipples. They shoot sensations through my body, and I throw my head back.

"Whose girl are you?" Miles grits.

I clench my jaw. "Mine."

Miles pounds heavily into me. "Wrong. Whose dick is in you?"

"Yours," I moan.

"I think she needs a little more reminding. And a little punishment for lying to us," Sawyer says. Something cold drips over my ass. I jump, automatically turn to look, and reach up to grab the blindfold.

"Uh uh." Hands grab my wrists and hold them down at my hips. Fingers rub the cold liquid down my crack until they reach my puckered hole. They play with the rim, making me clench down harder. It sends euphoria through me.

"Ever played with your ass before, bunny?"

"No," I grit.

Miles pulls me down on him so I'm lying on his chest.

"Not even with your ex?"

Ben? Ben 'accidentally' slipped in the wrong hole once, and it hurt like hell. I never let him try again.

"No," I say.

"Good. What a good fucking girl, keeping this for us."

Sawyer presses a finger inside. I stiffen. The pressure is uncomfortable.

"Relax, baby." Miles reaches a hand between us and plays with my clit. "He'll be gentle."

Sawyer pushes another finger in, pumping out gently with the rhythm Miles pushes into me with. I hold my breath. "Wait."

"You'll be fine, Cali." He keeps pressing. There's a bite of pain, and I clench my jaw. The pain quickly fades, adding to and replaced by pleasure.

"You think I'll fit?"

A gruff voice from across the room answers, "Not a fucking chance."

Sawyer chuckles. "Just you watch. Our girl is full of surprises."

Suddenly the fingers are gone, replaced by the head of his dick. As he presses gently, I tense. He's a lot bigger than his fingers.

"Easy, shadow. Tensing makes it hurt more," Miles rumbles.

Slight panic hits me. Miles is already filling me. I feel like there's no more room and no escape from the pressure. I struggle. Sawyer continues to press, causing a ring of pain to flare in me. I want to run.

I clench my jaw. Don't show weakness.

Miles plays with my clit, pulling my focus between the pain and the pleasure.

"What a nasty girl, you're doing amazing. Fuck, you almost have the tip."

Just the tip? I already feel so full.

Sawyer grabs my asscheeks, gripping them tightly. "There you go, good girl. You have us both now."

He stills, waiting for me to relax. I relax as the bite of pain dulls, and I'm left with the fullest sensation. Miles flicks my clit, and the sensation travels all the way to my ass. I moan.

"Oh, you like that? Taking both your men's dicks at the same time like a good little slut?"

As Sawyer moves in and out of me, the sensation becomes fuller. My pussy clenches, and both men groan.

"Jesus Christ, dude, she's trying to milk my dick."
"I can feel you in her. Fucking hell, you feel so fucking good."

I can't tell who says what anymore. Pleasure has overwhelmed me and made my brain foggy. I've never felt so full and pleasured before. I tense, feeling the orgasm creeping up on me.

Miles pinches my clit, sending pain shooting through me. "Don't you fucking dare come without saying who you belong to. Only good girls get to come whenever they want. And you lied to us."

I try to ride his hand to get that pleasure back.

"Cali," he growls. "There are people in this room who need to hear who you belong to."

I moan. The orgasm is creeping along the edges of my awareness, and it is the only thing I can think about right now.

Sawyer shoves roughly into me, sending pain shooting through me. It just makes the orgasm that much closer. "Who, Cali?"

"You!" I cry. Fuck, I'll say anything they want to hear to get them to let me come.

"And who else?" he grits. Miles finds my clit and rubs it again.

"Miles," I groan.

"Fuck, my name sounds so pretty when you moan it."

They work me up until euphoric weightlessness hits me. The orgasm takes over my body, and I float in the sensation. I'm pretty sure I cry out cuss words. The high lasts for so long. As I start to come down, they work me up again. All the sensations are overwhelming.

I arch my back. "No, no, please, it's too much."

Miles yanks my clit as they both shove into me. "It's not, and you can take it. Come again for us."

Pleasure spikes suddenly, and I come again, clenching on them, moaning something. They only let me ride for a second before they come at me again, playing with my body in all the right ways. I'm so tense it begins to hurt.

"Please...no," I groan.

They don't listen. Instead, they speed up, ramming pleasure I didn't think I was ready for through me.

Against my will, I come again.

I moan. I'm in a haze of pleasure and pain.

Vaguely, I feel Miles stiffen under me. His shout floats on the edges of my awareness, followed shortly by Sawyer.

"You see that, motherfucker? That's what you gave up the second you treated her like shit."

My thoughts swim. Is he talking to Ryder?

I'm being scooped up into a strong set of arms. "There you go. Atta girl, I got you. You did so good."

The pleasure is fading and replaced by relaxation. I allow myself to melt into his arms.

"Let's get you cleaned up."

The blindfold is removed. I blink and look around. Sawyer has me in his arms. My vision clears a little, and I see Ryder standing in the shadows next to a…

Holy shit. There's someone else here.

Fear hits me. I struggle to get away. "Who the fuck is that?"

Sawyer clenches me tighter. "He's not your concern anymore."

I've been here for how long and never seen another person? I kick out my legs in an explosive movement.

"Let me fucking go!" Another person could mean help. It could mean a way out of all this.

I slip out of his arms just enough to see, and what I do see stops me instantly.

CHAPTER 48

MILES

Cali screams, the sound high-pitched and blood-curdling. She really starts fighting Sawyer. I see him struggle not to hurt her. He drags her, cussing and screaming, upstairs.

"Miles." Ryder sounds calm, but I know he's anything but. "Who the fuck is this?"

I glance in disgust at Ben, who's been bound and gagged the whole time. Ryder's job was to pinch his nose closed if he made too much noise. A job he took great joy in.

"This is the piece of shit who hit her."

Ryder stiffens.

"Don't fucking worry," I snap at him. "I'm going to kill this one."

I yank the gurney back into the cell. I know I just got off, but I'm still disturbed. I need this kill.

Ben rolls his eyes and shakes his head, trying to get away.

I grab the cage of rats. "Let's get started, shall we?"

CHAPTER 49

CALI

Sawyer dumps me in his bathroom.

"Shower," he snaps and stands in front of the door.

I shove my hands into his chest. "You have my ex in your basement? Did he watch us fuck, Sawyer?"

Sawyer watches me with disconnected eyes. All kinds of thoughts roll through me. My ex just watched me fuck these men. These men who kidnapped me, call me theirs, and make all kinds of confusing emotions fill me.

The ex who treated me like shit. Who I hoped I'd never see again.

My ex who's tied up in the basement with psycho killers.

Fuck, why does he have to be here right now? My real life is intersecting with this fever dream I've been a part of and it throws me completely off.

I cross my arms. "Let me go. I want to see him."

Sawyer's eyes remind me of the first time he fucked me. Wild and unpredictable. Strands of hair have fallen out of his bun. His eyes narrow. "He's not your boyfriend anymore."

Anger fills me. "I don't care! You guys are sticking your fingers where they don't belong!"

Sawyer's jaw clenches. "He hit you. I think we're absolutely where we belong."

I start to argue, and Sawyer snarls, "I know he touched you. So forgive me if I don't want him to live."

Something odd skitters in my chest. Something warm. They're fighting for me. No one has ever done that for me.

I shake myself. They're going to kill him. I need to care about that. They're going to kill him and lock me away like I'm meaningless in all this. Like I have no voice.

Sawyer just stands there, silent. I grip the marble counter and stand up straighter, "I want to see him."

Sawyer gives me a deadly look and motions at the shower. "Get in."

"No!" I stare into his eyes. "You're just like him – not giving me a say in anything. Is that what you want?"

Rage dances in Sawyer's eyes for a second. I force myself to stand tall. He can throw a fit all he wants. I'm tired of this.

We glare at each other, the bathroom eerily silent.

Fear, anger, hatred, and hopelessness roll through me all at once. I throw my hands up. "What, you think I can't handle it? That I don't deserve to get a say in the death of a man who hurt me?" I lower my voice. "If anyone deserves to hurt him, it's me, Sawyer."

Sawyer stares at me for a second. Nothing happens behind his eyes, but his jaw clenches the tiniest bit.

"Fine." He steps out of the way.

I shove past him, racing to the basement. I rush toward the cell door and push it open.

I skid to a stop. Miles is standing over Ben with a cage over his bare abdomen. He's...tying it to him?

Miles turns to look at me, as does Ryder. Both cock their heads at the exact same time with blank looks.

There's silence for a second.

I cross my arms. "I'm not an annoyance that you just lock away when you want to mess with my life, Miles."

There's another second of silence. Miles gives me a look I can't interpret.

Ryder snorts. "Control your toy, Miles."

Sawyer's voice comes from behind me. "She wants to play, too." I whip around. He leans against the doorframe, almost filling it with his massive form. "Plus, I wanted to watch."

There's some kind of unspoken communication between Miles and Sawyer. I watch it in their eyes.

Miles shakes his head. "She doesn't belong here. Get her out."

Sawyer doesn't move.

Ryder starts towards me.

"No!" I glare at him. "Don't fucking touch me."

Ryder's dark eyes flare in challenge, and he's on me in a flash. His giant hand is around my throat, and before I realize it, I'm against the wall.

"What was that?" he says mockingly.

"Ryder!" Sawyer struggles to get between us. "My mark. Get your hands off her."

Ryder ignores him. He isn't squeezing, but his grip is firm. He leans into my ear, and I can just see Miles behind him. I'm hit with the smell of cologne and mint. His deep voice rumbles in my ear. "You're not the one who gives orders around here, little mystery. I'll fucking touch you if I want to. And there's nothing you or your little puppies can do about it."

I shudder in a breath. Ryder's voice is deep and swirls around me like intoxicating sin. God, why is this affecting me?

The fact he thinks he can bully me makes rage run through me. I lived with that long enough with Ben.

"Fine," I grit my teeth. "*Don't* let me go then, motherfucker. In fact, why don't you just kill me now instead of dancing around it?"

I hear someone suck in a breath. Miles moves toward us.

I raise my eyes to look into Ryder's deep brown ones. They're swirling with rage and something I can't put a finger on. His fingers tighten to the point I can feel my pulse racing against them, and I start to feel lightheaded.

That's it. It went too far, and I got a reaction. Victory runs through me. This big bad man wants to be in charge so much, but I'm the one controlling his actions right now.

I pull in a breath and smirk. "What, the big bad wolf wants to kill me, but he can't because his men would never forgive him?"

It's a gamble. I don't know how Sawyer and Miles would feel about it. But I see Ryder's eyes snap in anger, and he leans into me. Sounds start to mute, and there's a roaring in my ears. I vaguely hear shouting, and then the pressure on my neck is gone.

I blink, heaving in breaths. The roaring goes away. I cough. I was right. They won't let him kill me.

I laugh. I'm not sure why I'm laughing, but I can't help it. I've never been more powerful while being powerless at the same time.

I straighten. Ryder is still right there, chest heaving. Sawyer is standing slightly in front of him. All three men look pissed.

I turn to Miles. "He hit *me*, not you. Tell me what you're going to do to him."

CHAPTER 50

RYDER

My vision clouds around the edges. I can barely focus on anything but the wild, curly blonde hair of the infuriating woman in front of me. My skin feels hot. What the absolute fuck? Nothing gets to me. Nothing. I learned how to turn it off a long time ago. Dad would only beat me harder if he got a reaction. But this woman? She's gotten to me worse than anything in a long time. And now, she has the audacity to openly try to get between us.

I want to trample her down until she's helpless under me, helpless and completely at my mercy. My dick jerks at the idea.

Miles says, "I'm going to kill him, Cali."

She holds her head higher, a bunch of emotions rolling across her face.

I shake Sawyer's hands off me and cross my arms, trying to get myself back under control. I try to think of something I can feel and focus on that instead of everything else. I have a hangnail on my left thumb. I scratch at it. It's just like when I'd calm myself before

Dad would beat me. I need something else. I need to do something else to take this back.

I look into the woman's crystal blue eyes. "See that cage...Cali?" She turns her nose up at me.

"Miles is going to put burning coals on top. The rats will have nowhere else to go but inside your boyfriend's belly. It'll be agonizing, and it'll be slow."

I see a flicker of disgust and fear run over Cali's pretty face before she hides it in anger.

I chuckle. "What? The killers are hot until they're doing what you know they do?" I lean down into her face. "How many people do you think Miles has killed, girl?"

"Ryder..." Miles says.

I snap my gaze at him. "You'd prefer to lie to her?"

He glares at me but stays silent.

"Over 30." I turn back to Cali's angry face. "Handpicked, each one. Brutalized each one. Do you know what they usually die from?"

Her furious gaze is on me. We're so close her breath puffs out onto my face. I just want to lean into her and suck all the breath out of her. Make her fight and cry and beg for it back. Make her submit to me.

I keep my face blank. "Internal damage. It's a rough way to go. Slow. Fists don't kill quickly."

Cali's gaze flicks to the man on the gurney and back to me.

I need her to snap out of this stupid crush she has on my men. I lean in, "Isn't that what this guy did to you? Fists?"

"Ryder!" Miles barks.

I don't look at him. I'm trying to protect him. This gorgeous woman brings nothing but prison and life sentences. And the breakup of my family. I'd rather him hurt briefly than for the rest of his life.

"Think about it, Cali." I stand. "Now. If you want to be so involved, why don't you help?

"Ryder, no."

I whirl on Miles. Fear swirls in his eyes, but I know it's not fear of me. It's for her. Which makes me even angrier.

I grit, "If you want her to like you so bad, then stop hiding things from her, Miles."

"It's not that." He swallows roughly.

"Get the coals," I tell him.

He crosses his arms. "She's not one of us. I won't make her do that."

"I'll do it." Cali's voice comes out strong. I ignore her and lower my voice, "Oh, but you want her to be like us, don't you?"

Miles gives a tiny flicker of a reaction, then nothing.

"How do you think she'll be like us if the thought of what we do makes her sick?" I lean into him. "This. Will. Never. Work. Get it through your head."

"Stop this." Miles shoves into my chest. "You're acting like an ass because you're jealous."

I cross my arms, defensive anger running through me. Jealous? I'm not jealous. My stomach clenches. I'm trying to protect these men from their own lust and stupidity.

"No," I tell Miles. "I'm telling it like it is. The sooner you see reality, the less it'll hurt."

"So you all are just going to talk about me like I'm not here?" Cali crosses her arms.

Both men look uncomfortable. I'm uncomfortable. I feel sick. I hate fighting with my men. But if I need to do it to keep them safe, I will.

I say, "Try to keep him quiet, Miles. I have some work to do upstairs. Don't want to be disturbed by his screams."

I leave the room, refraining from slamming the door. My body feels hot and heavy. God, I need to hurt someone. Hurt, or fuck. Or both. I want to act on impulse and fuck both my men right there in front of Cali. To show her who really owns them.

But I don't. Because I don't react. I won't give her the satisfaction of another reaction from me. She'll pay. And she'll pay soon enough.

I move into my office and shut the door. I try to get to my work. It's just early enough that the stock market just opened.

I try to focus on my computer, but the data rolling across the screen fades into each other. I'm fucking pissed.

She got to me. How in the fuck did she get to me? The way her hateful little eyes looked up at me made me want to hurt her until she cried and begged me to stop. She'd look so pretty on her knees, covered in blood. She'd taste so sweet on my blade.

My dick hardens.

God fucking damn it.

Images of them fucking her just a bit ago flash in my mind. The way their two powerful bodies almost ate her up completely. The way she stretched painfully to allow both of them in. Her whimpers of pain. The sounds Miles made and the way Sawyer threw his head back in ecstasy.

My dick is so hard it hurts.

I growl and try to focus on my computer again.

God, their cum dripped out both her holes. I wanted to shove their faces in it. Suffocate them in it until they turned purple and begged for forgiveness.

I jerk to my feet. Enough. I refuse to get turned on by this.

She's nothing but a game. My men will get tired of playing it. So why do I feel like we're just getting started?

CHAPTER 51

CALI

Ryder walks out, and I'm left with both men. And Ben. Neither Sawyer nor Miles move for a second.

Rage fills me. Not once did they ask my opinion. I look with disdain at Ben.

Both men look uncomfortable.

"Give me the coals."

Miles snaps his gaze to me. "What?"

"Give me. The coals," I grit.

Ben starts thrashing and yelling behind his gag.

"No." Miles shakes his head and turns away. "This isn't for you. Ryder is gone. Go upstairs."

"No." Adrenaline pumps through me, and I stand my ground. A mix of gratitude, anger, and fear rolls through me all at once.

"Cali!" Miles snaps. "Go upstairs! You don't have anything to prove to me."

I turn to Sawyer. He cocks an eyebrow. "Don't look at me, bunny. I'm all for it, but this is Miley's hunt."

"Don't call me Miley," Miles snaps.

Anger runs through me. Again, they're trying to take all choice from me, including the choice to live. I'm so done. I don't know how to act. I just lean into my anger, putting my finger in Miles' chest. His green eyes flare, and he looks angry.

I hiss, "I didn't ask you to be my knight in shining armor. In fact, I didn't ask to be here at all. If you're looking for a helpless woman you can save, you haven't found her here. So either get your fingers out of my fucking life or let me have a goddamn say."

Hurt flares in Miles' eyes for a brief second, and something twists in my gut. Then his eyes flash to anger and Miles snarls, "You know what? Fine. Sawyer, get the coal."

I hear Sawyer leave. Miles and I are locked in a stare. Anger swirls in his green eyes. It's a look I've never seen him direct at me before. It sends a mix of fear and anger into me. But it's better than pity.

Sawyer returns. I snatch the bucket from him and whirl on Ben. His watery eyes are wide in fear. Acid drops in my stomach. Am I really about to do this? All of our history flashes in my mind. The days we got along and sat next to each other peacefully on the couch. The times he made me laugh, and the times he made me come. The bucket is metal and hot, and I can feel the skin on my fingers burning.

The screaming. The many things thrown at me. The nights he'd go through my phone, convinced I was cheating on him.

I pull in a breath and drop the bucket on top of the cage.

CAKE

ancake Mix
homemade pancakes

CHAPTER 52

SAWYER

Cali whirls on us with fire in her eyes. She looks wild and alive and afraid. I suck in a breath, her fear going straight to my dick. It jolts me out of my darkness for a second.

Cali gives me a double take, "What are you laughing at, pretty boy?"

I school my face. I didn't realize I was smirking. I say mockingly, "You, pretty girl."

"This isn't funny."

I raise my hands in surrender. "Believe me. Both of my men are about to lose their shit, and I'm not entirely sure you won't murder me tonight. Nothing is funny about this."

I feel the darkness swirling in me. That broken look on her face when she talked about Ben before, the fear on her face when we blindfolded her, and the absolute punch to the gut when I found out he hit her have me swirling in my demons again. I hate how easy it is to kick me back into my childhood.

That's because this is where you belong, son. I am your home. Lean into what I've taught you.

I shake my head.

Cali gives me a face. "I'm going upstairs."

I breathe in the fire spitting from her. It clears my mind for a second.

And then she's gone.

I move to chase after her, to get her brightness back, but Miles grabs my arm. "We need to talk."

I shake him off. "What?"

"How are we going to handle Ryder? He's hurt."

Look at you hurting the people you love. You'll never escape me, son. You're just like me.

I shake my head again.

Ben has started screaming behind his gag again. The rats are getting restless. It clears my mind for a second.

I can sense Miles looking at me. He asks, "What are we going to do about Cali?"

I watch the rats run from one end of Ben's stomach to the other. They know something bad is coming.

Miles snaps my name.

I whirl on him. "I don't know! I'm not killing her, Miles. She's mine." I can't keep the possessiveness out of my voice. Miles sees it, his eyebrows shooting up in surprise. I look away. I don't know how Miles is going to take it. But I think...I think this is more than a game to me. Cali brings clarity, fire, and life. I want to dig into her secrets. I want to own them. To own her. To own her soul. I'm not even slightly done with her.

And that scares me a little.

"Ours," Miles breathes.

"What?" I suck in a breath and look at my man again. He's bathed in the harsh light of the cell, all hard edges and sincerity.

"She's ours," he says.

We stand there, searching each other's eyes. I see nothing but sincerity in his. We've been at each other's throats endlessly recently. But right now? I feel like this is one thing we can agree on.

I dip my head in a short nod. Some of the tension goes out of him.

"I'll lock this up so she can't get to him," he says.

I let out a deep breath. For a second, the dark fog clears. I nod. "I'll talk to Ryder."

He needs to be handled with kid gloves. I need him to think it's his idea for her to stay. And I need to do it before he and Cali go at each other's throats and Cali ends up dead.

CHAPTER 53

CALI

This is insane. All of this is insane. I can't believe that they kidnapped him for me. It feels…good. No one ever cared about me that much.

Tears well up in my eyes, and I glance at the front door as I pass it. A mixture of emotions fills me. Day one Cali is screaming at me to run. Wiser Cali says that Ryder would be on me in a flash if I even set one foot outside. Stupid Cali says running is betraying them.

I couldn't stay downstairs one more minute. I dart into Sawyer's room and shut the door carefully.

Oh my god. Oh my god, did I just help kill someone?

I want to throw up.

No. No, Cali, we will not fall apart now. I splash some cold water on my face. I stare at the water as it goes down the sink as I try to zone out. No, don't think about it, Cali.

I glance around. It's silent.

Fuck. I need to do something to stop thinking. I need a drink.

No, I need to get drunk. I almost leave the room to find Ryder's whiskey, then pause. Ryder said he was getting some work done. The chances that he's in the office are high.

I look around the room helplessly. There are clothes scattered around, the bed is unmade, and Sawyer's dresser is an absolute mess.

I could look around. I've never been in here without him.

Ben was crying. Crying! Fuck. I start with Sawyer's dresser, looking around the top. There's receipts, cologne, change, watches, and junk. I rifle through it and find a loaded pistol magazine. I swallow. Is there a gun in here? I open drawers, trying to go quickly without missing anything. Nothing.

There's a large row of bookshelves along the wall by the window. I go to it. It's stocked with all kinds of books, sorted by the colors on the spines. In fact, it's the only organized thing in this place. I pull out a few books wondering if any of them were secret containers, but stop after finding nothing but real books.

I spin in a circle. I know it's a long shot to assume Sawyer would leave a gun lying around, but isn't that what killers do?

I check under the mattress. Nothing.

There is still the nightstand with a water bottle, charger, and a dirty shirt on top. I open the drawer.

Inside are three things: a book, a flattened penny, and a picture. I catch my breath and pull out the photo. It's of two boys with their arms around each other – maybe ten years old? They're dirty and standing in a room of filth, but they have the biggest smiles on their faces. The picture quality is terrible.

I flip the picture around. Nothing written on it. I look at the boys closer.

One has Sawyer's dark hair and blue eyes. He's giving the cheekiest grin to the camera. The other boy looks similar, maybe a little younger.

Something outside the room creaks, and I jump. I put the picture back in the drawer. But nothing moves.

Is this the brother Sawyer talked about?

I shudder out a breath and look at the penny. It looks like the coins my brother and I used to put on the train tracks, only to come back and find them squashed.

I check the rest of the room. I don't find the gun. It has to be in the house somewhere.

I'll bet they keep the good stuff in the office or their cars.

Tonight. Tonight, I should wait until they're asleep and then leave. Take my freedom back.

My stomach clenches, and I think about the smell of sweat, burning coals, and coconut. I'll never be able to go back to the person I was.

I come up with excuses. I need to have a gun when I run because something tells me they'll hunt me with all they have. I'd shoot it better this time. I'd have to. I have no other choice.

Why does the thought make my chest tight?

CAKE

Pancake Mix
homemade pancakes

CHAPTER 54

SAWYER

I find Ryder in the office. I step in and kick the door closed behind me.

He doesn't even look up from his computer. He looks dark and brooding, slouched down.

I cross my arms. "We need to talk."

"Nothing to talk about," Ryder grunts.

"Sure there is," I say. "You never told me if there were any hot guys in jail."

He jerks his gaze up to me.

I arch an eyebrow. "Kinda leaving me hanging here."

Ryder looks back down at the computer, his eyes dark and shadowed. "You'd have to call while I was there to know that shit."

I snatch a paperweight off the desk and play with it, tossing it up and down in the air. "I figured they'd be all over you. You know, hot prisoner, fresh meat."

Ryder grunts.

I toss the weight a few more times. "So how much is this case going to set us back?"

Ryder continues typing. "Why are you talking to me right now?"

"Grumpy?" I smirk at him. I know why he's mad at me. We defied him downstairs.

"Would you stop throwing that?" Ryder snaps.

I look at his huge frame. Goddamn, the man is handsome, all dark and brooding. I toss it again. "You gonna make me?"

He glares at me, then seems to catch himself and goes back to his work.

"What, too afraid I'd beat your ass if you tried?"

He doesn't even look up.

I slam my hands into the desk and snarl, "You gonna ignore me, Ryder?"

Ryder curls his lip at me. "Leave me alone, Sawyer. Don't you have something better to do? With your girlfriend, maybe?"

Adrenaline runs through me. I lean over the desk into his face, shutting his computer. I know he doesn't agree with Cali being here, but I need him to get on board. I just don't know how to get him there. So, I pick a fight with him.

"I have something to do," I hiss. "I'm doing it."

Ryder gives me no reaction. I see his eyes flare with the challenges I'm throwing him, but he doesn't take them. Instead, he pushes his chair back. "I need to run to town."

Before he can get to the door, I round the desk on him. I put my hand on his chest and shove. "Don't run from me."

Faster than I can register, Ryder's hand snakes around my neck, and he shoves me into the wall, pinning me there roughly and making me cough.

He leans into my face, voice low and angry. "Don't push me, pup. I won't be as careful with you as I was with your mark."

"Do your worst." I narrow my eyes in victory.

Ryder's dark eyes bore into mine, and he snarls in my face, "Don't you get it? I don't want to play with you. Fuck. Off."

He releases me like he can't stand to touch me.

I freeze.

Ryder walks out of the room.

I stare after him, my blood turning to ice. He's never once

322

pushed me away. In fact, he is always the one chasing after Miles and me, never letting us keep secrets from him and fucking us into submission when we fight him.

A car door slams outside, and I jump. I see Ryder's truck tear out of the driveway.

Fuck.

You should be used to this, Sawyer. People always leave. Even those who say they love you.

I swallow. Fuck that. Shut the fuck up.

I scratch my arm as I storm out of the room.

CHAPTER 55

CALI

Sawyer's bedroom door bursts open while I'm trying to comb the snarls out of my hair in the bathroom mirror. "Caliii," a voice singsongs.

I feel Sawyer's presence at the doorway. I refuse to look at him.

"Find anything useful?" he asks, his voice dark.

I force myself not to freeze. There's no way he could know I was looking through his stuff. "What do you mean?"

He chuckles lowly. "Oh, bunny. I thought you knew better than to lie to me."

I still don't look at him.

Sawyer stalks behind me and leans his head down behind mine. He sucks in a breath. "You know what happens to liars, Cali?"

"I'm not a liar." I throw my hair into a loose braid, trying to ignore him. Trying to ignore the way his very presence makes me hot.

Sawyer runs his fingers slowly up my spine. He chuckles again darkly. There's no humor in it.

"You're just built for me, aren't you, Cali? A fucking glutton for punishment."

His fingers run up the back of my neck, and he threads his fingers into my hair. Then he grips hard.

A jolt of pain runs through me, and I suck in a breath.

Sawyer jerks my head back, and my eyes fly to his blue ones in the mirror.

"Ah, she finally acknowledges me. Is that what it takes, Cali? A little force?" He yanks again, causing tears to well in my eyes.

"Let go."

Sawyer sucks in a breath and presses his crotch to me. He's hard.

"Let go," he mocks.

I snarl at him.

"Awww, look, the bunny is trying to be scary." Sawyer leans down while pulling my head to the right. He bites down hard on my exposed neck. Dull pain shoots through me, mixing with the sharp pain along my scalp. He bites down harder, and I jerk to get away.

Sawyer chuckles against me, releasing my neck. "You're so fucking cute."

"I'm not fucking cute." I try to whirl around. To pretend like he isn't making my pussy hot and my muscles tremble. Sawyer presses me into the sink. "Tsk, tsk, just let it happen." He leans down and bites my shoulder, crushing his teeth into my skin.

I cry out, wrestling against his massive body. I feel my skin bruising.

Sawyer releases me only to bite again, a little bit lower. He bites over and over, bruising and crushing my skin despite my struggle.

Each flare of pain shoots straight to my pussy.

"Fuck off," I stomp on his foot.

Sawyer doesn't even react. "Goddamn, you look beautiful covered in my marks."

He snatches me up and hauls me into the bedroom.

"Sawyer!" I cry out as he throws me on the bed. He crawls up after me immediately. I scramble back. "Stop! I don't want to do this right now."

Sawyer flattens my knees with one heavy, tattooed arm,

crawling up over my hips. "I don't think you realize..." He yanks my pants down. "You don't get a say right now."

My adrenaline spikes. Sawyer flashes a smile at me, his eyes dark and angry.

I hate that it makes my pussy wet.

"Does it turn you on knowing that you can't do a thing to stop me right now?" He yanks the boxers down my hips.

"No! You're fucked up." I swipe my hand across his eyes to get him off me.

Sawyer drops his head down to my pussy and sucks in a breath. "Goddamn. You're just a nasty slut, aren't you? You're wet as fuck." His breath puffs on my pussy. "God, I want to eat you until you're limp in my arms and you stop fighting me. And then I'll consume the rest of you until you can't tell the difference between us anymore." He yanks my legs back, so I'm completely bared to his manic gaze. "You'll keep no secrets from me, Cali. You can fight me, but you don't get to lie to me."

His mouth is so close to my clit, and discomfort rolls through me. I haven't showered.

Sawyer's sharp gaze studies me. "Tell me why you're weird about oral."

I glare at him. "I'm not being weird!"

"Don't fucking lie." Sawyer yanks me close to him. "You were weird with Miles, and now you're weird again. You're going to tell me." His fingers dig into my hips.

"Fine," I hiss. "You want honesty? Miles was the first one to ever make me come."

Sawyer freezes. His blue eyes rake over me, soaking in everything.

I narrow my gaze. "From head. I don't like head. So either fuck me like a man or not at all."

Sawyer's eyes flare in challenge, and in an instant, his head is buried in my pussy. He eats me with passion, alternating between licking and sucking and nibbling.

Pleasure fills me. "Fuck you, Sawyer. I said no." I arch my back, both trying to press into him and trying to get away from him. His assault on my clit is overwhelming and overstimulating.

I reach my hands down, trying to push his head away.

Sawyer watches me, slowing his assault and flattening his tongue, lessening the sensation while deepening it. He moans into me, continuing his pattern. Euphoria runs through me. Sawyer continues what he's doing without changing, keeping his eyes locked on mine, watching my every move.

I realize that I've stopped fighting him. I yank my fingers back in his hair. He moans, and his eyes roll back.

Fuck, I can't give up this easily. I'm supposed to be trying to get away from them.

I scramble to get away, and Sawyer yanks me back into him firmly.

"You're gonna have to direct me a bit, Cali. I haven't given head in...a long time."

I freeze. Oh fuck. I glance at him. The darkness is there in Sawyer's eyes, but mostly he looks aroused.

"Sawyer, you don't have to–"

"Shut up," he snaps, his gaze hardening. "Unless you're telling me how you like it or screaming my fucking name, I don't want to hear it."

I snap my mouth shut. He dives back into me, biting my clit hard.

I gasp and pull back from him. He follows, flattening his tongue again and rubbing my clit regularly. It causes sensations to rush through me again. I'm stiff, not sure what to do.

Sawyer pulls back. "Get out of your fucking head, bunny. You're going to fucking come today. You have no choice."

He dives back into me again, eating me with aggression. Despite everything, it feels fucking good. He listens to my body, moving with me. Every time I soften, he continues exactly what he was doing. He keeps at it until I stiffen. I'm going to come, and I don't fucking want to.

He looks up at me with victory in his eyes, his tongue shooting incessant pleasure through me.

"Sawyer..." I growl.

He bites down at the same time as he digs his fingers deep into my hips. I cry out, my whole body locking up. It's like fire fills my veins, and I close my eyes, pure pleasure rolling through me in waves.

Before I can come down off my orgasm, Sawyer pulls back and flips me over on my stomach.

Oh fuck. I can't see what he's doing. A sliver of fear runs through me, and I struggle to roll back over, throwing a look back at Sawyer.

He's pulled his pants down, his hard dick bobbing and stiff. I roll over to my back.

Sawyer crawls up over me. "One day, I'll find out who made you scared to close your eyes, bunny. And if they aren't already dead, I'm going to kill them for you."

He plunges into me, filling me up completely on his first thrust. I arch my back, a moan escaping me.

"Good girl. Fuck, you squeeze my dick so fucking nicely."

Sawyer pulls out slowly, then thrusts back in.

"What a nasty slut. You can't fight me. Your body submits to me, and soon enough, your heart will too."

My body freezes in fear. Fuck no. Absolutely not.

Sawyer reaches his hand down and plays with my clit. "Stop fighting me, Cali. It's useless."

He plays with my body so expertly. Euphoria skitters across my skin, and my muscles tighten.

"That a girl. Come for me, my pretty whore."

I do. I explode in sensation, every muscle tightening. Pleasure races up my spine, and my skin buzzes. Sawyer continues to pound into me, grunting. His abs tighten, and then he comes inside me, groaning my name.

We both lie here, panting.

I stare at the ceiling. My muscles feel like jelly. I feel so sated and exhausted. Fuck. He made me come. Multiple times.

Sawyer rolls over and throws an arm around me, spooning me.

Goddamn, I need a shower.

I go to move, but Sawyer just tightens his hold, pulling me to his chest. "Stay, Cali."

His arm is like a strong band around me. I relax back into his hold.

We lie in silence for a long while, both of us breathing slowly. Reality hits me. I know I need to get away from them if I value my life. But in this moment, it's oddly...peaceful.

Sawyer startles me when he speaks. "You like less direct pressure?" His voice is low and husky.

I blink.

"When I eat you out?"

My cheeks get hot. "I...uh. I don't know."

"What do you mean you don't know?" Sawyer raises his hand and traces around my collarbone until he finds the raised section of the brand. It's still healing and hurts.

I clear my throat. "I don't get...people don't eat me out very often."

"Why?"

"Ben never wanted to."

He stiffens at Ben's name.

We fall into silence again. I feel uncomfortable. I'm not sure what to say.

"You know he deserves what he's getting."

I squeeze my eyes closed for a second. "I'd rather not talk about it."

Sawyer silences.

I open my eyes and glance around the room. I want to talk about anything but that. "What's your brother like?"

Sawyer stops breathing for a second. Then he says softly, "Wild. More than me."

"That's hard to imagine," I deadpan.

Sawyer chuckles softly. "That's probably my fault. I raised him and didn't teach him better."

We're silent for a bit again.

I ask, "What's he doing now?"

"Drugs. He's in and out of jail."

I swallow. "Oh...I'm sorry."

"Don't be." He squeezes my arm. "Not your fault."

We lay there for a bit longer, and I squirm. "I really have to shower."

"So eager to wash me off of you?"

"I feel gross!"

"Fine. I need one too." He hops out of bed and offers me a hand. "But that just means I'll have to mark you with my scent again. And soon."

I groan but take his offered hand. When we get in, Sawyer insists on scrubbing me clean.

I snatch the soap from him. "I can do it."

"Let me." He winks at me. "Then you can do me."

I roll my eyes and start to lather up.

"Don't shower with Miles or Ryder, though. They're both water hogs."

Sawyer rubs right behind where I run my hands, cleaning right behind me.

I snort. "I don't see myself showering with Ryder. Ever."

Sawyer shrugs but doesn't say anything.

I pause. Wait. Does he expect that to happen? I look at the man in front of me. He's on his knees washing my thighs. "Is that what... will we all...shower together and stuff?"

Sawyer continues washing. It feels good, his huge hands being so gentle on my skin.

His silence scares me. I shouldn't have asked. This is just the game.

I step away from Sawyer. He grips my thighs and yanks me back to him, looking up at me through the falling water. "There are a lot of things I want, Cali. But you're not ready to hear them right now." He kisses the tops of my thighs and stands. "Let's just start with trusting me enough not to lie to me, yeah?"

I swallow. I don't know if I can ever do that. But I'm scared that I want to. Why the hell do I want to?

CHAPTER 56

MILES

I'm on my second trip upstairs to get more hot coals. The upstairs is quiet, with the exception of a shower running. My gut swirls with excitement and discomfort. I'm torn between watching Ben pay for the things he did and curling up with Cali in my arms.

Against my better judgment, I move back downstairs.

Cali looked at us with real fear again, and it made me sick.

Isn't that what this guy used on you? Fists?

Fuck. Ryder's words hit me right in the gut again, making fear and anger pour through me. I rip the door open.

Ben is thrashing, screaming into his gag. The rats have started digging into his flesh, their fur covered in blood. It looks agonizing.

I'm not like him. And I'm not like my father.

I drop the coals on the cage.

The rats scurry faster, sensing the heat. It smells horrible in here, like cooked fur and piss. I will the rats to dig faster so they don't get burned.

Ben's muffled screams are blood-curdling, every muscle in his body tense. Blood shoots to my dick. I like watching him suffer, completely at my mercy.

I lean over Ben's head, asking softly, "Is this how she sounded? When she was crying for mercy, and you beat her anyway?"

Tears track down Ben's face. He can't even hear me right now.

"No, she didn't cry." I stroke the top of his head. "She's braver than you. You're nothing but a pitiful coward." I brush a sweaty piece of blonde hair from his forehead. "Pissing yourself when you saw me. You want to know what she did when she saw us?"

A rat squeaks, frantic energy exploding in the cage. Ben fights against his bonds, helplessly straining. My dick hardens further.

"She fought us." A grin lights up my face. "She threatened to kill me."

The memory of her fire lights all my nerve endings up. Fuck, my dick is so hard it hurts.

Ben chokes out a cry. I yank my pants down, fisting my dick.

"That's right, she fought us with everything she had. She's still fighting us. Stupid, brave woman." I stroke myself, watching the tears stream down his gray, waxy skin. My balls tighten already.

"Did it make you feel powerful to hurt her, big guy?" I smack his face hard. "Look at me when I'm talking to you."

Ben's eyes close, and his whole body convulses. Fuck. He can't even listen right now. Pussy ass bitch.

The image of Cali's eyes spitting venom when she told Ryder to just kill her fills my head, and my body locks up in pleasure. It rolls through me, and I come, spurting streams of semen all over Ben's face. Fuck, she's so perfect and beautiful. And fucking stupid.

As the orgasm fades, I tuck myself back into my pants.

Fuck. It really stinks in here.

"We're not done yet." I pat Ben's shoulder and move upstairs. I step outside, sucking in a breath of countryside air. The high starts to fade, and fatigue fills me. I watch the only dark cloud in the sky against the deep purple of twilight.

Ryder's tone when he taunted Cali about my kills fills my head. He sounded so smug. So sure that I was just like the man who hit her.

I squeeze my eyes shut. I mean, we did kidnap her. She's not here of her own free will. Shame washes over me. As long as she's with us, she will never truly have a choice. A slave to new owners who are obsessed with her but still owners.

I rub a hand over my face. Where is Ryder? I need him to beat the feelings out of me. And maybe I'll beat him too for saying what he did.

As I turn to go back inside, I notice his truck isn't here.

Damn it. Where the hell did he go?

I march down the hall and pause in front of Sawyer's closed door. The whole house is quiet. I open it slowly.

It's dark in the room, and it takes me a minute to adjust, but when I do, I see Sawyer and Cali cuddled up in bed, sleeping. Sawyer has an arm around her. Her hair is wet, and from what I can see, they're naked.

Despite my mood, my dick twitches. I step into the room, shutting the door softly behind me. Neither of them move. I hear Sawyer snoring, and under that, I hear her soft breaths.

Fuck, they both look so peaceful. Soothing breaths fill my lungs as I watch them. Cali's lashes are dark against her pale skin, and her mouth is parted in sleep. Sawyer's freshly shaven, and his skin is smooth. I can smell the aftershave on him.

Damn. I pull in a deep breath. I should leave. Shower, make dinner, fight with Ryder. Then, tend to Ben so I can keep him alive just a little longer.

But I don't. I watch them sleep. I'm drawn to the bed like there's a magnetic pull. It feels like the closer I get, the more at peace my heart will be.

Fuck it. I strip my bloody clothes off and lay down beside Cali. I face her so I can see every tiny expression. She shifts a little, closing her mouth and moaning.

Goddamn it. Now I'm rock hard again.

Cali's breathing evens out, and I can't help it. I trace a finger along her forehead.

I can't sleep too long. I need to give the piece of shit IV fluids and patch him up. He doesn't get to die that quickly on me.

The gorgeous woman in front of me shifts. I saw her happy

there for a second. The way she looked at us after Sawyer made pancakes in the kitchen. Her gaze softened, and in that moment, she was the prettiest thing I'd ever seen. She looks now like she looked then. Like she stopped running and stopped fighting and let herself actually live.

I freeze. I swallow roughly, then trace my lips across her skin. "Is this what you look like when you feel safe, pretty girl?" I sit in silence for a bit, my chest warm with adoration. "I wish you could look like this every day."

CHAPTER 57

CALI

I hear Miles' whispered words. I pretend to be asleep, and he continues to trace my face for a little while longer.

A shiver runs up my spine. His words wrap around me in a warm embrace. Does he want me to feel safe? The thought makes the tension in my chest release and a tiny hint of hope bloom. But no. No! They're torturing Ben downstairs. And I'm next. Right? I try to scream at the sappy voice inside me who wants to melt for their protective behavior.

No. That sappy side will get me killed. I try to squash her.

It takes a while before Miles' breath also evens out. Thoughts race through my mind. This soft side from both of them is muddling what seemed so clear before.

Is this still the game? To make me fall for them? Because fuck, if I'm not tempted to believe them. They make me want to fall into their harsh but protective storms.

I swallow. Sawyer once said it would be easy to break me after I opened up. In fact, he himself told me it was dumb to open up.

Goddamn, I'm weak. Because that's exactly what I want to do.

It makes an ache form in the back of my throat. Opening up will never be something I can have. It's cruel to even think I could. God. I need a goddamn drink.

I shift my hands. Neither man moves. I push up slowly. Again, no movement. I'm between them, so I have to scoot to the end of the bed. I do so, laying the blanket back over Sawyer. I pad to the door.

Both men continue breathing heavily in sleep.

I take in a breath and crack the door open.

The house is quiet and dark. I listen for a while. Nothing. I step out. Ryder's bedroom door is closed. It's the middle of the night, so he must be asleep.

I move away from the hall and down to the kitchen.

There are no car keys on the hook.

Fuck. They must put those away at bedtime. I remember seeing a computer in the office. Communication with the outside world. My heart jumps at the idea. Part of me is excited. Part of me feels like this is wrong. They're trusting me, and I'm burning that trust.

The office door is cracked. I slip in, shutting it again behind me. It's hard to see, but the dark desk is shadowed with things all over it. I slip into the seat, feeling around.

Yes! Holy shit, it's here.

I pause before opening the laptop. I can't shake the wrong feeling. I mentally kick myself. I have every right to try and fight for my freedom.

I clench my jaw. Fight for yourself, Cali. You can't be a victim forever.

I open it, the blue light flaring over me, hurting my eyes for a second and making me blink.

"That's interesting."

The deep voice makes me jump. I hurl back in my chair, a small scream escaping me. I desperately search the room for the source of the sound. To my right, a shadowy shape sits in an armchair that I didn't notice on my way in.

I take a few steps back toward the door, my heart racing.

"You act like I caught you doing something wrong." Ryder leans back. I blink, willing my eyes to adjust.

"I…you scared me."

He says nothing. Then, he asks, "Trouble in paradise?"

"What are you talking about?" I straighten.

"What were you doing?" He nods at the computer.

I fumble, looking for an excuse. "I just wanted to…Sawyer said I could…"

Ryder arches an eyebrow, watching me struggle. Finally, I cross my arms and glare. "What were you doing spying on me?"

He steeples his fingers. "I wasn't the one spying, Cassie."

"It's Cali."

"Right." I catch a tiny smirk before he falls back into his indifferent look. "You have rules against getting on electronics."

"How do you…" I start.

His lip curls up. "They're my boyfriends, too. They talk to me, too. Not just you."

Too? Does he think we're dating? "We're not…" I pause. Because if the situation wasn't so fucked up, it absolutely looks like Sawyer, Miles, and I are dating. Damn, for a second there tonight, I felt like we were, too.

I clear my throat. "We aren't…a thing."

Ryder says nothing, continuing to look at me. "Why are you here?"

"I was kidnapped!"

"So you have no feelings for them?"

"No!" Emotions swirl through me, tightening my stomach. What the hell is wrong with me?

Ryder's voice lowers to a dangerous octave. "Really? Because either you have feelings for them, or you're leading them on, on purpose."

My gut clenches. I don't like how he looks at me like he can see right through me. "Leading them–what? What are you talking about?"

The cold blue light of the computer falls over his face. "They're obsessed with you. I've never seen them act like this with a woman before."

Strange warmth curls through me.

Ryder leans forward. "What are you doing to manipulate them?"

Manipulate them? *I'm* the one being manipulated! "I'm not!" I snap. "How, exactly, do you think I'm doing that?"

Ryder eyes me. "That's what I can't figure out." He cocks his head slightly. "Either you're playing a game, or you think you really like them."

I grit my jaw.

Ryder shakes his head. "I thought we talked about that. You've known them for all of what, a few days? How do you know you actually like them? They kill for sport. You don't really know them."

"I never said I like them!" I sputter.

He leans forward. "What's Sawyer's favorite book? What does Miles do to decompress?" Ryder stands, suddenly much, much taller than me. "What do they do when they're scared? Mad? Sad?" He stalks toward me.

"I..." I back away closer to the door.

"Answer me, girl," he barks.

"I don't know!" My throat tightens.

"That's right. You don't know." He leans toward me, his lip curled.

My back hits the back of the door. I shouldn't have fucking closed it.

Ryder moves until he's almost touching me. He's so tall my nose only reaches his chest. I crane my neck to look up at him. His dark features soak in the light in the room, sucking it into the void of his eyes. For a second, he looks sad.

Then I smell the alcohol on him.

Desire flares inside me. Fuck, it's been a long time since I've had a drink. I need one desperately right now.

Ryder looks down at me. "If you're not dating them, then you'll have no problem telling them you don't like them."

I swallow. Feelings I don't like swirl in my stomach at the thought.

"Right?" There's a warning in Ryder's voice. I get another hit of whiskey off him.

"Right," I grit.

Ryder takes a small step back. I spot the alcohol on the desk now. He follows my gaze, then looks back at me, his eyes lingering on my face. "You want some?"

I grit my teeth. Can he read my mind? Fuck yes, I want some. Ryder watches me in that unnerving way of his. He reaches for the bottle slowly, then lifts it to his mouth, taking a long swig while watching me.

My nostrils flare. Asshole.

Ryder snaps his hand out to grip my throat under my chin. He yanks me roughly to him, and I stumble into his chest with a gasp. With his other hand, he grips my jaw and levers it open. I open my mouth in surprise, and Ryder presses his mouth to mine, spitting a mouthful of whiskey into it.

I startle. The alcohol burns instantly, warming my mouth in a pleasant pain. I swallow, my throat burning with the liquid.

Ryder is still right there, holding me to him, his lips almost touching mine. We trade breath. His dark eyes are slightly wild. We're caught in each other's gazes for a second, his glossy eyes possessive and mean and afraid.

Then he releases me, stumbling back a step. He straightens, smoothing down his button-down. "Why don't you run?" he asks.

"What?" I catch my breath.

"Right now. I won't stop you."

"Because you'll put a bullet in my back."

Ryder pulls something out from the back of his pants and slams it on the desk with a loud bang. It's a pistol.

Adrenaline burns under my skin.

"I won't. Not right now," he says.

"Right now?" I narrow my eyes at him. "Yeah, that's comforting."

Ryder moves towards the desk and stumbles a little. Damn. Is he fucked up? I look to see if I could grab his gun before he can.

"Try it," Ryder says, his speech suddenly crystal clear. "Even drunk, I can still shoot you in a matter of seconds."

I freeze. Ryder smirks.

I think through his desire for me to leave. He wants me to run so he can make me disappear without making his men mad at him.

I straighten. "You're trying to cheat. You can't play the game behind Sawyer's back."

"Isn't that what you were trying to do?" Ryder motions at the computer.

I narrow my eyes. "I knew the consequences."

"So do I." He watches me.

"Oh yeah? For me, the consequences are my life. What are they for you?" Anger runs through me at how unfair this whole thing is. "A lover's spat? A little jealousy? So you get to fuck it out and everything will be fine. I'll be *dead*. Explain to me how in the fuck that's fair!"

Ryder crosses his large arms. "Life isn't fair, little mystery. I thought you were old enough to understand that."

The alcohol buzzes in my head. It's been so long since I've had a drink that it's already getting to me. I spit, "Oh, don't worry. I learned that a long time ago. My bad, you caught me in a human moment." I turn on my heel. "Have a good night, Ryker."

He growls at the wrong name, and I slam the door. As I do, my courage leaves me, and I run down the hall, slipping back into Sawyer's room. They're both still asleep in bed. Carefully, I crawl back between them, needing to at least pretend they can protect me from the emotions rolling through me.

Sawyer continues to snore, but Miles shifts and throws an arm around me. He mutters, "Where'd you go?"

"Bathroom." Tears prick behind my eyes. I want to say that I'm sorry.

"Mmmm," Miles mutters into my hair. Within seconds, he's asleep again.

Fuck. I don't want to play this game anymore. How do I get off this ride?

CHAPTER 58

RYDER

The house is in a sad state. There are dirty clothes everywhere, and there's almost no food left. My mind won't stop running.

As soon as the grocery store opens, I go shopping. As I move through the aisles, I try not to think about how Cali's pupils blew wide when I spit the whiskey into her mouth.

Fuck, she looked so beautiful and submissive. She can't even help herself. Fucking attracted to every walking red flag.

Attracted or trying to fuck us over. Or both.

When I'm in the cereal aisle, my lawyer calls. I pick up on the first ring.

"Hey, they're going to delay the suppression hearing. The officer is on vacation."

I grunt.

"I'm still working on our deal, but just so you know, I'm not getting anywhere."

Fuck. I squeeze my phone so tight that pain lances through

my fingers. I was worried about that. If this goes to trial, I'll be put away for years, possibly life. And what about Miles? It was his mark originally. How they haven't connected his DNA, I don't know. I don't want to uproot my family, but I'll leave the country if this falls through.

"You there?"

"Yeah."

"Okay. Just making sure you knew. I'd offer more, but I'm afraid this new guy's morals are going to get to him."

Someone rushes their cart around me like they're mad. I realize I've been blocking the whole aisle.

I hang up. I've prepared for this possibility. I have accounts set up in offshore shell corporations, and I always keep lines of communication open with Wyatt. I always knew there would be a chance we would have to leave. I feel a scratch at the back of my throat.

When I get home, I get to prepping more meals for my men. I got enough for Miles' favorite quesadillas and Sawyer's meat and mashed potatoes. I try to bury myself in this task. I'll deal with this and then the other stuff.

As I prep, I turn my shirt inside out before I get out the chicken. I don't want the salmonella all over the outside. I refuse to wear that apron Sawyer wears. He never washes it, and it's a miracle the man doesn't get sick more than he does. As I prep, I reach for the knife block.

It's not there.

I look through more drawers. Fuck. Where the hell are the knives? I look everywhere. They're not in the kitchen.

I look for Miles to ask where he put them. His room is empty, and his bed is still made. I frown, then head to Sawyer's room.

It's covered in dirty clothes, but his bed is all messed up. Fuck, his room is a mess. I always take care of the laundry when I'm here, and I forgot to do it after I came back. That blond bombshell is getting into all of my routines. I grab up the clothes and start a load.

I shoot a text to Miles: Where are the knives?

He responds back almost immediately: Basement.

I throw my hands in the air. What the absolute fuck. I march downstairs. Sawyer is down there, the TV on in the background. No knives to be seen.

"Where exactly did you idiots put the knives?"

Sawyer raises an eyebrow at me, then looks back down at his phone. "The sex room."

I mutter, moving over there, then stop short, looking at the new lock installed on the door. "It's locked?"

Sawyer huffs. "Yes, how else do you expect us to keep people out of it?"

"Unlock it." I glare at him.

Sawyer rolls his eyes and does what I ask. I find the knife block sitting on one of the sex benches, of all places. I snatch it, then slam the door.

I glare at Sawyer. "What, you expect your girlfriend to try and kill you? That's true love right there."

Sawyer won't look at me but he smirks slightly. "*You* threaten me with knives, and you call it love."

Despite myself, I think about that. Fuck. His neck does look so fucking pretty against my knife.

Sawyer drones, "Take your pissy ass back upstairs and pout alone. It's getting annoying."

Rage boils up in me so fast that I almost dart toward him to teach him a lesson.

Then he throws me a victorious glance, and I stop. That was exactly the reaction he wanted. He's trying to rile me up, just like he does to Miles.

I glare at Sawyer, then march up the steps. It feels wrong to be at odds with him. It's not the first time we've fought, but it doesn't feel right.

But I won't back down. I'm doing this for him.

I slice my chicken, then immediately wash the knife and cutting board to get rid of the germs.

As I'm cooking, Sawyer comes up and sits at the island. He stays silent, messing with his phone.

I see Miles and Cali walk past the kitchen window, toward the front door. Miles is in his jogging shorts. Cali's face is red and her hair messy. Miles must have taken her on a run. They're laughing, shoving each other back and forth like children.

My stomach sinks. Miles is going to be so hurt when she breaks his heart. He falls way too hard and way too fast. I don't want this to be the thing that breaks him.

Miles and Cali walk inside, still chuckling. Miles gives me a playful, single finger wave as they pass the kitchen, then continues on with his conversation. My eyes drop to both of their asses as they pass, headed to the bedrooms. Miles' ass looks tight in his shorts. Cali is in a pair of sweats far too large, but I can still see her cheeks bubbling out.

I catch Sawyer smirking at me.

I glare at him. "What?"

"Nothing." He grabs a tortilla from my pile and starts eating it. "Just looks like you want a piece of that."

I shoot him a deadly look.

"You know, you could have both." Sawyer bites a hole out of the middle and looks at me through it. "All of us, actually."

"No, I can't." I go back to prepping the food. "Someone has to be okay when reality hits."

"Jesus, you're being so dramatic." Sawyer glares at me, and it goes directly to my dick.

"Watch your tone."

"No, actually, I don't think I will."

Something slaps me in the back of the head, and I whirl. A tortilla lays at my feet. Anger rushes through me. Did he really just...throw that at me?

Sawyer winks. "I think you need to get off your high horse and chill the fuck out." He pushes up and goes to the sink, shoulder-checking me on the way.

I curl my lip. Sawyer is toeing every line he can. I know he wants me to snap. "Stop testing me, Sawyer."

He rolls his eyes. The man fucking rolls his eyes.

That's it. I've had enough.

I dart towards him, pinning Sawyer against the counter.

Sawyer faces me, a dark look in his eyes. "Jesus, calm down Ryder. You're being so emotional."

I snap my hand to the knife sitting on the counter. Sawyer sees the movement and hurls his body closer to me, ducking his head and trying to wrap me up under my arm.

I twist as he does, taking both of us to the ground, and turn so his body takes most of the fall.

Sawyer grunts, and I whip the knife around in a flash, pinning it to his throat.

"Knife in play, asshole," I hiss. "Relax."

Sawyer reaches down and grips my dick through my pants. He grabs me hard, shooting pain and pleasure through me. I lean the knife into him just enough that it slices into his skin.

Instead of submitting to my hold, Sawyer laughs and yanks my dick painfully. I jerk, doing my best to keep a steady hand on his neck.

"Careful, dick." I'm so close to his carotid.

"What, are you scared? Cut me, fucker. Make me hurt."

I shift so I can meet Sawyer's eyes. Usually he begs for this when he's almost lost. He meets my gaze with crystal blue ones. The clarity shocks me. The darkness is only at the edges instead of overwhelming him.

Sawyer spits up at my face.

I flip him so he's lying on his stomach and rip his shirt off in a violent move. He tries to get up, but I sit on his legs, pinning his head to the kitchen floor with my free hand.

"You want me to make it hurt?" I say, gripping his hair so hard he stiffens. "I'll make it hurt, you fucking brat. You're going to be crying for mercy by the time I'm done."

"I don't know," he says through clenched teeth. "I think you became kind of a pussy after you went to jail."

His words make anger zip through me and straight into my dick. I look down at his scarred back and admire my handiwork. My name is carved all over him, some "Ryder's" fresh, some old. I lean down, biting one of the newer marks. Sawyer hisses in pain.

"Oh, you're already crying? We haven't even started." I give a violent jerk to his hair. Sawyer's groan is sharp. "I didn't realize you had become such a pussy since I went to jail."

Sawyer laughs roughly. I see a tear has traced its way down his cheek. I lean up and lick it from him. Fuck. His suffering goes right to my dick. I rub it against his ass.

"Hurt me already, Ryder. Stop making me wait for it." He struggles.

I laugh. Fuck, I've missed this.

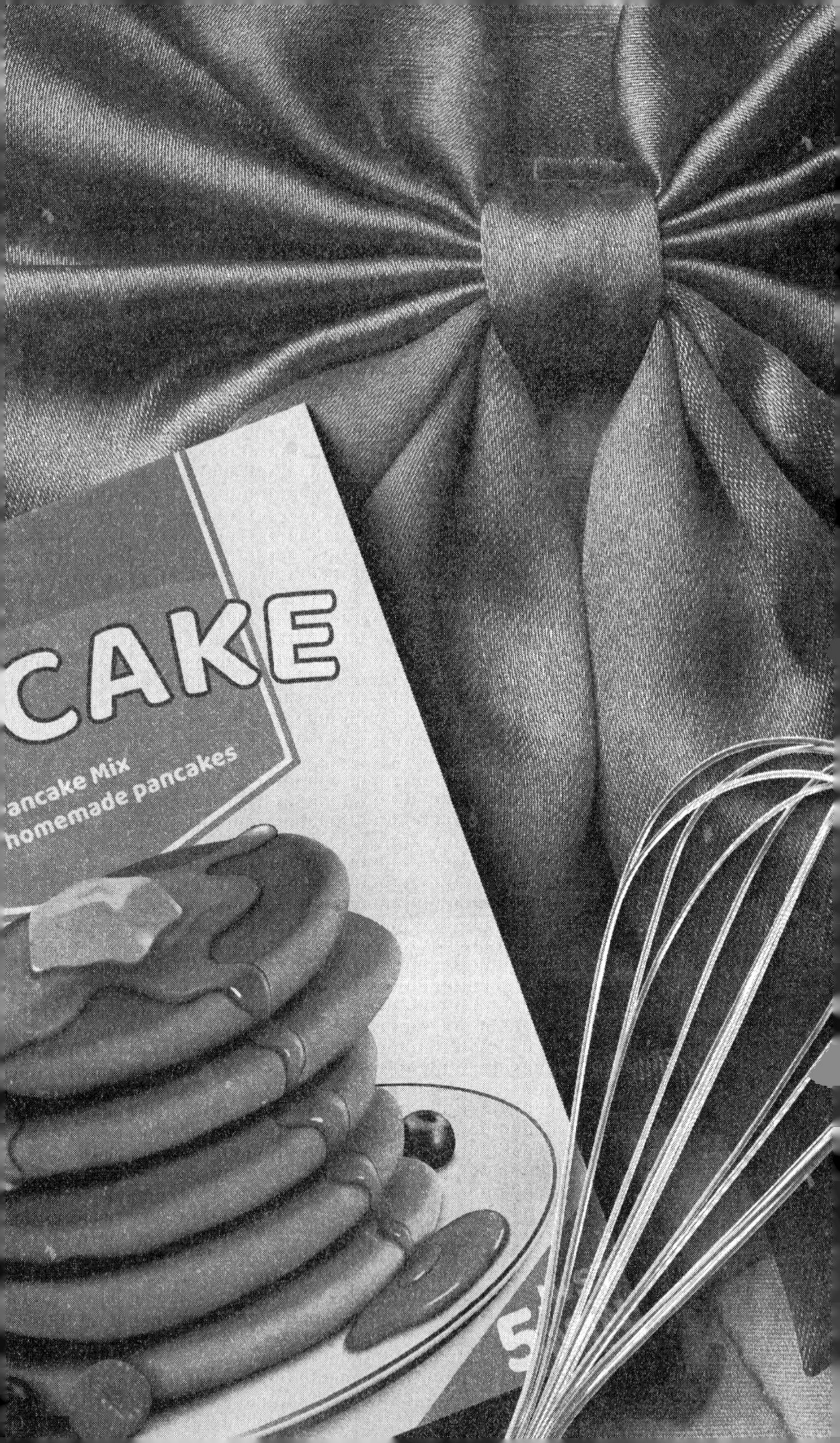
CAKE
ancake Mix
homemade pancakes

CHAPTER 59

SAWYER

Ryder's domineering hold makes me hard as a rock. I can't fight against his massive weight on my back. I feel the cold steel on my lower back, and despite myself, I jump. I've felt the bite of his knife many times, and I know it hurts like a bitch.

I soak in the fear and the adrenaline. I am painfully hard.

Ryder purposely draws it out, dragging the knife softly up and down my skin. Fucker. I try not to struggle.

"You've been quite the brat. I still don't know if you even deserve for me to do this to you."

Real fear runs through me, and the memory of him rejecting me last night comes flooding back. I try to push up, earning another sharp tug at my scalp. Tears prick my eyes.

"No, no. You don't have a choice anymore. Lay still and accept what I have to give to you, fucking whore."

A burning bite of pain digs into my lower back, and I stiffen. The pain is sharp and makes every instinct in my body scream to fight. I resist, lying still so he doesn't fuck up his mark. But damn, if it doesn't hurt just as bad as I remember it hurting. Each cut is like a hot brand to my skin, and I feel the blood pooling.

"Fuck, you bleed so prettily for me." The sharp pain is replaced by a tugging as Ryder leans down and licks the wound. Ryder groans into me, and I can't help but moan. A pleasured fog starts to wrap my mind in a buzzing peace.

Ryder leans up and goes to the next letter, alternating between cutting and licking until I'm in a haze of pain, and the world feels far away.

I vaguely feel him yanking my pants down.

"You don't deserve any lube, once again, Sawyer. You're the biggest goddamn glutton for punishment I've ever seen."

No, that's Cali.

Ryder gives a hard smack on my ass that barely pulls me out of the haze of the pain in my back. Fuck, it feels good to get lost in the fog.

I feel Ryder at my entrance.

"Don't tense up for me, boy. You know I'll take great joy in making this hurt."

I force my body to relax. Still, Ryder shoves inside me with brutal force, the way he knows I like it. I can't help the groan that rips from me. This pain is sharp and ripping, and he gives no leeway.

Tears well in my eyes against my will.

"Fuck," Ryder grunts, pulling out of me and pounding back in. "Jesus, you feel so fucking good. Does that hurt, brat?"

"No."

Despite myself, a tear leaks out of my eye.

Ryder smacks my fresh wound. "You're such a terrible liar. I love it."

I cry out this time, locked in pain. Out of the corner of my eye, I see Miles walk in.

"Ah, Miles. Want a piece of this ass?"

I squeeze my eyes shut, waiting for the pain to subside. It has to soon. Fuck, it burns like hell. Slowly, the throbbing lessens.

"On your knees, Sawyer."

I blink, realizing this wasn't the first time Ryder said it. His voice is gentle for a second, and then I make eye contact with him, and he smirks. "Miles is going to take your ass next. Don't you dare think about coming."

I stiffen and glance behind me. Miles has never topped a man before, although he's said in passing he thinks he'd be down.

Miles looks at me with open lust. "You okay with this?"

I look around for Cali. She's not here. "Don't fucking ask me that, it ruins the mood, fucker." I look down at the floor. "Either take it or don't, I don't give a fuck."

Ryder smacks my ass again. "That was an enthusiastic yes. Come here." He spits on his hand and grips Miles' dick. "Just like fucking a pussy."

"What would you know about that?" I grit. "You won't even talk to the one in your house."

"I think he needs something to shut him the fuck up, don't you think?" Ryder steps around me and kneels, shoving his dick into my face. "Jerk it. If you hurt me, I'll make what you feel right now feel like a butterfly kiss."

I grip his dick tightly, smelling musk and ass. I start stroking him as Miles pushes against my opening. I groan. He pauses.

"You're doing fine, Miles," Ryder says. "A little more pressure. Get past the ring."

Miles pushes in more. My ass stings from Ryder's earlier assault, and I groan. I jerk Ryder roughly. The pain shoots straight to my groin. I drop Ryder to reach down to grip my dick.

Ryder yanks my head back by my hair. "Did I say you could touch yourself?"

The pain in my back and my ass make my vision hazy. I look up at Ryder's huge body through half-lidded eyes. His eyes glint. "Where are my tears, Sawyer?"

Before I can prepare myself, Ryder lifts his arm and smacks me in the face so hard my ears ring. My eyes water. Ryder grips my chin, yanking my face up to him, watching the tears roll down my cheeks.

"There they are. Fuck, you're so hot."

Miles groans behind us. He's fully seated in me now. "Jesus," he mutters. "So...tight."

"Heaven, isn't it?" Ryder pinches my stinging cheek, causing me to jerk, and my muscles tighten around Miles.

Miles groans again, and Ryder laughs.

"Touch yourself," Ryder demands.

I do, stroking my dick hard, the pleasure immediately mixing with the fog, sending me into a state of euphoria.

Both of my men chase their pleasure using me, and it makes me that much harder. Miles doesn't last long at all before he's stiffening and groaning. Ryder jerks off over me slowly, sliding his hand up and down, dragging it out.

The one arm holding me up trembles. Ryder says something to Miles. He pulls out of me, and Ryder sits me back.

"I'm going to use your tears to make me come. You can finish, but only after I have. Understand?"

I nod.

"Eyes on me, Sawyer."

I flick my gaze up to him. Ryder's eyes are dark with lust and heat. He looks powerful, soft, and hungry. I see him swing back for another hit, but I don't close my eyes. The hit is hard, and my eyes water again. I let the tears stream down my face.

"Fuck." Ryder jerks himself over me violently, coming on my face. I blink, feeling the hot spurts of cum hit my forehead and cheeks. I wait with my mouth open, stroking my dick. My balls are so tight I'm about to explode.

"Come for me, brat."

I do, euphoria filling my body. I come into my hand in harsh bursts. Fuck, it feels so damn good.

As the high starts to come down, I feel sub-drop lock into place, and my emotions immediately drop.

Warm hands grip my shoulders and pull me up. Ryder wraps me up, pulling me into his body. "You're okay. You did just fine. Miles, get a warm cloth."

I close my eyes, burying my head into Ryder. The pain is intense, ripping through me every time I move.

Something warm strokes the side of my face.

"Let me get your face," Ryder rumbles.

I pull back slightly. Miles looks concerned. Ryder washes the cum from me.

I feel an odd, hysterical laugh in my chest. Usually, it's me or Ryder putting him into subspace, not the other way around.

"He's fine." Ryder bands his arms around me. "Grab a few painkillers and get me some hot washcloths and bandages."

I feel Ryder pull us to the couch. I sink down into him gratefully.

There isn't much talking. Both men tend to me, and I allow myself to relax fully. Fuck. Everything feels almost perfect.

Almost.

For the first time, I feel like I'm missing something from our group of three. I lift my head to look for Cali. I catch a glimpse of her in the shadowed hall.

I drop my head again, content. She's here. Peace washes over me. This is how I want it to be. All of us together, happy.

I know she'll fight it. But I won't let her. I'll force her to be happy with us. She's ours, and we're never letting her go.

CHAPTER 60

CALI

At first, I think Sawyer is going to say something about me creeping on them. But he doesn't. He just lays back down on Ryder's lap. The men continue in low conversation, oblivious to me being here. Miles laughs at something, his eyes crinkling up, and I can see the side of Ryder's face lift in a tiny smile. I don't think I've ever seen them look so happy. So peaceful.

After our run, I hopped in the shower. Miles was gone when I got out, and I found him here. I couldn't see everything that they were doing on the kitchen floor, but I heard it, and it made all the blood rush to my pussy.

This must be what they looked like before I got here. Happy.

I finger the silver circling my neck. I didn't miss how Ryder tensed up when I walked in with Miles and how Sawyer's body language changed when he saw Ryder's change. And I have no doubt that if I walked into the living room, everything would change right now, too.

I swallow. It's painfully clear that despite Sawyer saying I'm his and that Miles won't let me go, I don't really have a place here. I change things. I change everything. I've never been forced to be a fourth wheel before but damn...I don't like it.

I take a step back into the hall.

Last night was a bust. I made a mistake. I didn't know where Ryder was, and I ruined my chance to leave.

Tonight will be different. It has to be. For myself and for them.

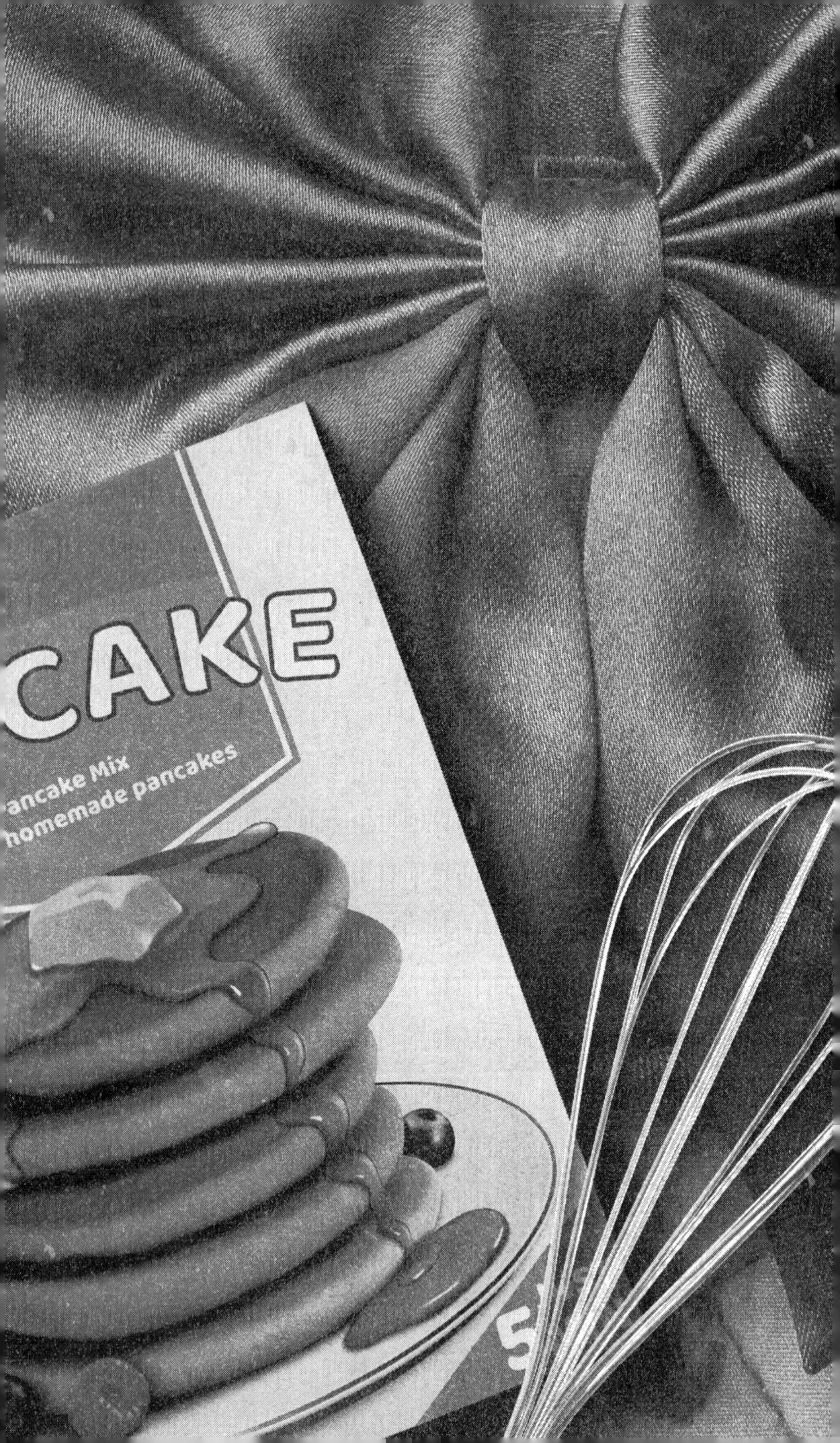
CAKE
ancake Mix
homemade pancakes

CHAPTER 61

SAWYER

Once the pain pills set in, I get up to help Ryder with meal prep. Miles joins us, too, snacking on all the foods Ryder has out.

Ryder wants to throw the chicken away. Miles tells him no and looks up the food safety rules for keeping food out.

Ryder still tries to throw it out.

I spot a few bottles of wine on the counter with the rest of the groceries.

"Hey man," I snatch them up. "Put this away."

Ryder gives me a weird look. "I was going to."

"No, I mean...we can't have these out. I'll put them in the basement."

Ryder puts the cheese down. "Enough with the fucking basement. We have cabinets for a reason."

I look through the bags to make sure I didn't miss anything. "I'm detoxing Cali."

Miles looks at me funny. "What the hell?"

Anger fills me at even having to voice the words. I snap, "I don't want her to get this."

Miles looks taken aback.

"Sorry." I sigh and run a hand over the top of my hair. "I just... try to keep this away from her."

Ryder just takes it all in, not saying anything. Both of them know my mother was an addict, and I've fought tooth and nail to try and stay out of her footsteps.

"I'm sorry, Miles, I didn't mean to snap."

He raises his hands. "It's all good, man. I'll keep it away from her."

"Thanks," I mutter, taking the stuff down to the basement and locking it away. Despite the painkillers, my back hurts like a bitch. I know I shouldn't be moving this much.

But there's something else I need to do. I've been wanting to do it ever since she talked about it. I snatch my keys and tell Miles to keep an eye on Cali. I still don't entirely trust her not to bolt when she feels the leash loosening.

Miles eyes my ass as I leave. "Think I'm gonna need another piece of that."

"In your dreams, pup," I growl and walk out the door.

I'm gone for a few hours. The whole time I'm away, my skin itches. I realize how relieved I've felt since she's been with us. I find myself looking for new abandoned properties to chase her through. Thinking about new ways I can push her. Make her come running to me. Make her realize that I'll provide everything if she only asks.

The woman has invaded every area of my thoughts.

When I return home, I instantly feel more peace knowing my people are close to me. I carry in my prize, knowing the men are going to give me shit. But they aren't in the living room. I set it down outside my room and move inside. "Cali?"

I'm met with silence. I check my whole room. The dirty clothes are gone, but she's not here.

For a second, my stomach bottoms out.

Fuck, she ran.

I dart to Miles' room and find her sitting on his bed, looking out the window.

"Ah, snooping through someone else's drawers?" I ask, but it takes a second for my heart rate to calm down.

She barely glances at me.

"Hey, what's wrong?" Discomfort fills me. I hesitate for a second, then sit stiffly next to her.

"Nothing." She gives me a fake smile.

My heart rate kicks back up. "Cali…" I warn. "What did I tell you about lying to me?"

She swallows. "It's nothing, Sawyer." Then she says lower, "Just sad."

Fuck. My stomach twists.

I grip Cali's chin and force her to look at me. Venom runs through me. "Who made you sad? I'll kill them."

She laughs bitterly and pulls her chin away. "It's fine. Just caught me in my feels. I'll get over it."

I snatch her up again. "Who, Cali?"

She tries to jerk away from me. "I said I'm fine."

My voice lowers, and the darkness creeps in. "Who?"

She snaps, looking into my eyes, her own glistening with tears. "What if it was you, Sawyer? What would you do then?"

Me? Something like pain twinges my heart. My chest grows tight. "What?"

"Yes, you." Cali turns her furious gaze on me. "You tortured Ben! You won't let me go, and you tortured someone, but you're so nice to me! You're so nice to me that it makes me confused. You're fucking with my head, Sawyer! And it's not fair. I don't…" Cali gasps. "Oh fuck!"

"What?" I scan her and don't see anything wrong. I grab her and turn her, looking for what bothered her. I don't see anything.

"You're bleeding!" she says.

"What?" I keep checking her.

Cali struggles to get away. "Your back. You're bleeding, Sawyer."

I glance down. Oh. My shirt is stained red. I must be leaking through the bandage.

"Cali, it's okay."

"You're bleeding a lot!" She darts toward the bathroom.

"Cali! It's fine." But she's disappeared. She comes back out with a wet towel and toilet paper. Part of me warms seeing her concern.

"I just need a new bandage." I pull my shirt up, twisting so she can see my back.

Cali is silent.

I want to turn around to see what she thinks, but I don't. Some part of me is afraid she'll think it's ugly.

I turn back around and stand, the strangest feeling hitting me. I feel ready to bolt. "Yeah. Anyway, just wanted to check on you."

"Wait." Cali looks at the things in her hand.

I pause. She looks like she's searching for something to say.

"Cali, I don't need your sympathy," I say, harsher than I mean to. Fuck, why is this so hard for me?

"Good," she snaps. "Because I wasn't going to give it." She takes a deep breath. "I want to earn more points."

It takes me a second to process those words. Wait. She wants to leave?

Pain lances through me. I had forgotten about the game for a second. The imaginary world I had built up in my head on the drive comes crashing down, and rage washes over me. I turn on my heel and stalk to the door. "No."

"Please!" Cali says. "I'll do anything."

I whirl, feeling the anger tight in my chest. I shouldn't have been so stupid, letting my emotions get involved. "Anything?" I say mockingly.

Cali throws the towel on the bed and puts her hands on her hips. "Anything," she says.

I desperately want to tell her that 'anything' is to stay. But seeing how much I've already fucked up this conversation, I don't see that going well. I'm mad at myself. "Fine," I snarl. "If you fuck Ryder, I'll give you points."

"How many?" Cali shoots back.

A snarl builds in my chest. "A hundred."

"That's not enough! Ryder will never fuck me."

I'm not so sure about that. I shrug. "That's a risk you gotta take. Either play the game or don't, Cali."

"That's fucked up, Sawyer, and you know it. Eight hundred, and I won't do it for any less."

I can't keep the bark out of my voice. "That's enough for you to leave."

"That's the point, jackass." Cali hisses and crosses her arms.

Darkness settles over my vision. I should have known better. Shouldn't have gotten my hopes up that she'd want to stay.

"Fine," I snarl. "But you don't get to tell him about the deal. Or Miles. And it has to happen within the next three days, or all points are off." I stalk to the door. "You hear me? You'll lose all of them. Good luck, bunny."

I slam the door and almost trip over what I brought outside the door. Miles is just coming out of Ryder's room.

"Jesus, who pissed in your cereal?" He glances at the box on the floor. "What's that?"

Betrayal swirls in my chest. But I shouldn't feel like that. It's my fault for letting myself feel something when I knew I shouldn't.

"Her cat," I snarl and yank my door open.

"What?" Miles sounds confused. "What's wrong, Sawyer?"

"I don't want to talk about it." I slam my door.

It bursts open a second later, and Miles steps inside. "Yeah, you can fuck off with that moody shit. Just talk to me. Did something happen?"

I drop on my bed. "I'm reading, can't you tell?"

"Must be very interesting air." He crosses his arms and leans against my dresser.

I snatch the book off my dresser and open it just for show, but I can't focus on any of the words. Oh my god. She saw her ex-boyfriend and decided she didn't want us.

I surge up. "Is that fucker still alive?"

"Who? Ben?"

Bugs are crawling under the skin on my arm. I try to shove past Miles. He reaches out a muscled arm and shoves me back hard enough I have to catch my breath. "Fucking talk to me, Cyrus."

I blink, focusing for a second. Miles looks concerned.

I can hardly say the words. They hurt to grit out. "Cali wants to leave."

Miles's gaze flicks across my face. He takes a second to respond, and when he does, the words are slow and careful. "Well, yeah. This isn't her home. She doesn't even have any clothes here, Sawyer."

"I brought her cat." I run a hand through my hair, laughing in disbelief.

Miles looks surprised for a second. "And she got mad?"

"She doesn't know." I grit my jaw.

"Jesus, dude." Miles blows out a breath.

"She saw her ex, and now she wants to leave."

Anger flashes on Miles' face.

"Get out of my way." I go to push past him.

He hesitates for a second, then lets me. "Don't kill him, Sawyer. His death is mine."

"I won't," I snarl. "But he'll beg me to."

CHAPTER 62

MILES

Worry floods me. Sawyer is unpredictable on a good day, but he's started getting better with Cali around. So what the hell set him off again?

I step back out into the hall. Loud meowing comes from a cardboard box.

Well, shit. He actually brought her cat? Sawyer isn't good at doing things for other people. Never has been. So, seeing him do this? A short burst of admiration fills me.

My door opens, and Cali storms out. "What the hell?" She stops short, seeing me and the box.

I raise my hands. "Hey."

Cali glares at me, her eyes spitting fire. Jesus. What the hell went down?

Another meow comes from the box. Cali flicks her gaze down. "What is that?"

I take a step back and motion at the box. She freezes, then slowly kneels down. She goes to open it, then glances back up at me like she doesn't trust me. That look hits me like a punch in the gut. As if I would ever let anything near her that would hurt her.

She opens one of the flaps and gasps. Her entire body freezes. She doesn't make a sound for a while. A black cat head pokes out of the box. Cali jumps into motion and gasps, reaching in and grabbing the cat. She clutches it to her body, rocking. "Weiner! Oh my god, Weiner, it's you. Oh my god." She holds the cat back out to take another look. The animal struggles, wriggling to get away.

Weiner? I frown.

She clutches it again, turning to look at me from the floor. Tears glisten in her eyes, all traces of the previous anger gone. Her eyes are pits of watery blue. She breathes, "Thank you."

I swallow. Fuck, she looks so beautiful right now. "Cali. I didn't–"

"How did you find him?" she cuts me off. Her look is so adoring that I completely stall out. I've never seen this look on her before. Fuck. I thought her fire was hot? This is the hottest thing I've ever seen. And I don't ever want it to go away.

Cali waits for an answer. I swallow again. I can't bear the thought of her stopping that look she's giving me. I do something I know I'll hate myself for and grit, "Lucky find, I guess."

She stands up, still clutching the writhing animal. "Seriously. I can't thank you enough."

The words pop out before I can stop them, "You can give me a kiss."

A smile covers Cali's watery face. I want to freeze this moment forever. I never want us to leave. Cali goes up on tiptoe and still can't reach me. I lean down, my breath ghosting across her lips. I don't kiss her, though. I want her to kiss me.

And she does. She presses her soft, full lips to mine and claims my mouth with hers. All my nerves tingle, and I open my mouth. She immediately licks out at my tongue. I grab the back of her neck and smash her mouth to mine, deepening the kiss and soaking in her essence. God, I want her all over me, in me, everything. We've stolen her body, and now I need her soul. And I'll get it. I need it like my next breath.

The cat struggles between us.

Cali breaks off the kiss, laughing breathlessly. I frown, hating that she's gone.

Suddenly, she seems to get uncomfortable and she squares herself away. "Sorry, uh, thanks."

I hate her sudden change in behavior. I reach out and grab her chin, turning her to face me. "Don't apologize, Cali. Ever."

After a small pause, a little smirk crosses her face. "Even if I told you I stole the last of your clean shirts?"

I laugh. As if I would ever be mad about that. I don't think anything this woman could do would make me truly mad. Even if she tried to run. I'd hunt her down, but I don't think I could be mad. She has a reason to run. We stole her. Well, Sawyer did. But now I'm complicit. She's just doing what she needs to do to survive. And I'm doing what I need to do to make us an intricate part of her survival.

My phone dings.

Sawyer: Bring her down here. Ryder too. He'll enjoy this immensely.

CAKE

ancake Mix
homemade Pancakes

CHAPTER 63

SAWYER

I wipe my blade off slowly in front of Ben. He's awake, thanks to the adrenaline I shot into his IV. Thank Satan for Miles' past military training because the man shouldn't be alive. But he is. Which means more fun for me.

I feel alive. Like I shot myself up with adrenaline, even though I didn't.

Ben trembles.

"Cali talked to me about you." I catch a glimpse of myself in the blade. "I know you did something to her. She won't talk about it because she's way too good to you, but I know you did something."

I trail the knife down Ben's side and cut into his clothes, baring his body.

The door opens, and Cali and Miles walk in. Ryder follows shortly behind.

"Ah, perfect. Now we can get started."

"He's not dead?" Cali gasps. She shrinks back into Miles for a second before she sees me watching her. Then she squares her little shoulders and gives me a defiant look.

A mix of emotions swirls in me, but anger is the biggest one. I'll teach her just what she's trying to protect. She can't go back to him. She's mine. Ours. And the sooner she learns this, the better off she'll be.

I yank Ben's clothes back until his shriveled dick and balls are exposed to the room. "Miss these, Cali?"

"What the fuck is wrong with you?" she growls.

"That wasn't a no." I place the cold steel against his balls. Ben starts screaming again behind his gag, and I glance at my men. They look interested and completely focused. This is what we do. This is what we thrive from.

"Ryder, you want to prep one more meal for me?" I lift an eyebrow, make eye contact with Cali, and cleanly slice through the skin, severing Ben's balls from his body.

The scream that erupts from him rushes under my skin, chasing the bugs away and filling my body with electric heat.

Cali keeps her gaze on me the whole time. She glares, eyes full of swirling fire. And that pisses me off more. She's mad at me for giving her abuser what he deserves.

I hold the bloody balls up in front of my face and ask in a mocking tone, "What was his favorite dressing, Cali?"

Her nostrils flare and she doesn't answer.

"Answer me, or I'll add his nipples to it."

"Dressing?" she asks. She's trying not to look at the dripping balls in my hand while I play with them. They feel like squishy bouncy balls in loose sacks.

Cali glances between me, the balls, and the man on the table. A bunch of emotions run over her face, too fast for me to keep track of. She grits her teeth. "You're fucked up."

"So you keep saying. Answer," I growl, my fists tightening.

Cali glares at me. "Maybe the nipples would make a good side dish."

I pause completely, looking at her closely. There's bravado on her face, and the pulse in her neck is racing. But there's also anger when she looks at him. For a second, I question myself. Is she mad at me or at him?

Cali turns her snarl on me.

Okay, me then. "Fine. Ryder, do barbeque sauce." I put Ben's balls on his chest, carve both of his nipples off, and then hand them to Ryder. He gives a dark chuckle and grabs them from me.

Ben's eyes roll back into his head, and he goes still. The fucker has passed out again.

I smack his face hard. "Wake up, coward. I've seen men handle ten times more pain better than you." I move to grab more adrenaline.

Miles warns, "Too much and you can give him a heart attack." I smack Ben's face again. He doesn't respond. I inject the adrenaline anyway.

Ben's eyes open, his skin clammy. I lean over him, ripping the gag out of his mouth. "Now, for that shriveled thing you call a dick."

CHAPTER 64

CALI

My heart is racing, and my palms are sweating. I've gone through every emotion while standing down here. I thought we were done with this. I feel sick watching the brutality inflicted on someone I know. But every time I see Ben's face, I flash back to the times he would come home and scream hateful things at me. I see his hands reaching out to choke me.

But a part of me says he still doesn't deserve all this pain. Maybe some of it was my fault. I'm not exactly an easy person to get along with.

Fuck. I don't know what to think or how to feel. I need a drink.

Miles pulls me back into his body, grounding me. I lean into his warmth.

"Please," Ben pleads, his voice hoarse. "I don't know what I did, but I'll do anything. My mom has money."

For some reason, him bringing up his mom makes me angry. He never did anything for that woman, and now he's offering her money?

Miles is hard behind me. Oh fuck. Does he like this? Do I like this? Sickness hits my stomach, and I struggle to get away from him. But it's not him who scares me. I'm feeling too many things at once while also feeling nothing. I feel like I'm watching all this from outside my body while still feeling everything that happens.

Sawyer chuckles, but there's nothing humorous in it. "You don't know what you did?"

Miles doesn't let me go, but he leans down and whispers, "You okay, shadow?"

No! Yes? Fuck, this is all too much. There's too much touching me. I try to push his arms off me.

In a smooth move, Sawyer slices Ben's dick off. I freeze. One second, it was attached, and now it's not. There's a roaring in my ears, and I stare at the bloody spot where his dick used to be. Dark red blood glistens.

Sawyer appears in front of me, looking like a vengeful, handsome god. He crouches down, eyeing me. "What, you can't tell me you'd miss that tiny thing. There's not a chance in the world he knew how to use it."

I swallow. Blood is dripping on my socks.

"I want to give him one more taste of you before he dies." Sawyer flicks his gaze up to Miles. There is some sort of communication between them.

"Cali?" Miles asks.

"What," I clear my throat. "What do you mean?"

"I'm going to fuck you with his dick one last time."

The roaring rings in my ears. I blink. What? He wants to do what?

Sawyer holds the appendage up in front of me. It's smaller than it used to be, but not by anything crazy. It looks like a super lifelike dildo. I can't believe all of this is real. It's not real, right? It's all so absurd that a laugh bubbles up in my chest. This can't be real life. But Sawyer just sits there in front of me, holding it. Faintly, I hear whimpers.

I shake my head. "Get away from me. I'm going back upstairs."

Sawyer gives me a dark look. "How fitting, the little bunny runs away when she gets scared."

I laugh harder. "You're literally psychotic. One minute you're nice and normal, and the next minute, you're waving my ex-boyfriend's dick in my face?" I shrug Miles' arms off me and back away toward the door.

Sawyer watches me, completely still. He looks like he's tracking me. Like he's hunting me. My skin crawls.

"So you still have feelings for him then?" Sawyer growls.

"What? That's where your mind went?" I laugh again. "You're fucking insane. No. I don't."

"Good, then you won't have any problem coating his dick in your pussy so I can shove it down his throat." He's still watching me with that unnatural look. I glance at Miles. His gaze is also dark but less unhinged than Sawyer's. He raises an eyebrow. "We won't make you, Cali."

"Like fuck we won't," Sawyer snaps.

"For the love of god." Miles turns to Sawyer. "Are you trying to woo her or traumatize her, Sawyer? Because sometimes I don't think you understand the difference between the two."

I just blink.

The door opens, and Ryder walks in. I snap my gaze at him. He has blue rubber gloves on and is carrying a plate. "I left the skin on. Thanks for not taking that off for me, you disgusting fuck."

Sawyer bounces up with a smile. "Thanks, bro."

Ryder hands the plate over and then leans back against the wall, looking me up and down. "Your girl is looking a little green, *bro*. This is rather PG for you. Still think she can handle you?" He turns to me. "There's no shame in tapping out. You did tell me the other night you have no feelings for them, right?"

Miles and Sawyer freeze. They both turn in my direction. Sawyer looks disbelieving.

I clench my jaw.

"Right, Cali?" Ryder mocks. I hear the warning in his voice. He'll tell them I broke the rules if I don't admit it.

"Yes," I growl. I don't want to look at them. I can't. Despite everything, I don't want to hurt them. I'd rather focus on Ryder's smug face. On reversing that look.

"Yes, what?" Ryder asks.

"Yes, I don't have feelings for them."

The room goes completely silent. My heart clenches. I feel like I did something wrong. I'm just playing the game. Right? But even that felt low to me.

I can sense Sawyer and Miles standing there, watching me. Fuck. They still aren't saying anything. I need to do something. Anything to get this to go away.

Sawyer says, "So you do want to fuck his dick."

Anger fills me. Fine, he wants me to believe I still want my ex? He can believe whatever he wants at this point. I say mockingly, "Sure, whatever. You seem to believe it, so it must be true."

Sawyer holds the appendage out to Ryder. "Fuck her with it."

Everything stills, and I freeze.

Ryder turns his lips down. "What?"

"You heard me." Sawyer watches me the whole time. He's mad. Beyond mad, he's fully gone.

Fear runs through me. I take a step back. Ryder stares at me for a second. His dark eyes are guarded, but he doesn't break his gaze from mine. Something flashes across his expression. Then he turns away from me. "No."

I freeze. He's not going to do it? My mouth drops open. "No?"

"Sawyer, take this disgusting thing." He tosses it at Sawyer. "She clearly doesn't want to."

Sawyer growls, "She's playing the game."

"I said no."

I stand in shock. Ryder snatches the plate back. "They're getting cold."

Fuck. He's not going to make me do it. Relief runs in cold rivers over my skin, and I feel weak.

Ryder leans over Ben. "Open up, baby bird. Sorry the hair is still on them."

Ben thrashes his head back and forth. With startling speed, Ryder snaps his gloved hand down, gripping Ben's chin. "I said, open."

Sawyer moves over to Ben. He grabs one of the two small items on the plate. They're covered in sauce.

"Enjoy, fucker." He drops it in Ben's mouth. Ryder forces his jaw shut. Ben thrashes, making sputtering noises. Ryder's massive form easily holds him down, his muscled arms barely flexing.

"Chew it, or you'll choke and die." Ryder chuckles.

I see Ben slowly chewing, and then I hear him gag. His body tries to jerk up, but he's held down.

"If you puke, you'll have to eat that too," Sawyer growls.

Ben continues to gag. Ryder reaches up and pinches his nose. "My cooking isn't that bad, fucker."

The room smells like sweet sauce and cooked meat. I feel the bile rise in my throat, but I force it back down. Not in front of them. I can't.

I glance at Miles. He's looking at me like I kicked his puppy. I turn my gaze away.

They force Ben to eat the second one, and he continues to gag. I'm not sure how he gets it down. Then Miles pushes off the wall. "My turn, fuckers."

He grabs the severed dick from Ben's chest. He rounds over Ben's head. "Small things do come as a choking hazard. Open his mouth."

Ryder complies.

Miles shoves the dick in Ben's mouth and pinches his nose.

Ben thrashes. Miles calmly holds him down, keeping him from spitting it out. "Shhhh, choking on your dick is a merciful way to go, believe me. You deserve much worse, but I don't want to traumatize our girl too much. You can thank her. Say: thank you, Cali."

All three men surround Ben like lethal killers. The black ink of their tattoos runs all up and down their arms, and I realize just how big they are compared to him. For the second time, warmth fills me. They're fighting for me. In the most fucked up way possible, but they're still fighting for me.

Tears prick behind my eyes. This is so fucked up.

Eventually, Ben stops moving. They continue to hold him for a bit. Then, Sawyer puts the plate on his body and wipes his fingers on Ben's shirt. "Well, that was fast. What's for lunch, Ryder?"

CHAPTER 65

RYDER

I'm tasked with making everyone a meal, so I throw some sandwiches together, bristling. They look at Cali like lost puppies.

They used to look at me like that.

I throw some barbecue sauce in the middle of Cali's sandwich and pour myself a healthy glass of whiskey from the office. I move to the couch to reach out to Wyatt. We knew him from the club we all met at. If we're forced to move out of the country, I know he'll have the resources to get us out under the radar.

As I'm typing, something black moves in the corner of my vision.

I stiffen, gaze locking onto the object. A black cat hops onto the couch, sauntering over to me.

What in the actual hell? For a second, all I can do is stare.

The cat arches its back, curling its tail down my arm.

I'm frozen. When I was seven, a stray cat attacked me. I came home with the claw marks, and my mother told me for weeks I was going to die of cat scratch fever.

The cat makes a little purring sound and climbs in my lap. I completely stop breathing.

"Weiner!"

The shout is sharp, and I jump. The little claws dig into my pants momentarily. Instantly, I'm stiff as a board, and my mom's concerned face flashes in my mind.

I blink to clear it away. This is stupid. It's just a fucking cat.

"Weiner, where are you?" Cali comes darting into the living room. She slides to a stop and freezes when she sees me, her hair wild around her face.

"Sorry, I was looking for..." Her gaze darts to the animal in my lap. "Oh."

She stares at me quizzically for a second.

I return the look with a glare and ask through clenched teeth, "What in the absolute *fuck* is a cat doing in my house?"

She just stares at the animal in my lap. Her stare turns to a glare, and she hisses, "Traitor."

The cat starts rumbling, and I jump. I glance down at it. I can see its little gray claws in its paws.

"Would you get your stray?"

Cali looks at me for a second longer than I'm comfortable. "Yeah." She walks up to me and then pauses. She brings with her a fresh wave of coconut. She smells just like Miles. It makes my dick twitch.

"I will if you give me a glass of that." She nods at the whiskey by the couch.

I hesitate. Sawyer would be heartbroken.

The cat moves in my lap, making me stiffen again. Fuck it, she can dig her own grave. I won't help her out of it. "Sure, whatever. Just get this thing."

Cali grabs the animal off my lap, but as she does, it digs its claws in, causing pricks of pain to dart through me.

"Fuck!" I swipe the cat off my lap. Its claws rip through my jeans as I do.

"Weiner," Cali hisses. "What the absolute hell?" She carries it away.

I brush the hair off my lap. My heart is pounding. I want to look up cat scratch fever.

No, that's stupid. I'll be fine.

I feel the pricks pounding with every heartbeat.

Cali comes back into the room, crossing her arms when she gets to the end of the couch. She waits for a second. It's like she can see my internal panic.

"What?" I bark.

"My drink?" She raises a delicate eyebrow.

Oh. I mutter under my breath, then move to the office to get her one. When I come back with it, she's sat herself down at the opposite end of the couch.

I go to hand it to her, but she says, "No. I want yours. No telling what you put in that one."

I stare at her for a second. Then I put her glass to my lips, taking a swallow, leaving her a healthy amount.

"There. Satisfied?"

She watches me, then shrugs and reaches out. When our fingers brush, a little jolt of electricity goes through me.

I sit back on the couch. I'm not the one she has to worry about spiking drinks.

Cali takes a deep drink, her lips covering the same spot on the cup mine just did. It makes me wonder what her lips would feel like against mine.

She swallows the drink like she's desperate. For a minute, I see the stress around her eyes. She stares across the room, out the back windows. We're quiet for a while.

Discomfort fills my bones. Why the hell is she still sitting here? If she thinks just because I wouldn't fuck her with that man's disgusting dick that I like her, she's deadly wrong. Her intoxicating scent drifts over to me. I close my eyes. Focus, Ryder. I'm about to get up and work elsewhere so I can focus when she says, "So you don't like cats?"

"I didn't say that."

"Weiner hates men." She throws me a glance.

"Then he has the wrong name." I snatch my drink, take a burning sip, and go back to my phone. I won't leave. I refuse to be uprooted by her any more than we already have.

"But he acts like a dick. Entitled and mean. So he's appropriately named."

I take a sideways look at her. "I think it's you who hates men."

Cali bristles for a second. "Only the ones who deserve it."

I take a sip of my drink. "Who deserves it? What infraction must a man commit to deserve your hate?"

Cali brings the glass to her lips and doesn't answer me.

The alcohol burns in my throat. "Look at you wrong? Not cater to your every need? Not snivel at your feet?"

She barks a laugh. "I get it, Ryder, you don't like me. No need to beat a dead horse."

We sit in silence for a bit again. She continues to just sit with me.

She hasn't tried to run since I've been here. Does she really want to leave? What possible benefit would she have to stay? I ask gruffly, "What are you doing?"

"Drinking."

"No. Here."

Cali finishes her drink in one go. "You know what, I have no idea." She stands.

At that moment, Sawyer stomps upstairs. "Let's go, bitches!"

Both of us glance towards him. He snatches a sandwich off the counter.

"Time to plant!" he says around a mouthful. "What do you think, Cali? Will we grow little bone shrubs? Little teeth trees?"

He throws her a mean look, and she grimaces.

I turn back to my phone.

"Family trip. You too, Ryder," Sawyer says around a mouthful. "Mmm, barbeque."

I clench my jaw. We used to be a family. But whatever the hell this is right now? It's not a family.

"Ryder." Sawyer's voice is low. I glance up. There's something about the genuine look in his eye that cuts straight to me.

Fuck. Fine.

Jesus, I'm getting soft. And being soft in this world means only one thing: loss.

CHAPTER 66

MILES

Cali comes bursting into my bathroom. She clocks me washing my hands. "Oh, sorry."

I quirk up an eyebrow. She said she had no feelings for us. It hit me right in the chest, and now she's pushing in here like she owns it? I growl, "What's the hurry?"

"I need...do you have mouthwash?"

I snatch it from under my sink. I restocked everything the other night. I was being sentimental and decided she wasn't going to try and kill me with anything. Now I'm mad and embarrassed. Clearly, this means more to me than it does to her. That's fine. I'll get her to the point I'm at. She won't have a choice. I just need a minute.

When Cali grabs the mouthwash from me, I catch a whiff of alcohol.

I freeze and stare at her. Cali takes a swig of the mouthwash.

"Cali..." I look her up and down. "Have you been...drinking?"

She shoots me a look that I know she tries to make innocent, but there's a tightness around her eyes.

"Shadow..." I growl.

She spits into the sink. "What, Miles? You aren't my dad." She wipes off her mouth. "So what if I drink? It's my life and my choice."

Shit. Sawyer is going to lose it. Drunk women have always triggered him. He hasn't said for sure, but I'm convinced his mom would use when she abused him. The one time all three of us tried to have a foursome with a girl, she came out of the bathroom with her eyes glassy and smelling like alcohol. Sawyer snapped on her. I think he genuinely forgot who she was. Ryder and I had to rip him away from her, and that was that.

"Cali..." I snatch the small woman up by her shoulders, forcing her to look at me. "How much did you drink?" Fuck, I can smell it strongly on her. She's going to have to stay far away from him.

Cali turns her angry gaze on me. "I swear to god, Miles. You can't control every part of me! I just watched you *kill* my boyfriend." She swallows. "Please, for the love of god, give me this one thing."

My heart squeezes at the pain in her face. But I can't back down. Not when it comes to her safety. "You're going to have to puke, Cali. Now." I shove her towards the toilet.

"What?" She screeches and fights me. "Get the fuck off me!"

I don't let up and shove her to her knees.

"Cali!" A voice booms in my room. It's Sawyer. "Where are you? Are you fucking him in the bathroom?"

I freeze. Sawyer boots the door open. "You know there are sexier places to fuck."

He takes us both in, his demeanor instantly changing. "What's going on?"

"Cali feels sick," I say. "She's going to have to stay."

"I do not!" Cali struggles to get up, and I reluctantly let her go. She brushes herself off. "I'm fine. Jesus. Let's go."

Cali storms past Sawyer, and I try to keep the wince out of my face. He pays her no mind and watches me with narrowed eyes. "What the fuck was that, Miles?"

"Nothing." I straighten. "She said she was going to puke, and I tried to hold her hair back."

Sawyer doesn't look like he buys it. I lower my voice. "She didn't take downstairs very well. Cut her some slack."

Anger flashes across his gaze. "She shouldn't feel bad for that sick fuck."

I glare at him. "Yeah, well, not everyone's brains work the same way yours does, Sawyer. She's not seasoned like the rest of us." I push past him into my room. "I think she should sit this one out."

"She seemed like she wanted to go."

Jesus. If I push this too hard, he'll suspect something is up. Maybe it'll be fine. I just won't let her get close to him.

When we load up into the truck, I sit Cali in the back, farthest away from the driver's seat, and I sit right next to her. She gives me a sour look but doesn't argue. Thank god. Every now and again, I catch whiffs of alcohol, but it isn't strong.

Sawyer throws the body in the trunk and drives us down the road.

Cali looks out the window like she's soaking it all in. I realize with a bit of guilt that she hasn't seen much of the beautiful countryside because we haven't let her.

"Where are we going?" she asks.

Sawyer glances at her in the rearview mirror. "A pretty spot I picked out just for us."

Ryder is silent. I worry that he'll use this as another reason to kill Cali, and I'm not sure what Sawyer was thinking of bringing her with us. Scratch that. I know he's not thinking, at least not with his head.

We drive through the countryside for a while. At one point, Cali giggles softly. I shoot her a glare. She gives me a sleepy, dopey-eyed look.

Fuck it all to hell, she's drunk.

CHAPTER 67

CALI

We drive for just under an hour. No one says anything, and I keep glancing between all the men. They look so shadowy and menacing and hot. Good lord, they're hot. With all their tattoos and violence. And dickishness.

The alcohol has gone to my head. Since when do I like assholes?

Okay, since forever. I ought to know better than to drink on an empty stomach. And fuck, if the dark looks Miles keeps shooting me make me want to jump his bones. He's mad at me for saying I have no feelings for him. Well, he can suck it up. I don't owe them anything.

Still, the guilt gnaws at me.

The longer we drive, the more the landscape looks like where I grew up. I'm thrown back into memory lane.

"You know, this looks like where I grew up." I watch as my breath clouds up the window briefly.

Sawyer throws me a look in the mirror. He also looks a little angry. It just makes him all the hotter to me.

I smirk at the nickname. "If I'm a bunny, you guys are the wolves." I giggle a little. "The big bad wolves."

Miles elbows me and growls, "You're embarrassing yourself."

I catch a tiny smirk on Sawyer's face. I glower at Miles and turn back to the window. Such a fucking killjoy tonight.

It's fully dark by the time we slow. We pull off a gravel road. The headlights flash across a few smaller crude oil tanks.

We stop, and Miles helps me get out. His strong hand steadies me when I stumble on the gravel a bit.

Sawyer jumps into the bed of the truck, and Miles leans into me, pressing me into the truck. His coconut scent surrounds me, and my pussy starts to throb.

"Don't let Sawyer know you're drunk." He catches my eyes with his mesmerizing green ones.

"I'm not drunk," I say, running my hands up his chest, but my words are drowned out by the dragging of a tarp. Okay, I'm a little buzzed. Who gives a fuck?

"Cali, a hand?" Sawyer calls.

I give Miles a wink. "Sorry, babe. My other man needs me."

Miles freezes for a second, then releases me.

Oh fuck. Did I just call Sawyer my man? Jesus Christ, what was in that drink? I flee, rounding the truck.

Sawyer has Ben's body laid out on a blue tarp on the ground. He's leaning on an ax. "Ah, there's the pretty little captive. Have a seat, I want someone to talk to while I get to work."

My stomach churns for a second, but the alcohol washes it to the back corner of my mind. I haul myself up on the tailgate.

"So." Sawyer swings the ax a bit but doesn't raise it. "You like wolves, little bunny?"

I cross my arms. "They're pretty animals."

He throws me a smirk. "And rugged."

I glare at him. "And stinky."

Sawyer huffs and swings the ax down. It chops through Ben's ankle, and I jump. It makes a crackle and snap, and suddenly I feel sick.

Sawyer heaves the ax up again, and his leg is separated at the knee. Dark blood leaks down the tarp.

I swallow. "Easy, babe," Miles mutters from my side. I jump. I didn't hear him come up.

Sawyer looks up at me. His eyes are still angry, but not as bad. "You grew up here?"

I squeeze my eyes shut. I don't like fighting with him. The alcohol rages through me. "Yeah. I mean, I don't know. Where are we?"

Sawyer chuckles, and there's another snap. "If you grew up in the country, you should know how to shoot a gun better."

I snort and shoot him a dangerous glare.

"What?" Miles asks.

Sawyer heaves the ax again, and I look away. Another snap. "She took a shot at me when I grabbed her. Shoots like Ryder here. Wide and crazy."

I glance over my shoulder. Ryder is leaning back against the truck door, one foot propped up. His voice is low and unbothered, "Right. You know I shoot better than either of you."

"Right." This time, the whack was meatier, and I slap a hand over my face.

"So Cali," Sawyer sounds cheerful, "Raised in the countryside. By mom? No dad, I'm guessing."

I snap my gaze to him. "What's that supposed to mean?"

He chuckles and looks at me. "Well, look who you fell for. Older men whose red flags are so bright they're damn near on fire. That's fatherless behavior."

A snarl of defensiveness rolls through me. "First of all, I haven't fallen for you. Kidnapped, remember?"

"Mmm." Sawyer leans on the handle, his glare mean. "So, no dad then?"

I clench my jaw. "I have a dad." He didn't raise me. I barely know him.

Sawyer goes back to his work. "So, did you like growing up here?"

I keep my eyes off the mess he's making and watch his muscles as they move. "I guess. I didn't get to go out much. I was a bad kid."

"I thought you said they beat that out of you." He pauses long enough to catch my gaze. "You were reformed."

"Well, yeah. Beat and prayed it out of me," I scoff. Why are we talking about this? I thought he was mad at me.

"Prayer, huh? Hear that, boys? She's good at begging." Sawyer wipes his forehead, leaving a dark streak. "Think you can beg for this cock when we're done? Maybe throw some worship in, too? I can be your god for the night."

I sputter. The warmth from the alcohol slows my response. Because damn, if that didn't make me horny.

Sawyer sees me struggling and smirks.

I shoot back, "Sorry, I don't believe in God anymore."

"What about Satan?" He leans on the ax. "I can be your devil if that's what you prefer."

My cheeks flame. Sawyer does look like a demon, his huge body splattered in blood.

"All done." He chucks the ax down. "Let's get him scooped up." He starts dragging the tarp toward the oil tanks.

CHAPTER 68

MILES

Ryder tried to hide it, but I saw how his gaze snapped to Cali when she talked about her childhood. He stared at her like he was soaking up every word, his body frozen.

Sawyer kept throwing glances Ryder's way, too. He knew exactly what he was doing.

I had no idea Cali experienced anything like that. It makes me sick. What little I know of what Ryder went through makes me murderous.

You're not any better than them, murderer.

I watch my boyfriend chop up Ben's body. And for the first time, I don't fight that voice.

If being the villain in Cali's life makes it a safer place for her to live, maybe I'm okay with it.

Maybe I am like my dad.

And maybe, in this case, that's the kind of man that Cali needs.

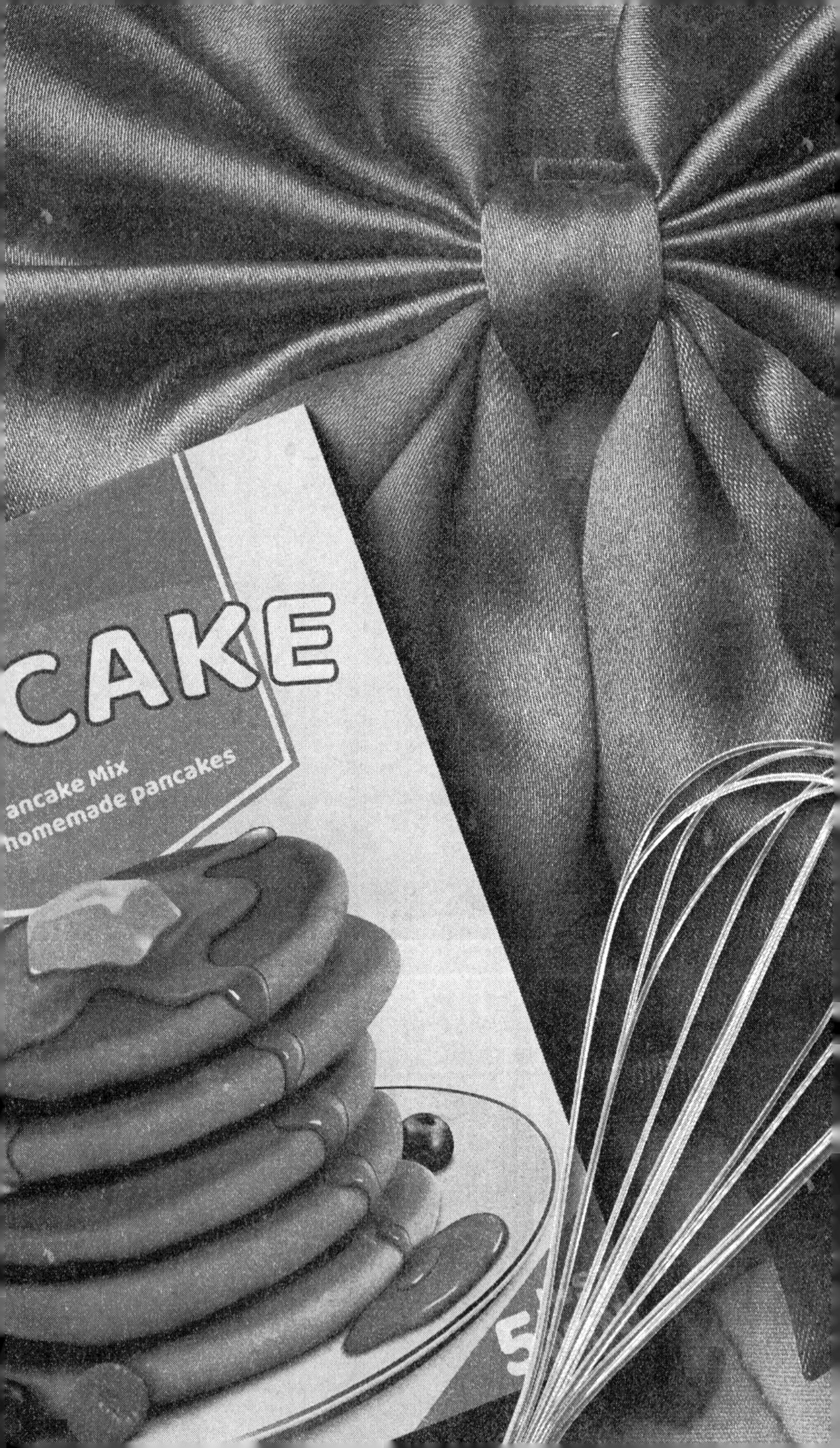
CAKE
ancake Mix
homemade pancakes

CHAPTER 69

SAWYER

We drag the tarp to the tanks. They aren't too big - not over the short tree line - and I scramble up the ladder.

"What are you doing?" Cali asks.

I move to the valve and open it. "Laying him to rest, bunny."

"Here?"

I peek over the edge, and she's looking around. God, she looks cute. Despite the fact she's mad at me, she's hanging on my every word like a little puppy.

"Well, yeah. We'll be able to look at this for years and remember. Much more romantic than burying it. Hand me a piece."

Cali stands there, frozen. I notice again how pretty her hair looks in the dark. It's almost translucent with the truck lights shining through it.

Miles moves past her and grabs a piece.

"C'mon up, you can help." I pat the metal beside me.

Before she can say anything, Miles snaps, "No. She's fine."

Jesus, he's being unusually bossy today. I shoot a glare at him. Ryder has stayed by the truck, texting someone again. That's fine. He doesn't have to like it, but he can't try to claim that we aren't including him.

Cali moves to the ladder, arguing with Miles. "I want to see."

He looks like he's going to throw her over his shoulder and run. Holy fuck, hunting them both down would be hot. My dick twitches. But even I know that's too risky right now. Not here.

Cali climbs up next to me. Her necklace glints dimly in the night, and my mark of ownership makes me fully hard.

"Whoa." The gasp comes from those pretty little lips. Goddamn, she's fucking gorgeous. And I can't believe she's mine. Ours. She doesn't think she is, but I'll purge that thought from her head. She won't dream of saying something as stupid as she did earlier.

I regret my deal to let her fuck Ryder to get points. At this moment, I hate that I'm a man of my word. I'll just have to make sure that it doesn't happen.

"You can see so much from up here." Cali looks around. The metal makes a hollow thump as she shifts.

"Pretty, isn't it?" Just like her. I give her a meaningful stare. She catches me watching and suddenly looks bashful, and if it isn't the cutest thing ever.

"Hey! Fucker." Miles bangs on the ladder, handing up a limb. "Focus, please."

At this rate, I'm going to throw *him* in the tank. I shoot Miles a look, snatch the arm, and drop it into the narrow opening of the tank. It hits the bottom with a hollow bang. These have been abandoned for a while. I checked them and the family history. It's perfect to keep animals from digging up the pieces and dragging them all over for the cops to find. Plus, I think it's romantic. I can take them here on dates, and we can reminisce and have picnics under the moon.

I drop another piece in with a bang.

Cali jumps at the sound and then giggles.

I flash her a smile. "Oh, you like that?"

Miles hands me another. Blood drips all over the container and myself. We brought lye to clean the majority of the mess up, although I have to use it sparingly to keep the integrity of the metal.

Cali watches as we put the rest of the body in. I leave the lid partially open to allow bugs to come in and assist in the process. Him being found eventually is not my worry, but I do need the DNA to decompose enough that it can't be traced back to us.

After I throw some more pieces in, I see that Cali is staring at the sky. I look up. It's scattered in bright stars. Being so far from the city lights, it's absolutely scattered in bright stars as far as the eye can see.

I look at Cali again. Her skin looks pale and smooth, and I trace my gaze down her neck, wishing I could see my brand. Good lord, she's the hottest, most infuriating woman I've ever seen. And normally, the only time of day I give women is to hate fuck them and throw them away.

Something stirs in my chest. It's not entirely unpleasant, but my body immediately tenses. Am I feeling…affection? Fuck. Every time I've felt this, the object of my emotions has been ripped from me. How could I do this to myself again?

I steel myself. I won't let Cali go anywhere. She can say all kinds of stupid things, but I'll *make* her fall for us. She might think she has a choice, but that's the farthest from the truth.

"Cali, let's go!" Miles shouts and hits the edge of the tank.

Cali glances at me with a small smile, and my tough guy act fades. Lord, I *want* her to want me. How fucked up is that? I'm the biggest glutton for punishment I've ever met.

"They're pretty," she says softly.

For a second, jealousy runs through me. I want to be able to make her smile like that.

I grab Cali's chin and tilt her face toward me. She smiles again, but this time, it's at me, and my heart nearly stops. I lean down to kiss her, brushing my lips to hers. She responds, flicking her tongue out.

And that's when I taste the alcohol.

It hits me like a bucket of cold water. Suddenly, I'm frozen, and it's not me and Cali anymore. I'm thrown back to the times my mom would force me to take a shot before sucking off her John's. My mom's voice is here, her voice deep from years of smoking.

Falling for the girl? How predictable, son. I thought I taught you to play a better game than this.

I stare at Cali, my ears ringing. She looks confused.

My mom's voice comes crystal clear right by my ear. *This whore doesn't want you. She's playing you so she can get what she wants and run. All women are the same, Sawyer. They could never love you.*

Fuck! My ears ring. My mom can't be here. She can't be here right now. I haven't heard her in so long. I thought she was gone.

Suddenly, I can hear everything all at once. Shouting, my mom laughing, metal banging. A form pushes past me.

I sit back, trying to focus. The alcohol is still in my mouth. Fuck, it's still in my mouth. I scramble to get down the ladder and barely make it before I hurl everything beside the tank. I'm puking so hard that I can barely breathe. My body shakes, and tears come out of my eyes.

Fuck, why was Cali drinking?

Pure pain cuts through my chest and squeezes until I can't breathe.

She's not your mother, Sawyer. She's not.

I shake my head, my chest tight.

Where did she get the alcohol from?

I can still taste it. Flashbacks roll across my vision. Scene after scene, smell after smell, sound after sound. As fast as they come, I try to push them away. I grip the gravel so hard it digs into my palms.

A rock skitters in front of me, and I glance up. Ryder looks down at me, his gaze concerned. He doesn't say anything and just holds out a hand to help me up.

I stand, looking around and heaving in a shuddering breath.

"We took care of the trail and the tarp," Ryder says softly.

I smell alcohol on him, too.

I snap my gaze to his, suddenly focused. "Did you give it to her?" My chest gets tight again. I know Ryder drinks, but it's on occasion, and he always tells me so I can avoid him if I need to.

He crosses his arms.

I shove his huge shoulders. "Did you give it to her, fucker?"

"If you must know, she demanded it."

Red-hot anger burns under my skin. He allowed it. Not only did he allow it, he didn't tell me about it.

"Oh, so you just what, *had* to give it to her? The tiny woman with no weapon and no leverage?" I clench my fists. Ryder did this on purpose. He's trying to get between us.

And that makes me murderously angry.

Ryder's voice is low like he's placating a child, "I am not her babysitter, Sawyer. She asked for it, and I gave it to her. You need to take that up with her."

My head swirls with anger. Oh, I fucking will. I'll teach her to never touch booze again. But this on top of it? I can't handle this.

I turn and march back to the truck, my steps in the gravel and the crickets the only sound. Fuck! I hate the quiet out here. I feel the shaming voices screaming in my mind. I smack them away before getting in the car.

They have no place here. Only I have a place here. And I'm about to fuck shit up.

CHAPTER 70

CALI

The drive back is silent except for the hum of the engine and full of deadly tension. My buzz is completely gone now. I'm not entirely sure what's going on, but I know I fucked up. It hurt more than I care to admit seeing Sawyer's reaction to kissing me. In fact, it felt like a white-hot knife had pressed through my heart.

Am I really that repulsive? I mean, hell, he's kissed my pussy before; how is my mouth any different?

I know how. I let my guard down. And I could tell he did, too. For a second, that moment on top of the tank felt perfect. It felt like he...saw me.

And then it all came crashing down. As I should have known it fucking would. I kick myself for my stupidity while I also want to cry.

Miles is mad at me too. I can feel the anger radiating off him. In fact, I never thought I'd say this, but Ryder is the only one who isn't pissed at me right now. He threw me a quick look of sympathy getting into the car. Or at least, I thought it was. It was only a flash of change from his usual indifferent look. Maybe that was his victory look. He finally won. They can all kill me and continue on with their happy, killer lives.

I don't look at any of them. I can't. I look at the dark landscape passing by, wondering if it's indeed worth it to just jump out of the car now. I reach out to the armrest, and Miles drops a heavy hand down on my thigh, pinning me to my seat. He squeezes once in warning.

When we get back, Sawyer storms into the house first. Ryder follows, and I just sit in the truck.

"Go." Miles nudges me.

I stare straight ahead. "And walk into my death?" I give a strained laugh. "I think the hell not."

"He's not going to kill you." Miles reaches across me and opens the door. "But I have no doubt you'll get punished."

"For what? Drinking wasn't one of my rules." I cry as Miles shoves me out of the car. He follows closely behind me, laying a heavy hand on my shoulder, preventing me from bolting.

"For not listening," he grits.

"What, am I a toddler now?"

"You're acting like one."

I dig my feet in, but it does no good. In fact, it only pisses Miles off more. When we get to the front steps, I see the blood from Ben across the concrete. My primitive brain takes over, and I bolt.

At least, I try. Miles snatches me up faster than I can register, throwing me over his shoulder and hissing, "Take it like a woman, Cali. Stop running."

"I will never stop running from you." I struggle to get out of his strong grip.

"Then you'll spend a lifetime getting punished." Miles smacks my ass and hauls me inside. He drops me right inside the door. I collect myself, looking down my nose at him and mockingly brushing myself off. He just gives me a blank look.

I sense a large body behind me. Before I can turn around, Sawyer wraps me in his heavy arms and says in a cold voice, "Hello, bunny."

I stiffen but don't fight him. So we're back to 'bunny' now.

"Hello, Sawyer."

He chuckles. "Miles, I left something on the counter for our sweet thing here. Grab it for me."

Sawyer picks me up effortlessly and brings me to the couch, sitting so I'm forced to sit on his lap. As much as I'm pretending to keep it all together, my heart is pounding. I have no doubt he can feel it through my skin.

I jump as Sawyer's hot tongue traces up the column of my neck. "Are you afraid?"

I grit my teeth. I know he feeds off of fear, and I refuse to give it to him. I've done nothing wrong. "No," I say.

"Tsk, tsk, another lie you're feeding me," Sawyer says against my skin. "Want to explain to me why you were drinking?"

Anger runs through me. "I don't see how that's any of your business."

Miles walks back into the room, holding a glass of water.

Sawyer tightens his grip. "Everything about you is my business." He lowers his voice, "Everything. I thought you had learned you can't keep things from me. But apparently not. You'll tell me what you're running from when you run to alcohol."

I clench my jaw. His voice makes goosebumps skitter up my neck. "Why, so you can manipulate me even more?"

"So I can protect you," Sawyer growls.

I laugh bitterly. "So you're going to protect me from my past? I think you just want to know so I can't surprise you anymore. I think you're scared of me. And I think you're scared I'll win your stupid little game."

The room falls eerily silent. I look at Miles, and he glances between Sawyer and me, an unknown emotion flickering behind his stony expression. I wait for Sawyer to reply. It weirds me out that I can't see his face. What is he thinking? Is he mocking me? Angry at me?

Finally, Sawyer's voice comes out low and dangerous, "You are far more than a game to me, Cali. You stopped being a game a long time ago."

I suck in a breath, stupid goosebumps prickling on my arms.

"And I'm going to protect you from yourself, stupid girl. You

413

want to be out of your mind? You want to drink?" Sawyer motions at the drink in Miles' hand. "Give me that."

I stiffen. "What is it?"

Sawyer reaches out and grabs it. "It's a roofie."

"What?" I try to jerk away.

"If you make me spill it, I'll give it to you with a needle," Sawyer growls. "I was trying to be nice."

I watch the glass closely, still struggling to get away. Every time I move, the liquid sloshes. "This isn't nice! You're a psychopath!"

"So you keep saying," Sawyer says blandly. "You want to escape so badly, I'm giving it to you. Take it, or I'll force you to. And I don't think you want that."

My muscles shiver. "What are you going to do to me?"

"You have till the count of three."

"No, wait!"

"One."

Panic runs through me. I try to escape, but his huge arm pins me on his lap.

"Two."

I know he isn't bluffing. I know he'll gladly do what he threatened.

"Th–"

"Wait!" I reach toward the glass. "I'll fucking take it."

Sawyer lets me take it from him. I glance at Miles, who stares back at me with dead eyes. He clearly isn't going to help. I don't know why I looked to the man who killed Ben to help me.

Sawyer barks, "Stop stalling."

My hand shakes, and I bring the glass to my mouth. Fuck, I don't want to be at their mercy. I don't think they'll kill me, but I'm sure they'll do anything just shy of it.

Fuck it. I'm not going down without a fight. I throw the glass back into Sawyer's face and scramble up. There's sputtering as I twist to hurl myself over the back of the couch to get away from Miles, too.

I leap over the couch and dart toward the front door before a huge form slides in front of me. I run right into a solid wall of muscle. I try to scramble back. It's Ryder. He snaps a hand around my neck and under my chin, forcing my gaze up to his dark one.

"Did you just disobey one of my men?"

I glare at him, swinging a foot out to kick him in the nuts, but he just holds me out away from his body with his long arms. I hiss, "Fuck you! I fucking hate you!"

Ryder simply squeezes my neck harder. "Do you want so badly for this game to add another player? You think I won't like breaking you until you forget who you are? Until you come crawling to me and begging for everything you need? You don't get to disobey Sawyer."

Ryder's grip is making the world grow dim and my ears ring.

"Bring it on, motherfucker," I slur. Let him fucking try. Let them all fucking try. I may be caught, but they will never break me.

There's a sharp jab to my thigh, and I try to jerk away, but moving feels like I'm trying to swim through cotton.

Then, Ryder drops me, and the world comes roaring back. All three men stand over me, looking down at me with blank expressions. Sawyer is holding a needle. I cough and rub my thigh. I know that with whatever he just gave me, I'm fucked. I'm about to be at their complete mercy, and there's nothing I can do about it.

I'm getting whiplash from how quickly they switch things up on me. I start laughing. They're killers. I'm not sure what the fuck else I expected.

"What are you laughing at?"

I glance up at Sawyer. "Just a funny way to go, you know? You almost had me. You played your game well. Had me eating right from your palm. You deserve this kill – you played well."

The room goes completely silent. Sawyer crouches down, grabbing my chin in his warm hand. "Oh, Cali. I'm not playing you. And we're not going to kill you. Far from it. In fact, if you beg, I might even make it feel good."

A wave of dizziness hits me, and I squeeze my eyes shut.

"Good girl. Just submit. It'll be easier for you." Someone picks me up, carrying me. The swinging in the air makes nausea boil in my stomach. They set me down on my back on the couch. I sit up as all three of them round the corner, blinking away the lightheadedness.

"Oh yes, please run again. How far do you think she'll make it? My bet is the front yard." Sawyer smirks at me.

Miles crosses his arms. "I won't let her. She'll fall and hurt herself."

"You're no fun. Ryder?"

The huge, silent man looks me in the eye and doesn't answer. I stare back, returning his look with a challenging one of my own. I refuse to break eye contact, even as another wave of lightheadedness swirls in the back of my head.

Finally, Ryder smirks. He looks like he's thinking about slicing me up, and a wave of tingles runs over my skin. Despite all odds, my pussy also gets hot.

Sawyer approaches me and straddles my waist. "We're going to teach you what could happen if you keep drowning yourself in alcohol."

I look up at Sawyer, a tingle of numbness running through me. Sawyer grins down at me. "Get me off."

"No," I spit.

"Get me off of *you*."

I struggle to pull away, but Sawyer is heavy as shit.

"C'mon, Cali. I'm not even doing anything to you," Sawyer mocks. "Get me off."

Anger fills me, and I snap my hand down to punch his nuts. His arm shoots down quickly as he backs up. He snatches up both my wrists and pins them to the back of the couch. I struggle, but I can't break his iron grip.

"Cali, I'm not even trying." Sawyer ducks his head down to look me in the eyes. "See how vulnerable you are?"

I bare my teeth at him and snap my head forward, knocking my forehead against the bridge of Sawyer's nose.

He hisses, jerking back, but doesn't let up on his grip. "Now you've just pissed me off. And you're no closer to getting free." In a violent move, Sawyer whips me down so I'm lying on the couch, and he's straddling me. The movement makes the world spin again, and this time, it takes longer to stop. I feel hands tugging at my clothes.

When I open my eyes again, my breasts are exposed, and my

pants are pulled down to my knees. Miles is holding my hands above my head, and Ryder sits on the coffee table next to us. I try to struggle, but it feels like it takes forever for my limbs to respond.

Sawyer hovers over me, blood dripping out of his nose. "You can't even fight us, Cali. But you were so desperate to not feel. To escape whatever it is you're running from. So desperate that you put yourself in a stupid position."

I watch as his blood drips down on my chest. I can't even feel it because my skin is so numb, and that scares me. I heave for breath. He put me in this position.

"Fight me, Cali."

I do. I try. But it's like I've become a prisoner in my own skin. I try to buck in anger, but his body feels like it weighs a million pounds.

Sawyer chuckles roughly, then yanks his pants down. His dick pops out, hard and veiny. There's a drop of precum at the top. He strokes it, looking down at me. "Stop me, Cali."

My emotions become fuzzy and slow. The anger flares and then fizzes flat. I slur, "Fuck you."

Sawyer leans down so his dick is closer. "Make me."

I pull down on my arms. It feels like I'm pulling from a million miles away.

He rubs his dick on my pussy and groans. "So fucking wet. Do you like this, Cali?"

A fuzzy sensation shoots through my clit through my body. Fuck, it feels good. My world is growing distant, but I can feel my clit like it's the only sensitive part left in my body.

"Does it turn you on, knowing that you can't do a thing to stop me? That I'm going to take what I want from this pretty little body, regardless of what you say?"

I force my eyes open. They want to close. I want to sink into that warm nothingness that is beginning to blanket my body.

"Wake up." That voice was different. It sounded like Ryder.

I force my eyes open again. Sawyer is perched at my entrance. His muscles are flexed, and he holds back, meeting my gaze with his fierce one. "You know, this isn't the first time we've done this before."

417

What? What the hell is he talking about?

Sawyer chuckles. "It was actually the first time we fucked. But you wouldn't remember. The drugs work a lot faster with alcohol." And he shoves himself in all the way.

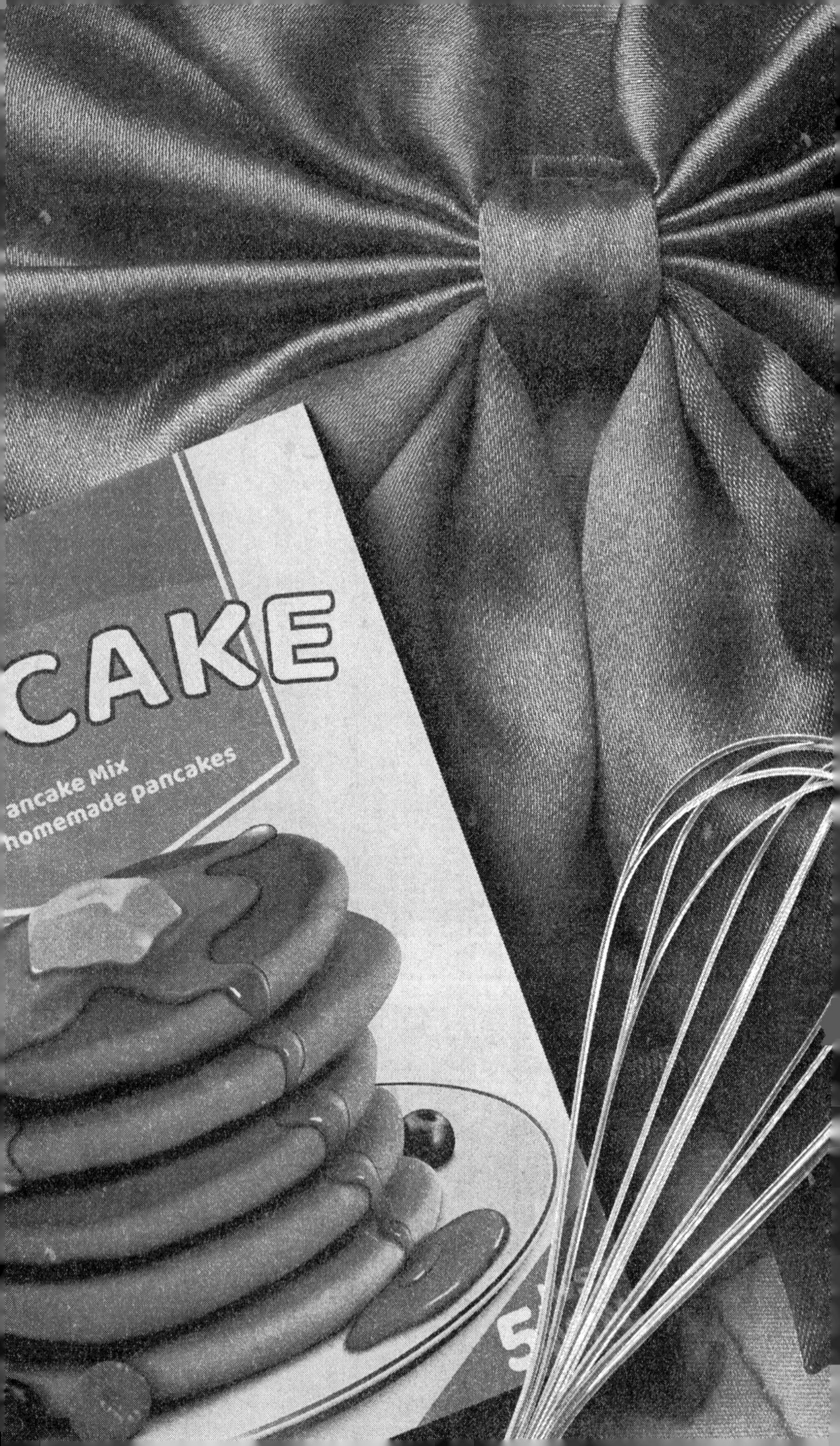
CAKE
ancake Mix
homemade pancakes

CHAPTER 71

SAWYER

Fuck, she's wet as hell. Her pussy sucks me in like it's hungry for me. I pump into her, watching her eyes roll back in her head as she lets out a little moan.

Jesus Christ, she's gripping me so tightly. I use her to stroke my dick, pulling all the way out, then back in again. I put my thumb down on her clit and swirl. I want her to feel as much as she can. I want her to feel me everywhere. To know that she's mine. That she can't escape me even if she tries to hide in alcohol.

My men watch me, lust in their eyes. That makes me get harder, and I jerk faster into her, swirling her clit until she stiffens. I lean down into her ear and say, "You really ought to protect yourself better from men like us, Cali."

She's barely awake, but I feel her body fully stiffen, and her pussy pulses over my dick. That drives me to the edge, and I come inside her with a shout, pushing in as far as I can go. My whole body tingles with the high, knowing she can't fight me. Hell, at this point, she might not even know to fight me. God, that makes me want to take her all over again.

I pull out, eyeing Miles above me. "Your turn."

He lifts an eyebrow. "Not my style."

I shiver in the aftershocks of pleasure. I glance down at Cali. She's fully out now, laying limp in front of me, her pussy leaking my cum. My dick twitches.

I turn to Ryder, turmoil roiling in my veins. I promised Cali that if he fucked her, I'd let her go. And I'm still mad at him.

"So you're playing our game now, huh?" I deadpan.

Ryder leans back, crossing his arms. "I don't really have a choice, do I? It's play your game or get pushed to the edges of this relationship."

His unaffected manner makes the old anger roll through me again. "Oh, so you want to get close to me, and you do that by giving her alcohol? That's your best plan yet."

Ryder levels his gaze on me. "Once again. She asked me for it."

"So you'll give a prisoner whatever she asks for?"

"Is she really a prisoner?" Ryder snarls, "I see the way you look at her. The way you talk to her. You've fallen for her. Which is the most dangerous thing you could have done."

He tries to hide it, but I see the hurt that rises in Ryder's eyes.

Miles clears his throat. "Ryder, we aren't trying to push you out."

Ryder's arms are flexed, and he grips his knees. "It doesn't matter if you're trying to or not. You're doing it."

"It doesn't have to be that way! You can get to know her."

Ryder laughs, the sound harsh. "Get to know a stranger so I can keep my men? That's a little fucked up."

I watch them argue, tension filling my chest. My stupid, impulsive ass made Cali a promise. If I push Ryder toward her, I'll inevitably have to let her go. If I don't and keep going down this path, I'll inevitably lose Ryder.

I hate that there's even a hesitation. Things have been rough with Ryder for the last few months. I've been on my bullshit, and that always turns him into an aggressive, closed-off monster. Which is fun as hell in bed, but the man doesn't know how to turn it off.

And neither do I.

Ryder stands, about to leave the room, and Miles lifts his hands in frustration.

"Listen." I clear my throat and shift. "Regardless of what happens with her, we need to figure our shit out."

Ryder snorts. "Really?"

"I'm trying, okay, jackass?" I snap. I clench my fists. The next words are hard to force out. "We need to talk. Like, actually talk."

Miles gives me an odd look. "Are you okay? Having a stroke?"

"You know what? Forget it." I also stand to leave.

"No, wait. I'm sorry." Miles lets out a breath. "It's been a long day. I'm sorry. You're right."

I pause.

"We need to talk. I'll start." Miles turns to Ryder, who looks disinterested. "I know you see how important she's become to us. Thank you for not...killing her. I know you wanted to."

Ryder's jaw flexes. "I still do."

"And you don't. Even though it's tearing you apart. So...thank you."

Ryder looks like he wants to say something else, but he doesn't. Miles waves his hand at me. I press my lips together.

Ryder cocks an eyebrow at me. "Got something to say, Mr. 'Let's Talk'?"

"Don't push your luck," I grit.

Miles turns a harsh glare at me.

Fine. I know I need to extend an olive branch. "Thank you," I force out.

Ryder smirks. "Couldn't hear you."

"Okay, way to turn it into something childish." Miles tosses his hands up. "Why don't you two go hate fuck or something?"

"He doesn't deserve it." Ryder turns on his heel.

I don't deserve it? I dart to my feet, and I chase after him. I'll communicate all right. All over his dick. With my fucking nails.

CHAPTER 72

RYDER

I step out onto the front porch. The harsh wind whips around me, but it feels good compared to the hot house. Ever since Mom got sick, she has kept the heat turned way up. I sweat doing my work. Often, I bring it out here, even though the winter weather makes it hard.

Dad pulls into the driveway. He gets out of the car in his work clothes, shivering as he runs up to the house.

"Dad." I follow him inside, hit again with the oppressive heat. "Can I come with you guys?"

"No." He doesn't even look at me. "Evelyn, are you ready?"

"Please!" I run in front of him. "All my work is done. I want to go."

"The hospital is no place for you." Dad brushes me off.

My eyes fill with tears. He acts like I'm a kid. I'm twelve now.

"Please, I won't make a sound."

"Don't ask me again." Dad ignores me, shuffling my mom to the car. She's thin now, just bones. She damn near looks like a ghost, huddled in her blanket against the car headlights. I fold her new clothes every day, but you wouldn't know. She spends so much time in blankets.

I watch as they pull away, the cold chapping my cheeks, a sense of helplessness running through me. Every time my dad takes her to the hospital, I beg to go. Every time he says no. Mom says she doesn't want me catching anything like she did.

I watch the road for hours until my toes and hands go stiff and numb. I recite my prayers over and over. As soon as I'm done with one, I start another.

Mom has stopped helping me with school. Stopped tucking me in since my bed was on the second floor. Stopped doing the dishes and cooking our food.

A lump forms in my throat. It feels scratchy. Fuck, am I getting sick too?

I watch for hours that night. My dad doesn't return. I later discover that my mom died at the hospital.

And when I find out, I can't react. I don't. It feels like I'll never feel again. I just go back to folding laundry over and over. I can't seem to get it right. It'll never be right.

CHAPTER 73

CALI

The hangover from whatever drugs Sawyer gave me hits like a truck. They must have moved me to Sawyer's bed because when I wake up, I'm here, looking at his posters of half-naked women. My entire body hurts, and I groan.

"Cali?" Sawyer asks from somewhere behind me. He comes around the bed. "You're awake."

"Fuck off," I groan. A wave of nausea rolls through me.

I feel a cold hand against my clammy forehead. I try to swat him away. This time, I can't hold the nausea back, and I vomit off the side of the bed.

"Oh shit. Hang on, Cali."

A trash can appears in front of me.

I wave Sawyer off. I don't even want to look at him. I don't want to talk to him, feel him, or listen to him breathe. "Go away."

"You need to drink some water."

My head pounds, and it's everything I can do not to hurl again. His voice is making it worse. Everything is making it worse. The lights, the smell, everything. "Get out."

"Cali…"

"Go!" I yell. "I don't want to talk to you, okay? Fuck you, Sawyer. Fuck you. Just please, go." My body trembles, and he glares at me.

"Cali, you need help."

I puke again.

Sawyer gathers my hair back. When I've puked all I can puke, I brush his hands off me. "Seriously. Go away."

Sawyer's jaw clenches. His hair is down for the first time, and it falls in his face. I slide back into bed and roll away from him. I'm so tired. So damn tired.

I hear Sawyer cleaning up the puke. For some unknown reason, it makes my eyes tear up.

"I don't need you to take care of me," I try to growl.

Sawyer says nothing.

I'm confused by all the emotions rolling through me, and him being here, acting like I'm weak, is too much for me.

"I hate you, Sawyer," I say softly.

All sounds freeze. I stare at his bookshelf wall for so long, feeling tears prick my eyes.

"Cali…" His voice is hesitant.

I squeeze my eyes shut. I don't want him to see that I'm crying. That I'm weak.

"Please. Just go."

I hear him walk to the door. He pauses for a long time.

"Fuck off." I hiss with as much energy as I can.

The door shuts softly. Unreasonably, it makes the tears spill over my eyes, and I sob.

I *am* weak. I'm weak because I care. Because I wanted him to care. He doesn't care. He just wants to win his game.

At some point, I fall asleep.

I wake up to the door opening. I crack my eye open to growl at whoever it is. Halloweiner gets dropped in the room, and the door is shut again.

"Come here, boy," I rasp.

My cat saunters around, sniffing at various things, ignoring me completely. The relief at seeing him is so overwhelming that I start crying again. I cry until I fall asleep.

When I wake up for the third time, there's water and a banana on the side table, and my cat is cuddled up with me. I feel a little better, and I snatch up the drink, downing it. Wiener cracks an eye open to glare at me for moving.

"Fuck," I moan. Flashbacks from Sawyer fucking me fill my head. Anger fills me at the same time as my pussy pulses. What was it he said right before I passed out?

Right. Sawyer fucked me before we even met. He always said I was his.

A mix of powerful emotions runs through me, and I turn my head into the pillow and cry. Again. Fuck. Ben is dead. My friends and family don't know where I am. And I'm here, getting both turned on and mad about these psychotic, possessive psychos. I hate my body's reaction to all this. And fuck, it's getting to be more than my body. I felt something else entirely for Sawyer, sitting up on that oil tank. For some reason, that makes me cry harder.

I fall asleep again, and when I wake up, my cat is gone. I sit up. I feel much better, almost like I have a mild hangover.

I get up and go to the bathroom. There's still no toothbrush for me. I snatch up Sawyer's and groan with the minty taste of the toothpaste.

The bedroom door snaps open. "Cali?" Miles rushes up to me, pausing when he sees me brushing my teeth. "You okay? I heard you..."

I glare at him in the mirror, then go back to brushing my teeth. He was a part of that bullshit, and he doesn't get let off the hook.

Miles crosses his arms and leans into the doorframe.

"How long have I been out?"

"All day and night. It's afternoon."

Good. I still have time to act on the deal Sawyer made me. I have one day left.

I finish up and brush past Miles. He follows me. "Do you need anything?"

I continue with the silent treatment, crawling back in bed.

Miles sighs, running a hand through his dark hair, looks around, then sits on the floor, facing me.

I frown. No, this won't do. I swing my legs back out of bed and pad out of the room.

"Cali, where are you going?" Miles gets up.

I move to the hall and down toward Ryder's room.

"Cali, you need to rest."

I ignore him, walking into Ryder's room and slamming the door.

CHAPTER 74

RYDER

My door opens as I'm folding laundry to put away. I glance over my shoulder and start saying something to Miles, but it's Cali who walks in, all legs and messy hair. My dick twitches at the sight of her, and it makes me mad.

Cali slams the door, giving me a careless glance, then heads right for my bed.

I freeze. What is she doing?

"Oh," Cali says, pausing. Her cat is curled up on my bed. The animal won't leave me alone, and it freaks me out. Every time I get one of the boys to get him out of my room, it manages to sneak back in.

"What are you doing?" I ask her.

The tiny woman doesn't answer and just climbs on the bed and puts her soft body under the covers.

"Excuse me?" I narrow my eyes at her. The animal gets up and cuddles in the crook of her knees.

"They won't leave me alone, so I came in here." Cali closes her eyes, her eyelashes dark against her pale skin.

"You know there's a whole house."

Cali looks sick. Sawyer has never spiked one of my drinks before, but he did Miles', and he didn't get out of bed for two days.

For a second, seeing Cali pale, curled up under blankets, makes me flash back to my mother before she died.

My chest gets tight, and I clench my jaw.

I shake the clothes I'm folding out more vigorously than needed. "Cali. Get out of my bed."

"Must we talk?" She groans.

"No. Get out of my bed." This is not how I pictured her in my bed. Not that I pictured her here. Ever.

She throws an arm over her head.

"Cali..."

"Ugh, I thought of all of you guys that you would be the least chatty." She looks at me but doesn't move.

I glare at her. "Oh, chatty will get you to leave? Fine then. Let's talk." I think about ripping her out of that bed and physically throwing her down the hall. But the way her eyes look sunken into her head makes me pause.

I go back to my folding. "I'll tell you about the five rules of trading."

Cali groans, and it makes me smirk. She must have quite the headache. I launch into an in-depth discussion about the stock trade, bidding, and selling as I fold my laundry. I take deep care in my folding, making sure that everything is just right. If it isn't, I start over again.

Cali listens for a while, annoyed at first, and then I think she falls asleep again. When I've finished my laundry, she's sleeping with her mouth open, little snores coming out. She looks so vulnerable and soft. Nothing like the hate-spewing, angry woman she normally portrays herself as.

Fuck. She damn near looks innocent. I clench my jaw. For a second, I see how she would get Miles to fall for being her knight in shining armor. She bleeds vulnerability when she turns off the fucking tough guy act.

It's mid-afternoon. I move back out to the office and find Sawyer lurking in the hallway.

He scares me a little, and I jump. "What the fuck, Sawyer?"

He pushes off the wall. "Is she okay?"

"She's fine." I prowl past him, headed to the office. He and I fucked after our fight, and it made things feel a little less tense between us.

Sawyer follows me. "She needs to drink more water."

I scoff a little. "Is your conscience getting the best of you, Sawyer?" But I thought the same thing. Not that I care.

Sawyer doesn't answer. I sit down to work at my computer, and Sawyer lingers. He hovers in the background, going from window to window. He moves incessantly, seemingly unable to stay still.

"Would you stop?" I snap. I'm trying to figure out a few more details should we need to leave the country, and his nerves are making me unsettled.

Sawyer looks at me with hurt in his eyes.

I run my hand through my hair. Fuck, I didn't mean to be so harsh. "Sorry," I pause. "You're making me nervous. Don't you have something to do?"

"Well, yeah." He doesn't do anything.

I shake my head, going back to my work. Eventually, Sawyer starts to leave the room. I know exactly where he's headed.

"Don't go in there, Sawyer," I say, possessive energy running through me. It scares me a little.

"Why not?"

I glance back at my work. "Because she doesn't want you to. Just give her some space."

"That's bullshit!"

I sigh. How did I get put in the peacekeeping spot between my men and their prisoner? The prisoner who is currently lying in my bed, getting her coconut smell all over my sheets.

Sawyer's voice lowers, "I just need to make sure she's okay."

"She's okay." I meet his blue gaze. God, he looks tortured.

I lower my voice, "I think the better question is, are you?"

Sawyer fights with himself for a second, then looks stricken. His voice comes out a whisper, "She kicked me out."

I don't say anything. His vulnerability surprises me. He hasn't let me in on anything meaningful in his life in months.

"She always...I guess I assumed she..." Sawyer looks at the ground.

I clench my jaw. I see where this is going. He's fallen for her. Completely. He doesn't even know what to do with himself now.

Which makes me steel myself. I can't fall the same way. Someone needs to be strong for the family. I grunt, "You can't strong-arm every part of your relationship with her, Sawyer."

He plays with a chip in the doorframe. "Sure I can."

I huff. "That may work with Miles, but not everyone is Miles." I turn back to my work.

I feel him staring at me.

"Are you fucking her?"

The question startles me. I glance up to see Sawyer looking intently at me, studying me.

Heat runs through me, embarrassment filling me for some reason. "No, Sawyer. I'm not fucking your toy." I usually only fuck people I have an emotional connection with. Even when we play with others, I usually sit back and let the boys play while I watch. But with her? Fuck, there's something about her that makes me want to play. Her fire is intoxicating. Makes me want to stamp it out. Teach her some goddamn respect.

Sawyer continues to look at me – like he doesn't believe me. I feel my cheeks heat again. Can he tell what I'm thinking?

Finally, he relaxes. "Okay."

Unreasonable anger fills me. It almost seems like he's relieved I'm not messing with her.

I growl, "Why – am I not allowed to? The only one not included in this game?"

Sawyer shrugs, and that possessive anger rolls through me again. I snap, "Answer me, Sawyer."

He winces. "So I might have made a stupid little bet with her that..." he trails off.

"That...what?"

He looks uncomfortable. "That if she fucks you, I'll let her go."

I stiffen, my skin getting hot. Anger runs through me, and for a second, I think about darting to my feet and fighting him. Then reality slams back into me.

She's off-limits. I shouldn't care. Right? Fuck!

Sawyer shrugs, stepping out of the room.

"Wait!" I chase him into the hallway. "You did what?"

"I'm sorry, man. I didn't think you'd want to." Sawyer looks embarrassed. "Was I wrong?"

"No!" I clench my hands into fists.

Sawyer looks me up and down. "Okay? Then why are you mad?"

I don't know. Fuck, why *am* I mad? Because it feels like I'm kept out of the game at every turn? Because they want to keep her fine, soft body all to themselves? If this is a game of keep-away, they're doing a pretty fine job of it. The previous anger from the other night rolls through me again.

"It's fine." I take a stiff step back toward the door. Just keep your hot little fuck toy to yourself, fuck what I think.

"Ryder–"

"Save it." I slam the door.

I don't want her anyway. They can have her. I don't like blondes anyway. Shame that she has a perfect body.

And pretty eyes. They'd cry so perfectly.

Sawyer is playing a dangerous game, and I don't think he knows it, but he just gave me all the cards.

CHAPTER 75

RYDER

Cali stays in my room until the evening. I'm finishing cooking a meal when she appears in the kitchen.

She must be starving. She's so little, and she eats almost nothing.

Not that I've been paying attention.

Both men are sitting on the couch on their phones, but they immediately put them down when she comes in.

"Cali," Sawyer says and stands.

She turns to me like he isn't there. "What's for dinner?"

Anger flashes over Sawyer's face.

Fuck if I don't almost smile. She's ignoring him to talk to me.

"Burgers," I say.

"Cool." Cali slides into the island chair, her back to the men. She looks better than she did earlier. And...shit. She's wearing one of my shirts.

My dick bobs.

Sawyer stands, but Miles grabs his arm and yanks him back to the couch.

"So," Cali says, looking at me with those haunting blue eyes. "You like to cook?"

"Yep." I go back to my work. I feel her watching me closely. The meat is almost done, and I change the paper towel under the spatula a final time to make sure there's no raw meat on it. The room is full of sizzling meat and tension.

Cali ignores the tension and flips her hair. "I hate cooking. More of a baker myself."

I watch the action and wonder what it would be like to grab that curly mess while I have her pinned against the wall?

Sawyer and Miles' attention is locked on us. I keep my victorious smirk down. I know Cali is only talking to me to get back at them, and maybe to try to get in my pants, but I can't help but enjoy it.

I set a plate in front of her. "Well, that's not surprising. You were probably raised to bake more than cook, yeah?"

She arches an eyebrow at me in surprise. Then, she gets suspicious. "How'd you know?"

Those were the standard roles taught to the women in my home, so I figured it would be the same with her. If anything she said about her upbringing was true.

I shrug. "Lucky guess."

She still eyes me like she doesn't believe me. "Did you stalk me too?"

I raise my eyebrows. I saw Sawyer's tab on my computer. I know he went through her phone.

I lean down, looking her in the eyes. "No, little mystery. I think most people have an expectation of privacy, and I don't violate that unless I'm asked."

I look at the men behind her. "I, for one, stayed off your phone." I straighten.

Cali looks confused for a second, looking at me and then glancing behind her.

Miles looks appropriately ashamed.

She stares at him, then sputters, "Did you?"

Sawyer looks angry. He turns his flashing gaze on me.

I wink and go back to my cooking. You want to make me a

player in your game? Oh, I'll play. I grab a burger off the pan and let it sit for a minute, tossing on the buns to toast.

"Cali, let us explain," Miles says softly.

"You too, Miles?" Cali hisses.

Silence.

I grab the food and place it in front of her. Her cheeks are red, and her eyes are glassy. Fuck, if it doesn't shoot straight to my dick.

Tears always get me hard. Goddamn it, dick. We're only playing with her. We're not getting involved.

Cali snatches her food up and starts to build her burger. I grab the condiments and veggies from the fridge.

She takes a bite, wrapping her pretty little lips around the burger, and I'm stuck staring. She's eating the food I made for her. Cali makes a tiny moan, fluttering her eyes.

"This is good."

I hold back a groan of my own. I love that she's eating what I made her. It'll help her get better.

"Cali, you can't just keep ignoring me," Sawyer says, and I watch out of the corner of my eye as he marches up to the kitchen island.

"This is good," Cali says to me again, trying to ignore him, but the fire blazes in her eyes. She's pissed.

I smirk.

"Cali." Sawyer grabs her shoulder.

Cali whirls on him and, almost faster than I can track, hits the side of his face with an open palm. The crack sounds loud in the room. Everyone freezes.

"Get. The fuck. Off me." Cali is shaking.

Sawyer's eyes are dark. Miles is standing, looking like he doesn't know if he needs to intervene.

Cali straightens, looking Sawyer right in the eye. The entire house is silent.

"Stop me, Sawyer," she mocks.

Sawyer is angry. His eyes are dark, but he just stands there.

Cali cocks her hand back like she's going to hit him again. He doesn't flinch.

His voice comes out low in warning, "Cali..."

"Make me stop," she swings her hand towards him, then pauses

443

right before she hits him, cupping his face in a gentle mockery.

Sawyer grips her hand, forcing it to stay on his face. "I won't hit you, Cali."

"Do it," she hisses, trying to yank her hand back. He grips her tighter.

"Hit me, Sawyer!" Cali throws her face in his. "Fucking hit me! You won't!"

Sawyer clenches his jaw.

"Hit me!" She screams, yanking her hand away.

He lets her.

Cali scoots off her stool, scrambling away from him. She heaves for breath, throwing him and Miles a wild look.

"You think you're so much better than Ben because you won't hit me? You kidnapped me! Took me away from my home for nothing. I did *nothing*." Her chest heaves. "You've been through my phone. You know I didn't call the cops on you."

Sawyer crosses his arms. "You did! You called 911 the day we saw you at the gas station."

"I didn't—" Cali stops, a look of realization coming over her face. Then it's flushed with pure fury. "I called 911 because Ben hit me that night, Sawyer. Choked me out in the kitchen!"

Sawyer gives her a disbelieving look. Cali continues to heave for breath. I don't know her that well, but she looks like she fully believes what she's saying.

Sawyer's face transforms from disbelief to shock. A quick flash of devastation flicks over his face before he flashes me a helpless look. For a second, I want to help him.

I have no idea if she's telling the truth.

Cali whirls, marching over to me. "I'll do the dishes."

Sawyer stands there, heaving for breath. He's frozen, and it makes my gut twist a little. I've never seen Sawyer freeze before.

The moment doesn't last long. He catches me looking at him, and his face transforms. With a snarl, he darts out of the kitchen.

Miles is still standing there, looking torn. For a second, I think about running after Sawyer and fucking that defiant, tortured look out of his eyes. But then Miles follows after him, and I'm left alone with Cali.

She continues washing the dishes.

What does that mean for us if she didn't call me in? I wouldn't believe her, but I haven't been through her phone, and Sawyer has, and he looked like he believed her. I don't know. And I hate not knowing.

Cali continues washing. She isn't washing them right, and it makes my skin crawl. I see all the spots she's missing, even leaving some bubbles on the pans as she sets them up to dry.

Wrong. All of it is wrong.

I gently nudge her out of the way with my hip. "Here, I'll wash. You dry."

She glances at my hard-on, then back at me. Her pupils widen and I think she's going to call me out on it, but she doesn't.

She switches, trying to dry the ones she just washed.

I gently take them from her.

She tries to snatch them back, "Sorry, did I not do it right, Your Highness?"

I bump her, shooing her arms out of the way like a pesky fly.

"You did fine," I say, grabbing a new sponge from under the sink – I don't use dirty ones on these – and begin my routine. I don't know much right now, but I do know that I can't let my men get sick.

Cali watches me, seething. I feel her anger burning across my skin, and it doesn't help my hard dick.

Once I'm as satisfied as I can be, I place the pan on the drying rack for her.

She says nothing. I ignore her and dig into the next ones. I'm almost done before I glance back at her.

She pretends like she wasn't just watching.

"So." She pulls a breath in. "Is that it?"

"What?" I growl.

"That." She waves at the sink. "Is that what's wrong with you?"

Heat runs under my skin, and I'm immediately defensive. "Sorry, am I bothering you, Your Highness?" My cheeks burn. I'm self-conscious about my compulsions, but I've gotten so used to people who've seen them a hundred times that I forgot what it feels like to have a new person see them.

Cali snatches up a pan to dry it. "Sawyer is bipolar as fuck. Miles thinks he's my fucking knight in shining armor. And you...obsess over dishes and laundry?"

I grip the sponge so hard it flattens completely in my hand. I didn't realize she was paying attention when I folded.

Cali gives a small shake of her head, twisting the towel in her hands. "I expected worse, honestly."

It floors me for a second. I fully expected her to make fun of me. Mock me. Throw some fire in my face about how fucked up I am.

But she doesn't. She just throws the towel on the counter. "I'm going to bed."

For a second, I feel something like respect for her. I don't unfreeze until I see her heading down the hall toward my room.

My dick jumps at the thought of having her in my bed again. That absolutely cannot happen. I can't get involved. I can't.

"Get your own room," I growl at her.

Cali stops. "Weiner is in there, so that's where I'm going to be."

I switch immediately from respect to lust. Oh, this insolent fuck. Christ, if I don't want to wrap my hand around her pretty throat and choke her until she changes her little tune. I growl, "I'll throw him and you out."

Cali turns back, and I catch a sly look. "You're scared of him. I don't think you will."

She turns on her heel and stalks out.

Heat flares under my skin. She noticed that too? So she wants to fuck around and find out? I'll play her game. I'll play Sawyer's game. Fuck it, game on.

I march after her down the hall, and Cali slams the door right before I get there.

Oh, hell no.

I rip the door open. Cali is stripping off her shirt, exposing her small, feminine back. She doesn't even look back at me. She pulls her pants down and steps out of them as she walks out of them, completely naked, toward my bed.

I'm frozen, drinking in her beautiful body. If possible, my skin gets hotter. She's so much smaller and softer than my men, and it makes me so hard it's uncomfortable. Her ass is perky and sways with every step she takes. I want to put my handprints all over it. Bite her until she bruises. Make her scream.

Fuck it, I'm done holding back. I'll teach her to turn her back on her enemy.

CHAPTER 76

CALI

Suddenly, a huge hand wraps around the back of my neck, and I'm whirled to face him. I gasp. Ryder walks roughly into me, backing me until my body hits the wall. Just as quickly, his hands wrap around both arms, and he picks me up until I'm eye level with him. He presses me into the wall.

"You want to play, Cali?" he growls, his voice dark and rumbly, sending goosebumps all over my skin. He holds me up like he doesn't even notice my weight. I know I'm supposed to fuck him to play Sawyer's game, but a shiver of fear runs through me.

"Answer me." Ryder shakes me, staring me down with those dark, ruthless eyes. My pussy soaks, and I bite back a moan.

"Put me down."

Ryder's eyes crinkle in a mean smirk. "No."

I kick my feet, but it does nothing.

"Now, now." Ryder tosses me on the bed. I bounce and immediately scramble to get up, but he's on me in a flash, pinning me down with his heavy body.

Ryder chuckles as I fight to get away. "You want to tease me with that fine ass body and think I won't just take what's mine?"

I shove against him, trying to push up on the bed. "I'm not yours!"

"You're lying in my bed. Naked. With my man's brand on your chest and collar around your neck. How does that make you not mine?"

A mixture of mint and Ryder's manly scent surrounds me, and it makes me weak. He sits up, pinning my hips under his. I'm forced to watch as he grabs the bottom of his shirt and slowly yanks it over his head. He's shredded and covered everywhere I can see in tattoos. There's not a blank space of skin anywhere but his neck and the palms of his hands.

"Close your mouth, Princess. You're supposed to look like you don't want it."

I snarl.

Ryder just laughs, his white teeth flashing, then undoes his belt slowly. I watch his tattooed hands and fingers work, moving with familiarity and flow. With a yank, he pulls the belt from his pants. I can see the imprint of his dick. It's straining against his jeans. I've seen it briefly before, but right here in front of me, it looks huge.

My heart hammers. Fuck. What have I gotten myself into?

Ryder throws the belt down on the bed with a thwack, and I jump. He smirks and reaches into his pants, pulling out his dick.

I gasp. It's big. And not only that, it's lined with two tattoos. I look closer. They're Sawyer and Miles's names.

"You like that?" Ryder watches me eyeing it.

I snap my gaze to his and clench my jaw.

"I bet you'll like it when I claim you with it, too."

Excitement and fear run through me. "No," I say.

Ryder snaps a hand down to my throat, and his other clamps over my eyes.

My world goes black, and my heart races.

"No," I gasp, this time in fear.

I feel his hot dick rub against my pussy.

"Mmmm," he groans, thrusting against me. "Your heart is flying, little mystery. Are you afraid?"

I clench my jaw.

Ryder's voice comes against my ear, gravely and hungry, "Why are you afraid? Are you afraid you'll like it when your enemy fucks you? When he makes you come all over his dick while you say you don't want it?"

Heat floods my pussy.

"Oh, I think you like that. How embarrassing. Keep being afraid, little mystery; it's doing something for me."

"Bastard."

I feel him notch at my entrance. My body trembles, and he groans, "Yes. Good fucking girl."

I try to get away, but he's there pursuing, stretching, filling, chasing me. My nerve endings are on fire as he pushes deep inside me. He lets out a shaky groan.

His dick rubs against a spot inside me. I arch my back, pushing into his hands that are holding my face and neck.

A hot mouth closes over my nipple, and his tongue flicks it. I buck into him as sensation shoots through me. He licks and sucks and nips until my nipple is hard and throbbing, then he goes to the other.

"Ryder," I groan, trying to protest.

"Ryder, what?" he mocks. "Ryder, please? Ryder, stop? Ryder, make me come?"

"Fuck you," I say.

"You're the one getting fucked, Cali." With that, he pulls out and slams back inside me. Pain shoots all the way through me, and I cry out.

He doesn't stop. He continues to pound in and out, filling me to the max. He leans on my throat, pushing my head down and making me lightheaded. I hate that I can't see him.

"Goddamn, you feel so fucking good. Such a good little whore for Daddy."

His words make my clit pulse, and I moan.

"Good girl. Buck up into me."

I can't help it. He's hitting me almost right, but not quite there. I shift to try to get the spot.

"I'm going to use this pretty little body to get off, and you're going to be a good little girl and take it." Ryder picks up his tempo and moans.

Suddenly, his hand is gone from my throat, and a sharp smack comes to my right nipple.

I scream, electric pain coursing through me. I cover my breasts with my hands.

"Atta girl. There's that fear again." Ryder groans again then there's another electric hit of pain, this time on my clit. I stiffen, waves of pain and pleasure hitting me as my orgasm crashes around me and my pussy clenches around his dick.

Ryder laughs, then stiffens. He yanks out of me, and hot streams of cum hit all over my torso. The hand against my eyes shakes, and then suddenly, it's gone.

I blink, my eyes blurry.

Ryder moves to the bathroom and I see the scars all over his back. I suck in a breath. It looks like he was whipped.

I hear the shower turn on, and he comes back out shortly, bringing toilet paper. I sit up. He eyes me and wipes the cum off me.

"You should shower."

I cross my arms, suddenly self-conscious. "Are you saying you're dirty?"

Ryder waves his hand at me. "Dishes, laundry, that's what's wrong with me. Go shower."

I glare at him but hop out of the bed. Anything to get away from him. That was hot and mind-blowing, and I was supposed to be the one to orchestrate that, but I don't think I did anything.

When I go to shut the bathroom door, Ryder grabs it.

"What are you doing?"

He pushes in and leans against the doorframe, crossing his arms. "Last time you were in here, you broke my mirror."

It's still missing from the wall.

"Are you babysitting me?"

He raises an eyebrow. "Get in the shower."

He's clearly going nowhere. I march to the shower and get in, shutting the foggy door behind me. The water is deliciously warm, and I relax in pleasure.

I hear a meow and see Halloweiner has come into the room and is curling around Ryder's legs. What the absolute fuck? I've never seen him love a man as much as he does Ryder.

Ryder's voice fills the room. "How do I get rid of this cat?"

"I don't know."

I turn my face into the stream of water. He lets me shower for a bit, then asks, "Why don't you like being blindfolded?"

I freeze. Not this again.

"You may as well tell me, Cali. I'm like a dog after a bone. I won't let you up as easily as my men did."

I glare at him through the door. "That's private."

Ryder snorts. "I was just dick deep in your pussy. How is that any worse?"

I grab the bottle of shampoo, yet another shitty brand that will fry my hair, and squirt out a handful. But it smells like him, and my horny brain is oddly satisfied. "Why don't you tell me about the scars on your back."

There's silence.

I laugh. "I didn't think so. Not so brave when it comes down to it, huh?"

The water rains down, and I scrub the soap into my hair. It feels fucking amazing.

"My dad beat me when I was a kid."

I freeze, glancing out into the bathroom. Ryder looks chill, still leaning against the doorway, with Halloweiner cuddled up on his feet. He raises an eyebrow.

"Oh," I say. "I'm...sorry."

"Don't be. Why don't you like being blindfolded?"

I close my eyes and take a deep breath. Who cares? It's not like it's a big deal. "My grandma always made me look away when she was beating me."

There are no sounds except the water beating down on the tile. I stand there for a minute, my face burning, then rinse my hair out. When that's done, I scrub the rest of my body.

I dare a peek out at Ryder. His entire body is rigid, and he's lost the relaxed look.

Fear runs through me. Oh my god, he looks murderous.

"She's dead," I say quickly. I'm not sure why. She doesn't deserve my protection. But...I can't bear to see what happened to Ben happen to her. I just...can't.

My face burns again. Not that he'd care that much. I'm not sure why I even said that.

"Can you get out? I'm going to dry off."

For a minute, I don't think he will. Then, he does, and the door shuts with a soft click.

I let out a breath as a tiny hint of disappointment fills me. What the hell?

I yank the water off and step out. I don't need him anyway. It was a mistake, but maybe I just fucked my way into a win at this fucked up game.

But my god, those scars were bad. Way worse than what I went through. I towel off aggressively. Life is so unfair.

CHAPTER 77

CALI

Ryder won't let me leave the room, and I don't want to see the other men anyway. It feels like the longest night of my life. I don't move, knowing Ryder's huge, naked body is lying next to me. I can feel the heat off him. My traitorous pussy gets wet thinking about all those muscles and all that ink. His dick is…I hate to admit it, but it felt so fucking good. And the tattoos down the side of it? Clearly, the man loves his pain.

I stare into the dark, expecting Miles or Sawyer to come bursting in. I can't tell if I want them to or I don't. But no one does.

I shift. Getting naked was a bad idea. A horrible idea.

My pussy screams that it was the best idea.

Just when I think I won't, I fall asleep at some point in the early morning. When I wake up, the other side of the bed is empty. My hair is ratty, and I have a headache, but otherwise, I feel fine.

I played Sawyer's game. I won. I need to tell him so he'll let me go.

My feet drag as I get ready. I tell myself it's not because I want to keep that I fucked Ryder to myself. It's because I don't want to see Sawyer. I'm still mad at him.

Finally, I work myself up enough to march into the kitchen. I'm not sure what I'm going to say, and I expect to face all of them, but it's just Miles on his phone on the couch.

He went through my phone. And held me down for Sawyer. I glare at him and yank open the fridge. Which is nothing compared to what Sawyer has done, but I'm still pissed.

"Good morning to you, too." Miles throws me a smile.

He looks like he's forgotten the past few days. I slam the fridge. "Don't you guys have something less healthy? Like cereal?"

He nods at a cabinet. "Top on the left, sunshine."

"Don't call me that," I mutter. He brought Halloweiner. That has to count for something.

"Okay, someone needs an attitude check." Miles stands. "Pump the breaks on the food."

"I'm hungry." I pour a bowl of Fruit Loops.

"You can eat after." Miles stalks up, looking me up and down. "Get your shoes on."

"For what?" I snap.

Miles snaps his hand out and grabs my arm faster than I can track. "We're going on a run." He starts towing me behind him.

"Let me go!" I try to tug away. His grip is gentle but firm.

"No. You've pouted long enough." Miles tows me into his room where my shoes are. He waits for me to put them on, one brow raising when I hesitate.

A thrill goes through me at the dark look he throws me. He says calmly, "If you want to find out, keep fucking around."

"I'm not—" but I put my shoes on. Before I can do anything else, Miles snatches me back up again and hauls me out of the room and then out of the house.

The sunshine is bright, and I blink and put my arm up to shade it.

"Let's go." Miles starts jogging slowly down the driveway, dragging me with him.

"I don't want to run!" I yank my arm away. The last time he took me on a run, I about died. My legs turned to jelly, and I'm still a little sore.

"Too bad." Miles tosses the words over his shoulder.

I glance around. No one else is around.

"I think you know what'll happen if you run from me, Cali."

I slowly start jogging toward him, grumbling, "You said a run. You didn't say it had to be with you."

"Pick up the pace, princess. I know you can go faster than that."

I go a little faster, the gravel crunching under my shoes. The morning sunshine is bright on the fields, the sky gray-blue, and the air crisp. Once I go fast enough for his liking, Miles shuts up. It's just the sounds of our feet and the birds. And my heaving for breath.

It feels like death – just like last time. Before long, I taste blood. Miles keeps us going for longer than I think I can make, and then finally, he stops.

I bend over, gasping for breath. The man isn't even breathing hard. Fucking god of fitness over here.

"You did good, sunshine."

Miles' cheery tone makes me hate him even more. I flip him off, and he chuckles.

"We'll walk back. Keep moving. It'll help you catch your breath."

I don't even have the energy to argue. We walk in silence for a while. Finally, I catch my breath, and for half a second, I feel good. The fresh air feels amazing, and I feel freer not being trapped in that house.

Not that I'd tell him that.

"Cali." Miles clears his throat. He sounds serious and I shoot a glance his way.

He rubs the back of his neck, a light layer of sweat over his skin. I hate that he looks good enough to lick.

"I'm sorry for looking through your phone. It wasn't my place, and I should have asked."

I stutter a step, then stop fully. Did he just...apologize? I can count on one hand the times someone has apologized to me in my life.

Miles stops walking and looks back at me with a surprised look.

I shut my mouth. "Uh..."

"And I'm sorry for...what you've gone through. We've all been a bit harsh."

I sputter. "A bit?"

Miles nods. "I'm sorry."

I wait for more. More arguing, more excuses, more anything. But he just keeps walking. I snap my mouth shut.

"What about Sawyer?"

"What about him?"

"Is he sorry?"

Miles shakes his head. "You'll have to ask him."

"Nope, not good enough." I glare at Miles.

He gives a soft chuckle. "I'm not Sawyer, Cali. I can't tell you what's in his head."

"But surely you have an idea. He is your boyfriend, after all."

Miles shrugs. He's silent for a bit, as if he's debating what he's going to say next. Finally, he says, "All I know is he's the most unhappy I've ever seen him. He hasn't been the same after you kicked him out of his room."

Good. That's what he deserves. All the same, my heart clenches.

We continue to walk, the sound of our shoes and the birds loud. I don't know how to act. The truth is, since I've shut Miles and Sawyer out, I've been the most unsettled I've been since I got here.

But that's a good thing, isn't it? I'm a prisoner. So why haven't I tried to run in a long time?

Fuck, I wish I never drank the night we sat up on the tank. I wish we could have stayed in that little pretend bubble. Miles was pissy with me, but now I know he was trying to protect me. Ryder ignored me, or pretended to ignore me. And Sawyer? Fuck.

I've fallen behind Miles. I clench my fists. "Miles."

He doesn't turn, but he slows. "I guess, for what it's worth... thanks for trying to help me. The other night."

His muscled back tenses and then relaxes. "You don't have to thank me, Cali. There isn't anything I won't do for you."

Against my will, warmth runs through me, and I realize that I actually believe him. Which scares the living shit out of me.

We walk in silence. Miles grabs my hand as we get closer to the house.

I freeze. "What are you doing?"

He holds it gently. If I yank, I can get it away. Because of how oosely he holds me, I let it rest there.

"Touching you," he says simply. He rubs his thumb along the op of my hand, sending goosebumps up my arm.

We walk like that, hand in hand. I should pull my hand away. try to convince myself he wouldn't let me if I tried, but I know hat's not true.

His soft, strong presence makes me want to just wrap myself n him. Fuck, if his hand alone doesn't make me want to jump his pones.

Miles must feel the tension because he throws me a heated glance.

We're close to the house now. I think he's going to walk us nside, but instead, he guides me to the back of the truck.

"What…" I gasp as Miles drops the tailgate and lifts me onto it.

"Miles, what are you doing?"

He runs both hands down my thighs, down my legs, and to my hoes. "Getting the lactic acid out." He winks at me and pulls both hoes off, throwing them in the truck bed and grabbing one of my eet.

I yank it back in embarrassment. They're sweaty.

Miles flashes me a dark look and snatches it back up. "Let me ub your feet." His grip softens, and he clenches his jaw. "Please."

This is weird. It feels uncomfortable. This powerful man is sking me for something that he could clearly take if he wanted to.

I relax my leg.

One-half of Miles' mouth turns up in a smile. He massages my oot, then rips the sock off, his warm fingers pressing on the tight pots, rubbing the run out of it. He switches to the other foot, ubbing and easing and stroking.

It feels so good. I feel my body starting to relax.

Miles starts up my calves, and I yank my leg back.

"I…haven't shaved." My cheeks burn. They still haven't let me lave a razor.

"I don't give a fuck, Cali." Miles grabs my leg and pulls me back. "There's nothing about your body that could turn me off."

WANNA PLAY A GAME?

He massages the tension out of my muscles. Pleasure runs up my legs, my muscles tingling. Miles' hands are doing something to me. They're possessive and strong and gentle.

I risk a glance at him. He's looking at me with barely masked heat and affection.

I glance away quickly, and my stomach flips.

Miles' hands move up to my thighs. I'm wearing his boxer shorts with the waistband folded multiple times, so he has access to my bare legs.

He strokes up and down, sending electricity up my legs and right to my pussy. With his right hand, he massages almost all the way to my pussy, and I suck in a breath.

Miles pretends like nothing happened, then does the same on the other side.

I should stop him. I should say no.

Miles rubs the fatigue out of my thighs until they tingle. He brushes up and over my pussy multiple times. He just pretends like it was an accident. My whole body is on fire, and it's not from the run.

Miles grips my thigh, tugging me slightly to him. I look at him from under hooded lids. His gaze bounces between my eyes and then down to my lips. He licks his, then looks back up at me. "Can I kiss you?"

I suck in a breath and hold it. Miles' eyelashes are dark and thick, and his pupils are completely blown.

I nod slightly.

A devilish smirk crosses his handsome face, and he yanks me toward him. I yelp, and he yanks my boxers down at the same time as he lifts me so they slide off my hips.

"Miles!"

I gasp as he buries his head above my pussy. He takes a deep breath in, making my cheeks flame. Miles places a kiss above my clit, then looks up at me, his eyes twinkling.

I try to push his head back, but he grabs both my hips and pulls me into him.

"Don't take it away, I'm starving."

"Miles." I grab a handful of his soft hair. "I'm sweaty."

He groans against my core, sending delicious tingles through me.

"Please, Cali."

Fuck. I throw my head back and angle my hips slightly into him.

Miles unleashes on me, fucking me fervently, eagerly, like he really is starving. His deep moan makes me gasp, the tingles against my clit already tightening my core in pleasure. His tattooed fingers dig into my hips, dragging me as close as he can to him. He grabs my clit in his mouth, shaking his head from side to side, shaking a glorious feeling into me.

I moan. Miles sneaks a hand up, sliding two fingers into me. They rub against my G spot, making my whole lower body tighten. As it does, he glances up into my eyes. He continues to work me, getting me on the edge of an orgasm faster than I've ever experienced.

Miles winks, and I come undone. Euphoria races through my body, and I lock up in pleasure. Wave after wave hits me, his fingers and tongue carrying me along. When I start to come down, I pant for breath.

He's still watching me.

A thought crosses my mind, and before I can think too hard, I smirk. "Good boy."

Miles' eyes flash, and in an instant, his hand is out of me and he's up in the truck bed, pushing me down. He grips my throat, a fiery look in his eyes. "What was that, pretty girl?"

I flash my teeth at him. "Good. Boy."

Miles is ripping his shorts off and on me before I can scramble back. His dick sinks into me, and he moans. My back arches against the rough grooves of the truck. Fuck, it feels so good to be filled right now.

Miles gives me no time to adjust. He pounds into me, a feral look in his eyes.

"You want to be a brat?" He squeezes my neck harder, then drops his head to behind my ear and pulls in a greedy breath. "Goddamn, you smell good."

He licks up my neck, causing tickling tingles to explode along my skin.

"Fuck, Cali." He drops his head to my shoulder, then moves it along to my armpit.

I struggle to get away. He holds me down effortlessly, lazily pumping in and out of me.

"God, you smell good enough to eat."

"Miles!" I squirm, and my cheeks heat.

"Don't you dare try to hide from me." He thrusts in heavily. "You don't get to be embarrassed about the things I love."

He reaches a hand down to play with my clit while he licks up the side of my neck. His tongue, fingers, and dick send me close to the edge again, and I tense.

Miles pounds into me, chasing his own high. His rhythm change sets my orgasm back a step. He instantly changes back, slowing and deepening his thrusts. He nips at my skin, breathing me in again. "Christ, you taste heavenly. I can't get enough, Cali."

His low voice saying my name makes goosebumps break out on my skin. He plays with my body until I'm right on the edge again.

"Such a good girl. Give me another, Cali."

I do. This orgasm is stronger than the last, ripping through me. I cry out, gripping onto him and digging my nails into his back. He grunts, keeping the same pace and dragging my pleasure out.

When I loosen my hold, he starts pumping into me, chasing his own high. "Jesus, Cali. You feel so fucking good."

I moan, and he thrusts harder, slapping into me. Then, with a shout, he pushes in and stills, coming inside me.

He collapses on me, wrapping me up and flipping us over so I'm laying on him.

We both catch our breath for a bit. I feel relaxed and sated. For a moment, peace fills me.

The sky above us is bright blue, and somewhere, a bird chirps.

"Cali." Miles shifts.

"Right." I move to get up. "Sorry."

"No." He grips me, hugging me to him. "Stay. I mean, if you want to. I just had something to say."

I glance at him. I don't like the change of tone.

"I...don't be mad. I kind of lied to you about something."

I sit up and move off him. Dread boils in my stomach.

"Wait." Miles sits up, holding my hand. "You know when I said...when you asked about Weiner?"

"Yes..." Where is he going with this? I glance around for my shorts.

He bites his lip. "It wasn't me who brought him here." He takes a breath. "It was Sawyer."

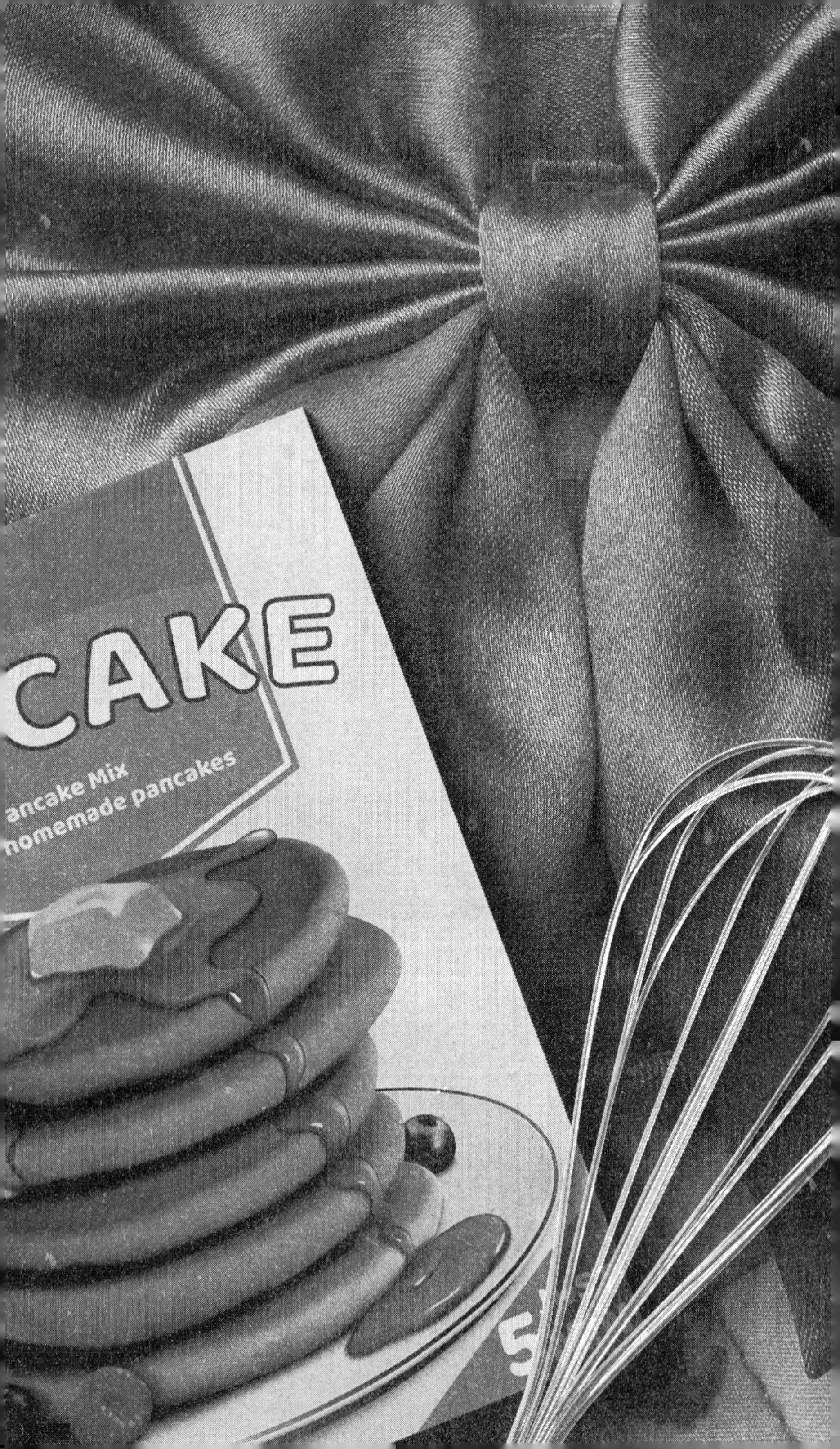
CAKE
ancake Mix
homemade pancakes

CHAPTER 78

SAWYER

Ryder dragged me out shopping with him. I didn't want to go. In fact, I'd rather stick pencils in my eyes, but here I am, glaring at the women's clothing aisle.

I can't get Cali out of my head. I've never been this messed up over a woman before.

Did I kidnap her when she hadn't done anything? Could it really have been chance? But no! The cop said someone at the gas station called. She called 911 that night. I saw her in her car talking on the phone.

My thoughts run in the same circles they have been all night. The clerk. It could have been the clerk.

Fuck! I slide aggressively through the rack of clothes, looking for her size. These clothes are trash. Nothing I'd like to dress her in, but there aren't a lot of options in this town. I snatch things off the rack, angrily stacking them on my arm.

It doesn't matter how I got her. I have her now. She's wormed her way into every part of my life, and I'm never letting her go. She can fight me all she wants, but it won't work.

Ryder's phone rings. He digs it out of his pocket with the hand not holding the cat food and steps back to take the call. I snatch a few more things.

Ryder comes back, looking tense.

I stiffen. "Everything good?" What if something happened back home? Did she run?

"Yep." Ryder flashes a fake smile.

I glare at him.

"She's fine, Sawyer," he snaps.

That part looked truthful.

"Fine. Let's go." I walk the clothes to the counter. Being away from them makes me twitchy. I don't like it one bit. I'll only be content when she's within my reach.

Is she okay? Has Miles gotten her to drink more water? Fuck, I'm going to do that when I get back.

CHAPTER 79

RYDER

That phone call changes everything. I didn't want it to happen, but I knew it could.

Sawyer is anxious to get home, and I let him rush us. I let him drive so I can shoot off some texts. This needs to get done, and it needs to get done fast.

And the men can't know anything about it. I hate to have to do this. My gut clenches. They'll try and stop me.

But I can't let them. Not this time.

CHAPTER 80

CALI

I take a shower after our run. Miles pops in while I'm there and fucks me against the shower wall. I'm fully satisfied and exhausted by the time we're done. Miles offers me a razor, and I accept. He looks on disapprovingly as I clean up a bit, and when he turns the water off, I laugh and shoo him out so I can do my hair in peace. The curls are getting beyond messed up using men's shampoo all the time.

"Let me help," Miles pouts, crossing his arms, still gloriously naked. I glance over his ripped body, dark with tattoos.

"Are you the hairdresser, or am I?" I raise an eyebrow. "I'll be out in a minute."

"You can teach me."

I finger my hair in exasperation. "How about you get me a comb, a blow dryer with a diffuser, and some fucking conditioner."

Miles laughs, and then his eyes grow serious. "Wait." He darts out of the room and returns with his phone. "Say it again."

I glance at him. He looks at me seriously. "You're going to have to tell me exactly what you need. I don't understand any of this."

Is he serious? Warmth floods through me. I list off a few of the essentials.

"Great!" Miles eyes me again, lust apparent on his face.

Despite myself, I laugh and shove him back. "I'll be out in a minute."

He grins. "I'll see if the boys are still in town. They can pick that up." He throws me one more heated look, then steps out of the bathroom.

I let out a breath. I feel...happy. I glance at myself in the foggy mirror. My eyes are bright, and my skin is flushed from the run and the heat and...Miles. Goddamn, Miles. How long has it been since I've felt this happy? I honestly don't remember.

I pick my fingers through my curls. I work through my hair for a while, trying to get the worst of the tangles out. It doesn't feel nearly as good as when Miles does it.

When I finally step out of the bathroom, I'm cold. I search Miles' dresser for some clothes to wear. Weiner meows, rubbing between my legs.

"I know you're hungry. I'll get something out of the fridge."

I hear Miles' door open.

I throw some boxers on. "Hey, could you also get..."

It's not Miles. I jump, covering my tits with my arm.

Ryder looks me up and down, his gaze heated. For a second, we stare at each other. Then he shoves his hands in his pockets. "Miles went to the store."

"Oh." I scramble to find a shirt. I'm not sure why. He's looking at me with a mixture of heat and something I can't quite place. Last night rolls over me in a wave of lust.

Fuck. I can't be feeling that for him. He's an ass.

Ryder watches me silently as I finish dressing. I feel the heat creep across my skin under his dark stare.

"Do you...need something?" I ask.

Ryder continues to watch me. "Do you still want to run?"

I freeze, staring at him. His dark eyes are a mystery. I can't tell what he's feeling.

What is he doing? Does he know Sawyer's deal? Is this some

kind of trick?

"This isn't one of Sawyer's games. Genuine question."

"I..." I glance around. Do I want to run? For real? What would Miles think? What would Sawyer think? Fuck, why am I hesitating?

I could go back to my apartment. For a second, I struggle to remember my routines there. I've been here for so long that I've gotten used to it.

Is this Stockholm? Holy shit, this is Stockholm.

There's no way they'd let me go. Ryder's made it clear I'm a liability.

I clear my throat. "No, I wouldn't run."

He cocks an eyebrow. "You can answer honestly."

"I don't need you shooting me in the back." I cross my arms. "So no, I wouldn't run."

There's a flicker of emotion, then it's gone. "I'm not going to kill you, Cali. I'm giving you a chance to run. I'd suggest you take it."

Wait. He's giving me a chance? I frown and take a step back. What is going on?

"I have a whole new identity set up for you. You can start over."

I hear buzzing in my ears. Is this for real? I glance at Ryder's expressionless face. He doesn't care. He can't get rid of me fast enough. He fucked me once, and now he's done.

Pain grips my heart.

"But we have to go now, Cali."

"Wait, why?" I shake my head, trying to clear it.

Ryder's face is stony. "Do you want to go or not?"

No, this isn't real. This is a test. I need to talk to Miles.

"Where's Miles?"

"At the store." He continues watching me with a cool gaze. Halloweiner arches his back against Ryder's legs.

"What about Sawyer?"

"I'll take that as a no?" He crosses his arms.

"No! That's not what I said. Just...give me a minute." I pace back and forth.

"We don't have a minute, Cali. Either you want to go, or you don't."

"Why are you doing this?"

Ryder looks impatient. "Isn't this what you've wanted all along?"

Yes. It is. But not like this? But, this is my chance. I need to take it.

"Okay." I eye him. His expression doesn't change. He simply turns to the door. "Let's go."

And that breaks my heart further. "Wait!"

Ryder stops. So many things run through my mind. Why are you doing this? What if this hurts them? What if it hurts me? But instead, I say, "Promise me on their lives you won't kill me."

Ryder turns back, his look solemn. He watches me for a second. "I promise on their lives, Cali. If you disappear and never breathe a word about us, you'll never see us again."

CHAPTER 81

RYDER

Cali is shaky at best. I thought for sure I'd have to fight her. I was about to reach for the zip ties in my back pocket, but she finally gave in. All she has to grab is her cat, which doesn't take her long. Guilt and something else tugs at me. I do my best to ignore it, but it fights desperately for my attention.

Cali keeps throwing glances at me and looking around the house for the others.

She won't find them.

I get them in the truck and head off toward the city. The car ride is silent.

My attorney's conversation keeps running through my mind. *New evidence. Sawyer and Miles. DNA.*

Fuck! The last thing I wanted is for them to get tangled up in this. I'm a shit person for letting it go on this long. We should have ripped the cord earlier.

I should have ripped the cord earlier. Should have done it before I got involved. Fuck, why did I get involved? And why is this so damn hard?

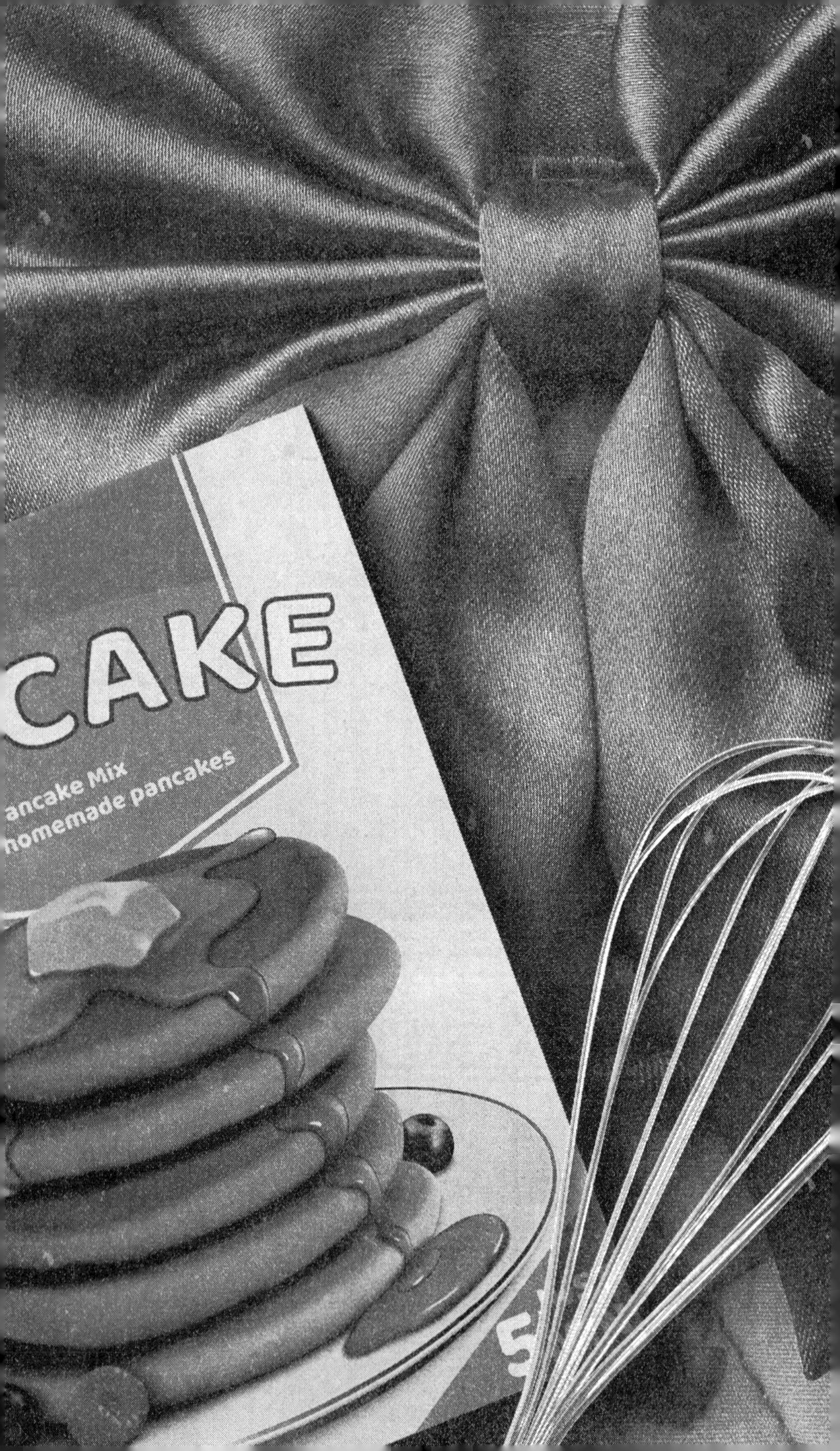
CAKE
ancake Mix
homemade pancakes

CHAPTER 82

SAWYER

30 MINUTES EARLIER

A s soon as we get back, I head inside. I haven't talked to Cali since our fight in the kitchen, and I've waited long enough.

Miles comes into the kitchen with wet hair, grinning like an idiot.

He brushes past me. "Going to the store!"

I glare at him. He looks like he just got fucked – all happy and glowing. He probably did. Jealousy runs through me. Clearly they've made up, and she still won't talk to me.

I've decided I'm done giving her a choice: We're going to hash this out here and now, whether she likes it or not.

The front door slams.

"Sawyer!" Ryder comes in after me. "We need to talk."

"Busy." I head toward Miles' room, where I imagine Cali is.

"It's about Cali."

That makes me pause. I turn. Ryder looks at me and arches a brow. "You remember that deal?"

My stomach clenches. Did he fuck her?

Ryder smirks. "Your girl screams so prettily."

I freeze. Is he for real right now?

"Squeezes the dick so tightly when she comes. No wonder you guys like her."

"You motherfucker," I snarl. Ryder crosses his arms. "Time to let her go, Sawyer."

"No!"

"That was the game, wasn't it? I fuck her, you let her go."

"I'll never let her go." I stalk up to him, stopping just shy of him and clenching my fists.

"Whatever happened to being a man of your word, Sawyer?"

I'll never let her go. I can't. Just the thought sends panic through me. "For her, I'll break it."

There's the tiniest change in Ryder's expression, then it's gone. I whirl back around to head to the room before a loud clatter makes me turn back around.

Ryder is on the ground, having taken an island chair down with him. He has a hand on his chest.

"What the fuck?" I growl.

Ryder heaves for breath. I move to crouch next to him. "You good?"

Ryder grabs onto me. "Chest hurts. Just...help me up?"

Fuck, what's wrong with him? I grab his shoulders, and as I do, I feel a sharp stab in my thigh like a bee sting.

I glance down. Ryder is finishing pressing the plunger of a syringe into me. I can't process it for a second. What the hell?

Ryder straightens, his face looking sad.

"What the fuck?" I can only stare at him. Did he just give me that?

Ryder raises his hands in a calming manner. "It's okay. Everything will be fine."

"What's going on?"

Ryder eyes me. I don't like that look in his eyes. He walks toward me, heading between me and the hall.

Between me and Cali.

Oh fuck. He's going to do something to Cali.

I dart down the hall.

Ryder is fast. He snatches me up and yanks me back roughly. I whirl, trying to throw a punch at him.

He grabs onto me tighter, burying his head in my back. "I won't hurt her."

"Don't fucking touch her," I snarl, struggling.

"Calm down," Ryder grunts, wrapping me in his arms and yanking me back. He's big and fucking strong as hell. I struggle, then go completely limp, trying to get him to drop me.

Ryder drops his body with me, not letting go of me.

"She doesn't want to be with you. You have to let her go."

"That's bullshit!" Dizziness hits my vision. Oh fuck. I'm going to pass out before I can get to her. "She never said that." Frantic energy runs through me. Something is wrong. That phone call he got. Something is wrong.

Miles! Where is Miles?

Ryder rolls his huge body on top of me. I fight to escape, but the damn drugs hit me harder than I expect.

"I'm trying to take care of our family."

"Fuck you." There are two of him swimming in circles above me. I blink while thrashing. Fuck, maybe if I close my eyes, it'll be better.

I don't realize I've stopped moving until he picks me up. I struggle to fight again, but it feels like all my limbs are fuzzy and cut off. Everything starts to get distant.

"I'm sorry."

It's the last thing I hear before nothingness overtakes me.

CAKE

ancake Mix

homemade pancakes

CHAPTER 83

SAWYER

I wake up groggy, my limbs heavy. I glance around, trying to clear my vision. Grey walls. Low light.

Wait. Am I…in the cell?

I try to move, but I can't. I glance down. I'm…tied to a chair?

Oh fuck. Ryder. Cali.

Adrenaline races through me. Cali. Where is Cali?

I shout for her, but I know this room is padded. Not much will get out, but I still try.

How long has it been? Fuck, fuck, fuck. If he kills her, I'll never forgive him. Fuck! What if he kills her?

I rip at the zip ties so hard the chair falls over. I hit the ground with a thump, all the breath knocked out of me.

Jesus Christ, I feel like shit. My head pounds, and I feel like I'm going to throw up.

But that doesn't matter. Nothing does. Cali is the only thing that matters anymore.

I struggle for a while, not getting anywhere. Ryder knows how to tie someone down and has multiple ties, and now I can see handcuffs around my ankles.

Helplessness washes over me. Oh my god, I'm going to lose her. The last thing she's going to feel for me is hate.

My chest hurts. Everything hurts. The bugs are back, skittering up and down my arms.

Fuck, I don't want her to think that I hate her.

I jerk back and forth on the ground so hard that I throw up. There's not much that comes up since I haven't eaten much in the last few days. I've been worried about her. Trying to figure out how to fix what I fucked up.

"Cali!" I cough her name. "Please, Cali, come back."

My throat tightens, and heat pricks at my eyes. I glare at the spot of bile. It's a dark puddle compared to the pockmarked, stained gray floor.

I zone out, staring at it. I didn't realize how much it looks like my mom's old carpet.

We never mop down here. Why don't we ever mop down here?

CHAPTER 84

CALI

Halloweiner screamed for the first part of our drive. He's finally quieted down, but I sit anxious, praying he doesn't pee. He's only in a cardboard box, and any little thing could set Ryder off.

Ryder looks calm. He hasn't said a word to me, just drives in silence. It puts me on edge. He said he wouldn't kill me, but does his word mean as much as Sawyer's?

My heart squeezes. I've taken a step that I can't come back from. I just threw away everything that I had with them, and my chest tightens. I can't help but feel like I did something wrong.

This is wrong. So wrong. But I deserve my freedom. It's what I wanted, right?

As we get closer to the big city, I start recognizing the roads again. My stomach churns.

I finally break the silence. "Where are we going?"

Ryder glances over at me. "I got you a hotel. You can stay there while you get your feet back under you."

"Why can't I go home?"

He looks uncomfortable. "Do you really want the cops sniffing at your door, asking where your boyfriend went?"

"Ex," I correct, looking back outside. "He's not my boyfriend."

There's silence.

"Your DNA is on him too, Cali. You realize that, right?"

I clench my jaw. "How am I supposed to get a job?"

"I kept your name similar. Callie Smart. You have a new social, and I'll leave you with enough cash to get settled. You're a capable girl. You can get it figured out."

The hum of the tires fills the car.

My voice is low, "Why are you doing this?" Is it because we fucked?

The muscle in Ryder's jaw flicks. We sit in silence for so long that I don't think he's going to answer me.

When he does, his voice is low and hoarse with emotion, "I'm trying to keep my family together. Wouldn't you?"

I continue staring out the window. More and more cars flash by. We're getting close. I hear him loud and clear. I'm not part of their family. I have no place with them.

He's right. I've known them, what, two weeks? They're killers. I'm not. Well, maybe I am now. I don't know.

"My family." A family I'm not part of. That makes my throat tighten so badly, and I think I'm going to cry. And for the life of me, I can't figure out why that hurts so damn bad.

We enter the city, and Ryder pulls up to a tall building with mirrored walls all the way to the top floor and stops. I glance around. We're here? This is too fancy.

Ryder faces me. His voice and tone is even. "You know that if you say anything about us to anyone, I'll kill you."

I have no doubt about that.

"Don't go back to our house. Don't go back to your old place. When I say new life, I mean it."

Fuck. This morning, I was showering with Miles, happy for the first time in a long time. Now, everything is changing. Again.

Suddenly, I don't want to get out of the car.

Ryder reaches across to the glove compartment. I catch a whiff of his cologne. He smells good as hell, and I hate myself for noticing. I'm such a fool.

Ryder shoves a stack of cash at me. "The hotel is paid for three weeks. This should be enough for rent and a down payment." He hands me paperwork and a box. "ID, social, birth certificate, and a phone."

I look down at my hand. There's more money than I've seen in my whole life.

"Where..."

"They're expecting the cat. Do you have any questions for me?"

I blink, then glance at Ryder's dark eyes.

I clench my jaw. I don't even know what to ask.

Ryder's eyes dart between mine, down to my mouth, and then my throat. "Oh, and one more thing. I'm going to need that necklace."

My hand flies to the necklace. "What? It's mine. Sawyer gave it to me."

Ryder lifts a dark eyebrow.

I clutch it. I don't want to give it back.

Ryder sighs like I'm dumb. "There's a tracker in it, Cali."

My heart stops for a second. A tracker? Sawyer put a tracker in my necklace. Jesus, of course he did.

I stutter out, "It won't come off. It's locked."

Ryder grabs a tool out of the glove compartment. "Lean over."

I don't want to. For some reason, giving this up feels like I'm giving him up. Even more so than running.

"Cali, I'm in a hurry." Ryder grabs it with one hand and uses a tool to clip off the lock with the other.

I suck in a breath and glance at the circular metal in his hand. My neck feels...empty. I can't keep it. I can't, but I want to.

"Can I..."

Ryder puts it in his pocket. "Sorry, Cali. Start your life on your own terms. Forget about us. Do all the things you want to do."

I stare at his pocket. Fuck. This hurts.

"Cali...I have to go."

I glance up. His gaze is soft. "I'm sorry you ever got tangled up with us in the first place."

I still don't move. Someone honks.

Ryder sighs and gets out of the car. He grabs Halloweiner from the back and opens my door. Cool air wafts in, and I shiver. He reaches around me, unstraps me, and his warm hands guide me out of the truck.

Then I'm standing on the sidewalk. The sounds of people and the street fill my ears.

"Remember. Callie Smart. I have all your paperwork inside that stack." He nods to the money in my hand.

He moves around to the front of the truck, and I'm frozen. This is wrong. It's everything I wanted, but it's wrong!

"Wait!" I take a step forward. "I've changed my mind!"

Ryder throws me a look over the truck bed, then gets in the truck.

"Wait!" I start running forward, but he pulls away from the block. And suddenly, I'm in the city with a stack of money, a new name, and completely and utterly alone.

CHAPTER 85

MILES

Ryder texts me while I'm on my way back from the store. Went for a drive. Be back in a bit.

I smile at the text. Actually, I've been smiling a lot. I know things aren't perfect, but I feel like we can work things out with Cali. She was meant for us. Built for us. And Ryder, too, if he can get his head out of his ass.

I hum on my way back inside. The house is silent, so I assume they all went out. I putter around for a bit, doing some chores, then picking up my guitar again. It's been a long time since I've even wanted to play, but I do now. I'm excited to give Cali her things. God, I hope I got the right stuff.

As time drags on, I start to look at my phone. They've been gone awhile. Where the hell did they go? I know Ryder and Sawyer will take care of her, and she'll take care of herself, but something starts to feel off.

Finally, I hear the truck rumbling up to the house. I grin, meeting them at the front door.

But it's only Ryder. And the look on his face instantly sobers me.

"What's wrong?" I bark, immediately focused. Ryder has dark circles under his eyes, and he looks stressed.

He waves me inside, shutting the door carefully behind him. "Sit."

"What the hell? Where's Cali and Sawyer?"

"Sit," he barks.

My stomach tightens. Something bad happened.

"I don't fucking want to sit. Tell me!"

Ryder glares at me.

"Jesus Christ." I throw my hands in the air when Ryder uses his big body to herd me back toward the couch. He moves my guitar before pushing me to sit.

Oh my god. Something horrible happened.

Ryder runs a hand through his hair. "I don't know how to say this."

"Where are they? Are they safe?"

He throws me a tired look. "They're safe. For now."

"What does that mean?"

"Would you let me explain?" he snaps. "My attorney called. There's new evidence against you, Miles. And Sawyer. Some hotshot detective is starting to put our kills together."

My stomach sinks all the way. Fuck. That's bad. But what does that have to do with Sawyer and Cali?

"And what we offered them to look the other way isn't enough." Ryder drops his head, raking his fingers through his hair. "We have to leave the country for a bit, Miles."

My stomach is in knots. "Okay? Where are the others?"

He looks up slightly. "Sawyer is safe. I had to...he didn't agree with my methods to keep all of us safe. So I had to make him safe."

Adrenaline fills me. "What the hell does that mean? And Cali?"

"Also safe." Ryder glances at his phone. As he does, the sound of a low-flying plane moves over the house. It's so low that I jerk my head up.

"Good. Our ride is here." Ryder stands.

"What do you mean?" I'm so confused. "Please, Ryder, where

are they?"

Ryder sighs. "Sawyer is in the basement."

I give him a weird look and snap, "No, he isn't. I've been here by myself for the past few hours."

"He is. He's in the cell."

I dart to my feet. Okay, something is definitely wrong. Ryder put Sawyer in the cell? Why in the world would he do that?

The world slows to a stop. Ryder did something to Cali. Fuck, he did something to her.

"Ryder!" I grip his shoulders and shake him. "What did you do to Cali?"

The look he gives me is tired. "She ran."

I shake him again. "That's bullshit!"

"She did." He roughly shrugs my hands off him. "She was a prisoner here, Miles. What did you expect? I've been telling you this all along."

My world drops out from under me. She...ran? But she was so happy when I left. Glowing and happy and content.

I snap my gaze to Ryder, a snarl building in my chest. "You took her."

He starts toward the front door. "She left of her own free will, Miles. We have to go too. Once the cops catch wind you guys are here, they'll be knocking down the door."

I lunge after him. "I could care less about the cops. Where's Cali? Did she leave on foot? Where did you take her?" My heart is racing, and my ears are ringing. Normally, I'm calm, but more fear fills me right now than I've ever felt.

Ryder ducks out the front door, and I follow him, freezing at what I see on our street. It's a goddamn crop duster. A fucking plane sitting right there on the road.

What the hell is happening right now?

Ryder strides up to the pilot, exchanging words.

Sawyer. I dart back inside and down to the cell, ripping the door open.

Sawyer is lying on his side, bound to a chair.

"What the fuck?" I bark, darting toward him.

He blinks groggily.

"Fuck! Sawyer, are you okay?"

"Cali," he groans. "Ryder did something to Cali."

I glance around. Fucking hell, I don't have a knife with me.

"I'll get you out. Just hang on." I dart upstairs, then realize the knives are still in the sex room. I cuss, running back downstairs to get one. When I finally do, I cut the zip ties, only to realize he's cuffed to the chair.

"Fucker!" I hiss. "What did he do to you?" I sit Sawyer back up.

He shakes his head slowly, slurring his words a little. "Drugged me. That mother...fucker."

"What did he do to Cali?" I ask.

Ryder's voice comes, making me jump. "I didn't do anything to her."

"Right," I snarl.

Sawyer hisses, "Did you kill her?"

Ryder looks calm. "You didn't let her have a choice. So I let her choose."

"What?" I run my hand through my hair. "Unlock him. Right now."

Ryder puts his hands in his pockets. "Sawyer, the cops are after you too. We have to go. I have everything set up, and our ride is outside."

"The fuck?" Sawyer spits on the ground. "All I care about is Cali."

Ryder winces slightly. "She's safe. Please, Sawyer."

Silence. I stare at Ryder. This has to be some big joke. This isn't real, is it?

Ryder narrows his eyes. "Don't make me fight you to keep you safe."

What? My stomach clenches, and I squeeze my fists, my body getting ready to fight.

He gives me a sad look, "You too, Miles?"

Rage boils up in me. "Me too? It's you, Ryder! You're doing all this!"

He snarls at me. "Oh yeah? Well, what about this?" He holds up something in his hand. I squint to see it.

Sawyer sucks in a breath. Is that...her collar?

Ryder tosses it at Sawyer. "She doesn't want you. You kidnapped her. Whatever you think you have with her is Stockholm. You'll forget about her soon enough."

"The fuck it is!" Sawyer yells. "You took that off her."

"We need to go." Ryder looks at me. "Please, Miles. Work with me."

"Work with you?" I sputter.

"Don't make me make you."

My rage boils over. "Oh! So you'll preach about choices, but you'll take away our choice? What if we don't want to go, Ryder?"

He throws his hands in the air. "I'm trying to keep you safe! What will it take to let me help you?"

"Let us get Cali back," Sawyer growls.

"Not gonna happen," Ryder glares at him.

I narrow my eyes. "You know where she is."

Ryder shoots me a dark look.

"Jesus!" Sawyer stands, but his legs are still cuffed to the chair, loud clanking filling the room. "Tell us!"

"No! Get on the plane. Now." Ryder motions at me.

"Not unless you tell me where she is." I cross my arms. I know Ryder could beat me in a fight. He's bigger than either of us, and Sawyer won't be any help tied to the chair and drugged. Ryder could force both of us on the plane right now, and he knows it. His gaze is tortured.

"I can't tell you." He swallows. "We're going to Wyatt's island. You know he keeps track of everyone to come and go. She'll go on a list. The same list we're on. You know he knows everything about us and keeps tabs on us. She would never escape our lifestyle. Never."

I swallow. Wyatt is brutal. He guards his secrets viciously. Which is great for a hideaway. Horrible for anyone he doesn't know.

Ryder grips the side of the doorway. "You don't even know Cali. This is just an obsession. You'll get over it, and then what? Her life will be ruined because you couldn't get your dicks under control!"

Sawyer snarls, "It's more than that."

Ryder runs his hand down his face. "You haven't even known

her a month. How can it be more than that?"

"It just is, okay!" Sawyer looks like he struggles to find the words.

I step in. "It's more," I say. "Cali is...everything we didn't know we were missing."

Ryder clenches his jaw. The room is silent and full of tension.

Finally, Ryder rips his hands off the doorway. "If you get on that plane with me right now, I'll tell you where she is."

My heart fills with hope.

"In three months."

"Three months?" I sputter.

"Yes," he barks. "I need to know you're over whatever honeymoon stage is messing with your heads. And I don't want you to ruin her life because you couldn't get it figured out."

Three months? Three fucking months? Fucking hell, she could be anywhere in that time!

Sawyer nudges my hand and growls, "Fine. We'll do it."

I whirl on him, disbelief running through me. "The fuck we will! I'll give him thirty minutes. Max."

Sawyer shoots me a dark glare and taps my foot again with his. He's trying to tell me something.

The rage wrestles in my chest.

"Unlock me." Sawyer turns back to Ryder.

Ryder doesn't move. "You give me your word you'll get on that plane?"

"Yes!" Sawyer snaps. "We'll get on the fucking plane. Get these fucking cuffs off me."

Ryder looks between us. "And you?"

I grit my teeth. Fuck. I don't know why Sawyer is agreeing to this, but I have to trust him. He's as messed up as I am over this girl. "Yes," I growl.

"Good." Ryder bends down and unlocks Sawyer, giving him a hand up. "We don't have much time. If there's anything sentimental here, grab it. I'm burning the place down, and then we're gone."

CHAPTER 86

SAWYER

The small plane takes us a few hours to the coast. We stopped a few times for fuel, and then we hit a private airport with a bigger, but still private, plane. The same one we used to take back when we hunted with Wyatt.

I puke a few times on the flight. Every mile between Cali and us rips at my heart. I've never felt more tortured.

She's getting away. I swore I'd never let her go, and now she really has a chance to run. To forget about us. And that breaks me into pieces.

I hate that I don't have the strength to fight Ryder right now. How could I let this happen?

Miles is unusually quiet the whole time. Ryder talks about his plans, but neither Miles nor I say anything.

As we're boarding, my resolve almost crumbles. I can't leave the country knowing she's here. I turn to leap off the stairs, but Ryder is behind me and grabs my arm, pushing me roughly into the plane.

I whirl on him, and darkness closes in around my vision

I'm gripped roughly. "Sit down. You're going to hurt yourself." Ryder backs me to a seat, and when my knees hit it, they crumble. The plane is roomy, and it's just us, but Miles sits next to me.

I'm useless right now. The thought damn near makes me want to cry. I can't do anything to get Cali back. I grip the collar I gave her. I haven't let it go since we left the house.

The plane takes off, and the sadness gripping my chest slowly fades out, replaced by anger.

If she really ran, I'm going to beat her ass black and blue, then brand the rest of our initials into her. Because clearly, she didn't get the message the first time.

Ryder paces up and down the aisles, occasionally disappearing into the back and the front. When Ryder disappears into the cockpit for the 20th time, Miles leans over into me. "So what's the plan?"

I lean back and close my eyes. "We're gonna get our girl back."

He grunts. "I'm not waiting three months."

"Me either."

"He's not going to tell us where she is."

I crack my eyes open to check around the room. Ryder isn't here. "That doesn't matter."

"What do you mean?" Miles turns to me.

"She has a tracker on her."

I hear Miles sigh. "Dude. He took her collar."

"I know."

I crack my eyes open to look at him. He's stiff. "Don't fuck with me. Are you for real?"

"Yes."

Miles jumps to his feet, then glances at the front of the plane and sits back down. "Where?" he hisses.

"In her arm. I had one put into the birth control I gave her." I've never been more grateful to be thorough.

Miles looks at me for a minute, then claps me roughly on the back. "Oh my god! Genius! Have I told you I love you recently?"

I wince. "No need to hit me." But I can't keep the slight smile off my face.

Miles sits back, his face flushed. "Oh my god. We can get her back."

We're silent for a bit. It's not just a want. I *need* her back. She started as revenge, but the longer she stayed with us, the more I knew she was different. And the more I learned about her, the more I needed her. I need to unpeel all her layers. I still do. Examine every secret. Make her understand, once and for all, that she's mine. Ours.

Miles' soft voice startles me. "Do you really think she ran?"

I clench my jaw. I've been running that possibility around in my head. I don't want to believe it, but it's not outside the realm of possibility.

Miles is silent. "I hope she didn't."

I grit my teeth. "She'll pay if she did."

We are silent for a bit. Then, Miles says, "We didn't exactly make it easy on her."

I snap my head to look at him. Miles gives me a torn look. "We didn't make her at home."

"What are you talking about?" Anger rolls through me.

"She had nothing. She had no clothes, for Christ's sake. Nothing personal."

"I prefer her naked anyway," I mutter.

"Sawyer," Miles snaps. "Did we give her a room? A bed? A goddamn toothbrush? What about deodorant and shampoo? Did we even ask her what she likes to eat?"

My gut cramps. Shit. We didn't do any of that.

"I brought her cat."

"A few days ago! That should have happened at the very beginning."

My chest tightens. Fuck. I didn't mean to ignore all those needs. I clench my fists. Oh my god. What if she actually did run? What if I drove her away?

I feel sick again.

As soon as this plane lands, we're going to get our girl. And I'll do better this time. This is my last chance. Because after this, I'm never letting her go.

CHAPTER 87

RYDER

ONE WEEK LATER

I'm washing the dishes, and I can't get Cali out of my head. The way her body moved under me. Her soft skin and wild hair. Her attitude, her fire.

Her fear.

I clench my jaw.

God! The woman is infuriating. She's not even here, and she's still in my thoughts.

I drop the sponge in the sink, realizing that I've washed most of the dishes without noticing. I can't remember the last time I did that.

"What are you doing, boss?" Miles comes into the small kitchen, leaning against the counter.

We're still settling into our new house. It's on one of Wyatt's islands scattered around Japan. But this one is empty, save the runway and the house, and full of rocky cliff faces, forest, and beach. There's perpetual gray skies at this time of year, and it's hauntingly beautiful. Despite all that, it still feels like something's missing.

"Dishes," I mutter.

"Sawyer wants to talk to you."

I glance at Miles. Sawyer hasn't seemed like he's wanted to talk at all today. He's been fidgety and on edge, constantly checking his phone. Something is up. I've been waiting for them to talk to me about it.

I feel bad for not telling them that Cali wanted to come back with me. Her panicked face in the rearview mirror has haunted me ever since.

I cross my arms. "Okay."

I follow Miles to the living room, where Sawyer stands stiffly. He has dark circles under his eyes, his hair is wild, and I don't think he's slept a single full night since we've gotten here. My chest tightens at that knowledge. I thought he'd be a little better by now. If anything, he's worse. And that hurts me.

I eye him, "What did you want to talk about?"

Sawyer glances at Miles, then back to me. "We're going back to get Cali."

My stomach tightens. I thought that might be what he's been worked up about. "No, you're not. The cops are looking for you. And in case you missed it, we don't have a plane."

Sawyer just stares into my eyes, unbothered.

Warning bells go off in my head. He's planning something. "What are you doing?"

"Giving you the courtesy you didn't give us. A choice." Sawyer glares at me.

I grit my teeth. "A choice for what?"

"Come with us, or stay here."

I shake my head, leaning back. "You can't go anywhere. Wyatt doesn't have any more flights out for two months."

Sawyer shrugs. "He doesn't, but his pilots do. You're not the only one with money around here, Ryder."

I glance at Miles. He cocks an eyebrow. Shit, they're serious. They must have bribed the pilot to come back when I wasn't looking.

I shake my head, running my hands through my hair. "You were supposed to give me three months."

"That's too long," Sawyer snaps.

"No, it isn't! What are you afraid of? That she'll forget you?"

A tick runs across Sawyer's jaw. Miles looks uncomfortable. So that's it. They're afraid that because she ran, she doesn't want them.

A pang of guilt hits me hard.

I growl, "What if you bring her here, and she fights you for the rest of her life? Would you still want it?"

Sawyer answers immediately, "Yes."

I glance at Miles. He shrugs. "She wouldn't. We fucked up before. We won't again."

I see the conviction in both their eyes. They won't give this up. I tried, and they won't.

Miles' voice comes out soft, "If we bring her here, you won't have to worry about her betraying us. There's nowhere for her to go. No one for her to talk to."

I clench my fingers tighter. "There's always that possibility."

"So get to know her so she doesn't!" Miles says. "Not everyone is like your family, Ryder. We won't lose her."

The room is full of silence. My heart pangs. I don't want to lose anyone. I want to hold my men so close they can't get themselves killed.

Miles asks softly, "Safety concerns aside, do you have anything against her?"

Do I? I've been torn on this all week. She's feisty, opinionated, and reckless. Beautiful and strong and continually running around in my head. But...she's not in my routine. I didn't vet her. All of a sudden, she was there, in my house and my room, destroying my stuff. Turning me on without even trying.

Miles looks so fucking scared of my answer it makes me want to reach out and give him a hug. Promise him I'll never leave him, regardless of what psycho he brings into our home. Hot little psycho.

I suck in a deep breath. I can't believe I'm about to do this. "There's something you need to know. About when Cali ran."

CHAPTER 88

CALI

I pace the length of my room for the five hundredth time today. My legs buzz with energy, and walking does nothing to get rid of it.

I shake out my hands and glance at the bed. "Should I?"

Halloweiner ignores me. He just twitches his tail and continues to pretend to sleep.

"Ugh. I'm doing it." I snatch up some cash and my fake ID. I glare at the phone Ryder gave me. Will I want it? It was completely new - still in the cellophane - and there's nearly nothing on it. I spent the first day creating a fake email and making social media accounts for my fake name.

I snatch it up. No one goes without their phone anyway. I don't want to stand out. It's weird how quickly I got used to not having it when I was with the boys.

No! Fuck, Cali. Stop thinking about them.

I square my shoulders, checking myself in the mirror before I go. Ryder left an obscene amount of money with me. On the third day, I finally got out of my own depressed filth and bought all new clothes. It didn't even make a dent in the cash.

I readjust my shirt. It's uncomfortable. I miss the oversized shirts that smelled like them. I catch a glimpse of the hair care on the counter. The same exact things I asked Miles to get.

My throat clenches.

Christ! Get it together, woman. We're happy now. Smile.

I plaster on a fake grin and march downstairs. There's a hotel bar here, and it's been on my mind endlessly. I've told myself I won't go. Then I've told myself that I will — that I'm my own woman and can decide what to do.

Sawyer can go fuck himself.

Ugh, Sawyer. My heart cramps. He thinks I hate him. I never got to tell him thank you for Halloweiner. And I never will.

Tears well in my eyes for the thousandth time this week.

I blink angrily. Jesus fucking Christ, Cali. What the hell is your problem?

I've researched Stockholm religiously. It's what I have. Clearly. Right?

I reach up to feel for the collar again, knowing it isn't there. It feels like part of me is...missing. It's for the best. Ryder said I wasn't part of his family.

Flashbacks from the nightmare I've had every night this week hit me. Sawyer is chasing me through the dark, screaming that he hates me. That I betrayed him.

I break out in a clammy sweat, sliding into the stool at the bar. There are a few other people here.

"Can I get you something?" The middle-aged bartender asks.

"Um, yeah." My hands are shaking. Fuck. I sit on them. "Wine, please. Anything red."

"You got it."

He slides a glass over to me. I slide back my payment and grab it to have something to do with my hands.

I need it. I really need this drink. My stomach churns at the thought of drinking it. An irrational voice pops in my head: Sawyer would be disappointed.

Fuck. Stop thinking about them. They were assholes, remember?

Assholes who gave you no choice and traumatized you.

Who cared about you and protected you in a way no one else has before.

I watch the bartender serve some others their drinks. He barely rinses the glasses out, turning them over on sticky counters. Ryder would hate it.

A middle-aged man keeps throwing me glances from the other side of the bar. He looks average, like every other worn-down businessman on a trip. He smiles and waves at me. At first, I want to ignore him, but then I force myself to react. I'm here for a distraction. I need a distraction.

So when the man slides over, and I feel nothing but annoyance, I stamp it down.

"Hey. This seat taken?"

"Nope." I clench my glass and give him a small smile, then look out over the rest of the bar.

"In town for business?" the man asks.

Oh fuck. What do I say? "Uh, yeah. You could say that."

He gives me a genuine smile. "What do you do?"

Suddenly, I feel jittery. I already hate this fake ass conversation. It pops out before I can stop it, "Hairdresser."

I swallow. Is that what new Callie will do?

"Oh. Cool." The man takes a sip of his beer. "I work for Amix."

I give him a blank look. His eyes are brown and dull.

He chuckles. "Oil company."

"Oh." Someone kill me now. I glance over the room again.

"You looking for someone?" He turns to check over his shoulder.

"Oh. No." I settle back toward the bar, tapping my fingers on my glass. I should drink it. Take a sip. Dull the horribleness of this conversation and escape for a bit. But, for some reason, I can't. I keep seeing Sawyer's face on top of the tank.

The man keeps up with it. "So, what do you do for fun?"

"I..." the question floors me. What do I do for fun? I draw a blank. For the last week, I've sat lost in a hotel room in a strange city, doing nothing but crying over men who are bad for me. I think back to the old me. This. This is what she did for fun. Drink. And mindlessly scroll social media.

It hits me suddenly how empty I used to feel. How empty I feel again.

I swallow harshly. My eyes cloud with tears. I didn't realize until I met the men how much I had lost myself. They helped me find it again without even trying.

"Uh...you okay?" the man asks.

"Yeah. I...cut hair for fun."

As I'm talking, a man comes up to the bar carrying flowers. He drops them off by me. "Someone said to give this to you."

I turn, looking around. What the hell? I look back at the bouquet, and my heart stops.

Purple and white blooms. They're foxglove and hemlock.

I push back from my stool, heart racing, and check the room again. I don't see anyone. There's a little card with the flowers. My hand shakes as I reach for it, adrenaline running through my body.

Nice shirt. But you looked better in mine.

I drop the card. Oh my god. He's here. I back away from the bar, then whirl, half walking, half running. I'm almost to the elevator before a hand grips my shoulder and yanks me back into a hard body.

"You lost, little bunny?"

CHAPTER 89

CALI

A thrill runs through me. I know that voice. How is it possible?

I yank away to look at him. But Sawyer's arms band tighter around me, pinning me to his chest.

"Wanna play a game?"

His dark voice sends shivers down my arms. My chest heaves. I'm surrounded by the smell of cologne.

Sawyer squeezes tighter, just enough to hurt. "Yes...or no?"

I gasp, the old fight filling me. "No."

Suddenly, I'm shoved away. I stumble a step before turning. Three figures, all in white Ghostface masks, stand there, blocking my way to the front of the hotel. They're big and menacing, dark tattoos tracing down their arms.

One of them cocks his head, saying mockingly, "Run, bunny."

The fire that I lost this whole week runs through me. I feel more alive than ever. And I do. I run faster than I've ever run. I dart down the hall toward the stairs, ripping open the door to go up. I take the stairs two at a time, darting up them as fast as I can. My breath comes in pants, but I feel like I'm flying.

Fuck, they're here! All I can feel is excitement as I run.

There's a bang as the door to the stairs slams. I scream.

"What a good girl, running from us." The voice echoes, then gets dark and menacing. "But you won't get away this time."

His voice shoots straight to my pussy, and my adrenaline spikes.

I reach the third floor, where my room is, and yank on the door to get in. It's locked.

What? I yank again. It doesn't open.

Scrape, scrape, scrape.

"Caliiiiii. Come out and plaaaay."

A white mask appears on the stairs below me.

I scream, darting up the steps. I reach the next level, heaving for breath. It's also locked.

What the fuck? I dart up the next steps, my heart pounding. I skip the next level, running

up and up. I hear their measured steps below me.

"You're going to pay for being such a naughty girl."

It feels like I'm taking each step in slow motion. I look back, catching their white masks. They're catching up to me, and that gives me a sudden thrill.

I make it to the top. There's a single door, and I try it.

It's unlocked, so I burst through it. It opens to a hallway leading to yet another door.

"We're going to fuck you so hard you'll regret the day you ever ran."

I rush through that door, then stumble to a stop. It's completely dark in here. I blink. Well, not completely dark. There are windows I see, letting in a little light from the evening nightscape. This is the penthouse.

I hear their voices outside and run further in, tripping over something. I cuss, pain tearing up my shin.

The door opens, flooding the room with light for a second.

The men step in, and the door swings shut, enveloping us in darkness again.

"Give up now, Cali and Ryder won't make you cry...too much."

"Fuck off," I shoot back. I scoot farther into the room.

There are a few dark chuckles. I can only see vague shapes and the faint white of their masks.

"You know all of us love taming brats, right?"

I turn a corner and bump against something soft. A bed? Is this a bed? I pat around, crouching down. It is. I feel around. There's enough room under it.

I slide under just in time. A dark form steps around the corner.

I watch him look slowly around the room. Who is it? I squint at his hands. Sawyer? Miles?

He looks down at me, eerily still. Can he see me? No way. Not with the mask on.

"Hello, Cali."

I scream.

He reaches down, grabbing me by the hair. He yanks just enough to bring tears to my eyes. "Come out to play, pretty girl."

The other two walk in.

I feel the steady threat on my scalp. I hesitate, suddenly not eager to face their wrath all at once.

The pull comes again, this time a clear warning. Tears spill over my eyes, and I cry out.

"Come out."

I elbow my way out. The one holding my hair doesn't let up. He pulls me into a kneeling position and tilts my head back so far I'm staring at the ceiling. He lets out a heady groan, running his nose up the column of my neck. I can't see the other two, but I hear one right in front of me, then silence.

I try to look, but there's a sharp jerk on my scalp. Fingers brush across my throat.

"So delicate."

"Such a pretty thing."

"Mine."

The voices come from all over. I try to swallow. My body tingles with excitement, and my pussy is wet already.

"Did you miss us, Cali?" the voice growls in my ear.

"No."

Another sharp tug. "Lying only gets you punished more."

"Yes," I gasp.

"Mmmm. She wants this." Suddenly, the hand in my hair is gone, and there's a hand around my throat, lifting me up and throwing me on the bed.

"Why don't you show us how much you missed us?"

I glance at them surrounding the bed. In the dark, I still can't tell them apart, but the one on the right sounds like Sawyer.

Adrenaline courses through me, and I do something totally stupid that makes me feel more alive than I've ever been.

"I missed you this much." I hold out both my middle fingers with a tiny space in between them.

The guy at the foot of the bed rips his mask off and lunges for me. It's Miles. He grabs me around the waist, lifting me up and slamming me against the wall. He cushions my head against his hand, keeping it from hitting the wall. Miles growls, "Oh, I love it when you play."

In a matter of a few brutal yanks, my new clothes are shredded off. Miles yanks his pants down, and his hands are immaturely all over my breasts. He groans, gripping them tightly, sending pleasure straight down to my pussy.

"Wrap your legs around me."

"Fuck you."

There's a dark chuckle, and he leans down, biting my neck hard. I scream, automatically wrapping my legs around him. My clit presses against him, and I groan. I missed this. Needed this. Needed them like I needed my next drink, only worse.

"What was that? Are you being a needy whore?" Sawyer comes around to the side of the bed, his mask abandoned. "Groan for me again, whore. I want to see those pretty little lips sing."

Miles adjusts himself and thrusts inside me in a violent motion. I scream from the intrusion, stiffening.

"Yes," Sawyer says, gripping his dick. "Fucking gorgeous. Do it again."

Miles pulls back, then slams into me again. I grunt, my body stretching to take him.

"Jesus Cali...you're soaked," Miles says.

All I can do is moan as I clench around his length. It feels like forever since I've had this, and I'm already floating in pleasure. My clit rubs against him in this position, bumping every time he moves.

Miles must notice, ducking his head to look into my eyes. "Do you remember the rules, pretty girl? You don't get to come unless those eyes are on mine."

He flexes into me. Oh god, I want to come already.

Ryder is standing at the foot of the bed, arms crossed, his dark gaze fixed on us.

"Eyes." Miles' voice is gritty and full of lust.

I look at him. His eyes bounce back and forth between mine. Then, he reaches his hand between us and pinches my clit.

I come, clenching around his dick tightly, pleasure exploding, then floating through my body.

"Good girl. Good fucking girl," Sawyer groans. "What a pretty little obedient slut."

I open my mouth to argue when Miles steps back from the wall. I cling to him, about to fall. He pulls out of me quickly, and Sawyer grabs me. "On your knees, Cali."

I turn to face him, but he whirls me around so my back is to him, forcing me onto my hands. "You think you deserve to look at me after you disobeyed? After you ran from us and broke the only rules?"

Sawyer smacks my ass once, the shock going through me. Miles grips my chin, forcing me to look at him. "Good?"

No more smacks come. I wait, tense, but Miles just waits. They remember that I don't like to not see. I nod, tears filling my eyes.

"Good tears or bad tears?" Miles asks.

"Good," I choke out.

More hits come, these ones harder. I stiffen, but take them. The pain flows through me, mixing nicely with the pleasure, sending all my nerve endings buzzing.

I feel Sawyer playing with my asshole, and I automatically clench.

"Oh no." Sawyer spits on me, rubbing his fingers around my ass. "You don't get to shut me out. Not anymore."

He presses a finger into me, and I groan.

"Miles. Eat her."

"Gladly." Miles drops down underneath me, and I pause as he grabs my clit in his teeth and yanks.

Smack! "Say, sorry for running, daddy."

"Fuck you," I groan.

The bite to my clit makes my entire body jolt. If it weren't for the two pairs of hands grabbing ahold of me, I would have run.

Smack, smack, smack. Sawyer hits the same spot over and over, causing blooming hot pain to burn on my ass. I look up to see Ryder watching it all. The smacks don't stop, and I cry out, trying to get away. They don't let me.

It feels amazing, but I'm missing something. I want Ryder to join.

Ryder tilts his head, slowly reaching his hand down to yank his pants down and pull his dick out. The tip glistens in the faint light, and my mouth waters.

The pain is making my eyes water, and tears drip down my face. He groans.

"What, too cowardly to join in?" I ask.

It's the wrong move. Or the right one, I don't know. But Ryder is on me in a flash, yanking my hair back and smacking his massive dick in my face.

"You want to choke on my cock, girl?" His voice is gravely and low. "See how far down my men's tattoos you can make it?" He yanks again. "Maybe I'll let you back up for air, maybe not. Brats don't deserve to breathe."

Ryder clenches his fingers in my hair, and my mouth parts in a groan. He puts his dick on my tongue.

I take him into my mouth, groaning as his taste fills me. I lick around his head and down his shaft. He groans, tightening his hold on my hair.

Miles and Sawyer continue messing with me, Miles eating and Sawyer using his dick to tease my opening.

I'm so turned on I can't help it.

"That's enough," Ryder growls. "My turn to pick the game." And with that, he thrusts his dick down the back of my throat.

I immediately gag. Ryder doesn't let up, pushing further in and groaning as my body tightens around him, trying to gag him out.

"Yes, pretty girl," he moans. "Choke on me. Choke on Daddy's dick."

Ryder pulls back just enough for me to take a breath, and when he does, Sawyer pushes all the way inside my ass.

I scream, and it's immediately silenced by Ryder pushing all the way down my throat again. He gathers my hair and taps my nose. "Eyes, Cali. Look at me."

I blink up at him, barely able to see his dark look through the wash of tears.

"Yes," Sawyer groans. "Take all of us like a dirty little slut. Look at our nasty whore. You look so beautiful taking us like this."

I look over to see Miles playing with himself. I hover on the edge of another orgasm. Ryder periodically denying me air makes all the sensations come more strongly. I feel his dick twitching, and I know he's enjoying it from how stiff his entire body is.

Smack! Sawyer times it just as Miles nips my clit again, and I come undone. I shatter into Miles' mouth, shuddering and trying to cry out around Ryder's dick.

"Fuck yes, Cali. Yes." Sawyer pistons in and out of me. None of them let up, pushing me to another orgasm. I come again, this one more sensitive, more powerful, and more painful.

I scream out around Ryder's dick, and he pulls all the way back, twitching. I gasp for air, trying to catch my breath. Miles continues to assault my clit, and harsh sensations run through me.

"Please, no more."

"Oh, you lost the right to stop coming when you ran, bunny. We're only getting started."

And he's not lying. They play with me, and Ryder fucks my face until my arms are shaking and my eyes are rolling back in my head. At some point, Miles comes all over his hand, reaching over and painting it on my tits. Ryder smacks my cheek to keep me awake, but the haze of lack of oxygen and pain has me tight.

I come again, painfully, fully crying and snotting around Ryder's dick. With a barely contained groan, he yanks out of my mouth, coming on my face. I pant, collapsing to my elbows. Sawyer pushes inside me one more time before he also comes. He pulls out, coming on my back.

They let me down carefully, brushing the hair out of my face. I'm sticky and covered in come and so exhausted that my eyes keep shutting.

"Good girl, you did so good. Sleep. We'll take care of you," Miles says.

"When you wake up, you'll be ours forever. There will be no escape then," Sawyer coos.

I struggle to keep my eyes open.

"Sleep, pretty girl. And then the real punishment can begin."

The blackness overtakes me.

CHAPTER 90

CALI

I stir, feeling arms around me.

"Shhh, I got you," Miles whispers. "Sleep."

The world rocks, and suddenly I'm wrapped in his coconut scent. I press into his chest, groaning. I'm not asleep, but I'm totally drained from the adrenaline and orgasms.

"She out?"

"Yeah."

"Get her in the car. I'll get her stuff."

The voices are harsh. My stuff? My boy! I crack my eyes open. Lights pass by overhead as Miles carries me down the hotel steps.

He says, "We'll get Weiner, don't worry."

I'm slowly waking up, but I'm not fully awake until Miles slides me into a van and sits next to me. I sit up straighter, looking around the strange car. "Where are we going?"

"Home." Miles leans over to strap me in.

Home. I don't even know what home is anymore. What does that mean? His home or mine? And was mine really home anyway?

There's nothing tying me to that apartment anymore.

The other two come down shortly with a cat carrier I've never seen with Halloweiner inside. They put it all in the backseat.

Sawyer slides in next to me. "Ready for round two, bunny?" He looks haggard and tired.

My voice comes out rough, "Round two?"

Ryder pulls away from the curb.

Sawyer looks straight ahead, avoiding eye contact with me. "Oh, you thought the game was over?"

"Is that why I'm back? The game?"

A muscle tightens in his jaw.

I swallow. The tension is thick. I've had so many things I wanted to say to him all week, including some angry cussing, but it all gets bottled up in me, and I don't know what to say.

Sawyer won't even look at me. Won't yell, won't beg for forgiveness, nothing. My chest clenches.

Ryder looks expressionless. I swallow, and some of the orgasm high fades away.

Maybe I didn't mean as much to them as I thought I did. Every fake conversation I've had with myself this week circled back to one thing: they were complete without me. I'm not part of this family, so why am I back? Sawyer couldn't stand to lose?

Anger fills me, but mostly at myself. Of course I overestimated my role in this game. They're the hunters, and I'm the prey. Nothing more.

Sawyer confirms that by not looking at me.

Miles puts his hand on my thigh, rubbing his thumb back and forth. He clears his throat. "Cali..."

"Let's not talk." Looking out the windows on either side would require me to look at them, so instead, I look straight out the windshield.

Miles stiffens but does as I ask. The ride is silent. I'm not sure where we're going, and honestly, I'm not sure I care. Fuck, I'm an idiot.

When we pull up to an airport, I try to choke back the tears and that makes me angrier. I can't even lose with dignity, I have to embarrass myself by crying?

Miles shifts to face me. "Hey, hey. Are you okay?"

He sounds genuinely concerned, and I can't help but let loose a strangled sob. Here comes the embarrassment.

Sawyer gives me a dark look.

I try to shove both of them away and climb out of the car so they don't see me break, but Miles blocks me with his huge body. "Cali! What's wrong, baby?"

I sob harder.

"Is she hurt?"

Suddenly, I feel hands on me, turning my face to Sawyer. I cover my eyes with my hands.

"Sub drop?"

The overwhelming feeling of pain hits me in the chest, and there's no fighting it. I lean over my knees and start sobbing heavily.

"Talk to me."

I'm beyond talking. I cry and cry until the pain eases enough for mortification to seep through. Miles is rubbing my back. My breaths slow to hiccups.

The men are silent. I don't think I can raise my head to look at them. I don't even know what to say. I wanted it to be more? I wanted them to care about me more than the stupid fucking game? God, I'm an idiot. An idiot.

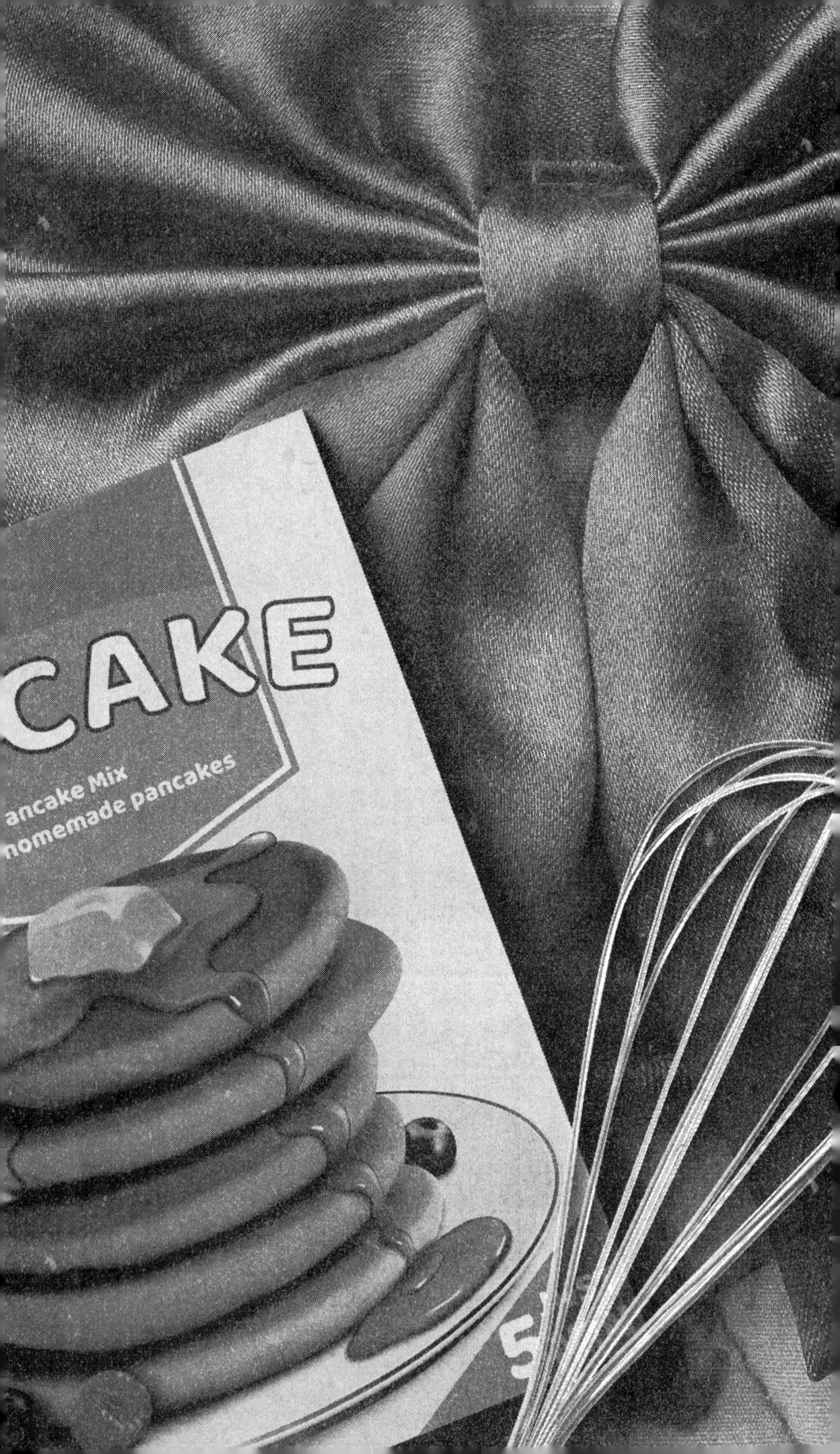
CAKE
ancake Mix
homemade pancakes

CHAPTER 91

SAWYER

I clench my jaw so hard it hurts. Cali won't talk to us. She looks devastated to be back with us, and that absolutely breaks me.

I wanted to say everything to her that I had rehearsed in the mirror. But when we got in the car, and she sat next to me, breathing and real, a bolt of fear hit me. What if she doesn't feel the same way? What if she laughs in my face? After my mom, I've never let another woman in.

"We have to go," Ryder says softly.

"Right." I snap back to business. We have a flight to get on. It gives me something to do other than sit in these uncomfortable feelings. I carry Cali's things to the plane. Miles walks her to the stairs, and she doesn't even fight him.

And that hurts. I'd rather her fight than cry her eyes out and give up. Where the hell did this come from?

The plane ride is silent. Cali curls up on one of the seats and doesn't say anything to us. I run my hand through my hair for the hundredth time.

Did we fuck up? Was she happy without us? God, she looked so excited to see us in the bar. I almost came in my pants seeing the look of fear and lust that ran across her face.

We didn't come in time. She was already ready to leave us. That thought angers me.

When we finally get close, Ryder pulls me into the back of the plane. "I can't take this anymore," he hisses. "The tension in here is thick enough to cut. You need to talk to her."

"In case you noticed, she won't talk."

Ryder crosses his big arms. "And why do you think that is?"

"I don't know!" My chest constricts.

Ryder raises an eyebrow. "You don't know?"

"Yes," I hiss. "If it's so obvious, why don't you fill me in, big guy?"

Ryder sighs and runs a hand down his face. "You have to communicate, Sawyer. Tell her how you feel."

My gut clenches. "How am I supposed to do that?"

"I don't know! I can't do it all for you, Sawyer." Ryder throws his hands in the air. "If you really care about her, you'll suck it up and apologize."

He walks back to his seat. Fear floods me. When Miles and I get into fights, I just pretend like nothing happened, and we go back to living as if nothing happened.

I steel myself. I can learn to apologize. Right?

I don't think I can bear it if I apologize and she runs again. I can't lose her...again. I don't think I'd survive it.

CHAPTER 92

CALI

I watch out the window as we descend. The morning sun shines off a thick layer of clouds. I see an island in the middle of the ocean as we descend through them. It's mostly forest, with a few cliff faces and some rocky beaches. Curiosity fills me. Where are we?

When we touch down, and the plane comes to a halt, Miles holds out his hand.

"Where are we?" I ask, standing without his help.

"Home," he says simply.

My chest clenches. I want someplace to call home.

I step outside onto the tarmac. The air is colder and more humid than I'm used to, the water in the air instantly clinging to my skin.

Miles grabs my hand, gripping tighter when I try to yank it back. The other men follow as we walk up a path into the trees. The ground is wet and mossy, covered in gray boulders. The trees open up to a clearing where a quaint, two-story house sits. The roof is flat, the windows are bordered by storm doors, and all the lights are on inside. It looks warm and dry. Despite myself, I find myself pulling towards it.

When we get to the front door, it's not locked. Sawyer pushes it open. "Welcome home, Cali."

My heart stops.

Wait, home? As in, my home?

Miles pushes me gently inside. We're in a small entryway attached to a hallway. I pause. Miles pushes me down the hall where a living room opens up on the right. Suddenly, I'm hit with a familiar smell. It smells like apples and cranberries. Like my apartment. I whirl around.

Miles gives me a gentle smile.

Ryder pushes past us with the luggage. "You'll have to take your shoes off in the living room, Cali. The floors are tatami."

I glance down. They look like woven straw mats.

"Here, I'll get those." Miles grabs the luggage from Ryder and starts heading upstairs with Sawyer. Poor Halloweiner is howling.

"I'll take care of him," Miles says. "We have a space upstairs for him to settle in."

Suddenly, they're gone, and I'm left standing with Ryder. He looks just as good as I remember, with a dangerous aura surrounding him. I'm not sure where we stand, and I shift.

"You hungry?" Ryder asks.

Starving actually. I nod. He walks me to the kitchen. The downstairs is shaped like a big square, with the steps to the upstairs in the middle.

"What do you want?" Ryder opens the pantry.

"Uh, whatever." I slide into the dining room table and look around.

He tosses me a bag of chips. "Eat those while I warm up some real food."

I open it hesitantly while he heats something up in the microwave.

I glance at the table. "I followed your rules, you know."

"I know."

I look up at Ryder. He's staring at me with heat in his eyes. The microwave dings. He looks at me for a second longer before opening it.

I eat my food in silence for a bit. He watches me silently. It's unnerving.

"Would you stop?" I mutter.

"Stop what?"

"Stop...looking at me."

Ryder lifts an eyebrow. "Why?"

"Because," I grumble while heat runs through me. "It's weird."

He huffs. There's silence again, but I don't feel the burning weight of his stare.

"You know they were sick over losing you."

I jerk my head up. Ryder is looking at me again.

They...were?

"I told them about what happened." Ryder moves to the sink, avoiding my gaze. "When I dropped you off."

I'm not sure where the question comes from, but it pops out before I can stop it. "What about you?"

Ryder's large back almost blocks the small window over the sink, and he stiffens with the question. "What about me...what?"

I glare at my food. "Were you sick? You promised I'd never see you again the last time I saw you."

Ryder looks down at the sink. He's quiet for so long that I don't think he's going to answer. Then he says softly, "I'm not good at this communication shit either, Cali. You're going to have to accept that if you're with us."

I'm just supposed to accept that they won't talk to me?

Ryder says in a voice so soft I almost don't hear him. "And that was the first promise I was happy to break."

What? Is he for real right now?

"I'll take that if you're done." Ryder nods at my dish.

"Oh, yeah." I get up, handing it to him. His dishes thing.

Ryder nods, immediately rinsing it out.

"Is there...what are the rules with the dishes so I know how to do those right?"

Ryder glances at me, startled. He immediately tries to hide it. "Oh. No, don't worry about it."

I pick at a dent in the counter. "Okay..."

He hesitates. "I just have...a weird thing with germs."

I lean back against the counter. "It's okay. You don't have to explain it to me."

"No, I do." He takes a deep breath. "The others know, so you should too. I've had it ever since I was a kid. It's hard to break."

Heavy footsteps come down the stairs, and Miles pops around the corner, closely followed by Sawyer.

"Ready to see your room?" Miles asks.

I glance at Ryder, then back at Miles. "My room?" I parrot back. I have...a room here? The tightness in my body lifts for a second.

"Yep, c'mon."

I slowly follow Miles upstairs. Sawyer follows behind me, and I feel his stare on my back. My skin tingles. I feel the unspoken tension between us.

Miles walks me back straight from the stairs into a big room full of windows and a walkout porch, looking out into the misty forest. There's a king-size bed in the room, and it's light and airy. The room is full of light furniture, and I do a double take. On top of the dresser are some knick-knacks from my apartment.

I blink. But how...? I move up to them, running my fingers across them, then whirl.

Miles holds up his hands. "We went back to your apartment before we got you. Don't be mad. There's more stuff in the bathroom and in the closet."

Sawyer crosses his arms, leaning against the door frame.

"Mad?" I glance at the things again. The thoughtfulness makes tears prick behind my eyes.

Miles sits on the bed. "We have to talk."

I stiffen.

He rubs the back of his neck. "Sawyer and I wanted to... apologize."

I freeze completely, staring at Miles. Did I just hear him right?

"There are some things about how we met that we'd like to change," Miles says. "Not taking you, I'm not going to apologize for that." He looks down, then makes eye contact. "But we never made you feel at home. Didn't let you have a say."

I can't move. I can't even swallow. This is so beyond what I expected that I'm shocked.

I glance at Sawyer. He looks uncomfortable and glances at the floor when he sees me looking at him.

Miles continues. "This isn't an excuse because there is no excuse, but I think you should know that I..." He clears his throat. "I overstep sometimes." He takes a deep breath. "My mom's boyfriend killed my mom when I was a kid."

The room is silent, and even Sawyer stiffens.

Miles shifts. "That's irrelevant, but I don't want anyone to feel what my mom felt, so I...step in maybe when they don't want me to."

My stomach bottoms out. Oh my god. "Miles, I..."

He waves me off. "I didn't tell you that for your pity. I don't need your pity. I'm just trying to fill you in. And apologize."

I close my mouth. I don't know what to say. My head is swimming in response.

Miles stands. "Don't say anything. Either of you. I'm just...sorry. I'm going to check on Weiner."

And he's gone, leaving me and Sawyer.

I'm still frozen, trying to figure out what is going on. Am I dreaming? They aren't acting normal. I mean, they are, but I've never seen this side of them before.

Sawyer stands there for the longest time, looking uncomfortable and watching me.

There are so many things that I could say, but I'm not sure what. I clear my throat. "I guess I uh...never said thanks for Weiner."

Sawyer rolls his eyes. "He's sassy."

I huff, "Yeah."

"Fits his owner." Sawyer raises an eyebrow.

I laugh, turning to check out the dresser. It's already full of my clothes. "You guys brought my stuff?" I move to the bathroom.

He follows me, leaning on the bathroom door frame. "Yep."

My hair stuff is on the counter. I check the drawer. I have a toothbrush! That fills me with more excitement than it should.

"You might be missing some panties, though."

I shoot a glare at Sawyer that has no power behind it. "Pervert."

He gives me a bored look. "I prefer them used. I left you just enough to fill that order for me."

I move past him and shoulder-check him as I go. I check out the rest of the room, finding item after item hidden away, and when it becomes too much, I explore the balcony.

Sawyer comes out after me. I lean on the railing, staring at the forest. There aren't any leaves on the trees, but the moss fills the forest with green.

Sawyer says, "You know, typically when you go through someone's house, it's easy to get an idea of who they are."

I glance at him. He looks just as handsome as I remember him, his hair piled into a bun, showing off his sharp jawline and dark stubble.

"Yours was different." Sawyer's blue eyes look out over the forest. "You had a bunch of old stuff from your childhood that wasn't your style anymore. Some things that were gifts. Random shit. Nothing that screamed Cali."

I wince, looking out into the forest. Back then, I spent most of my time binging social media or fighting with Ben. I didn't have a personality other than make it from one day to the next. I couldn't. I was just trying to survive.

Sawyer says softly, "I think you've been running long before you met us."

I clench my jaw.

"We're more alike than you think," Sawyer says, looking at me.

"Yeah?" I ask.

"Yeah." He glances at his hands, picking at the skin around his nails. I can vaguely hear the men talking downstairs.

"I hope..." Sawyer pauses. "I know I haven't been the best. Not when it comes to taking you — I won't apologize for that shit, and I won't let you go, even if you ask." He throws me a dark look. "But, with the other stuff that Miles talked about."

I turn to look at him. Sawyer clenches his jaw. It's weird seeing him so uncomfortable.

"Like what?" I cross my arms.

He says, "Shit, this talking thing is hard."

"Like *what*, Sawyer?" I arch an eyebrow.

He clears his throat, then turns away to face the trees. "I didn't listen to you and made you want to run from us. For real. And for that, I'm sorry." He clenches his hands.

"I want to start over. I'll do better. Maybe here, you can stop running." He turns to look at me, blue eyes boring into me. "Because I stopped running when I met you. With you, the game became a reality. And for once, I was comfortable living there."

His words wrap around me like an embrace. I've seen a lot of versions of Sawyer, but this one? This one seems the most genuine. Against my will, tears fill my eyes. Fuck.

Sawyer says softly, "So just know, we want this place to be a safe spot for you to find yourself. And maybe when you stop running from yourself, you'll stop running from us."

I blink. I don't know how to respond to that. Because I do want to stop running. I want it so fucking badly.

Sawyer straightens. "Jesus Christ, that was harder than shooting someone."

I snort. I can't help it. It's not funny, but all the stress from everything boils over.

Sawyer tosses me a fake glare. "I'd rather kill someone."

I turn back to go inside, hiding a smile. "I'm sure."

"Oh," Sawyer follows me in. "I hope you know you're not done getting punished, by the way. Not by a long shot. In fact, get ready, because we have another game. If you'll play."

"What?"

Sawyer goes to my closet and pulls out a pile of clothes topped with running shoes. "Put these on, and when you're ready, come downstairs."

I eye it and him. "Is it a cheerleader outfit?"

Sawyer just winks and walks out, shutting the door behind him.

CHAPTER 93

CALI

The clothes turn out to be bright orange leggings and a neon yellow jacket - sans bra - and the material is sweat-wicking. I come downstairs in it.

All three men stand around the kitchen table. They've also changed and are in dark clothes. They look at me hungrily. The mood has changed. I feel like I walked down into a trap, and I pause.

"Hey, bunny." Sawyer smiles slowly. "New game."

My stomach clenches, but excitement runs through me as well.

"You have a thirty-minute head start. You can go anywhere on the island. If we catch you, we'll do whatever we want to you." Sawyer slides a map across the table. "There's a shack on the island. It's a safe zone."

I grab the map.

"Oh, Ryder's playing so here." Miles clunks a large hunting knife down on the table. I snap my gaze up to Ryder. He winks at me.

"Tick tock, bunny. Time starts now."

My heart hammers. I snatch up the knife and dart to the front door. Their jeering whoops and whistles follow me out. And I'm filled with joy and satisfaction.

Once outside, I'm hit with the humidity again. I slide to a stop, looking at the map. Fuck, I don't know how to read one of these, but I head in the direction I think the safehouse is marked. It's close to the edge of the island, and I hit the beach so I don't have to run through the woods.

Exhilaration runs through me. Two can play this game.

It takes me longer than I'd like to find the shack. It's a small garden shack sitting in a group of trees, almost invisible from the shoreline. My heart is pounding, and I heave for breath. I know they expect me to go in it. So I dart up and prop the door open. I hesitate. These clothes are going to be impossible to hide in, and they know it. I debate for a minute, then yank them off and throw them inside, leaving me in just my panties. I dart back into the woods to find a place to hide, not even cold from all the running.

When I spot movement, it's a large, quiet form just inside the tree line. I catch my breath. Ryder. He prowls forward, eyes locked on the shed. He's covered in a fine sheen of sweat, but his breathing is completely controlled. He smirks, seeing the door propped open. To get there, he has to walk right past my spot. I stay crouched, my heart hammering.

Just as soon as he steps past, I dart up.

Ryder crouches and whirls. I have too much momentum and run into his body, angling my knife into his side. "Don't move."

Ryder laughs but complies. "Oh, pretty little woman. What are you going to do with that knife?"

I pant. "Cut you if you aren't careful."

In a move too fast for me to combat, Ryder spins out of my hold and is on top of me, pushing me to the hard, freezing ground. His strong hand grips my wrist with the knife. "Since the moment they told me about you, I knew you were going to be trouble."

"Get off me!" I screech, struggling to get away. But it's half-hearted.

Ryder gets up on his forearms, leaving just enough weight on me to keep me pinned. "What if I like my women helpless and at my mercy?"

"You sound just like Sawyer," I hiss.

Miles' voice comes from behind me. "He rubs off on people."

I crane my neck to look, and Ryder takes that opportunity to rip the knife out of my hand and place the cold blade on my neck. Miles stands over me, smirking. "In multiple ways."

"Where is he?" I growl, looking around as best I can without moving my neck.

"Here, bunny." Sawyer steps into my field of vision. He rubs his dick. "I almost came watching my naked girl jump on my boyfriend waving a knife." Sawyer crouches down, looking into my eyes. "Cut him a little next time, will you?"

I feel my pulse pound in my neck and glance at Ryder's dark gaze. The black pupil has almost overtaken the brown. "You ready for your punishment?"

"For what?" I narrow my gaze.

"Running," Sawyer says simply.

"You told me to!" I struggle slightly, and he just turns the knife so the flat is against my neck and presses on my windpipe.

"Do you just do everything you're told? I swear you've fought us at every turn."

I struggle to kick my legs, but my pussy is hot and pulsing. I can't get over how much their nearness affects me. Sawyer laughs at my pathetic attempts.

Ryder growls over me, "You want to get away so bad?" He gets up, and suddenly, the huge weight over me is gone. "Go. Run."

I scramble up. They surround me with predatory smiles.

Sawyer growls, "Run, Cali."

I do. I take off again towards the water. The fear runs through my blood, and I break the tree line before I'm snatched up again and hauled back against a chest. "What an obedient little pet. You ready to cry for me?"

Ryder throws me to the ground, and I catch myself in the sand, turning to face him. He stands over me, slowly unbuttoning his pants. The other two circle around me, so my avenues of escape are cut off. Not that I'd actually run again. My mouth waters, and I say weakly, "Stop."

Miles chuckles. "At least pretend like you mean it, Cali."

Ryder gets to his knees and flips me on my stomach. He immediately pins me down with a heavy hand on my lower back.

Ryder leans over me, "Sawyer has his mark on you. I'm going to add mine."

What? I start struggling for real this time, but I'm only sinking deeper into the cold sand.

"Cry for me, and I'll make it feel good."

Real fear runs through me, but it's met with a flood of wetness in my pussy.

I go to look behind me again, and Miles grabs my chin, forcing me to look at him. "I'll be your eyes."

I feel Ryder snap my panties off. "I'm gonna fuck you while I put my name on you, Cali."

Miles says, "He's gonna push into that hot pussy from behind now, Cali."

I feel Ryder's dick press against my pussy. I struggle to get away, feeling the grains of sand against us. I gasp, "The sand."

"Hurts, doesn't it?" Ryder pushes into me with a single stroke, and I cry out, the stretch of his dick and the sand cutting into me.

"Good girl. Such a fucking good girl." Miles strokes the side of my face. I clench around Ryder, who groans. He waits a minute as I stretch, then pulls out and slams into me again. Pain mixes with pleasure and fear, and I moan, trying to look back.

"Eyes, Cali," Miles demands. I look at him. The mist has beaded up on his eyelashes. "That's a good girl. You're safe. We'll keep you safe."

Ryder ruts into me, spiking my pain and pleasure. Sawyer stands over us, stroking his dick.

"Cali," Miles says. "Do you trust us?"

I look between him and Sawyer. My first reaction is fear but after our talk in the house, I look both of them in the eyes and nod.

Miles smiles softly, then nods back to Ryder.

Biting pain bites into my right asscheek. I yelp, jumping.

"Atta girl, let me hear you," Ryder moans.

The pain comes again, blinding. I feel my flesh ripping apart. I hold my breath for as long as I can, then let out a high moan.

"Fuck." Ryder pumps into me.

"You're doing so good, Cali. He's almost done." Miles still grips my chin, stroking my cheek with his thumb.

I cry out as the pain rips through me again.

"You're done. All done."

"Damn, shadow. Your ass looks pretty with his initials."

Ryder lets off my lower back, plunging into me. He reaches a hand around to play with my clit, grinding little pieces of sand into my sensitive flesh. It's too much. There are too many sensations all at once, and I pull away to relieve them.

Ryder doesn't let me. He continues slamming into me, and pleasure fills me against my will. He plays with my body just enough to rile me up more and more. My body tenses around him, and I come in an explosion of pain and pleasure. I scream, buzzing and euphoria flooding me. Ryder stills, coming inside me with a roar.

"Good girl, Cali. You're our perfect girl," Miles groans. As I come down off the high, Ryder pulls out of me.

"Knees, Cali," Miles demands. "I need to feel that perfect mouth on me, just like the first time we met."

I gladly comply, scrambling up in the cold sand. The cold mixes with the heat running through my body, sending delicious tingles through me.

Miles has his dick out already, and I eagerly take him into my mouth.

"Me too, Cali." Sawyer steps up next to him, and I eagerly grab his dick in my hand. There's sand all over my hand, and I try to brush it off.

"No," Sawyer grabs my hand. "Make it hurt, Cali."

Miles shoves to the back of my throat, and I stare up at him. He throws his head back, abs flexed. Both men groan, and my pussy floods, knowing I'm bringing them both pleasure. I switch back and forth between them, sucking one then the other eagerly. I almost come from that alone, grinding on nothing.

"Here." Sawyer moves his foot toward me. "Ride my shoe."

I hesitate, then scoot awkwardly toward it, settling over his running shoe. It feels rough and soft and perfect. I continue sucking and pleasuring them while I ride. My asscheek is on fire, and it just adds to the sensations.

Fuck, I think I'm going to come. My eyes roll back into my head.

"Come for me, baby," Sawyer groans, shoving his dick back into my mouth. I suck him down, riding to ecstasy. I come hard, pleasure exploding through my whole body. Sawyer comes down my throat with a shout, grabbing my hair and pulsing into me. Miles also stiffens and swells in my hand, shooting his cum all over my face and Sawyer's body.

I groan. It's the hottest thing I've ever experienced. Sawyer pulls me off him, and before I can collapse, Ryder grabs me. He picks me up, cradling me against his warm chest.

I shiver, cuddling into him.

"Goddamn, Cali. You're the best thing to happen to us." Sawyer moans. Ryder starts walking us back down the beach. The other men follow, and they take me all the way back to the warm house.

I shiver when we get inside, loving the heat. Ryder sits with me on the couch while Miles grabs a washcloth and some antiseptic.

I sit on the floor, leaning my stomach against the couch so he can clean me up. And for once, it doesn't make me nervous.

My emotions are high and swirling after everything.

Sawyer gets up. "I have something for you, Cali." He returns, holding a small box, and puts it on the couch in front of me. I stiffen and open it slowly, gasping.

It's my collar, with a new lock, this one shaped like a heart. It has three inscriptions on it. I look closer. A guitar, a bunny, and a cat.

"This time, it's never coming off." Sawyer says softly, "Because you're ours forever."

It's all I can do to keep the tears out of my eyes as I nod.

"I get to claim you too," Miles says. "When you've recovered, Ryder is going to give us matching tattoos." He strokes my hair. "Guitars. Since you brought the joy back to my soul."

My throat feels tight.

Miles shifts. "Cali, fuck knows we haven't done it right in the past. And we won't do it right in the future. But we want you. And we hope that one day, you'll want us back too. For real."

I look at all of them, hope and fear running through my heart. Because, despite everything, I do want them. I want to know all of their pasts and for them to know mine and to play all their fucked up games.

I consider not running. And for the first time, it doesn't fill me with dread.

I lean over and kiss Sawyer. Miles leans down and steals one too, then Ryder.

"Okay, enough with the sappy shit," I laugh. "Either fuck me again or get me some clothes."

Miles' eyes gleam. "Sorry. Legs broken. Can't get any."

I laugh. "Then I'll just be stealing yours."

"Fine with me." Sawyer winks.

"She's wearing mine." Miles looks around, realizing he doesn't have any with him, and darts up.

"Not a chance," Sawyer growls at him, starting to chase after him.

I glance at Ryder, and he rolls his eyes. "That'll never change. Now, spread your legs so we can do it again."

EPILOGUE

CALI

A FEW MONTHS LATER

"Would you sit still?" Miles yanks on my hair. "Can't." I shift again, delicious tingles running through me. It's Sawyer's turn with the remote-controlled vibrator, and the fucker is taking full advantage.

"Fuck, Cali. Sit fucking still." Miles gives another yank and leans over to look at his phone. He's trying a new braid that I said I liked and has cussed more than I've heard in a long time.

The men have opened up to me more in the past few months. Ryder has even let me do the dishes. And told me about his mom. In fact, all of them have told me about their families. I'd be lying if I said it didn't feel fucking good. The cops are still looking for them, so we haven't been able to go back, but that's okay. We've made a home here and I'm the happiest I've ever been.

The vibrator changes frequency again. I glance around, trying to see if I can spot Sawyer.

Suddenly, there's a startled yell from down the hall, and I jump.

Colorful cussing fills the house, and heavy footsteps march our way. Ryder appears.

"This fucking thing." Ryder hurls something small and dark at me, and I startle. The object bounces off my chest. It's a mouse. A mother fucking mouse.

I scream, darting up and yanking my hair out of Miles' hands. "What the hell?"

"Fucking hell, Cali," Miles groans. "I'm going to have to start over."

Ryder motions at it. "Your fucking cat just left that in my bed."

The mouse doesn't move. Oh my god, is it...dead?

A deep laugh breaks out, and Sawyer saunters into the room from the kitchen. "What, scared of a little mouse, Ryder?"

Ryder straightens. "No! It was in my bed. He won't stop leaving me things."

Sawyer smirks. "Awww, Ryder. No reason to be scared. You're like a hundred times bigger than it." He grabs the mouse gently and goes to throw it outside.

Ryder crosses his arms. "I'm not scared."

Sawyer winks at me on his way back, then turns to Ryder. "You know, cats bring offerings when they think you can't hunt. Halloweiner thinks you're the weakest of the group."

Ryder lifts a dark eyebrow.

Sawyer shrugs. "He's smart."

Ryder moves almost too fast for me to track, throwing Sawyer down on the couch by him. They exchange a few heavy blows, skin thudding on skin.

"Fucking children." Miles motions at me. "Come here, let me finish."

I watch the battle of strength on the couch in front of me. Miles yanks me back down on the floor between his legs.

The men wrestle until Ryder gets Sawyer pinned in a painful looking arm lock. Ryder says in a bored voice, "Relax, Sawyer."

"Fuck you," Sawyer spits back, wincing.

Ryder chuckles. He shifts enough to yank both their pants down and sinks slowly into Sawyer's ass.

I watch them, my pussy growing hot. I know Miles is watching too. His hands are moving in slow motion.

"Come here, Cali." Ryder orders while pounding into Sawyer.

Miles quickly finishes my hair. Normally, I'd fight. They'd make me listen to them, I'd go kicking and screaming, and we'd fuck until we couldn't anymore. Then we'd pass out and start all over again.

I straighten. "No."

Miles scoffs behind me. "No?"

Sawyer smirks.

I stand and step away from them. "No. This time, you listen to me."

All three men glance at me. A thrill runs through me at their attention. Affection fills their gazes, even in lust. My body tingles. These men have become more to me in the past months than I ever thought was possible. And for the first time in my life, I think I might be safe – in the most unsafe way possible.

I back away again. "My turn. You'll play by my rules."

Sawyer snorts, and Ryder smacks his ass. Miles rolls his eyes.

I wink at them. "Wanna play a game?"

THE END

Wanna Play A Game? is the first book in the interconnected, standalone series, *The Hunter's Club.*

AUTHOR'S NOTE

Ya'll are nasty, and I love you for it. If you want to connect with me and more nasty dark romance girlies, please join my Facebook group, Alina May's Book Babes! Or, of course, you can follow me on Tiktok or Instagram at Alina_may_author. I won't be responsible for the unhinged content you see there.

I'd like to give a special thanks to Sarah, Amanda, and Laurelyn for beta reading for me and to Paige for your unhinged torture advice. And of course special thanks to my editor and PA Taylor – you're the best! Only you would offer to edit a whole book last minute, and I love you for it.

55472691R00310